As a child, Fiona Harper was constantly teased for two things:
having her nose in a book and living in a dream world. Things
haven't changed much since then, but at least she's found a

Fiona Harper was constantly told off for two things when she was at school: staring out of the window and daydreaming, and talking too much. Not much has changed since then—she's still got her head in the clouds and she's still happily chatting away. The only difference is that these days she's paid for it as an author! She now lives in London with her husband and two daughters, and her career that puts her runaway imagination to use.

Fiona loves dancing, so clear the floor if you're ever at a party with her, and her current creative craze (one of a long list) is jewellery making. She loves good books, good films and good food, especially anything cinnamon-flavoured, and she can always find room in her diet for chocolate or champagne!

Fiona loves to hear from readers and you can contact her through fionaharper.com or find her on her Facebook page (Fiona Harper Romance Author) or tweet her (@FiHarperAuthor)

# THE
# *Doris Day*
# VINTAGE
# FILM CLUB

## FIONA HARPER

This edition published in Great Britain 2015
by Mills & Boon, an imprint of Harlequin (UK) Limited,
Eton House, 18-24 Paradise Road, Richmond, Surrey, TW9 1SR

© 2015 Fiona Harper

ISBN: 978-0-263-25339-9

097-0415

Harlequin (UK) Limited's policy is to use papers that are natural, renewable and recyclable products and made from wood grown in sustainable forests. The logging and manufacturing processes conform to the legal environmental regulations of the country of origin.

Printed and bound by
CPI Group (UK) Ltd, Croydon, CR0 4YY

# ACKNOWLEDGEMENTS

I'd like to thank everyone at Mills & Boon, especially Anna Baggaley, my very patient editor, and the lovely Victoria Oundjian, especially as it took quite some time to help this author see the wood of this book through the trees of her wayward imagination. I also want to say a huge thank you to all of M&B's marketing and promotion team, for their enthusiasm and hard work from day one.

Big thanks to my amazing agent Lizzy Kremer and also to Harriet Moore at David Higham Associates, for her calm encouragement in the midst of a deadline panic and her insightful suggestions.

My family definitely deserve my gratitude, especially my husband, Andy, who patiently listens to me warble on about difficult plot matters so I can get things straight in my head, even though he hardly ever knows who these people I'm talking about are, and to my lovely daughters, Sian and Rose, who cheer me on all the way, and who didn't moan (much) when I hogged the TV for months, watching every film of Doris's I could get my hands on.

Thanks to all my Facebook friends who helped me with football-related stuff. Sorry, those scenes ended up on the cutting room floor, but at least you have educated this football dunce a little.

Lastly, and most importantly, I want to thank Doris Day, for her captivating and charismatic performances that have charmed generations and continue to bring us joy and happiness, but also for her strength of character and resilience. The true story of the woman behind the Hollywood icon was the inspiration for this book.

# Chapter One

# Nobody's Sweetheart

When Claire Bixby was nine, she decided that one day she'd like to live in Hollywood, because she wanted to be in movies. Not that she wanted to be an actress. Far from it. No, Claire wanted to actually be *in* the movies, to live there, a place where the sun always shone, everything was Technicolor bright and families lived happily ever after together. There would be no more shouting, no more crying. No hearing the front door slam, one parent leaving never to return – even if she'd discovered she could breathe out more easily after he'd left.

However, as all little girls do, Claire grew up, and she came to understand that nothing was what it seemed in Hollywood. The houses weren't real. The outsides were just false fronts and the insides built on a sound stage, made up of plywood flats that could be wheeled around depending on where the camera needed to go. And while the sun might shine pretty regularly in California, she suspected that once the actors took off their make-up, they probably went home and shouted at the dog, or discovered their wife was cheating on them with her plastic surgeon, or maybe just went back to their mansion to sit there with the curtains drawn, wondering why their fabulous lives weren't really that fabulous and if even one of the hangers-on who buzzed around them knew what their real name was.

So by the time Claire had turned thirty-four, she'd never once visited Hollywood, preferring to keep it a dim and distant bubble of fantasy she wasn't quite yet ready to pop. As a travel agent, however, she did plan trips to Tinseltown for others, which was why on one sunny and rather muggy May morning, she hopped off the number fifty-six bus, thinking not only about the work of the day ahead but smiling slightly at the memory of her childhood naïvety.

She'd slowly been growing her business over the last two years and recently she'd taken the plunge and hired proper office space. It was only a couple of miles from where she lived in Highbury, North London. She'd moved into the premises two months ago, but she still loved turning the corner into an alley that led into a forgotten gem of a courtyard. Whilst most of the surrounding area had been levelled by the Blitz and had been reimagined into vast modern estates by some of Britain's top architects during the sixties and seventies, a few narrow streets had survived and tiny pockets of nineteenth-century buildings nestled amongst the landscape of grey concrete and geometrical shapes.

Evidence of the old workshops and shopfronts still remained in Old Carter's Yard. A couple of units were boarded up, yet to be renovated, but the others were filled with small businesses, many of which were wedding-related. It had started with a proposal-planning agency, of all things, and had grown from there. Now there was a bakery that did the most amazing five-tiered creations, a photographer's studio, a stationer's and even a wedding accessories shop, which did everything from garters and stockings to waterproof mascara for the big day and plastic tiaras for rowdy hen nights.

Claire walked across the cobbles carefully in her heels and smiled to herself as she saw the sign above the window. *Far, Far Away.* She still thought it was a great name for a travel agent's, especially for one that specialised in romantic get-aways, even though that hadn't been part of the plan when she'd left her job as an advertising executive at Webster & Templeton and had set up an office in her living room.

She gave the window display the once-over before turning the key in the lock. The old-fashioned bay window of what had once been a fishmonger's was now backed with a collage of elegant and romantic destinations: Paris, Venice, the Orient Express. A deserted Caribbean beach with a startling turquoise sea. A picture of a couple silhouetted by the sunset on the verge of what promised to be a meaningful kiss.

Knowing that brides-to-be were drawn to anything that hinted of weddings like a kleptomaniac to something shiny, Claire had draped white tulle around the window and had added a bouquet of silk flowers and a couple of wedding invitations. She'd then tossed a handful of rose petal confetti across everything, so it looked as if had been blown in by a soft wind. And at the bottom of the window in gold lettering it said, *After the perfect wedding, the perfect honeymoon* . . . Her post-wedding bookings had doubled since she'd opened up shop here.

She unlocked the door and stepped inside. Like many buildings in the Victorian courtyard, her shop stayed fairly cool in summer, but London was in the grip of a heatwave and this was the stickiest May on record for more than two decades. It had only been a short walk from the bus stop, but the back of her neck was already damp under her blonde bob and she could feel her tailored red shift dress sticking to her skin. Before she headed for her desk, she propped the door open to encourage fresh air to flow into the space.

She'd only just sat down in her office chair when she heard a rap on the glass of the open door. She looked up to find one of her fellow 'wedding ghetto' traders leaning against the jamb.

'Hey,' Peggy said, smiling. Today she was in all her vintage glory. Her platinum blonde hair was curled to resemble Marilyn Monroe's and she wore a fitted pale pink dress covered with small white polka dots. The look was finished off with matching pink stilettos with spotty bows at the toes.

Claire had been friends with Peggy even before she'd rented the office in Old Carter's Yard. It was through Peggy, who worked two doors down at Hopes & Dreams as a proposal planner, that Claire had discovered the shop space had been available to rent.

Claire smiled back. 'Hi. Need help with a proposal?'

Peggy nodded and came and sat down in the chair opposite Claire. 'Nicole asked me to pop down. We have a client who wants to pop the question – sunset at the top of the Eiffel Tower. That bit we can manage, but we'd like you to handle the first-class Eurostar tickets, and give us suggestions of half a dozen romantic hotels in Paris. He hasn't got a five-star budget, but he'd like it if his fiancée-to-be didn't guess that.'

Claire smiled. 'I know some great little boutique hotels on the Left Bank, where you get a bit more pizazz for your euro. What sort of timescale are we looking at?'

'Their anniversary is on the fourteenth of July. He'd like to do it then.'

'No problem.' Claire opened her browser and clicked through a couple of hotel websites. 'I'll have preliminary details to you by the beginning of next week.'

Peggy clapped her hands together and grinned. 'You're a star! And I'm so glad you took this office over. It's so much more fun coming down for a visit than sending off a boring old email.'

'I'm glad too.' Carving a name for herself in the travel business had been hard. She needed a niche, she'd realised, and thanks to Peggy and Hopes & Dreams she'd found one. Six months after she'd started doing bookings for them she'd moved from general travel planning to concentrating on romantic trips of all kinds – proposals, honeymoons, special anniversaries.

She'd even planned a couple of holidays to help couples conceive. Okay, well, she didn't actually *help* them conceive – that was up to them and God – but giving them some much-needed time together where they could relax and let nature take its course, *that* she could manage.

'How about a Frappuccino?' Peggy asked, nodding towards Sweet Nothings, the organic café and bakery just at the entrance to the yard.

Claire frowned. 'It's only ten past nine and you're having a break? I thought you were supposed to be just "popping down".'

Peggy's smile didn't fade one iota. 'I'm still working,' she said sweetly. 'We'll discuss the Paris trip while we slurp.'

Claire shook her head gently and considered Peggy's tempting offer. When she arrived for work in the mornings, she usually dived straight in and didn't surface again until her stomach started to rumble, but this morning her throat was dry and a fine bead of sweat was tickling its way down between her shoulder blades. 'Oh, go on then,' she muttered.

Peggy sprung up from the chair, grinning harder. Then she held out her hand. It took Claire a couple of moments before she worked out what was going on. Rolling her eyes, she fumbled through her purse then dropped a ten pound note into Peggy's hand. 'I want change!' she yelled after the polka-dotted figure that practically skipped out of the shop.

There can't have been much of a queue in Sweet Nothings, she thought, because less than a minute later she sensed a presence in the doorway, hardly enough time to blend the ice, let alone dowse it in ice-cold milk and espresso. 'I need to talk to you about the film club meeting tonight,' she said, still looking at her computer screen. 'How do you feel about being our new treasurer?'

A dark silhouette strode into the shop. 'You know I'd do anything for you,' a smooth, deep voice said.

Claire's head snapped up.

'Treasurer of what?' Doug Martin asked.

Claire shook her head. 'Nothing you'd be interested in,' she said, laughing. She saw enough of Mr Martin as it was. 'Sorry, I thought you were someone else.'

He took a couple of steps into the office. 'A *boyfriend* kind of someone else?'

Claire fought hard to keep her denial unspoken. She pasted on her best professional smile. 'How can I help you, Mr Martin?'

He smiled at her indulgently. 'Doug. I thought we agreed you were going to call me Doug.'

They had. And it did feel rather old-fashioned to be talking to a customer that way. He was a nice enough man, maybe a little closer to forty than she was, with an unthreatening, slightly boyish face.

'Okay, Doug . . . What can I help you with?'

He didn't have a chance to answer, because Peggy swept back in the door, a giant Frappuccino in each hand. She took one look at Doug and stopped in her tracks. 'Oh, sorry . . . Didn't realise you had company.'

Claire shot her a 'save me' look. Peggy just trotted over to the desk, popped Claire's drink down two inches to the left of a coaster and whispered so Doug couldn't hear. 'Not a chance. Both you and I could do with a few more Y chromosomes in our lives.'

Claire's brow lowered. *You have him then*, she mouthed.

Peggy gave her a dazzling smile and headed for the door. 'I couldn't possibly poach a client, but you never know . . .' She blew a kiss at Doug, who received it gratefully. 'If things go well, he might be knocking on my door soon anyway.'

Claire resisted the urge to throw the fountain pen sitting on her desk at Peggy and impale her to the doorpost with it. She did *not* need more Y chromosomes in her life. She'd only recently got free of one man and she wasn't about to fill his space either quickly or indiscriminately.

And, as harmless as Doug was, he just didn't float her boat. 'So . . .' she said, turning her attention back to him, hoping he hadn't heard their muttered conversation. 'Where do you want to go this time?'

Doug dropped into the chair Peggy had recently vacated and looked intently at her. 'I think an island in the South Pacific.'

Claire looked over her shoulder at the world map that sat behind her desk. 'Any bit of the South Pacific in particular? It's a pretty big place, and there are thousands of islands.'

When she turned back, Doug looked deep into her eyes. 'Somewhere secluded . . . romantic.'

'Uh-uh.' Claire nodded, but her eyes narrowed. She had a funny feeling she knew where this was going. She winced as she asked the crucial question. 'How many travellers?'

He leaned even further forward and gave her a meaningful look. 'I'd like it to be two. How about adding a wedding on a secluded white sandy beach beneath the palm trees?'

'Doug,' Claire said wearily 'we've been through this before.'

He shrugged and shifted his weight so he was sitting firmly back in the chair. 'You can't blame a man in love for being hopeful, can you?'

Claire sighed. She'd like to, but the truth was she needed to build a customer base with more Dougs. Well, not exactly like him. She could do without the shameless flirting and the twice-weekly proposals, but she needed more repeat customers who kept coming back because she'd done such a good job the last time they couldn't imagine booking a holiday without her. It was happening, but slowly.

'No,' she said, finally answering his question. 'But I've told you before that I don't love you, Doug. I hardly even know you.' No matter how many hours he spent emailing or phoning each month. The downside of having a brand-new shiny office was that he now had the opportunity to moon over her in person.

'Well, you could always make time to try to get to know

me, ' Doug said. He brightened. 'I know . . . Let's forget the wedding and just do the honeymoon!'

Claire couldn't help but laugh. There was something about Doug's irrepressible optimism, at least, that was attractive. 'Now, do you really want me to book this trip for you, or are you just wasting my time?'

His face fell and he sighed. 'I really want you to book me the trip. Mother says the Cook Islands are on her bucket list and since her time in this mortal realm is coming to a close, I'd better take her there before the year is out.'

Claire smothered a smile. From what she'd gleaned about Doug's mother, she suspected the old lady would outlive them all. 'The Cook Islands . . . Now we're getting somewhere.' She stood up, walked over to a rack full of brochures, pulled one out and flicked to a page that showed the kind of luxury resort Doug's mother would appreciate, then handed it to him as she sat down again. 'What you need is to find a nice girl who likes to travel.'

And doesn't mind a twenty stone chaperone with a blue rinse, she added silently.

Doug, to his credit, was already bouncing back from her refusal. 'But *you're* a nice girl. And you must like to travel, otherwise why become a travel agent?'

Well, he'd hit the nail on the head there, and there were more than a few destinations on her own bucket list that were still unticked.

'I do like to travel. And I will . . . But I've been very busy getting the new premises up and running and all my time and energy has gone into that.' And money, she added silently, but he didn't need to know that, did he?

Anyway, she didn't like to travel alone – not that she was

about to take Doug up on his offer to be his Girl Friday on a deserted tropical island. She wasn't that desperate. But the last time she'd been away was that horrible trip to Prague with Philip, the last-ditch attempt to do something romantic as their marriage had been falling apart. For some reason, hearing the rumble of case wheels in the pre-dawn quiet just didn't seem as thrilling any more.

And she wasn't about to fill the space he'd left behind just because she wanted someone to talk to on a long plane journey. She was enjoying her freedom too much. A few years of staying put in London was a small price to pay for being able to do what she wanted, to fly as high as she could, without those little comments, sharp and penetrating as sniper's bullets, bringing her smashing back down to earth again.

'Well, if you won't come to Rarotonga with me, how about an evening out in the West End?'

Claire blinked and refocused on Doug. She sighed. 'We've talked about dating too.'

'Oh, it's not a date,' he said with a surprisingly straight face. Only the glitter in his eyes gave him away. 'It's a party.'

Claire opened her mouth to ask what the difference was, but he barrelled on.

'Jayce Rider, the guy who took over the Hamilton Hotel and turned its fortunes around is a friend of mine. He likes to throw parties for people in the travel industry and he's planning one a week tomorrow. I thought you might like to come with me. For purely business reasons, of course.'

She hesitated. Actually, she'd been looking to develop relationships with a couple of high-end London hotels, hoping to be able to give her treasured clients a little bit of luxury at a discount. The Hamilton would be perfect.

She kept her expression neutral as she looked at Doug. 'I'll think about it.'

He grinned back at her, reminding her of a puppy who'd been scolded only moments before, but was now wagging its tail, transgression already half forgotten. 'I'll pick you up at eight,' he said, as he rose from his chair and saluted her farewell.

Claire half stood in her chair as he disappeared out of the door. 'There'll be ground rules!' she yelled after him. He didn't shout anything back, so she wasn't sure he'd heard her, but, even if he had, she suspected he might find a way to circumvent them.

She let her bottom bump back down into her office chair and then slumped face first onto her desk. The morning was already so clammy that her cheek instantly stuck to the polished surface.

Was that what Doug's little visit had been all about?

Had he used her guilt at saying no to an all-expenses paid honeymoon to manoeuvre her into saying yes to the party? Which she hadn't actually done, she reminded herself, even though it felt as if she had.

She peeled her face off the desk and sat up, then stared at her computer screen, thinking she ought to book the whole blooming trip anyway – two tickets, first class but non-refundable, and twin rooms all the way so he had to share with his Gorgon of a mother. Hah! The cancellation fees alone would make him think twice before he pulled another stunt like that on her, before he started messing with her head—

She inhaled sharply.

*Claire, you're being paranoid.*

Not every man she met was out to use her as a pawn in his twisted little games. She had to remember that.

She scrubbed her face with her hands and stared out through the open door across the courtyard to Sweet Nothings, and suddenly remembered her Frappuccino perched on the edge of the desk. Half the ice had melted and one side of the swirl of cream had sunk into the liquid, making it look like a rapidly fading iceberg. She took a sip anyway. It was warmer than she would have liked, but at least she wasn't in danger of brain freeze.

After a couple of slurps of the cool liquid she began to feel a bit more normal again. She laughed softly at herself.

Stupid woman. Of course Doug wasn't manipulating her. Everything he felt and thought was instantly written all over his face. He didn't have it in him to scheme and push and lie. Doug Martin had that going for him at least.

The gravity of this revelation hit her. Her eyes opened wide as she reached the bottom of the Frappuccino and it made a loud vacuum-like sound. That meant Doug had one up on almost every other man who'd played a significant role in her life, which made him a much better prospect than she'd given him credit for.

Yikes. That was a seriously sad state of affairs.

She laughed again and shook herself as she aimed the empty Frappuccino cup towards the bin and scored a mental point for getting it in first time. She stood up and reached for her purse. Maybe she should go and get herself a fresh one. If she was starting to consider Doug Martin as prime boyfriend material, the heat of this sticky May morning was definitely getting to her.

# Chapter Two

## Just One Girl

The Doris Day Film Club met on Tuesday evenings in the upper room of The Glass Bottom Boat, a shabby little pub on the fringes of Highbury and Islington that had, as yet, escaped the clutches of developers who wanted to transform it into yet another fashionable and minimalist wine bar. Some of the other pubs in the area were cool and grungy, the kind with bare plaster and sanded floorboards that had live music and open mike nights. The Glass Bottom Boat was just plain grungy.

There was no air conditioning in the upper room, just walls covered with red flock wallpaper, a carpet guaranteed to make one's eyes hurt and rickety tables and chairs that had been stained with dark varnish in an effort to make them look 'rustic' instead of just old and broken. The only way to get more air into the room was to wedge the two large windows open as wide as they could go, which wasn't far, seeing as they were almost glued shut with four decades' worth of paint and half the sash ropes were missing.

It was a small space, only needing twenty people to fill it

to the rafters, so on this muggy evening, the eight members of the Doris Day Film Club fitted in quite comfortably.

The room's saving grace, and the only reason the club continued to meet here month after month, was the massive, state-of-the-art 52-inch flat-screen TV that almost filled one wall. The landlord had installed it when the last World Cup had been on, and had intended to play sports on it twenty-four-seven, but on Tuesday nights it belonged to the Doris Day Film Club and them alone.

On the table nearest the window was Bev, dressed in a pastel blouse and beige slacks. She was giving a younger woman the highlights of her last visit to the chiropodist. Candy, a yummy mummy in her late thirties, was suitably grossed out but trying to hide it, while simultaneously studying her own stiletto-encased feet under the table and wondering if bunions were looming perilously close in her future too.

On the table next door were Kitty and Grace, two vintage fashion queens in their early twenties, who thought anything retro was cooler than cool and never left their houses without their eyeliner wings and crimson lipstick. Kitty was flirting with George, bless him, the lone male of their intimate little society. Everyone had assumed he was gay at first, but it turned out he was just a sweet old bachelor who'd fallen in love with Doris at the age of eleven when his mother had bribed him with a quarter of gobstoppers to accompany her to the flicks to watch *Move Over, Darling*. He'd never been able to find a woman to match Doris after that, so he'd never tried, didn't think it would be fair to his bride to always play second fiddle to such perfection. Of course, he didn't mind it when a pretty young thing like Kitty gave him a bit of attention, even though it made him blush furiously.

Finally, gathered round a square table that had one of its legs propped up by a folded beer mat, were two of the three-strong committee. Claire sat in the central chair and stared at the gossiping group with vague dismay. It was getting harder and harder to start on time nowadays. Quite a few unlikely friendships were budding. Never in her life had she been in more need of a loudhailer.

'Ladies!' she began.

'And George . . .' Maggs, her vice-president, sitting beside her, interjected.

'Ladies and George!' Claire said, just that little bit louder. The din continued. Claire sighed.

Maggs tutted beside her. Two years ago they hadn't had this kind of problem, but two years ago she, Maggs and Claire's grandmother Laurie had been the only members of the club. Now it was a victim of its own success.

Claire had never actually volunteered for the position of president; she'd kind of inherited the role after her grandmother had died. Gran had started a Doris Day Appreciation Society back in 1951 and had roped her best friend, Margaret – always known as Maggs – into being the second member.

The society had been hugely popular in the fifties and sixties, filled with members who'd been drawn to the independent and charismatic woman they'd seen on the cinema screen, but numbers had dwindled in the seventies, when Doris had stopped making films and it became less than cool to have a squeaky clean image.

Maggs had insisted that Claire take up the mantle of

president when the position had become vacant. In honour of her grandmother, she'd said. Claire had been flattered at the time, but now she suspected Maggs preferred the vice-president's role, because she got to boss people around without actually doing very much.

Claire hadn't really minded. Watching Doris Day films with her grandmother had been the happiest moments of her childhood, afternoons when she'd escaped the tense atmosphere of home, when she hadn't had to watch what she said and did or be careful that she wasn't too noisy. Gran had never minded if she wanted to sing or skip around the flat or laugh out loud.

Thinking of noise brought her back to the decibel level of the current moment. That, and the fact that Maggs jabbed her in the ribs with a bony elbow. She was one of those wiry old ladies, the sort whose strength belied their tiny frames. 'I used to be able to do a wolf whistle that could stop traffic three streets away,' she said, looking from noisy club member to noisy club member. 'It hasn't been the same since I got my false teeth, but I could always give it a go?' She raised her eyebrows and began to lift two fingers towards her mouth.

'Not a good idea,' Claire said wearily. 'If they shot out and hit someone, we could be sued, and funds are low enough in the kitty as it is.'

'Might be worth it, just to get some peace and quiet,' Maggs muttered, surveying their unruly members with disdain. She turned her focus to the empty chair on the other side of Claire. 'Talking of money . . . Where's our new treasurer, anyway?'

'She'll be here any second.'

Right on cue, the door flew open and Peggy burst in, wearing the same pink dress she'd had on earlier, so tight it only just allowed her to trot in her five-inch heels.

'You're late,' Maggs said, switching her laser-beam stare from Claire to Peggy.

Peggy just grinned at her. 'That's because my first job as treasurer was to negotiate next year's rent for the room with the landlord. Not only is the price staying the same, but he's agreed to throw in a round of cocktails each meeting too.'

Claire's eyes widened. She was about to ask just how Peggy had managed that – Bruce, the landlord, had never been anything but surly with her – but then she got a prime view of Peggy's rear end as she bent over to put her vintage handbag on the floor and pull out her notebook, and she had a sneaking suspicion just how their new treasurer had accomplished it.

Maggs nodded sagely. 'I knew there was something I liked about that girl. I've always been partial to the odd gin sling.' As if to prove the point, she pulled a hip flask from her handbag and added more 'va-va-voom' to the already generous gin and tonic in front of her.

Claire decided not to remind the older lady just how vocal she'd been when Claire had suggested Peggy for the post of treasurer. She'd called Peggy a 'slip of a thing' and had campaigned long and hard for Bev, who she'd strong-armed into coming from her Pilates class, to take the job, even though Bev had said flatly that she didn't want to do it.

Maggs leaned across Claire and held out her hand. 'Can I borrow one of those for a second?' she asked Peggy, nodding at her shoes with the polka-dot bows. Peggy opened her mouth to ask why, but Maggs waggled her fingers impatiently. In the end, Peggy just sighed and handed one exquisite shoe over.

Maggs took it by the toe and rapped the heel on the table three times so loudly that the whole room fell silent. 'There you go,' she said to Claire, and handed Peggy back her shoe.

All eyes turned to Claire. She stood up. For just a split second nothing came out of her mouth.

It was stupid. She should be over this by now, not only because she'd been leading these meetings for almost a year, but because her previous job had required her to give numerous presentations. However, while she was good with people, fabulous one-to-one, there was always this jab of panic every time she got up to talk to a group. It hadn't worn off in the slightest over the years. There was something about this intense moment of silence, when every eye was trained on her, that made her feel like an insect on a microscope slide. Her throat always went dry and her fingers tingled.

She breathed in through her nose and cleared her throat.

She smiled at the small group of women – and George – in front of her, nursing their Diet Cokes and their warm white wines. 'Hi, everyone. Welcome to this month's meeting of the Doris Day Film Club. First, an order of business before we get going with tonight's film: we've had a suggestion… Instead of running film night once a month as usual, we'll meet weekly and have a Doris Day Film festival over the summer: twelve weeks, taking us from now right through to the end of July. Would all those in favour please raise—'

She was cut off as someone gave the slightly temperamental door behind her a shove then barrelled into the room, almost sending her flying. The whole group turned to look at the newcomer. Their visitor, a young woman, stared back at them with undisguised terror.

'Is this the Dor—' Her gaze darted from face to face. She paled as she spotted the red lips and eyelashes of the vintage crew and started to back away. 'Um . . . Never mind. I think I'm . . . um . . . in the wrong place.'

She attempted to reverse, but hadn't counted on the fact she'd moved a little bit sideways as she'd fallen into the room and she ended up backing into the wall and hitting her head on a wall light, almost dislodging its tasselled orange shade.

'No, you're in the right place,' Claire said softly. 'This is the Doris Day Film Club.' She indicated an empty chair next to Kitty, the nearest of the vintage girls. 'Please join us.'

The girl remained frozen. Claire realised she was younger than she'd first thought, maybe only in her late teens. She wore a football shirt and shapeless jeans with battered trainers on her feet. There wasn't a lick of make-up on her face and her thin dark hair was parted severely down the middle and hung lank down either side of her face.

'We'd love to have you.' She held out her hand. 'I'm Claire, the president of the club, but that doesn't mean much except I do the boring stuff and get custody of the library of films we watch each meeting.'

The girl looked at her hand as if it were a live cobra about to strike. Panicked, she glanced at the door, but Claire had stepped forward when she'd starting talking to her and was now blocking her escape route.

Eventually, the girl's shoulders slumped. 'I'm Abby,' she said, so quietly that Claire hardly heard her above the noise of the drinkers who'd spilled out onto the street below the open windows, eager to escape the cloying heat of the pub's dark interior.

Kitty straightened her spine and twisted to stare at Abby as she bypassed the empty seat next to her and scuttled round the back of the tables and chairs to find a spot in the corner tucked away behind Bev and Candy.

'Hang on, I know you, don't I?' she said.

Abby didn't answer, just dropped into the chair, hunched over and folded her arms tight.

Claire looked between the two of them. A couple of the others were scowling, thinking Abby a bit rude, but it hadn't been disdain Claire had seen on Abby's face. It had been fear. Strange, because Kitty was a friendly, open-hearted girl of twenty-three, whose passion for all things vintage was unrivalled, her only flaw a tendency to open her mouth and let whatever entered her head spill out of it.

Despite the snub, Kitty grinned at their new member. Abby, however, didn't see it, as her eyes were fixed steadily on the beer mat on the table in front of her.

'Abby Preston, that's right. You used to go to St Joseph's, same as me. My younger brother Gus was on the football team with you. He was always moaning that you got to play centre midfield instead of him. He was well miffed that you were the best on the team!'

Abby looked up. Her long straight hair had partially fallen over her face and she didn't brush it out of the way. 'Really?'

Kitty nodded. 'Really.'

Abby looked down again at the table, but Claire noticed that she now wore the barest of smiles.

'Well, it's lovely to have you with us for the evening, Abby,' Claire said, as she took her seat, 'and don't worry, if it's not your cup of tea, you don't have to come back next time.'

Much to everyone's surprise, Abby shot to her feet again, sending her chair skittering backwards into the wall. 'But that's just it! I *do* have to come back next week!'

Claire gave a slightly nervous laugh. 'No . . . honestly. We won't *make* you stay!'

Abby shook her head. 'It's not you I'm worried about,' she explained, with a wobble in her voice. 'It's my mum. She's blackmailing me.'

'Blackmailing?' Claire repeated quietly.

Abby nodded, her jaw tight. 'She says she gave birth to and raised a little girl and that she's tired of me going around looking like a football hooligan and that it's high time I learned to be a bit more ladylike.'

'I see,' Claire said slowly, not really sure she did.

'My mum says exactly the opposite,' Kitty said brightly. 'She keeps asking when I'm going to stop showing her up by dressing up like a pantomime dame!'

There was a murmur of sympathetic laughter from around the room.

'My mother was always going on about the fact my slip was showing,' the old lady sitting next to Abby said. 'She said I was the untidiest child she'd ever seen.'

Claire watched Abby take in Bev's spotless pink blouse, the crease in her nylon trousers and her perfectly permed hair. Bev smiled back at her. 'Mothers and daughters,' she said. 'Some things never change.'

Claire frowned. 'The demanding parent thing I get, believe me. But what I don't get is why it has anything to do with us . . . the Doris Day Film Club?'

Abby sighed. 'She often pops in downstairs for a drink and she's seen you all going through the pub looking . . .' she broke off to glanced around the room '. . . well, looking like *girls*, and last week she came home with a flyer for your meetings and stuck it to the front of the fridge with a magnet. She says it's this or a spa weekend.' Abby paused for a moment to let a shudder ripple up her spine. 'And since neither of us have got the money for one of those, here I am.'

Claire shook her head, but she was smiling at the same time. 'I'm sure she's not going to actually—'

'Oh yes she is!' Abby blurted out. 'She's hired the whole pub out for her fortieth birthday party in six weeks' time, and she says she's getting desperate. No way am I allowed to show her up in front of her friends.'

'Stand up to her,' Peggy said, folding her arms across her chest. 'She can't force you, can she?'

Abby looked quite fierce. 'Actually, she can. She bought tickets to the Arsenal–Man United game for me when I was broke. I'm saving up to pay her back, but now she's holding them hostage. If I don't turn up at her party in a dress with…' she didn't elaborate, twirling of her fingers near her head '. . . hair and . . . m-make up, she says she's going to flog them on eBay.' And then she sat down on her chair with a thump, looking more miserable than ever.

Bev, who had six grandchildren and was always hoping for more to mother, leaned backwards and patted Abby's hand in a matter-of-fact way. 'Don't you worry,' she told her. 'If there are two things this lot aren't short of, it's advice – whether you want it or not – and fashion sense.'

'I'm not sure any amount of fashion advice is going to help me,' Abby said mournfully, 'but thank you.'

Bev nodded. 'Don't you get het up about that right now. You got here for the meeting, just like your mother asked. We'll start worrying about the rest of it next time. All you need to do now is sit back and enjoy the film. You can do that, can't you?'

Abby gave her a weak smile and nodded.

'That's sorted then,' said Bev, and turned back around to face the front of the room.

Claire took her cue. 'Right . . . we might as well get on and watch tonight's film. I was going to go for *Tea for Two*, but now I'm wondering if we should go for one that will give Abby some good fashion ideas.' She opened a large zip-up case that held her entire collection of Doris Day DVDs in sleeves and flicked through it. 'Any suggestions?'

'*The Pajama Game*!' said Kitty loudly. 'It's based on the fashion industry, after all.'

Maggs snorted at the young woman. 'Don't be daft. It's hardly as if Abby needs a nightie for her mother's party, and Doris spends a lot of the rest of the film in factory work clothes.'

Kitty pouted. 'It was just a suggestion.'

'What about *Do Not Disturb*?' Candy said. 'I remember how that dress she wore to the party at the hotel took my breath away the first time I saw it.'

'Oh, my, yes!' Kitty said, almost jumping out of her seat, sulk forgotten. 'All those sequins! And do you remember...? The lining of the coat matched!'

'Maybe . . .' Claire said as she continued to thumb through her collection, frowning slightly. For some reason she wasn't sure that this floor-length dress in orange sequins was going to be Abby's thing.

'I know,' Peggy said firmly beside her. '*Pillow Talk.*'

There was a general buzz of agreement. Claire looked up. Almost everyone was nodding – except for Abby, who was looking at them all as if they were talking a foreign language.

'*Pillow Talk* it is,' Claire said, smiling as she slid it from its sleeve. 'Great choice, Peggy. Jean Louis created the whole wardrobe for that film. It shows Doris in some of the most spectacular creations of her career – smart, simple, elegant. In other words, perfect.'

She dimmed the lights and a reverent hush fell over the room.

The opening credits rolled and a sense of both peace and nostalgia swept over Claire as the jaunty little title song played and an anonymous pyjama-clad couple threw pillows back and forth at each other from their respective beds. She let out a long breath.

It had been a long day, and she hadn't realised she'd need this moment to switch off and unwind until it had come upon her. Now, for a glorious ninety minutes, she could sit back, relax, and lose herself in a world where wrongs were always righted, love always triumphed and even the most scheming scoundrel could be redeemed.

# Chapter Three

## Never Look Back

When the film finished, Claire turned the lights back on and the members of the Doris Day Film Club started to gather their belongings together. Claire noticed Kitty and Grace turn to Abby, expectant looks on their faces.

'Did you like the film?' Grace asked. Of the two, she was definitely less talkative, preferring to emulate some of the screen goddesses of old and maintain an air of mystery. She was tall, with a long neck, aristocratic features and vibrant red hair. Her eyes were always slightly hooded, and Claire was never quite sure whether it was in an effort to look sexy or because she thought feigning boredom was cool. She and the *shoot first, think later* Kitty were certainly an interesting pair.

Abby looked from one to the other, as if she was surprised girls like that would start up a conversation with her, and then a slow, shy smile spread across her lips. She nodded. Kitty and Grace gave each other a knowing look.

'What did you like best about it?' Kitty asked, grabbing Abby's arm.

Abby's eyes widened, then she thought for a moment. 'I liked her . . . Jan. I mean, Doris. She seemed nice.'

'That's why we love Doris too,' Kitty said, while Grace just flicked her hair back over her shoulder. 'There's something so warm and approachable about her, even while she's looking glamorous in all those epic clothes and—'

'She's sexy too,' Grace added in her husky voice.

'Yes,' Kitty said, 'but she's sexy without being in-your-face about it.' She shot a look at Grace as she said that. 'And then there's the whole "perpetual virgin" thing . . . I think it's kind of romantic . . . I think I'd like to be thought of that way – sexy but unobtainable.'

'I don't think anyone's going to mistake *you* for a perpetual virgin!'

Kitty pinned her with a fierce look. 'Well, that's better than being like you! If a man ever does get into those knickers of yours, he's going to find they've frozen solid!'

Grace just flicked her hair again and turned away.

Kitty leaned in closer to Abby and took on a confidential tone. 'Okay, I had some insecurity issues a while ago, and maybe I tried to solve them by seeking male attention—' she glanced towards the blank screen of the television '—but watching these films has made me think that maybe I'd like a bit of old-fashioned respect.'

Abby nodded, looking uncomfortable at Kitty's massive overshare.

Grace's perfect mask of calm showed signs of cracking. 'Sorry,' she said to Kitty, while keeping her eyes fixed on the garish wallpaper. 'I've been trying to develop some of that Bacall-like rapier wit and sometimes it runs away with me.'

Kitty rolled her eyes but her expression softened. 'Forgiven. Anyway, we're drifting from the point . . . What we're trying to do is tell Abby that Doris is all about the fun and the romance—'

'And the fashion,' Grace added seriously.

Claire was sliding the DVD of *Pillow Talk* back into her storage case. She'd been listening to the conversation. 'Actually, Doris ended up hating the image people, and the media, had of her. Her real life wasn't like that at all,' she said.

Kitty and Grace looked at her, their expressions slightly blank. Abby looked at the floor.

'We all love her because she's bright and perky and happy on screen, you're right,' Claire continued, 'but she had a lot of tragedy in her life. The real Doris Day is a lot more complex than people think.'

'Oh, I know,' Kitty said, nodding absent-mindedly, and then she grinned, 'but the *clothes*! Did you see the clothes, Abby? Which ones were your favourites?'

And with that, Kitty inked arms with Abby and steered her towards the door. Grace wafted along behind them. Poor Abby looked stuck halfway between awe and terror. Who knew if she was going to come again next meeting – which would be next week, rather than next month, as the membership had unanimously embraced the idea of a Doris Day film festival. Claire supposed it depended on how desperate she was for those Arsenal tickets.

She looked up at Maggs, who was hovering near the committee table, and gave a heavy sigh. 'They don't get it, do they? Those girls? They don't know the truth about

Doris. All they can see is the pastel colours, the dazzling smile, the voice of an angel . . .'

They didn't know what Claire knew – the one reason she'd really started to love Doris Day in her own right, not because her grandmother had – that Doris was tough. She was a survivor. Claire wanted to be just like her.

'It'll come,' Maggs said, strangely reasonably for her. 'After all, you didn't get it at first.'

Claire nodded. She hoped Maggs was right. It was one of the reasons she'd wanted to keep the club running after Gran's death. Gran had known the truth too, drawn strength from it. Her life hadn't been easy either.

There wasn't much clearing up to be done after club meetings. Usually, there'd be a bit of chit-chat after the film, then people would drift off one by one until it was just her, left to give the place a quick once-over before she turned out the light and shut the door, but tonight Maggs was hovering.

Claire straightened the lampshade that Abby had bumped into. Maggs didn't seem to be making any moves to leave, so Claire glanced over her shoulder at her, just in time to see Maggs finish taking a quick nip from her hip flask and hide it back in her handbag.

Claire frowned, but didn't say anything about it. Instead, she asked, 'George not giving you a lift this evening?'

Maggs shook her head. 'I told him to go on without me.'

Claire stopped fussing with the shade, which would just not consent to stay horizontal. 'Oh? Are things okay between you two?'

Maggs shrugged.

Claire turned to look at her. She'd thought Maggs and George might have been developing a little 'thing'. Maybe she'd been wrong, but she hadn't failed to notice the way that at some club meetings, as the film rolled, George wouldn't be watching Doris on the fifty-two inch screen all the time. Sometimes he'd be watching Maggs.

It wouldn't be such a bad thing, even though Maggs had scoffed at the suggestion. Claire knew how lonely she'd been after Sid had died. They'd been married for thirty-eight years, after all. It had to leave a horrible hole.

She put a hand on Maggs's bony shoulder. Maggs, her full height at five feet and one inch, looked up at Claire, her expression guarded, eyes searching. 'I just don't know,' she said quietly, revealing more than she ever had on the subject before. 'He's a sweet man, but he's not . . . ' She looked away.

*He's not Sid,* Claire finished for her silently. She got that.

'Well, I'll give you a lift back if you want,' Claire said and continued to bustle around while really doing nothing. It was better if she pretended she hadn't seen that mistiness in Maggs's eyes.

When Claire had been a child she'd always thought of her grandmother's best friend as 'that funny lady', but as she'd grown into an adult, she'd come to appreciate the other woman's dry humour, her mastery of the snappy comeback. They'd found a new kind of closeness since her grandmother's death, bound together by her absence in a much stronger way than they had been by her presence.

Maggs sniffed and gave Claire a faux-offended look. 'I'm not too old and frail to get the two-seven-one, you know. Those louts who like to ride on the top deck don't scare me!'

Claire turned to have one last go at the lampshade, mainly to make sure Maggs didn't see her smiling at that comment.

If anything, those 'louts' were more likely to be cowed by Maggs than the other way round. 'I know that,' she said, turning back, 'but my car has air conditioning and I can give you door-to-door service.'

Maggs adjusted the light cardigan she'd slung over her shoulder. 'I suppose I can keep you company, if you want. There's something I need to talk to you about, anyway.'

'Club business?' Claire asked absent-mindedly as she flicked off the lights and they both exited onto the landing.

'Not exactly,' Maggs muttered as she followed behind.

\*

Given the fact she had something to say, Maggs was very quiet on the drive home. She didn't speak until they were almost there. 'I had a letter from your father,' she announced suddenly, staring straight ahead, looking for all the world as if she'd just told Claire she had a hairdressing appointment in the morning.

Claire didn't decide to brake hard – she just did – causing both her and Maggs to fly forward until their seat belts engaged, digging into their chests then flinging them back into their seats again. She turned to stare at Maggs, only half aware her fingers were making dents in the steering wheel.

'What . . . ? I mean, how . . . ?' She shook her head, kept on shaking it. 'How did he know your address?'

Maggs shrugged and glanced at her. Now that Claire was looking at her more carefully, she could see that Maggs wasn't as blasé about the whole thing as she'd first thought. There was a tension around her mouth, as if someone had pulled a drawstring round it, crinkling its edges.

'To be honest, I have no idea, but he wrote to me anyway.'

Claire realised that her little Fiat was blocking the narrow Victorian street, lined with parked cars on both sides. It was only a matter of time before some other motorist started honking their horn or swearing at her. She slid the car into gear and eased away slowly. 'What did he want?'

'To see you.'

The urge to brake hard again was strong, but Claire managed to beat it. Instead, she concentrated on indicating left and turning into Maggs's road. 'Why now?' she whispered, more to herself than her passenger.

Maggs sighed. 'He didn't say.'

Claire's brows lowered and pinched the skin at the top of her nose. Of course he hadn't said. Her father had never felt the need to explain anything he did, had only saw fit to issue orders. She stewed on that thought as she performed a perfect parallel park outside Maggs's house.

'But reading between the lines,' Maggs continued as the car came to a halt, 'I'd say he's ill.'

Claire realised she was squeezing the life out of her steering wheel again and deliberately peeled her fingers from its warm surface. 'I don't care,' she said. She could feel Maggs looking at her, and Maggs kept looking until Claire gave in and twisted her head to stare back at her. 'I don't.'

'He's your father,' Maggs said simply.

She nodded. She knew that.

'If anyone knows the pain of not taking an opportunity to make things right while you can, it's me.'

Claire sighed. There was a difference. Maggs had had a silly quarrel with Sid the day before he'd died and the following morning she'd been monosyllabic with him at breakfast. He'd told her she was being childish then went out to fetch a pint of milk from the corner shop. She'd never seen him again. Not until she'd had to identify his body. Heart attack. No one had seen it coming, not even Sid, who'd declared himself as fit as an ox until the day his body had so unceremoniously contradicted him.

'It's not the same,' Claire mumbled. She hadn't seen her father since she was eleven. But she'd never been sad she hadn't had the chance to say goodbye properly; she'd been glad. Glad he'd never come back. Glad she didn't have to go and spend weekends and half the school holidays with him. Glad her mother slowly stopped being the quiet, shrunken woman he'd turned her into.

Maggs made a noise of grudging agreement, then she delved into her ever-present patent black leather handbag and pulled out a crumpled envelope and held it out to her.

Claire stared at it. She didn't even want to touch it.

When she refused to respond, Maggs folded the envelope in two and tucked it into Claire's handbag, which was nestled in the passenger footwell. 'Never say never,' she said quietly before she kissed Claire on the cheek, then reached for the door handle. 'Because never is a very long time,' she added, as she gently unclipped her seatbelt and got out of the car.

Claire tried to look cheerful, but it felt wrong, as if her smile was sitting wonky on her face. She waved her farewell and, when Maggs had disappeared inside, she put the car in gear and drove away.

# Chapter Four

## I Can Do Without You

Claire slid her key into the bottom lock of her front door, only half aware of what she was doing. An image of her father, stern and disapproving as he sat in his favourite armchair, would not be dislodged from her head. She hated that it was lingering in her brain like a squatter almost as much as she'd hated being summoned to see him all those years ago.

Her mother had always kept a nice house, had taken pains to make it feel welcoming and homey. They'd had yellow walls in the hallway and lounge, so it would always feel like the sun was shining even when it wasn't, her mother had said. But Claire couldn't picture that when she remembered standing there, frozen with fear, outside the living room door.

Her memories were bleached, making the light weak and pale blue, like the morning after a snowfall. Even now the thought of that cold light made her shiver.

The longer she'd stood there hesitating, the more the image of her father behind the door had grown in her mind, large and imposing, like one of those statues of Lenin she'd seen in a history book, until he and his stupid armchair had filled the room.

Eventually, she'd pushed the door open with her finger-tips, secretly hoping it would stick, but it had always swung open; he'd been fastidious about DIY. Getting the walk and the expression on her face just right had been of the utmost importance. Too bright and bouncy and he'd think she was being flippant. Too dour and slow and he'd say she looked guilty.

She closed her eyes and shook her head as she dealt with the top lock. He wasn't there any more. Not in that house where she'd grown up. Certainly not in her life. He really shouldn't still be here, deep inside her skull. A rush of warmth tingled from her fingers up to her face. She was angry with him for making her think of him when she'd erased him from her consciousness so completely. Angry with him for contacting her. For pretending for even the tiniest millisecond that he cared.

Anyway, festering about the past was not the way she'd chosen to live her life. She'd learned that much from Doris Day at least.

She pushed her glossy black front door open and moved to step inside, but it bounced back and smashed her in the face.

Ow.

She frowned, rubbed her nose and tried again, this time keeping her distance. Once again the door sprang back towards her. Seriously? Had there been that much junk mail since this morning that it was blocking her progress into the hallway?

It was possible. She only owned the upstairs of the Victorian terraced house. She and the downstairs owner shared this front door and the decent-sized hallway. Her neighbour didn't know the meaning of unsubscribing from a mailing list, and because he really just used this flat as a crash pad, she was always having to hoover up his unwanted mail and shove it in the recycling. What did 'Mr Dominic Arden' want with five different subscriptions to geeky-looking magazines about cameras and microphones for anyway? Surely nobody could be that sad?

And then there were the takeaway leaflets. Not just the ones that came through the door if you wanted them or not. He was such a good customer when he was here, obviously, that every greasy kebab or curry shop in the whole of north London had put him on their mailing list and sent him regular vouchers and leaflets about special deals.

She took a deep breath to steady herself and gave the door one final hefty shove. Whatever it was that had been blocking the door moved, but it felt a whole lot sturdier than a wodge of glossy leaflets advertising fifteen per cent off home delivery Chinese.

Frowning, she stepped into the hallway. She'd have to clear up whatever it was, otherwise she'd just have to fight her way through it again in the morning. She reached for the light switch beside the door, cheering herself up by imagining shoving all the junk mail through his letterbox from that day forward, letting him deal with the recycling Everest when he finally returned home.

Her fingers, however, never made it to the switch, because no sooner had she got one foot inside the door she tripped over something. Something hard and metal and rubbery at the same time. She came crashing down on her knees, her hands shooting out in front of her to stop her face hitting the black and white tiled floor.

She stayed there on all fours, shaking slightly and trying to make sense of the usually ordered universe of her hallway. Slowly, she reached out to the right and felt for whatever it was that had caused all the trouble. She found thin metal rod and then a sturdier strut, and by the time her fingers had gripped the blocky rubber tread of a wheel she'd got the whole thing worked out.

It was a flipping bike! *His* flipping bike. Mr Downstairs. Mr Come And Go As I Please, Not Minding Anyone Else Arden. Claire hauled herself to her feet and, without moving them for fear of being felled again, leaned towards the wall and switched on the light.

The bulb promptly exploded.

Of course it did.

The hall was plunged into darkness once again, but for a flickering moment she'd glimpsed the hulking bike lying across the hall floor, sprawled across a heap of brightly coloured leaflets and polythene-wrapped magazines. She would have kicked the stupid thing if she hadn't been scared she'd tangle her toes up in the spokes and injure herself further.

Carefully, she felt around for the frame of the bike and then lifted it to stand against the wall, where it had undoubtedly started off the evening. However, her neighbour had thoughtlessly parked it too close to the front door, not caring that she wouldn't be able to enter, and then had gone off to bed or God knows where without a care in the world. It was totally and utterly typical of him.

Honestly, she didn't know how her grandmother had put

up with him for so long! Claire had inherited both flat and bothersome neighbour after Gran's death and even though she'd lived here for a year now, he'd probably only been in residence for a couple of weeks of that time – a few days here, a few days there – but she was already hoping he'd just up sticks and move abroad for good one day and stay permanently out of her hair.

Thankfully, she knew this hallway like the back of her hand and, with the help of the dim glow of a street light across the road, she made it to her flat door without further incident. Once inside, she exhaled and slumped back against the closed door. For a moment, she just concentrated on breathing.

There was no point in getting all het up about things she couldn't change, was there? *Que sera, sera* and all that. She doubted her Neanderthal of a neighbour was ever going to amend his behaviour. What she needed to do was take a leaf out of Doris's book and smile in the face of adversity, have a 'thumbs-up' attitude rather than a 'thumbs-down' one. After all, Doris had had a lot more tragedy in her life than an inconsiderate downstairs neighbour. According to her autobiography, the men in her life had done far worse to her than that.

First, she'd mentioned the musician husband who'd beat her and even once threatened to kill her and their unborn child, then her sadness at the failure of her second marriage after only eight months. She'd adored him, but he hadn't been able to handle her growing fame. Then, according to Doris, husband number three had kept an iron grip on her career, becoming more of a father figure than a life partner. After his death, it transpired his lawyer had embezzled more

than twenty million dollars from Doris – almost the entire
fortune she'd spend her career building – and had left her
half a million dollars in debt. Years later, she'd still never
been sure if her husband been totally duped by the lawyer
or if he'd had some hand in the shady dealings. Marriage
number four hadn't ended that happily either.

In the light of that, Claire could surely endure a mountain
bike and a ton of junk mail!

She breathed out again and let her shoulders relax. There.
That was better. Maybe she'd even find it funny in the
morning.

Whatever will be, will be. Whatever had happened, had
happened. She couldn't change it, so she might was well
ignore it, move on . . .

But her knees complained as she started to walk down
the hallway towards the living room. She looked down to
discover red marks on both of them and a tiny cut on her
right leg, where she must have sprawled into the upended
mountain bike. That horrible warm, itchy sensation that had
come over her on the doorstep when she'd been thinking
of her father returned, but she attempted to bat it away like
a pesky fly.

She decided to watch TV for a bit before heading to bed,
her system still too pumped full of adrenalin for her to drop
off yet. She collapsed onto the sofa and reached for the
remote, but as she flicked through the TV channels, she
found herself staring round the room more than paying
attention to the screen. The itchy sensation wouldn't leave.
She had the horrible sense that bothersome insect of a
feeling had landed and was laying eggs, that it would just
keep growing and breeding no matter what she did.

Ugh. She shuddered and attempted to distract herself by looking around the room.

While she'd moved her furniture in, she'd also kept some of her grandmother's stuff, including a glazed bookcase and a bureau with a roll-top that stuck. The floral wallpaper was the one she remembered from her childhood, so old it had gone out of fashion and come back in again, but it matched Claire's modern retro-inspired sofa and armchair perfectly.

She sighed.

God, she missed her gran. Her nose stung and a tear appeared at the corners of both eyes. She kept staring at the large cream peonies on the wall, watching them blur in and out of their pale sage background until the moisture evaporated and the urge to give in and just sob abated. She realised she'd stopped on some show with loud-mouthed people arguing over the contents of abandoned storage lockers and shook her head. Gran would have hated this programme. No class. No class at all.

With that thought in her mind, she aimed the remote squarely at the screen and turned the TV off, then rose and hauled herself to bed. Suddenly, she felt very, very tired.

*

Claire tossed and turned all night, partly because of the heat, despite the fact large sash windows in her bedroom were open both top and bottom, and partly because every time she woke, she realised she'd been having a conversation with her downstairs neighbour in her sleep, letting him know just how inconsiderate and selfish she found him.

She really wasn't doing very well at this live-and-let-live, whatever-will-be stuff, was she? It was stupid that something so trivial was affecting her this way, but ever since Maggs had mentioned her father's letter earlier that evening she'd felt as if everything was topsy-turvy.

It didn't help that in her dream conversations her neighbour hadn't had a face. On the rare occasions he'd returned from wherever he'd been overseas he seemed to live a nocturnal existence. She'd heard doors slam, been woken by his music at unearthly hours, had to haul his bin back from the path after bin day, because he'd already left and someone would probably nick it if it stayed there too long, but she'd never once laid eyes on him.

At four-fifteen she let out a growl of frustration, threw back the sheet and got out of bed. There was only one way she knew to deal with this kind of thing. She needed to do something concrete, something to get these words out of her head.

It had been so hot that she'd been sleeping naked, so she pulled on her white shortie PJs with the large red hearts on them – a Christmas gift from Gran two years ago. It had been a joke between them, seeing as they resembled the ones Doris wore at the end of *The Pajama Game* – and stumbled into the kitchen. She grabbed the reporter's notebook and biro she often used for her shopping lists and started to scribble.

Halfway down the page she stopped. It looked terrible. The sort of thing a lazy school child would scrawl as a forgery explaining that the family pet had digested their homework. It carried just as much weight and looked just as convincing.

She stood up and put the kettle on, deciding a nice strong cup of tea might help bring her to her senses, then reached into the dresser she'd found in a local junk shop for her good writing paper and rummaged in her pen pot for her fountain pen.

Yes, she had writing paper. The proper kind. It was the colour of clotted cream with ridges that felt nice if you ran your fingertips over the surface. Gran had always stressed the importance of a good 'thank you' letter, especially after birthdays and Christmas, and Claire had found it was one convention in this day of emails, status updates and Tweets that she didn't want to let go of.

She made her tea and then sat down again, her eyes feeling slightly less gritty and her hand slightly more steady. She decided to use the scribbled note as a starting point and began to both copy and edit as her indigo ink swept across the page.

When she was finished, she folded it neatly into three and pushed it into an envelope with a tissue lining. It was a thing of beauty, and it seemed a travesty to be using stationery like this on a philistine like Mr Arden, but she hoped it would help her get her point across. She meant business, and this letter certainly screamed it loud and clear. She was tired of letting men ride roughshod over her and, while this might not be much, it was a symbol of something bigger. It was a start.

She licked the envelope, pressed the flap closed and then stood up. No time like the present, she thought, as she nipped out of her flat, padded carefully down the stairs, now illuminated with greyish pre-dawn light, and carefully and noiselessly lifted her neighbour's letterbox.

She paused just at the moment she prepared to let the envelope drop onto the varnished floorboards inside. Slowly, she eased the letter back out of the slot, and then, still gripping it lightly, she turned her head and looked at the sprawl of junk mail cluttering up her hallway.

If she posted it, it would probably just get buried under everything else. Better to put it somewhere he was bound to find it. Her eyes came to rest on the culprit of her sore knees, resting innocently against the wall.

Hmm. He'd used his bike yesterday, and even if he didn't use it again before he left, he'd still probably pick it up and put it back inside his flat. She walked over and placed the letter strategically on the saddle, then stepped back and surveyed her handiwork. There. That should do.

However, as she turned to creep back up the stairs, she had one last flash of inspiration . . .

Quickly, and before she could talk herself out of it, she grabbed the bike and rolled it forwards so the front wheel was *just* sticking a centimetre or two past the edge of her neighbour's front door. There. He wouldn't be able to miss it now – just like she hadn't been able to miss the stupid contraption last night.

She grinned naughtily as she tiptoed back up the stairs, thinking to herself that it was just as well Doris was still going strong in her nineties. Even though Miss Day was known to have a keen sense of fun, Claire wasn't sure she'd have been proud of what she'd just done if she'd been peering down from heaven.

# Chapter Five

# Anything You Can Do

Dominic's body clock was so screwed up he'd bypassed the sleepy stage of tiredness and now just felt a bit drunk. Reality swam in and out of focus when he opened his eyes. For a moment, he thought he was in yet another hostel or airport, but he soon realised the reason he didn't recognise his own bedroom ceiling was two-fold—firstly, he stayed here so infrequently he'd forgotten what it looked like and, secondly, somehow he'd turned himself around in the night, and now he was lying with one foot on his pillow and his head in the opposite corner of the bed, one arm dangling towards the floor.

*Food.*

That was the thought that entered his head, a primal and desperate signal sent direct from his abdomen to his brain, but the rest of him was so exhausted he couldn't decide whether he wanted to eat or throw up. Be that as it may, he still managed to flip himself off the bed and stumble into his kitchen.

Inspecting the fridge might be a risky manoeuvre. He'd gone straight out for a 'welcome home' drink with his mate

Pete as soon as he'd dropped his rucksack inside his front door and hadn't checked the contents yet. He couldn't quite recall if he'd remembered to empty it before he'd left back in February.

To be honest, he was happy to leave that riddle unanswered for now.

He turned his attention to the cupboards. There wasn't much tempting there, either. Packets of rice and pasta. A tin of kidney beans that he had no memory of buying – especially since he hated the things. Some Cup-a-Soups that were well past their expiration date.

His stomach growled and clenched.

Great.

It had finally made up its mind what it wanted: anything, basically. As long as it arrived within the next thirty seconds. He was just giving the can of kidney beans some serious thought when he spotted something brightly coloured lurking in the back of the cupboard. Before his brain even registered what it was, his hand delved in and retrieved it.

He laughed a little manically as he saw it and thought to himself, still smiling, that he was definitely still sleep loopy. Why else would the sight of a multipack of miniature cereal boxes be quite so funny?

He started tearing at the cellophane, which was a pretty stupid idea, he discovered, because as he battled with one end of the package, a box of Coco Pops fell out the other.

Ah, he'd already started them. He remembered now. This had been the joke gift Pete had given him on his birthday, quipping that Dominic couldn't even commit to something as big as a whole box of cereal.

He abandoned the boxes still imprisoned in the cellophane

for the one that had escaped. He ripped open the top and poured the contents into a bowl and ate it with a spoon that was technically too large for his mouth. He didn't care. It was just the first thing that his fingers had landed on when he'd raided the cutlery drainer on the sink.

He turned and sat on the table, legs swinging, as he munched his way through the first couple of mouthfuls. Once he'd shoved the third in, he realised that, as nice as they were, Coco Pops were a tad dry on their own. He glanced hesitantly at the fridge. Any milk he'd left in there had probably been growing bacteria for so long it had now evolved into an organism the size of a small Yeti.

And then he remembered . . .

The old bird upstairs had her milk delivered. Had done for years.

He checked the clock. Six-forty. If he timed it right, he could 'borrow' a pint, then go out and buy a replacement before she came down to fetch it in. He wasn't usually given to such petty thievery, but he was desperate. She was a nice old lady, with a great sense of humour and a twinkle in her eye. He was sure she'd understand.

He dropped his cereal bowl on the table with a clang, sending a shower of tiny chocolate pellets across the surface, and headed out of the kitchen. He was just salivating at the thought of all that ice-cold milk making his cereal pop when he opened his flat door, stepped outside and immediately found himself face down on the hall floor, something sharp digging into his arm.

He discovered it was a brake lever.

What the . . .?

He lay there for a moment, wondering if he was still

dreaming, but the insistent throbbing in his bicep where the brake lever had poked him made that unlikely. Slowly, he picked himself up and dusted himself off. He could have sworn he hadn't left the bike there last night. However, severe jet lag and a couple of beers could mean he was wrong about that. He probably shouldn't have cycled home.

It was then he noticed the crisp white envelope lying on the floor. It was addressed to *Mr D. Arden*. He kept an eye on it while he righted his bike and leaned it against the wall, then picked the pristine letter up and went to snaffle the milk from the front step.

Thankfully, some things never changed. There was a pint waiting for him, still cold enough to be beaded with condensation. He picked it up, keeping the letter in his other hand, and made a mental note to go out to the shops as soon as he'd finished breakfast. He knew a plastic carton wasn't going to fool her, but he'd leave a note, explaining . . .

Once back inside, he dumped a generous amount of milk on his Coco Pops then sat down on one of the kitchen chairs to read the letter.

*Dear Mr Arden,* it started. He snorted. That made him sound like his father. People hardly ever called him that. Most just used his last name, no pleasantries. Sometimes people used his Christian name, but a lot of his friends just called him Nic, mostly because he'd made it clear if they ever tried to shorten it to 'Dom' he'd flatten them. Whatever this letter contained, he guessed it wasn't going to be good news.

He read on . . .

*It has come to my attention that you are in residence again.*

He snorted again, smiling as he continued to shove Coco Pops in his face. *In residence?* That didn't just make him sound like his father; now he sounded like the Queen!

*As a consequence, I think we should establish some ground rules that allow us to cohabit harmoniously.*

Ah, the old bird upstairs. Once upon a time they'd got on fairly well, but maybe she was getting extra crabby in her old age. He stopped both reading and chewing to look at his kitchen ceiling. Come to think of it, he hadn't seen her for quite a while. How long had it been? One year? Two? One time he'd come back she'd been so quiet he thought she might have gone into a home.

He'd thought they'd had quite a good arrangement going. Most of the time she had the house to herself and when he was 'in residence' she was deaf enough that she hadn't minded his loud music or the fact his body clock was so messed up that sometimes he clattered about in the middle of the night and slept all day. Mainly, they'd just stayed out of each other's hair. It seemed that was about to change.

He carried on reading, Coco Pops forgotten, with a growing sense of apprehension.

*Firstly, I think we can all agree that the communal hallway is not a bicycle shed.*

His eyebrows rose and he let out of huff of surprised laughter. His upstairs neighbour was starting to remind him of Mrs McClure, his old headmistress, who had also had a lot to say about him and bike sheds – but it hadn't been about leaving his bike there, that was for sure.

*Secondly, each of us should be responsible for our own post and the disposal thereof. I'm sure the Amazon rain-forest will benefit greatly if you could cut down on your*

*magazine subscriptions and remove yourself from quite so
many takeaway food mailing lists.*

He picked up his spoon and shovelled another helping of
cereal in, frowning. Okay, this had been mildly amusing to
start with, but where did this interfering old busybody get
off telling him how to run his life?

*Lastly, I should remind you that it is your duty to maintain
any lights on the ground floor, just as it is mine to replace
those on the top landing. It seems the light bulb in the hallway blew last night so I'd be very glad if you could replace
it promptly and before you go away again, to prevent any
further accidents from happening.*

*Yours sincerely,*

*Claire Bixby*

Dominic stared at the letter. He wasn't feeling quite as
cheerful as he had when he'd picked it up. He chewed
and his frown lines deepened further. Claire? He thought
her name had been Laura or Lottie or something like that,
although he'd always erred on the safe side and called her
Mrs Bixby. He shook his head and threw the now chocolate
milk-splattered letter down on the table. But then that
generation were keen on abandoning their given names
for nicknames. Look at his grandparents . . . They'd been
christened Mavis and Reg, but everyone had called them
Teddy and Bob.

He sighed. Normally, he'd have blown this off, because
he'd have been away and the snotty letter thousands of
miles behind him in less than a week's time. However, the
shoulder he'd busted a couple of years ago working in South
America had been bothering him. And if it bothered him too
much, then he couldn't carry his kit, and that just wasn't

thinkable, especially now he was branching out, mixing his freelance camera operator work with making films of his own.

Stupid doctor had told him he needed to rest it, to let it finish its healing process without having to deal with the rigours of supporting a broadcast-size camera for hours on end, travelling in jeeps that would have laughed at the idea of suspension and sleeping in hammocks or on the ground.

He'd had the offer to work on a historical documentary for the BBC in China, about a plucky single lady from London by the name of Gladys Aylward, who'd travelled to China to be a missionary at the turn of the twentieth century. Not only had she ended up adopting over a hundred orphans, but she'd marched them over mountains and the Yellow River to escape the invading Japanese army.

Aside from the fact he was interested in the story, the job would put plenty of money in the coffers for his next directorial project, and would also provide some useful contacts. However, he needed to be fully fit by mid-July or they were going to have to go with someone else. He had some physio sessions lined up and an appointment with the specialist at the end of June, so he couldn't say yay or nay until then.

All in all, it meant just one thing. He was grounded. For now at least.

Which also meant he was going to have to play nice with the old lady upstairs. He blew out a breath of frustration. Whoop-de-do. Less than twenty-four hours back in dear old London and he was already having so much fun.

He threw his empty cereal bowl in the sink and headed out to the hallway to collect his bike and stash it back in his spare room. And while he was at it, he really ought to write a note – a not too sarcastic note, if he could manage it – and explain about the milk. That was really going to put him in her good books, wasn't it?

She had a point, he supposed. She probably wasn't too steady on her feet any more, and the last thing he wanted was to be responsible for a broken hip because she'd tripped over his bike. He had left it in a pretty stupid place, hadn't he? So stupid that he'd managed to fall foul of it himself. He shook his head and laughed softly as he lifted it up and manhandled it into his flat. It was only as he was resting it against the wall of his spare room-slash-office that he started to think about exactly just how stupidly the bike had been positioned . . .

He swore. Quite violently. And he didn't care if the old bat could hear him!

The bike had been left partially covering his door, hadn't it? Now he was properly awake, he could remember where he'd left it quite clearly, and it certainly hadn't been where he'd found it this morning. The old witch! There was no way he could have parked the bike blocking his own front door, no matter how tired he was.

He wasn't sure whether to have her arrested for assault or admire her for pranking him like that.

Looking at the desk full of unread *Video Monthly* and *HD Camera Pro* magazines, he walked over and rummaged for a bit of paper – any bit of paper – and a pen. He was going to write the sweet little old lady upstairs a note all right, but it certainly wasn't going to be an apology for stealing her milk!

# Chapter Six

## Ain't We Got Fun?

Claire woke with a start and immediately flipped herself over to look at her alarm clock. Sunlight was streaming through her thin floral curtains. Her heart was racing and she pressed a palm against her chest to calm it.

It was okay. It was still only just past seven. She wasn't late for work. She yawned and collapsed back down into the mattress.

She'd crawled back into bed not long after delivering her note to her neighbour, thinking she might as well be comfortable as she whiled the hours away until she needed to get up, but she must have dropped off to sleep almost immediately. Hmm. It seemed she'd been right – her plan of getting all of those churning thoughts out of her head and onto paper had worked. She actually felt quite refreshed. Even that image of her father in his armchair was receding, getting fuzzier and less insistent.

She stared at the ceiling, her mind drifting, and it inevitably flowed until she was thinking of the letter. She replayed what she'd written inside her head, listening to herself as she read it aloud. After a moment, she pushed herself halfway to sitting, rubbed a hand over her face then through her hair. She'd thought the wording had sounded formal and firm last night. Now, in the mellow sunshine of a May morning, it seemed a little . . . well . . . snotty.

It would have been a better idea to just write the stupid thing so she could get some rest, but leave it on her kitchen counter instead of delivering it straight away. She smiled to herself. That was the beauty of actual pen and paper as opposed to electronic forms of communication. It wasn't permanent, irrevocable, until it was in the hands of its intended recipient. With email that took a split second, but she'd bet her letter was still sitting on the bicycle saddle downstairs. She really didn't think Dominic Arden was much of a morning person.

Maybe she should just go down and fetch it, have a little read . . . She could always seal it up in a new envelope if she still thought it was fine, although it did seem a bit of a waste to use *two* such fine bits of stationery on one such unappreciative man.

She flicked the switch of the kettle on as she passed by the kitchen and headed for her front door. Quietly, still in her love-heart PJs, she crept down the stairs and headed for the bike.

Ah.

Too late.

Damn that man's nocturnal wanderings. Not only was her lovely envelope gone, but the bike had disappeared too. He'd definitely found it.

Oh, well. The tone might have been a bit sharp, but she stood by what she'd said. She stared at his front door. There was no movement behind the glazed top panels, no sound from inside. She let out a breath of relief. The confrontation would come eventually, but she was kind of glad it wasn't about to happen right now.

Before heading back upstairs, she turned and crossed the hall to open the front door, but when she stared down at where her glass bottle of milk should have been all she found was a plastic two-pinter with a scruffy note taped to it.

Huh? Since when had the milkman been buying his supplies at Tesco? And why was he sending her notes? She paid her bill online these days.

Frowning, she ripped the note off then hooked the plastic carton over a finger and used her free hand to unfold the piece of paper as she trudged back upstairs.

When Claire was halfway up, she stopped.

Of all the . . .

*Dear Ms Bixby*, it started. *Thank you so much for your very informative note.*

Claire's stomach dropped. The tone matched that of her letter perfectly, and she'd been right – it did sound snotty.

*I'm sure we can all agree . . .* it continued. Claire swallowed and started walking up the stairs to her flat again.

It was written perfectly reasonably and neatly – surprisingly neatly, actually, given that Mr Arden seemed such a pig the rest of the time – but somehow the words oozed sarcasm. Was that how her note had come across? She really hadn't intended it to. She closed her front door, deposited the milk on her kitchen counter and carried on reading, picking up at the beginning of the paragraph again.

*I'm sure we can all agree that you probably don't need to have your nose quite so far into my business. What I do with my post and what I eat really is no concern of yours.*

*I will, however, concede that I shouldn't have left my bike parked where it was last night, but I must admit I (wrongly) assumed that you would be safely indoors and watching* Countdown *with your cocoa by the time I came home, so I didn't think it would be a problem. I apologise for that.*

Claire bristled. This man didn't even know her! How dare he start making assumptions about her like that, as if she was a hopeless spinster who had nothing better to do with her life? The fact that some nights she really was home quite early, often curled up watching trashy TV while she did travel research on her laptop was neither here nor there.

He might have hit the nail on the head – accidentally, of course; she couldn't believe he had a perceptive bone in his body – but he didn't have to make her sound like a dried-up old prune. She'd get around to dating and romance sometime soon; it wasn't totally off the agenda, just not anything she was planning for in the immediate future. Besides, there was more to life than men, that was for sure. She didn't need one to make her complete, as her mother had. If she did find someone she thought she could spend her life with it would be an enrichment, not a necessity.

She shook her head and returned to reading the letter.

*So I apologise for leaving my bike in the hallway and for any inconvenience it might have caused you. I will try to keep it in my flat as much as possible. I have to say that I didn't appreciate the little prank you pulled. I honestly thought you'd be above something like that.*

Claire felt a blush creep up her neck. He was right. She was better than that. Most of the time. And there was she, just thinking he didn't know anything about her. How odd. Maybe he wasn't quite as much of a pig as she'd thought.

She sighed and shook her head. She didn't know what had come over her last night. She'd just been so . . . so . . . after Maggs had given her the letter from her father. Just thinking about it caused that itchy warm feeling come back, tingling in her fingertips, swirling in her head. She clapped a lid on it and tried to ignore it as she went back to reading the letter.

*I have to admit to 'borrowing' your milk this morning. However, I replaced it immediately and I shan't be repeating this act of felony.*

*I have already dealt with the light bulb in the hallway, so that should cause no further problem. However, if you have any future concerns relating to our shared space, feel free to contact me. If you don't, then please could you kindly butt out of my life? Perhaps I can suggest a hobby? Knitting or bingo. A social life. In any event, something to keep you entertained enough so that the urge to meddle doesn't become all-consuming.*

*Yours very sincerely,*
*Mr D. Arden Esq.*

Any goodwill her neighbour had created during his mostly reasonable letter evaporated. Not a pig? She was right about that! This guy was a fully blown warthog.

Mr D Arden *Esquire*? He was mocking her, just with those three little letters. It made her insides burn and her head spin. Before she had a chance to think it through, she ripped the little green cap off the plastic carton of milk and poured the whole lot down the sink. She didn't want any of his milk! She'd go out and buy her own. She didn't want to have any connection to him at all.

There were a few moments of satisfaction as she watched the last of it gurgle down the drain, but then she realised she'd run out of bread and the only thing she had left in the cupboard was cereal. She squashed the empty plastic container to put in the recycling with slightly more force than necessary. There was no way she was going to attempt Weetabix now. It would be like eating hamster bedding. There was only one thing for it.

She threw the carton in her recycling bin and stomped off towards her bedroom. She was going to have to go out for breakfast but, to be honest, the further away she got from here right now the better, otherwise there'd be blue lights and sirens and a puzzled Scenes of Crime Officer wondering how a man could drown in a pint-sized puddle of milk!

# Chapter Seven

# There's Good Blues Tonight

Dominic rang the doorbell, balancing a bunch of carnations and a bottle of wine from the petrol station in one hand. A few seconds later, the door opened and there stood Pete, all bearded six foot five of him, grinning. He slapped Dominic on the shoulder. 'Nic! Mate . . . come in. We're a bit behind schedule. Hope you don't mind if we eat a little—'

He was cut off by a high-pitched female shriek from the living room. 'Sammy! *Noooov!* Don't you dare—'

Pete took off running, Dominic hot on his heels. They both burst down the hallway and through the living room door. There they found Pete's wife Ellen, who was close to tears, and a small boy completely naked from the waist down.

Ellen put her hands on her hips, but her defiant stance was spoiled by the wobbling of her bottom lip. She looked at her husband accusingly. 'He pooed on the carpet. I told him not to but he pooed on the carpet.'

Dominic stifled a smile as he spotted the offending article right in the middle of the rug.

Pete shook his head. 'Sam . . . Mate . . . You know you're supposed to do it in the potty. Where's the potty?'

Sammy, wide-eyed and silent, pointed at the corner of the room, to a gleamingly clean Lightning McQueen potty. Dominic didn't blame him. Who wants to poop in a cool car? They should have got him Hello Kitty to do his business in.

Dominic looked at Ellen again. Her eyes were wild and she looked as if she was about to crack. Her hair was hanging out of what might once have been a ponytail, and her T-shirt was doused with ketchup stains. What had happened to the cool, slick girl he and the rest of his mates had envied Pete for snaffling first?

Obviously, Pete saw what he saw too. He scooped up his son and handed him to Ellen. 'Look, you deal with him and I'll deal with—' he nodded towards the lump of brown on the carpet '—that. Okay?'

Ellen nodded gratefully, then swept swiftly out of the room and upstairs.

Dominic couldn't help grinning as Pete dealt with his son's 'accident'. 'Nice work if you can get it,' he quipped, as Pete went to fetch a pair of hot pink rubber gloves from under the sink. Dominic dumped the flowers on the counter, put the wine in the fridge, then watched, smirking, as his best friend dealt very efficiently with the mess, disinfectant and everything.

Pete just shook his head. 'You wait,' was all he said, and, despite the fact he had just had to clean up someone else's poo, he was still relaxed and smiling. Dominic would have expected at least a couple of swear words. 'Well, that pretty much sums up my life at the moment,' he added as he peeled off the rubber gloves and disposed of them. 'What's new with you?'

Dominic launched into the tale of the bike and notes and the snotty upstairs neighbour. He'd only got to the bit where he'd tripped over the bike when Ellen returned, this time in a clean T-shirt, her hair down and with Sammy in his pyjamas. 'There,' she said, handing the boy back to his father, 'you can deal with *your* son.'

Dominic raised his eyebrows in lieu of a question.

Pete grinned. 'Anything smelly and revolting he does is apparently down to my genes. Ellie takes no responsibility for it whatsoever.'

Dominic chuckled. Ellen certainly had a point. He'd known Pete for ten years and there had definitely been a lot of smells and noises and other disgusting things at times.

'Right, ' Pete said, and hung his son upside down by the ankles. 'We're going to settle it once and for all . . . Where do poos go?'

'Potty!' Sammy yelled back. And then there was lots of giggling and shouting and squealing, mostly from the kid, as he tried to wriggle free of his father's grasp.

'So flipping well do them in there!' Pete said, dropping his son head first onto the sofa and proceeding to tickle him.

'Pete!' Ellen yelled, from the kitchen that joined on to their large living room. 'He's never going to go to sleep if you get him all worked up like that!'

'Okay,' Pete called back breezily, continuing to tickle Sammy, but putting a finger in front of his mouth to indicate they should carry on quietly. Father and son grinned at each other, then Sammy surprised Pete by launching himself at his father and clinging round his neck like his life depended on it.

'Luff you,' he whispered into Pete's neck.

'Love you too, mate,' Pete replied, his voice taking on a scratchy quality.

For some reason, Dominic found a bit of a lump in his throat.

'Come on then, trouble,' Pete said, standing then picking Sammy up round his middle. 'Time to say goodnight. Mummy first . . .'

He disappeared into the kitchen and the clattering of pans stopped for a few seconds, then returned. 'Don't forget Uncle Nic,' he said. Dominic expected Sammy to be shy, like he was last time he'd visited. Maybe a fist bump or a high-five would have done. But when Pete put Sammy down, Sammy rushed at him and gave him a hug almost as tight as he had done his father.

For a moment, Dominic wanted to just close his eyes and feel the warmth of Sam's small body. ''Night, monster,' he said gruffly, as Pete picked Sammy up once more and headed upstairs. While he was gone, Dominic drifted in the direction of the kitchen in search of a drink.

He found Ellen in there wrestling a heap of pasta into a pan of boiling water. 'Spag bol again, I'm afraid,' she said, smiling ruefully at him. 'I think we had that last time you came.'

He shrugged. 'It's home-cooked and I don't have to reheat it in the microwave, so it wins on both counts. Besides, you make the best spag bol in Islington!'

'Aw, you're so sweet,' Ellen said and left her sauce to come and give him a big squeezy hug. 'We've missed you.'

Dominic hugged back. 'I've missed you both too,' he replied. And he really had. As much as he moaned about Pete, he and his wife were the one constant in his ever-changing world. He gave Ellen a kiss on the cheek and, as she pulled away, he said, 'Can I help myself to a drink?'

Her mouth dropped open. 'Oh, God. What must you think of me? I haven't even offered you anything to drink! What do you want? Wine? Beer? Both?'

He smiled and opted for the beer. They chatted about nothing in particular until Pete came back down the stairs and joined them. He and Dominic rested their backsides against the counter of the galley kitchen and sipped cold lager out of the bottle. It was heaven.

'Oh, yes!' he said, after swallowing a swig. 'I didn't finish telling you about my upstairs neighbour.' And he launched back into the story again, embellishing it here and there just to make Pete and Ellen laugh.

'So, did she write back?' Pete asked.

Dominic nodded, smiling. 'You bet she did.' He put his beer down and pulled a crumpled, folded envelope from the back pocket of his jeans. 'Look at that.'

Pete took it from him and read it, chuckling, Ellen looking over his shoulder. 'I've always thought you were "an unbearable, egotistical lout" myself,' she said. And then the pasta boiled over. 'Flip!' she yelled. 'That's because you two are distracting me. Now get out of my kitchen so I can finish in peace!'

Pete saluted his wife and led the way back to the living room, where he and Dominic dropped down on different sofas. Pete handed the letter back.

'Ah, I think your new pen pal is sweet,' he said, giving

Dominic a patronising look. 'And she certainly is getting feisty in her old age! Maybe you should go and knock on her door, ask her out to an early bird dinner?'

Dominic looked at him. 'Don't be stupid. Why would I want to do that?'

Pete shrugged. 'Because this is the closest thing you've had to a relationship in ages.'

The grin Pete wore as he finished his sentence got right up Dominic's nose. He put his beer down on an end table and stared at his best friend. All traces of laughter had gone and his mouth was a thin line. 'If you've got something to say, just say it.'

Pete held his hands up in mock defence. 'Whoa,' he said laughing. 'What's got your knickers in a twist?'

'You,' Dominic said simply. 'You've been churning out the same old gag for years now. It's getting a little old.'

Pete shook his head, still smiling, but there was a narrowing in his eyes. 'It was just a joke, mate.'

Dominic picked up his beer again, took a long hard swig. 'Well, it feels like more than that when you just won't leave it alone. If this is your way of trying to tell me you think I need to find a woman and settle down, just come out and say it. Doesn't mean I'm going to listen, but at least have the guts to be honest about it.'

Pete looked back at him warily. Dominic knew his friend well enough to know that Pete was weighing up whether he should just blow the whole thing off by making another joke, or be serious about it. Dominic was secretly hoping he'd do the former. Why on earth had he picked this fight? It was all that snarky letter writing going on between him and Ms Claire Bixby, probably. For some reason she'd got him all riled up.

Pete eventually cleared his throat and looked down at the rug, the exact spot where the poo had been when Dominic had arrived. 'Well, I do think you'd be happier if you'd just—'

'For crying out loud!' Dominic waved the letter at him. 'I've got one bloody busybody trying to run my life already. I don't need you making it a double act!'

Pete's rather bushy brows drew together and lowered. He glared at that spot on the carpet now. 'Stop being so bloody oversensitive!'

'I'm not being oversensitive,' Dominic said tightly. No one had ever labelled him a drama queen – far from it – and he wasn't going to let his best friend start now. 'But it's hardly surprising, is it? I only see you once every couple of months and it's always that – or something like that – that are the first words out of your mouth. Admit it. You think there's something wrong with me, just because I don't want what you've got.'

Pete, whose expression was normally as jolly and open as a teddy bear's, frowned and his jaw tensed. 'Well, maybe there is something wrong with you. You've got to admit it, you've been on a romantic losing streak for a long time. It's been years since you scared Erica away. She was a great girl, you know.'

Silence, thick and complete, fell in the living room.

Dominic saw Pete's Adam's apple bob. He knew he'd stepped over a line.

'Well,' Dominic said, draining the last of his beer and standing. 'If you really think that, I might as well go.' He was tempted to throw the bottle at the wall, but he knew that would upset Ellen, so he just put it down carefully on the end table and walked towards the door.

'Nic! Mate!' Pete began to rise.

Dominic ignored him. 'Don't you "mate" me,' he said, as he passed his friend and walked out the door. 'Mates don't judge each other! Mates don't tell each other what to do! Mates support each other's decisions even if they don't agree with them.'

And then he walked out the front door and into the annoyingly warm night. He'd have really liked the salve of cold air on his skin.

Ellen rushed into the living room, wooden spoon still in hand. She looked at the open door, and then at her sheepish husband sitting on the sofa. 'Oh, Lord,' she said wearily. 'What did you go and say this time?'

\*

Dominic rode his bike home with little regard for traffic lights or pedestrians. He was really tempted to throw his bike in the hallway and be done with it, but he hauled it back into his spare room, muttering under his breath as he did so. The computer was sitting on the desk, its blank screen staring at him. He might as well check his email . . .

But he didn't check his email. Instead, he opened up his web browser and went to Facebook. He spent a while faffing around reading things on his timeline – 'meaningful' quotes, status updates about friends' pets, silly quizzes that everyone knew were silly but still did anyway. He discovered his knowledge of rock lyrics was legendary, that his Hobbit name was Ogbutt Merryfoot and that if he were an ice cream flavour he'd be vanilla – which he was quite upset about.

Eventually, though, he clicked through to what he'd really come here to look at, even though he'd been kidding himself he hadn't.

Erica's profile popped up in front of him. She'd changed her picture, he noted. One of her on holiday, looking tanned and relaxed. She'd smiled at him like that at the beginning of their relationship.

His finger hovered above the mouse button. He should unfriend her, he knew. He was going to. It was just . . . It seemed a bit petty, especially as they'd been broken up almost four years now. There wasn't any venom left between them. She'd moved on. New husband, twins, a house in the suburbs. And he'd moved on too.

Hadn't he?

Even though he knew he shouldn't, he clicked on her photos tab. Instantly, scores popped up. Erica out with the girls. Erica cuddling her babies. Erica smiling with her new husband.

Obviously, he hadn't had trouble giving her what she wanted, what she *needed*. What she'd eventually told Dominic he was incapable of.

*You can't do it, can you?* she'd levelled at him. *You can't go anywhere beneath the surface. Or you won't . . . and I can't spend my life with a man like that, a man who refuses to open up to me and doesn't want me to open up to him. So I'm sorry, Dominic, the answer is no. I can't – I won't – marry you. Not unless you can change.*

He closed his eyes and inhaled.

God help him, he'd tried. Really tried. But it hadn't been

enough for her and eventually she'd left, and he'd just got the offer to do that filming job in Madagascar, so he'd left too. Just started travelling. Hadn't really, truly come home again. Not in his head and his heart anyway. It was easier this way. Why kill yourself trying to do something you weren't cut out for? Better to stick to what you were good at, and what he was good at was travelling – and making films.

He didn't want it anyway. That's probably why he was rubbish at long-term anythings.

With a sigh, he realised he hadn't been angry with Pete because he'd been wrong, but because he'd been right. He was going to have to apologise, wasn't he? But Pete would just have to leave it alone after that, not go digging in that wound just because he could. It had been okay to rib each other like that when they'd both been young, free and stupid, but the dynamic had changed now.

He shook his head, shut Erica's profile down and turned his computer off. Look who was poking at old wounds just because he could. Pete had nothing to do with his little pity fest just now.

Stupid man, he told himself. You're happy as you are.

But, as he wandered into the kitchen to eat yet another tiny box of cereal – a poor substitution for Ellen's spag bol – he couldn't help thinking about what it would be like to have a little mini version of himself like Pete had, and just whether that might plug the growing hole inside him, the one that seemed to widen every time he got on an aeroplane.

# Chapter Eight

## Teacher's Pet

They'd already started watching the film when Claire heard someone slide in the door and shuffle into a seat at the back. She waited a few moments then glanced nonchalantly over her shoulder.

Abby. That was a surprise. When she'd been absent at the usual start time, Claire had assumed they'd seen the last of her.

As *Teacher's Pet* rolled on, Claire found her thoughts returning to the newest member of the Doris Day Film Club more than once. Although Abby seemed out of place in their little group, Claire couldn't help thinking that maybe fate had brought her their way. There was a lost quality about her that made Claire think of a scared stray animal.

If Abby's mother was as demanding as she sounded, Claire suspected they were on a losing mission right from the start. However, Abby had come to them for help, and for that reason alone they would try. Doris herself would almost certainly approve – although the strays she championed since her retirement from Hollywood tended to be the furry, four-legged kind.

In a strange way, Abby reminded Claire of the Clark Gable character in *Teacher's Pet*. He played a 'tough as nails' journalist who had a chip on his shoulder about other people getting the education he'd been denied. While Claire didn't think Abby had a chip on her shoulder about being a girl, she'd done what the hard-nosed newspaper man had done – instead of trying, she'd just given up and turned her comfort zone into a fortress.

'God, how I love that film,' Candy said, as the lights went back on again and the credits rolled. 'I love the fact that Doris was playing intelligent career women who could hold their own against any man back in the late fifties, before it was really fashionable. That scene where she tells Clark Gable off in the lift is pure gold dust.'

Bev and Maggs murmured their agreement.

'Despite the huge age gap between Clark and Doris, it still works as a romance,' Peggy said, joining the discussion. 'The characters are unusually three-dimensional for a romantic comedy.'

Kitty giggled. 'My favourite bit is when Clark kisses Doris in her office, taking her by surprise, and her legs buckle under her when she walks back to her desk.'

Grace sighed. 'I want to be kissed like that one day.'

Everyone turned and looked at her. It was the most she'd said all evening.

'Don't we all,' Maggs added dryly, and the whole room had a chuckle, including Abby, who then flushed and looked at the floor.

Claire stood up. 'Before we all head off tonight, I want us to put our heads together and see if we can find a way to help our newest member.' She glanced at Abby, who now looked as if she was about to slide off her seat and under the table. Claire understood the urge to squirm when one was the focus of attention better than anyone, but there wasn't any other way, and this was what Abby had asked of them, after all.

'Watching films is all well and good, and we all know Doris had impeccable style, but I think we probably have it within our small group to offer some practical help too.' She turned to look at Candy specifically, who had a very sensible head on her shoulders and always looked stylish, but Kitty started bouncing in her seat.

'We'd love to help, wouldn't we, Grace?'

Grace nodded coolly.

'We've already talked about it,' Kitty added.

Abby looked warily from one to the other. 'You have?'

The vintage girls, both in red and white polka dots this week – Kitty with white on red, Grace with red on white – looked at each other before continuing.

'If you'd let us . . . We'd really like to give you a make-over.'

Abby looked shocked, as if she'd just been announced the next Miss Universe, and maybe just as tearful. 'You'd do that? For me?'

Both girls nodded. 'You'd be helping us really. We love doing makeovers,' Kitty said, 'but Grace says she's getting bored doing them on just me. What we really need is a fresh canvas.'

'Fresh meat, more like,' Maggs muttered under her breath.

'Are you up for it?' Kitty asked, nodding encouragingly.

'Um . . . I think so.'

'Great!' Kitty said, clapping her hands together. 'How about we do it before the next film club meeting?

Abby looked nervously between them. 'I don't know. Maybe.'

'We're going to have so much fun,' Kitty said brightly, as she stood up, and she and Grace linked arms and scurried away, plotting furiously as they disappeared down the stairs.

The rest of the club members started to drift after them, but before Abby escaped, Claire went over to her. 'Are you okay with the whole makeover idea? It's fine to say if you're not.'

Abby looked grim for a few long moments. 'I'm as fine as I'm ever going to be with it, and I'll never get those tickets if I don't, so I suppose I'll just have to do it, no matter how I feel about it.'

'Is it a special match?'

Claire expected Abby to nod just as emphatically, but instead she looked flustered and her cheeks grew pinker. 'Kind of . . .' She looked at her trainers as she scuffed the offensively patterned carpet with one of them. Eventually, she looked up at Claire from under her hair. 'It's not so much who's playing, but who I was hoping to ask to go with me.' And then she blushed even harder.

'A boy?'

Abby's eyes stayed on the carpet. She nodded. 'I've known him since we were in primary school together. We bonded over a shared love of football and we've been friends ever since, it's just . . . every time I look at him, things seem to go a bit weird.'

Claire nodded. She remembered feeling that way about

boys when she was Abby's age, that swirly feeling in her stomach when you thought about them. The little kick of your pulse when you knew you were going to see them.

'Does he feel the same way?'

Abby's face told Claire everything she needed to know. 'I'm just "Abs" to him, his mate with the killer left foot, but I thought maybe if we could get away from the other lads, have some time on our own . . .'

Ah, it was all starting to make sense now: Abby's sudden and desperate need to embrace her hitherto undiscovered feminine side, why she'd come back to the Doris Day Film Club.

'Can't you talk to your mum about this? If you told her why you wanted the tickets, she might understand.'

Abby shook her head, her lips a thin line. 'All she wanted after two boys was a daughter she could fuss over and dress up and go shopping with, and instead she got me. I'm just one huge disappointment to her. She just thinks Ricky encourages me in my tomboy ways.'

Claire gave Abby what she hoped was a sympathetic look. 'Well, we – the club and I – are going to do everything we can to make sure you prove her wrong at that party. If you want our help, we'll pull out all the stops to make it happen.'

Abby stood up, looking concerned. 'Do you really think you can help me look like a girl?'

'I'm sure we can,' she said, smiling.

Abby smiled weakly back. 'Thank you, Claire.'

Claire watched her trail down the stairs, looking slightly less forlorn than when she'd arrived, and then she made sure everything was shipshape, switched off the lights and closed the door.

Much to her surprise, she found Maggs waiting for her on the landing. 'Well . . .' Maggs said. 'Have you read it?'

*Read what?* Claire almost said, and then she remembered. She hadn't used that handbag since last week and she'd made herself forget about the letter. Besides, she'd had other letters on her mind since then – a string of notes going backwards and forwards between her and her cheeky neighbour. On the one hand, he was driving her crazy, but on the other, she had to admit he had quite a way with words, and sometimes he could be quite funny.

No, she thought to herself. Do not be sucked in by surface charm. That was how her mother had got snared by her father. He'd seemed lovely while they'd been going out, courteous, strong, principled. It was only after she'd married him that she'd discovered just how iron-clad those principles were, and just how exacting he could be if anyone failed to meet his standards.

Okay, her downstairs neighbour was nothing like him – mainly because he had no standards whatsoever – but the advice was good all the same. Always look deeper. Always look beneath. Exactly what she hadn't done with Philip.

Her ex-husband proved her point quite nicely. He'd seemed the polar opposite from her father when she'd met him. He'd been romantic and affectionate and thoughtful, but she'd still fallen into her mother's trap. Maybe she wouldn't have if Mum had been around to warn her. Gran had tried, but Claire had pigheadedly refused to listen, and then, after a few years, when she'd really realised what he was like, she'd been too stubborn and proud to admit she was wrong.

Anyway, she didn't want to think about Philip. It was

over. In the past. She was moving on, just as she had done with her father.

They started walking down the stairs, and Claire could feel Maggs looking at her. 'What?' she asked.

'Well? Have you read it?' Maggs said, rather impatiently. It was only then Claire realised she'd been so lost in thought – hijacked first by Mr Dominic Arden and then her ex – that she'd forgotten to answer her.

'Sorry,' she said laughing. 'Away with the fairies. And, no, I haven't read it. I don't intend to. I told you that last week.'

Maggs didn't say anything. Didn't mean she wasn't communicating heaps.

'I know you think it's a mistake,' Claire continued, 'but I can't do it. What happened, happened, and I have no desire to revisit it. What was it that Doris's brother said about her? Something about her never being concerned beyond what the momentary problem was . . . That's how she's managed to say stay so bright and sunny in the face of everything that happened to her, and I think I'm going to adopt that philosophy.'

Maggs just grunted softly. 'That all sounds very pretty, but don't forget . . . the past has a habit of coming back to bite you in the derrière whether you want it to or not.'

'Don't you worry about my derrière,' Claire said, as they emerged into the lounge bar of The Glass Bottom Boat. Kitty, Grace and Abby were sitting at a small table, the vintage girls talking animatedly, Abby looking slightly bemused. George was hovering near the door. He looked as if he was about to say something as Claire and Maggs approached, but Maggs just gave him a little wave and carried on out the door.

'Claire said she'd give me a lift again this week,' she said, as she swept past, too late to see George's expression turn from hopeful to crestfallen. Claire didn't miss it though.

She almost said something to Maggs, but Maggs was wearing that inscrutable, don't-try-to-mess-with-me expression that Claire knew only too well. She'd say something, all right, but with Maggs timing was everything. She'd just have to pick her moment carefully.

They walked slowly down the street in silence. This week she hadn't been able to find a space near the pub, so she'd had to park down the side of the playing fields opposite, but it was a nice night for a walk – warm, not as sticky as recently, and the proximity to midsummer meant that it wasn't fully dark yet and a slash of turquoise edged the horizon, despite the fact it was past ten.

Claire walked, trying to keep her mind on the sound of her shoes on the cracked paving stones, on the hum of a city summer night – dogs barking, neighbours arguing, someone somewhere playing a radio too loud so the music drifted between the houses and out into the almost-deserted park. But her mind refused to focus on these concrete, present day things. Now that Maggs had brought him up, it kept drifting back to her father, images of him, memories. She felt as if her mind was a runaway car, which kept veering slowly off in the wrong direction and then she'd notice and grab the steering wheel and coerce it into going back onto the route she'd planned for it.

She didn't want to think of him.

If anything, she should want to think of her mother, who'd been wonderful and loving and resourceful. She'd been gone ten years now. If she'd known their time together was going to be cut short, she'd have asked more questions. Or maybe not. In her twenties, she wouldn't have known the right things to ask. Maybe it was only now she was older with one bad marriage behind her herself, that she wished she could ask Mum if it had been the same for her.

At least she'd separated from her toxic husband. Why hadn't Mum left her father? Why had she waited for him to do it to her? Why hadn't she ever stood up to him? After he'd left, she'd blossomed into being the bright and funny and strong woman Claire would always choose to remember her as.

Suddenly, a question popped free, one she hadn't realised she'd needed the answer to until it left her mouth. She glanced across at Maggs. 'Did he ever hit her? My mother?'

They kept walking, but something about the atmosphere between them changed. The air grew stiller, thicker.

He hadn't ever hit Claire, although she'd always been afraid he might. She could remember a specific look in his eye that had always made her stomach quiver. A tingle of cold ran up her spine now, just thinking about it.

Maggs kept her focus straight ahead. When they reached Claire's car, she stopped and turned to face her. 'Honestly? I don't know . . . Maybe.'

Claire nodded.

She was starting to fear she'd known the answer for a long time, but just hadn't dared face it.

She unlocked the car and opened the door for Maggs. When they were both settled inside, before she turned the key in the ignition, Maggs spoke again. 'I know Laurie was always worried for your mother when he got into one of his moods. We didn't talk about it. People didn't in our day. It was the sort of shameful thing you just swept under the carpet, but I guessed she suspected what her son was capable of.'

Claire shook her head. 'I don't understand it. How did such a lovely woman as my grandmother raise such a cruel, dysfunctional son?'

Maggs let out a heavy breath. 'You don't remember much about your grandfather, do you?'

'No,' Claire replied slowly. Just a vague memory of a stern man with white hair.

'I keep thinking about him recently,' Maggs said quietly, all the usual sass and sarcasm gone from her voice. It made her sound younger, less invincible. 'I never liked him, you know, not even right back at the start. Maybe I was jealous he stole my best friend, or maybe I just saw a little bit into Laurie's future. I don't know . . .' She breathed in sharply. 'Anyway, I think he had a lot to do with how your father turned out.'

Claire shook her head. She'd never heard Maggs talk like this before. Maybe it was the gin she'd been nipping from her hip flask that evening. In the darkened room while they watched the film, she'd seen little flashes in the gloom as the street lamp outside had reflected off the shiny metal.

She pondered that as she turned the key in the ignition and revved the engine, shattering the fog-like silence that had settled around them.

'I'm surprised Gran didn't ever marry again after he died,' she said, her tone light, as she indicated and pulled away. 'She was still a very attractive woman, even into her fifties.'

'I thought the same about Cathy. Your mother wasn't short on admirers once your father had cleared off, you know.'

Claire nodded. She had memories of a couple of well-dressed men coming to the house with bunches of flowers, of them taking her mother out to dinner while Mrs Winfield from next door babysat, but there hadn't been many and they'd usually disappeared after four or five dates.

That had been sad too. Mum had been so pretty and funny. She'd had a way of making everyone feel included, as if she'd allowed them entrance to a special club where everything would always feel safe and warm and fun. When Claire had asked if she had a boyfriend, her mother had laughed the suggestion off. She'd said she was much more interested in taking care of Claire, and it wasn't the right time to get serious about anyone.

At the time, Claire had assumed this was just another selfless act of love on her mother's part, but now she wondered if there had been another reason.

'Runs in the family, doesn't it?' Maggs said, as they navigated the narrow back streets almost empty of traffic. 'First Laurie, then Cathy . . . And you haven't seen anyone else since Philip.'

That was just what Claire needed to pop her out of this rather maudlin mood she and Maggs had created between them. She chuckled softly to herself. She should have known better than to broach this kind of subject with Maggs. 'Don't be daft,' she replied. 'It's completely different. It's not that I don't want to, it's just not the right time. I need to focus on the business at the moment . . .'

She trailed off and her mother's voice echoed in her ears: *It's just not the right time, Claire, love. I think my focus should be on you at the moment . . .*

She shook that thought away as she craned her head to

see out of an awkward junction. 'Anyway,' she said, pulling out the trump card she'd almost forgotten about, 'I've got a date tomorrow.'

She could feel Maggs's beady eyes on her as she concentrated on the road. 'Oh, yes?' Maggs said, her pitch as high as Claire imagined her eyebrows were. 'Anyone nice?'

Yes, Claire thought to herself, but that was the problem. Nice and not much else, but telling Maggs that wouldn't get her off her back. However, there were a few pertinent facts about the man in question that might.

'His name is Doug Martin and he's a client. And before you ask, yes, he's single. He's also rich and very attentive. He's taking me to a party at The Hamilton.'

She risked a sideways glance to gauge Maggs's reaction. Maggs was looking suitably impressed. Claire smiled to herself. Distraction manoeuvre complete.

'Sid and I went dancing there on New Year's Eve once,' she said wistfully. 'It was the toast of the town then. Shame that it fell into such disrepair.'

'It will be again, if the new owner has anything to do with it,' Claire said, 'and there'll be some very useful contacts at that party.'

'Hmm,' Maggs said. 'You're going out with a rich, attentive man and the thing you're most pleased about is what it can do for your career. Now tell me, what's wrong with this picture?'

'Nothing,' Claire said haughtily. 'Mixing business with pleasure is how us youngsters do it these days.'

'Ouch,' Maggs said, and let out a reluctant chuckle. 'Touché, Miss Bixby. But just you make sure there's more pleasure than business in this scenario, okay?'

She made the turn into Maggs's road. 'I'll do my best.'

'I know that look,' Maggs muttered. 'You've worn the same one since you were a little girl. It's your "I'm pretending I'm listening, but really I'm going to do my own sweet thing" look.'

Claire pressed her lips together and tried not to smile. 'Learnt it from you.'

Maggs mimed taking a bullet to the chest. 'And the hits just keep on coming.'

Claire pulled into a space outside of Maggs's house and yanked on the handbrake. 'You can't go all superior on me, otherwise you'll have to admit you were a bad influence.'

'All I'm saying, is that you could do with some male company,' Maggs said, as she opened the door and eased her slightly creaky body from the car. 'You work all the time and when you're not working, you're doing club stuff, or hanging out with girls.'

'And George,' Claire reminded her, smiling just a little too sweetly.

'You're on a roll today,' Maggs said, her tone grudging. 'I shouldn't have taught you so well.'

Claire got out of the car and came round to where her grandmother's best friend was standing and gave her a hug. Maggs shook her head, but smiled as she did it, and let Claire press a kiss to her papery cheek.

'I've told you before not to meddle in my love life,' Claire said, 'not until you've got one of your own, at least.'

'You're no fun,' Maggs said, as they pulled apart.

'You want me to turn the tables on you? I saw the way George looked when you blew him off this evening. Crushed doesn't even begin to cover it.'

Maggs shook her head. 'He's too young for me.'

'So? What's wrong with a toy boy?'

'I'd eat him for breakfast.'

Claire laughed. Maggs probably would as well. Poor old George. Damned if he did, damned if he didn't. 'See? You need to start taking some of your own advice, Dr Maggs. You accuse me of not moving on, but I don't see you doing much of that yourself.'

'I'm practically in the grave,' Maggs said wearily. 'If I "move on" too much, I'll just fall straight into it.'

'Now you're just getting dramatic,' Claire said, although she knew Maggs was okay when she was hamming it up. It was when she closed right down, didn't show a thing, that Claire got truly worried about her.

Maggs sighed as she headed up her garden path. 'I do hate it when you're like this,' she said, with more than a touch of the martyr about her.

Claire smiled to herself as she got back into the car. 'When I'm like what?' she called out.

'Right,' Maggs replied, as she opened her front door and disappeared.

# Chapter Nine

# By the Light of the Silvery Moon

Claire was having the strangest dream. The sun was warm on her skin and the waves of a clear turquoise sea lapped against the edges of the little rowing boat she was sitting in. Okay, that didn't seem strange at all. In fact, it was rather lovely, and if that had been all there was to the dream she probably would have enjoyed it.

She glanced down and saw a flash of something in the sand and rocks thirty feet below. At first she thought it must be a little fish, the sun glinting off its scales, but then she realised the shiny thing wasn't moving.

The thought slid through her head like a whisper. *Treasure* . . .

She stood up, prepared to dive in, and that's when things got strange. Instead of hearing a splash and discovering her body slipping through the cool water, there was something more akin to a *boing* and she bounced right off it. It was as if the whole surface of the sea had turned into a stretchy, rubbery, see-through skin and as hard as she tried she couldn't break through. It was most frustrating.

Eventually, she sat down, cross-legged on the undulating

surface and folded her arms. The waves ran under her, making her bob up and down, just as if she'd been on a trampoline and someone else was jumping on the other end.

The only sounds were the gentle rustle of her hair in the breeze and the slap of the waves against the hull of the boat. She wasn't sure how the boat didn't just sit on the water like she did, rolling over onto one side, but it didn't. Apparently, it was just her having this strange problem.

As she sat there, wondering what to do next, she started to think she could hear music. At first it was just a tickle at the corner of her consciousness, and she wasn't even sure if it was coming from inside or outside her head, but then it grew louder.

Outside. Definitely outside.

She got excited again. Perhaps it was mermaids. Anything seemed possible in this strange place she'd found herself in.

The music grew steadily in volume, a bass beat thrumming through the rubbery sea surface and vibrating on her bare legs. Maybe not mermaids after all. Not unless they were the kind that didn't like operatic arpeggios, but pounding metal verging on the edge of goth . . .

That was when Claire woke up. The boat, the sun, the strange waves were all sucked back into her subconscious. The music, however, remained.

She sat up and pushed the hair out of her face, trying to make sense of it all, waiting for the music to disappear with the rest of the dream. It didn't. It just carried on thumping, like the beginning of one of those headaches she got sometimes that sat right behind her left eye. She put one foot on the floor and felt the vibration of it through the polished boards.

It became crystal clear that this had nothing to do with the dream and everything to do with the nightmare who lived downstairs.

Okay. This was it. She'd just about had enough.

Not only had there been the whole bike incident, and the letterbox that ever-spouted pizza delivery leaflets. She'd also had to deal with his bins again. He hadn't pulled them forward on rubbish collection day, so she'd had to do it. She'd have left them, and rejoiced at the thought of him rotting away in his own mess, if it hadn't been for the very real possibility of attracting rats. Or foxes. It was bad enough pulling his stinky dustbin to the kerb, but she wasn't about to gather up the contents once they'd been strewn halfway down the street by a vixen looking for a nice juicy chicken carcass.

Of course that had meant yet another note. And yet another cheeky reply.

She knew she should have left it at that, but for some reason letting him have the last word didn't sit well with her. Her pile of posh stationery in the kitchen was diminishing rapidly, along with her live-and-let-live, *que sera, sera* philosophy. She was doing her best to ignore everything but the troubles each day brought; it just seemed that each day brought a new batch from Mr Dominic flipping Arden.

She stood up and marched across the bedroom. No more notes. This was it. It was about time the pair of them had some face-to-face communication. And, if her palm met the side of his face during that communication, so much the better.

She stomped down the stairs, growing angrier with each step, because she knew the volume of her neighbour's music was robbing her of the satisfaction of knowing he'd heard them too.

When she got to his front door, she knocked on it. Sharply, but loudly.

Nothing. At least, nothing but that infernal music. What was he? Seventeen?

She tried again, this time pounding with her fist. Still nothing. She waited again. Five minutes she stayed there, alternately knocking then folding her arms and staring at the door, her toes tapping in impatience. Once or twice she found she'd accidentally fallen in with the rhythm of the music and that just infuriated her further.

Eventually, she stormed off back upstairs and slammed her front door as hard as she could. So he wasn't just an inconsiderate, lazy, pasty-faced technology geek, but a coward too. She should have known.

She went back to bed and rummaged through the drawer in her bedside table until she found the earplugs she always took on long plane journeys. She squished them into her ears and lay there, shoulders tense, armed folded across the top of the sheet and stared at the ceiling.

It was no good. She could still hear it.

At least she thought she could. It might just be the memory of all that noise echoing off the inside of her skull, like hearing an extra chime after the church bells had stopped ringing. She turned over and shoved her head underneath her pillow.

*Please let him leave soon*, she prayed fervently, as she waited for her blood pressure to drop back down to normal. She didn't know when, but it had to be soon, didn't it? And she'd be crossing the days off her calendar with a fat red squeaky marker until he did.

\*

Dominic woke with a start. He was lying on his sofa in his living room and had no memory of how he'd got there. For some reason, he could hear the end of the last song on one of his favourite albums playing in his head, but all around him everything was completely silent.

He looked up and noticed his iPod, still lit up, sitting in its dock.

Ah. Now he remembered.

He'd been feeling particularly restless this evening. Probably because now he'd been back in the UK for more than a week, he was noticing that his days were kind of empty. He'd decided to listen to some good music to get this feeling of being trapped, grounded, out of his system. Somewhere in the middle of it, he must have fallen asleep.

Now, for most people that might have been impossible, but not for Dominic. He'd always been able to drop off anywhere, even when he'd been a teenager, and it had served him well on his travels most of the time. When he'd gone backpacking with uni buddies, they'd always complained about noise and hard beds and strange smells, but none of it had bothered him. He just closed his eyes and he was away.

Even staying in some of the *really* dodgy places his work took him to hadn't been that bad. If he ever did have problems sleeping, he stuck his earphones in his ears and played music, sometimes quite loud, reasoning that it was often silence punctuated by unexpected noises that woke him up. If he could choose something with a consistent volume level it became white noise, lulling him to sleep. It was the sudden quiet at the end of an album that often roused him these days.

The iPod blinked off and he sat up, stretched and yawned. At least he was feeling sleepy now. And it was dark. Finally, his body clock was returning to some sort of normal pattern. About time too. He stumbled off into his bedroom where he ripped off his clothes and fell into bed. A few seconds after he hit the mattress, he was sleeping the sleep of the innocent.

*

He was still in a pretty good mood when he emerged from his flat to go for a run at eleven o'clock the next morning. He looked out for a little white rectangle on his doormat and wasn't disappointed. Somewhere along the line, the war of notes between him and his upstairs neighbour had become a source of entertainment.

Hmm. A signal that he definitely needed to get out more. He had the research for a new documentary he wanted to do on free divers – the particular kind of mental discipline required, the tight-knit community of enthusiasts, the dangers – but it was desk work, his least favourite kind, and would hardly get him out the flat much. Pete had texted him a couple of times and he'd texted back, but they hadn't seen each other since that incident at his house last week.

Which meant he needed an alternative social life. One involving female company would be good, no matter what Pete said.

Just thinking about how his best friend had summed him up still made his jaw clench. Just because Pete had a point, it didn't mean he had to lay it on quite so thick. He'd exaggerated, as always.

Dominic frowned. No way was he a total romantic disaster! But Pete couldn't see that. All Pete could see was his little nest of domestic bliss and he measured – and judged – everyone, including his best friend, against that. The only problem was that Dominic knew Pete was so stubborn he was never going to let go of the idea that his best friend was a romantic pariah unless he was faced with incontrovertible evidence to the contrary.

A thought pinged inside Dominic's head, so clearly and so brightly, that he was sure that if he looked in the mirror, there'd be a glowing light bulb above his head.

That was it! The solution to both his problems in one fell swoop.

He'd find a nice girl to date and be as romantic as he could possibly be, maybe even take her round to Pete and Ellen's for a meal or something. Not that he'd be rubbing his friend's face in it . . .

Well, not much.

But, as he played out the scenario in his head, he started to feel a little restless. He didn't want a girlfriend, remember? He didn't want to do 'long term', not even if it caused Pete to eat a double portion of humble pie.

Hang on a moment, he thought to himself. You've been moving around too much, thinking of relationships in terms of days and weeks instead of months. He'd be gone by the beginning of September at the very latest. Why was he panicking? It'd be perfect. Long enough to wine and dine a girl, but short enough that no one was in danger of getting really serious. No hearts would be broken, and Pete would still have to eat his words. That is, he would if he and Dominic were speaking by then.

He sighed. It would blow over. Their fights always did. But he was still pretty peeved at the moment and he and Pete were both male and pigheaded, which meant saying sorry was not an option. The other option, the one they always chose, was to wait a couple of weeks for everyone to cool off, meet up for a pint and pretend that nothing had happened.

He'd call Pete next Thursday.

Which meant he was going to be spending a lot of time on his own until then. This was the downside of his life, the one he never noticed when he was busy travelling from place to place, one he didn't like much now it was taking great pains to point itself out.

It was hard to keep relationships of any kind going when he was only around for a week or so every few months. Every time he visited friends, they seemed to have moved on months and years – getting engaged, getting hitched, popping out sprogs – while he had stayed the same. Sometimes he had a few new stories or maybe another scar but, yep, pretty much the same. It was a bit like being a time traveller, only he'd travelled in Dominic years instead of light years.

Ugh. Well. He had this thing he'd been given an invite to for tonight. Maybe he should go to that. He knew the guy wanted him to do a documentary about him, but it really wasn't his kind of thing. Still, he could eat and drink on someone else's money and have a chance to tell the rather persistent businessman no to his face. Email refusals didn't seem to be working.

He decided to cheer himself up by reading Ms Bixby's

note before he headed out and started pounding the London streets in his trainers. He was starting to build a picture of her in his head, prompted by that first comparison to Mrs McClure: grey hair set like the Queen's, a polyester paisley dress straight out of the seventies, horn-rimmed glasses and the kind of matronly figure that suggested armour-plated boobs. If she was anything like his old headmistress, he'd win her round eventually. She'd scold him and call him an impossible boy, but when he left the room she'd smile secretly to herself.

He opened up the envelope and leaned against his front door, intending to post it through his own letterbox when he was finished. This note, however, contained none of the usual sarcastic gems he'd become accustomed to. In fact, it was rather bald and rather short.

*Dear Mr Arden*
*If you ever, ever play music again that loud at two o'clock in the morning, I will be contacting the council's noise pollution team. It was most rude and inconsiderate, but I suppose I should have learned to expect that from you.*
*Ms C. Bixby*

Uh-oh. He'd stepped over a line, he could tell.

Okay, maybe he'd accidentally stepped over plenty of Ms Bixby's lines since he'd been back, but somehow this felt like a big one, one that it would be very difficult to tiptoe back behind.

Had the music really been that loud? He hadn't thought so. He'd played it that volume before and she'd never complained.

He pulled his door key out of his pocket and opened his front door. Well, she'd complained now. He felt a bit bad, especially after she'd done his bins for him the other day. It can't have been easy for a crotchety old thing like her.

Oh, flip. He was going to have to do it, wasn't he? He was going to have to say the 's' word and . . . he swallowed . . . apologise. He headed for the kitchen and picked up his wallet. He could run later. What he needed to do now was go and buy a peace offering.

Now, where in trendy old Islington did they sell stuff like knitted toilet roll covers and crochet hooks?

# Chapter Ten
# Ready, Willing and Able

Claire arrived at The Hamilton at five to eight. She took a moment to gaze at the recently renovated hotel, now restored to its full Art Deco glory, before going inside. The exterior had been a muddy brown a couple of years ago, but now the stone was almost white, the black-leaded windows stark against its paleness. She skipped up a couple of steps and through the heavy revolving door.

Even though she'd visited quite a few times since it had opened, she always got a little tingle down her spine every time she stepped inside. This is how a good hotel should make you feel, like magic was in the air, like you were on a Hollywood set, full of love and laughter and singing and dancing.

Not that there was much singing and dancing going on in The Hamilton's lobby, and she suspected the suave-looking doorman might firmly eject her if she tried to tap dance along the exquisite black and white marble floor tiles or see if she could shatter the crystal chandelier with a high C. No, The Hamilton was far too classy for that, but the gold leaf, the clean elegance, made her think of the heyday of Tinseltown, something that made her heart beat a little bit faster. She could almost imagine Sinatra at the glossy black grand piano near the fireplace or Monroe trotting through the lobby in a sable coat, black-gloved palm splayed in front of her face to ward off the swarming photographers.

And there was Doug, looking completely at home as he lounged on the dark marble reception desk smiling and chatting with one of the staff. He'd insisted on picking Claire up, but she'd stood her ground and had insisted just as strongly that she'd meet him here.

He turned and spotted her and his whole face broke into a wide smile. Claire couldn't help smiling back. There was something very nice about someone being pleased to see you, even if they could be a bit of a pain in the backside sometimes.

'Claire!' he said, holding his arms wide and walking towards her. He had that easy confidence about him that meant he fitted in everywhere. He looked just at home in her shop as he did in this elegant hotel lobby. He never doubted that the world would open its tightly clenched fist for him, to give him what he desired. She envied him that. It had taken years after her father had left for her to believe she shouldn't feel guilty about anything nice that happened in her life.

She let him kiss her on the cheek and, when he offered his arm, she took it. 'You do remember though, Doug? This isn't—'

'A date,' he finished for her. 'Yes, believe me, you've been very clear about that.' He smiled as he said it and leaned in to press the brass plate for the lift button. 'But if I can't wine you and dine you, I'm going to make sure I introduce you to every person in the room and make sure Far, Far Away is the roaring success it deserves to be.'

They rode the lift up in silence and, when the doors whispered open, it was a revelation. She'd seen pictures of the new rooftop bar and terrace, of course, but being there in person was something else. While the rest of the hotel was all elegance and lovingly restored period features, The Terrace, as it was simply called, was one hundred per cent, cutting-edge twenty-first century.

The bar area sat in the middle of the roof, an imposing box of plate glass, furnished in brown and cream with sofas and chaises longues in weird organic shapes. Surrounding the bar was a wide terrace, filled with large square sectional sofas clustered round low tables with storm lanterns on them. Everything was clean lines, pared-down elegance, making way for the real star of the show – the London skyline.

The city lay glittering in the dusk beyond the low glass wall that ran round most of the terrace. In one direction, The Shard, another the London Eye and the Houses of Parliament. Turn again and you could invent a new game thinking up nicknames for the various strange buildings that were sprouting up around The Gherkin in the City.

Claire held her breath. This was perfect. Just the kind of place she wanted to be able to recommend to her clients, but all this perfection came at a price – she was just hoping she could convince Jayce Ryder that promoting The Hamilton as *the* top romantic hotel in London could benefit them both.

'Come on,' Doug said, hooking his arm through hers and leading her down wide marble steps into already packed party. 'There are a few people I want to introduce you to.'

She had that tiny little moment of stage fright again, at

the thought of having to sound sophisticated and impressive and like a smart businesswoman, but then it occurred to her that maybe she *was* all those things, and that she just had to relax and be herself, not always try to be the perfect version of herself that had only ever existed at the top of her father's measuring stick.

Doug led her effortlessly through the crowd. Whereas it would have taken her fifteen minutes to nudge and 'excuse me' across the room, people just seemed to ebb and flow around him. She looked her escort over once again. For some reason, away from her office, he seemed more dashing, less . . . desperate. How interesting.

And he certainly knew how to work a room. He went into action, introducing her to every person as they moved seamlessly from group to group. It seemed he knew everyone – journalists, hoteliers, restaurant and airline owners – and when anyone clapped him on the back and asked him how long it had been since they'd seen each other, he replied then smoothly moved on to Claire, singing her praises and making her sound so fabulous that after an hour her handbag was stuffed full of business cards.

She stood back and watched Doug order a martini from a waiter carrying nothing but champagne and marvelled at his ability to charm anyone into anything. She sighed. It really was a pity there was not one hint of a spark between them.

Doug received his martini and then he stood behind Claire, put his hands on her shoulders and turned her until she was facing the door that led onto the west side of the terrace. 'Now, Wonder Woman, who is it that you've been dying to meet all evening?'

*Jayce Ryder*, she whispered silently to herself.

Doug pointed to their host. He was deep in conversation with another man, a man who stood out from the rest of the corporate-looking crowd. Instead of a suit he wore jeans. Really old jeans, she'd guess, by the way the denim looked soft and worn in places. And instead of a shirt and tie, he wore just the shirt. White, which matched many around him, but it was so crumpled it looked as if he'd just lifted it out of an overpacked duffel bag and thrown it on. Maybe he had. He was the only person amidst all these 'travel' people who actually looked as if he might have just jumped off a plane from a far-flung destination.

'Want to go and meet him?' Doug said.

Claire nodded, and then realised he meant Ryder.

She took in a deep breath as they moved through the milling guests and approached the pair who were discussing something important and serious on a raised seating area in one corner of the terrace. The crowd thinned here, as if people knew instinctively the smarter of the two was someone important, and not to crowd him.

As they approached, the man Jayce Ryder was talking with turned his head. Claire's cheeks suddenly got hot and something down in the pit of her stomach wobbled. It was a purely physical reaction. Odd, because of the two men, the hotel owner was definitely the better looking, but there was something about the other man – the way his hair looked as if the only comb it had seen for days was his fingers, an air of recklessness around him that just worked for her.

'I don't believe it!' Doug was saying loudly beside her. 'Nic? Is that really you?'

The stranger, who'd been frowning up until now, as if he'd been trying to convince his brain that his eyes were playing tricks on it, suddenly grinned at her escort. 'Get out of here! Doug? Doug *Martin*?'

The two men laughed and hugged, leaving her and the hotel owner raising their eyebrows and smiling at each other.

'You two know each other?' Jayce said, as they thumped each other on the back then pulled apart, still grinning broadly.

Doug nodded. 'This fine chap and I went to university together, shared a flat with a bunch of louts whose names I can't even remember now, but we haven't seen each other in – what? – at least five years. He's always off somewhere, you know, reporting, or whatever he does.'

Ah, a travel writer, Claire thought. That made sense. No wonder he'd been in such deep conversation with Jayce Ryder.

'I've been trying to convince him to do a piece on the hotel,' Jayce explained, 'but he's a hard man to pin down.'

Doug laughed. 'That's why I haven't seen him in five years!' He turned to his friend. 'You ought to do it. It'd be a great project for you.'

The other man – Nick, wasn't it? Claire thought – just shrugged.

'As tempting as the offer is, it's not really the sort of thing I do.'

Jayce Ryder just flashed his famous smile. 'But you said you were – and I quote – "stuck" in London for a month or two. Maybe it's time for something different?'

'Well, like Doug says, I prefer working in more exotic locations.'

'London is exotic to someone from Bora Bora.'

Claire smiled to herself. He wasn't going to give up,

was he? Jayce Ryder obviously wanted this man to write an article on his hotel and he wasn't going to stop until he got it. She had to admire his ambition, but she also admired this 'Nick' person for sticking to his guns.

'I'll think about it,' he finally said, which was probably the most sensible thing to do, given the tenacity of their host. Still, the look on his face said he was as likely to say 'yes' as he was to suddenly run out and buy an iron for that shirt.

'That's all I'm asking,' Jayce said firmly.

Nick nodded sagely, then frowned. 'So, how do you know Doug?'

Jayce gave a rueful smile. 'Let's just say that Doug's lovely mother is a regular – and may I say, very exacting – customer of mine.'

This led them to launch into reminiscing about one of her more eventful stays at his flagship hotel in New York. Claire and Doug's old college friend looked at each other and smiled.

'So, are you Doug's latest . . . ?'

Claire laughed, maybe a little loudly, and shook her head. 'Oh, no. Nothing like that. I'm his . . . Well, I'm his travel agent.'

He smiled at her quizzically. 'In these days of internet bookings and last-minute deal sites, do we really need travel agents? Aren't you a dying breed?'

Claire sipped her champagne. 'Like a lot of industries, my one is changing, but that doesn't mean I can't carve out my niche. You know what those booking sites are like, don't you? Great prices, huge amount of choice, but how do you know the top featured hotels are there because they're really very good or because they've paid to promote themselves?

Those kind of sites are fine if you know exactly what you want, but it can be a little overwhelming if you don't.'

He was looking at her, his brown eyes warm, the slightest of smiles curling one corner of his mouth up.

'Okay, maybe not everyone finds it overwhelming,' she added hastily. This man didn't look as if he'd find battling a nest of snakes in the desert much of an inconvenience. 'But some people do. And it's time consuming – especially if you do your homework – and, even if you do, it can still end up being a bit of a gamble. In your line of work, you must know that not every hotel lives up to its professionally taken pictures and website blurb.'

He let out a hollow laugh. 'Don't I know it.' The smile stretched to the other side of his mouth. 'So that's where you come in.'

'Exactly,' Claire said, nodding. 'For those people who want personalised recommendations, not just for travel routes and accommodation. I do my research, talk to my contacts. I can suggest the best times for sightseeing popular attractions, little out-of-the-way places people didn't even know they wanted to visit, restaurants for every budget. I offer what they don't have – experience, contacts, a network of tried and tested travel options that people can depend on for quality and reliability. Think of me as the walking, talking guidebook for the people who don't mind paying a little bit extra for service and security.'

'And do you jump in their suitcases and pop out again to take them on guided tours?'

The twinkle in his eyes told her he was teasing her, but she didn't mind. It was nice to talk to someone who liked travelling as much as she did, who had probably been to some of the places she longed to visit. And the fact he wasn't bad-looking didn't hurt much either. Maybe Peggy had a point about the lack of Y chromosomes in her life. Just a little bit of simple male attention was making her feel a little giddy.

'No,' she replied, 'but sometimes I spend so much time planning the trip I wish I could go with them and do it all myself.'

He sighed. 'What a pity I never use guidebooks.'

'Not ever?'

He shook his head. 'Although, I never go anywhere without a good map, but I like to just land somewhere and work it out for myself, discover its secrets by exploring, talking to people . . . That's the whole fun of being in a new place.'

'I take it you're not a "top ten things to do in Paris" kind of guy, then?'

He laughed again. 'Guilty as charged, I'm afraid. I prefer places that aren't even on the tourist maps, if possible. What's the point in going somewhere someone has already been and just reading what they already discovered about it from a book?'

Some more people crowded onto their little bit of the terrace, searching for their host, and she and Nick stepped closer to the parapet. Claire took a moment to look out across the darkening sky over the city. The clouds above were a dusky indigo while those at the horizon were still burnished with the memory of the setting sun.

'Well, if there were more people like you,' she said, as she kept staring at the view, 'I'd be out of business before I was even established.' She turned her head slightly to look at him. 'But I have to admit, doing it your way sounds a lot of fun.'

She got an extra glimmer of warmth in those brown eyes as a reward for that comment. He opened his mouth and, just for the tiniest second, she hoped he would say something outrageous, like 'Let's jump in a cab, go to City Airport and catch the first plane we find.' But he didn't. Which was just as well, because hadn't she promised herself she was going to make sure she knew – really knew – the next man she got involved with?

'Would you like another?' he asked, nodding at her empty glass.

Claire blinked. She didn't remember finishing it. 'Yes. Yes, please,' she said and smiled at him as he took her empty flute and disappeared into the crowd. It was only after he'd disappeared amongst the bodies that she remembered she'd decided to stop at one glass. Oh, well. She'd never catch him up and she could always put the glass down when it arrived and 'forget' about it.

A cool breeze whipped above the parapet, causing her arms to tighten into gooseflesh. She folded them across her body and tried to warm herself. She turned round to see where Doug was and discovered that he and Jayce had drifted away, and they were now deep in conversation with two girls who looked like models. It was then she realised that avoiding more alcohol wasn't the only thing she'd forgotten. She'd been so engrossed talking to Doug's old college buddy that she hadn't even introduced herself to the man she'd come here to meet.

With a quick glance towards the bar, she scuttled over to join the group and hoped she wasn't going to become invisible in the company of two women at least a decade her junior and two dress sizes smaller.

# Chapter Eleven

## Send Me No Flowers

Dominic hummed as he worked his way back through the crowded party with a glass of champagne and a beer. He was glad he'd decided to come to this shindig after all. While it wasn't really his style—he'd have much preferred an evening down at The Glass Bottom Boat with Pete—things had brightened up considerably since he'd met . . .

He paused. That's right. They'd been so surprised to see each other again after all this time that Doug's matchless manners had slipped. Dominic didn't know the 'not girl-friend's' name. He grinned. He would inside of five minutes, though.

She was a little more prim and sophisticated than his usual type. Not that he didn't like sophisticated; he just tended to go for sporty girls. The women he usually met on his travels had battered plimsolls on their itchy feet, not stilettos. However, if he was going to prove he could be Mr Romantic maybe it was time to ditch the flower-child drifters and gypsy souls and try something different?

This blonde was certainly different and, although she was pretty and funny, he had the feeling she was going to be a bit of a challenge, which was perfect, actually. He needed something – or someone – to distract him for the next couple of months, because there was no way he was going to do a documentary on Jayce Ryder and his hotel chain to keep himself busy. He liked to tell the truth when he made his films and, as much as Mr Ryder kept bandying the words 'creative freedom' around, he had a feeling how it would go in reality. He'd end up being pushed into doing a hollow puff piece for The Hamilton and that wasn't his style at all.

The corner of the terrace where he'd left her was more crowded now, and he elbowed his way through the last bit. He caught sight of a green and white floral dress, cool and serene against all the corporate grey and black, and realised she'd joined Doug and Jayce again. She was talking animatedly and both men were hanging on her every word, ready to laugh every time she finished a sentence. It was odd – she came across as all buttoned-up, but there was something very open and warm about her too.

He joined the group just as she was coming to a high point. 'And you'll never guess what he did next!' she was telling the pair excitedly. 'I don't know whether to hoot with laughter or sue him for defamation of character!'

Doug wiped a tear from his eye. 'This is too funny,' he said between heaving breaths.

Dominic offered her the glass of champagne. Somehow she managed to smile, thank him and ask him if he could hold on to it just a little bit longer with one glance. He shrugged one shoulder and let her carry on.

She was digging around in a handbag that was the same shade of olive as the leaves on her dress. Eventually, she pulled out a crumpled piece of paper. 'Okay,' she said, shooting a smile at her audience, 'here it is.'

'That's the actual thing?' Doug said, eyebrows high. He looked as if he was fit to bust something. 'Can I see it?'

She nodded. 'Let me read it first.' She took a breath, composed herself and started to read what was on the paper.

'*Dear Ms Bixby . . .*'

Dominic kept on grinning. He was only half listening, too busy wondering how he could steer her away from the competition and have her all to himself again. A tiny neuron in his brain flashed and winked, trying to alert him to the fact he'd just missed something important, but he ignored it.

'*I'm very sorry if I kept you awake last night. I didn't realise my music would disturb you.*'

The neuron winked harder, almost spontaneously combusting with the effort, and Dominic, who was nodding, waiting for the rest of the story he'd half missed to be over, stopped smiling. He experienced a cold rush, similar to the feeling he usually got when he realised he'd left the house without something essential. He patted his pockets and found his phone, his keys and his wallet all safely there.

'Okay, this is the priceless bit,' Claire was saying. '*I was under the impression that you are a little deaf and the volume has certainly never bothered you before. However, I'm guessing you've recently had a hearing aid fitted, and I'll try to keep the noise down in the future, especially late at night.*'

Dominic froze. That lone neuron had finally done its job and now slumped exhausted in the corner, while a thousand others took up its cause and lit up his brain like a firework display. He took a good long slug of his beer.

It couldn't be. How had she got hold of that?

Wh-why? Why? Why? Like a broken record, his mind seemed to have got stuck on that word.

How could this attractive woman he'd just met at a party be reading the note he'd left for his upstairs neighbour this morning? Had some weird *Doctor Who* thing happened and it had slipped through a wormhole and ended up in her handbag?

She was giggling, really giggling now, which made her nose crease up and look cute. Dominic got stuck looking at it, looking at the bright smile underneath. It was way easier than trying to work out what parallel universe he'd slipped into.

'And he left the note on my doorstep along with a box of Milk Tray and the latest issue of *The People's Friend*. I mean, how rude can you get?'

'What a jerk,' Jayce muttered.

Dominic hadn't warmed to the hotel tycoon that much since first meeting him, but now he was starting to actively dislike him. What did he mean 'jerk'? A lot of thought had gone into those presents. He downed the rest of his beer.

It was then that Doug spotted him standing there, confused and scowling, an empty bottle in one hand and a glass of fizz in the other. 'Hey, you're back! I'm so sorry, Nic. Please forgive my rudeness. I forgot to introduce you to this lovely creature . . .' He turned and smiled at his guest. 'This is Claire Bixby.'

Those fireworks inside Dominic's head went for the finale. He put his mouth to his beer bottle and found it empty, so downed the champagne instead. 'Claire Bixby?' he repeated, weakly.

'Yes,' Doug replied, completely oblivious to anything but

the lovely woman in the green and white dress he'd brought with him. 'I'd like her to become the second Mrs Martin, but she keeps turning me down.'

'The second Mrs Martin?' he repeated, no less confused than before the introduction. Had Doug got married and divorced since he'd last seen him?

Claire raised a hand and shielded her mouth. 'Second after his mother,' she added with a wink.

'And, Claire, this is Nic—'

Dominic thrust out his hand. 'Nice to meet you, Claire,' he said quickly, cutting Doug off. He didn't know why he did that, just that he felt he needed a bit of time to gather his scrambled thoughts together before he revealed his true identity. That, and the fact he was on the verge of becoming the butt of the joke the other three were sharing.

She smiled back at him, began to say something, but then spotted the empty glass in his hand and frowned. 'Was that . . . mine?'

Dominic nodded. 'Terribly crowded,' he muttered. 'Got bumped. Let me just go and get you '

And with that he was away again, putting some distance and some cold air between himself and this Alice-down-the-rabbit-hole moment.

He shook his head as he searched for a waiter with a tray. No, that couldn't be Claire Bixby. Not *his* Claire Bixby. His Claire was old. Waspish. With armour-plated boobs. There had to be another one. That was the only explanation.

He lunged at a waiter with a tray full of champagne flutes and nearly went flying over a low sofa. Thankfully, he found his balance and righted himself, grabbing a glass at the right minute and almost spilling some onto the head of the girl sitting below him. He turned and headed back to Doug and Jayce and . . . Claire.

The straw he'd clutched at crumbled in his fingers. While there *could* be another Claire Bixby in London, what were the chances of her being in possession of his letter and knowing about his peace offering? The only thing he could think of was that maybe she was named after a relative like her mother or her—

Dominic felt as if he'd run into a brick wall at full sprint.

Her grandmother. And not Claire. He'd been right all along – the old lady upstairs had been called Laura or Laurel or something like that. Suddenly, it was all starting to fall into place, why his neighbour had been defying his expectations at every turn.

'Here,' he said, thrusting the champagne in her direction. 'I got you another one.'

She wasn't smiling so warmly at him now. Probably because he was being a little weird. But who *wouldn't* under these circumstances? 'So what happened . . . ? With the note and the . . . other stuff?' he asked.

She shook her head, as if she was weary of the subject and just wanted to be done with it. 'Nothing,' she said, 'I was so furious I haven't even thought about replying yet. Anything I might write would probably get me arrested!'

He blinked. 'But chocolates are nice, aren't they? Everyone likes getting chocolates.'

Both Doug and Jayce shook their heads. Jayce coughed. 'Rookie move,' he said. 'So obvious. If you really want to win a woman round, you have to be a lot more creative than that!'

Dominic scowled at him. The adrenalin was still pumping

hard through his system and he'd like to release a bunch of it via a well-timed punch. Mr Smooth over there was looking more and more like a prime target.

'I suppose it *would* have been a nice gesture—' Claire cut in.

Dominic spun to look at her, scowl erased. There. He'd known she was an intelligent woman the first moment he'd set eyes on her.

'If he hadn't meant it as an insult,' she finished.

Dominic opened his mouth but no words came out.

'I mean, all those references to knitting and cocoa and hearing aids!' Claire said, a firm and very defined little line appearing between her eyebrows. Her nose and mouth might say 'fun', but that brow definitely said 'stubborn'. 'He's obviously telling me – not too subtly, I might add – that I'm old and crotchety before my time!'

Dominic shook his head. 'I'm sure he wasn't—'

'Just because I don't live like a pig and have a sense of decency and a bit of consideration for other people, he thinks I'm a stuck-in-the-mud old busybody! I don't think those are bad qualities to have, do you? I mean, decency and consideration,' she added quickly. 'Not the stuck-in-the-mud bit.'

Well. When she put it like that . . .

He shook his head dumbly, worried that anything he might say would incriminate him further. Wow. He'd really got under her skin, hadn't he? And there was he, thinking it had all been a bit of fun . . . It really wasn't a good time to break the news, was it? Better wait until she'd stopped ranting, had a bit of time to let her blood pressure go down.

He shook his head, still unable to believe it. *This* was his upstairs neighbour? Crikey, if he'd known that, he'd have been knocking on her door a lot sooner.

He blinked as he watched her talk with the other two men. It was hard to marry this warm, animated woman up with the starchy, sarcastic notes he'd been getting for the last week. She seemed so nice in person. It didn't put him off much, though. If there was something he liked in a girl, it was a hidden impish side and, thanks to her extensive note writing, he knew Claire Bixby had one a mile wide.

'Sounds like a real catch,' Doug muttered, as she finished her tirade.

Claire snorted. 'I wish! If he ever did find a girlfriend, he's probably the type to mooch off her, then he'd move and be out of my hair for good.'

'It could happen,' Dominic said, frowning a little. The fact she assumed he was utterly charmless and useless was annoying him. She hadn't thought that way five minutes ago when she'd been smiling at him, fluttering those long brown lashes.

She swallowed a mouthful of champagne she'd just taken and shook her head. 'I severely doubt that.'

*There.* Right there she'd sounded just like one of her notes. The image of the crusty old battleaxe from upstairs and the woman in the leafy dress in front of him started to merge and blur. And to think he'd actually gone and bought her chocolates!

'Anyway,' she continued, 'I feel disloyal wishing him on a fellow woman. What on earth could she have done to deserve someone like him? I mean, he's a child – doing what he wants without any thought to the consequences for anyone else. He probably wouldn't know what to do with a grown-up relationship if it walked up and bit him on the nose.'

Dominic clenched his jaw.

She was wrong. So wrong. Why did everyone keep making these snap judgements about him? It had just been a couple of notes. Okay, and a badly parked bike. And some stolen milk. Possibly the Sisters of Mercy being played at full volume in the wee small hours of the night.

Ah.

Okay, *maybe* he could see why she hadn't taken a shine to him. But that didn't mean she was right about him. Not at all. Even if some of the things she said reminded him rather too sharply of Erica. Or Pete.

The subject changed then to the best hotels in the city, and, while Jayce discussed his competition, Dominic watched Claire. Now she'd stopped looking quite so affronted she'd melted back into the woman he'd first laid eyes on not half an hour ago. For some reason, he couldn't stop looking at her mouth. She had a really lovely smile. And she did it a lot. When she laughed, it wasn't an elegant tinkle but a throaty giggle, which was as infectious as a case of the measles. Jayce and Doug were both eating out of her hand.

The true magic was, though, that even though she had both men enraptured, it didn't change how she talked to them, she didn't flirt or wield that power the way many attractive women did. It was as if she didn't realise that she'd snared them. And that was the most captivating thing of all.

He felt his own anger melting away at the things she'd said about him. After all, he'd left her a rather unfortunate trail of clues. He couldn't really blame her for getting it all wrong – and it was hardly worse than the truck load of conclusions he'd jumped to about her.

A distinguished-looking gentleman joined their group and soon peeled the host away to talk to another cluster of people further along the terrace. That left him and Doug and Claire together.

'So, when are you off on your next jaunt?' Doug said, looking at him.

Dominic opened his mouth and closed it again. 'Soon,' he finally said, then glanced quickly at Claire, before frowning and pretending he was listening to something. 'Isn't that your phone?' he asked Doug.

Doug patted his pocket and shook his head. 'Don't think so. Even though it's noisy in here, it's on vibrate as well and I didn't feel anything.'

Dominic leaned forward a little. 'Are you sure? I thought I recognised that special ringtone you gave to your mother—' The theme to *Jaws*, if Dominic remembered rightly.

Doug looked a little panicked. He glanced towards the lobby, where it was quieter. 'I should probably go and . . . Just in case.'

Dominic nodded seriously.

'Of course,' Claire said, looking sympathetic.

And with that, Doug scuttled off, scanning his phone as he pushed his way through the milling party guests. Dominic felt bad about sending him off on a bit of a wild goose chase, but he had the feeling that his secret would be out in two minutes flat if he let Doug hang around.

Not that he wasn't going to fess up eventually, but he liked Claire, and if he was going to have a romantic entanglement over the next couple of months he'd really like it to be her.

Not to mention it would be rather satisfying to prove both her and Pete wrong in one fell swoop.

But he was going to have to play this carefully. Not lie, just . . . stall a little. He had the feeling she wasn't going to keep smiling that warm, crinkle-nosed smile at him if she found out he was responsible for her sleepless night last night – or the host of other inconveniences he'd accidentally put her through in the last week. She'd probably throw her champagne in his face then march away and never speak to him again, and he really didn't want that. Not now he'd decided he'd like to be more neighbourly.

A lot more neighbourly.

Claire watched Doug until he made it to the lifts. 'I think Doug and his mother have been responsible for keeping my agency afloat since it started,' she told Dominic. 'The first few years for any new business are tough, and they've been a godsend. Thank goodness, when Mrs Martin gets bored, she likes to jet off to a new place and see the sights.'

'You know,' he said, going with the first thing that fell into his head, 'that's not such a bad idea.'

Claire gave him a wry look. 'From your lips to God's ears . . . The travel agency is doing okay now, but I want to grow too.'

'What Jayce said was right. I'm between jobs at the moment.' He looked out over the London skyline. It was getting darker now, the lights of the city gold and orange and white against the velvety blue sky. Some people dreamed all their lives of coming here; all he seemed to want to do was escape it. 'And I travel a lot for work, but maybe it's time I took a trip just for fun. A week, maybe. I haven't had any proper time to relax in a long while.'

Claire's smile softened, but didn't dim. 'I think that's a fine idea. I'd offer my services, but I don't think I plan the sort of holidays you're after.'

He nodded and dived at the opportunity she presented him. 'Well, give me your card anyway. You never know.'

No, you never did. And, as she handed him the little rectangle of card with an elegant logo and simple contact details, he congratulated himself. That had been quite easy. Now he had a way to reach at her that didn't involve marching up the stairs, knocking on her door and getting slapped in the face.

'Do you have one?' she asked, as she put her business card holder away again.

Thankfully, he didn't. Never got round to it. What was so wrong with a number scribbled on a bit of paper when the need arose? And, even if he had a card, he wouldn't have presented it to her right now. That would have totally given the game away.

'No,' he said, and then his smile became just a little wolfish. 'But I can give you my number, if you like?'

She flushed a little as he said that. 'Okay.'

He kept smiling at her, and eased the cocktail napkin she'd been holding in one hand from her fingers. 'Pen?' he said.

She nodded and delved into the green handbag again and came up with an elegant brushed-metal ballpoint, not the half-chewed plastic thing he'd have had if he'd been even half that organised. 'Here,' she said, handing it to him.

He scrawled his number down on the napkin and handed it back to her. Before tucking it away in her bag, she retrieved the pen and pressed the end. He watched her write 'Nick' next to the number. On a reflex, he almost corrected her, telling her to lose the 'k' and why. The words formed in his head, but he didn't let them out of his mouth. Instead, he opted for humour. 'Do you get so many men's numbers on these things that you need to label them?'

Claire carefully folded the flimsy square then put both it and the pen into her handbag and clipped it closed. 'Oh, yes,' she said, her face serious, but her eyes teasing. 'Hundreds.'

He couldn't help it. He grinned at her. 'Well, just as long as you don't lose mine.'

She shook her head, feigned horror.

He leaned in, cupped her elbow in his hand, as he got close enough to smell her floral perfume. Lily of the Valley, he realised. Instead of air-kissing, as he knew everyone did to death at these parties, he pressed his lips briefly and softly to her cheek, just in front of her ear. She went very still and, when he drew back, her eyes were huge.

'I have to go now,' he said, 'but I have a feeling we're going to bump into each other again very soon, Claire Bixby.'

And with that he turned and walked away, through the crowds to the bar and then beyond to the lifts. He needed to retreat and regroup. If he stayed he'd want to keep talking to her, but Doug would return soon and make keeping his secret difficult. Better to leave now and work out how to best show Claire Bixby how very wrong she was about him.

When he got home, he sat in his living room, a beer open in his hand, and stared at the ceiling, smiling. Later, when he was watching a Bruce Willis film on one of the movie channels, he heard the front door go. He muted the TV and listened to her walking up the stairs, now able to picture those shapely calves and killer heels below the modest dress.

He let out a low and silent laugh. Suddenly, being stuck

in London for the next two months didn't seem like such a bad thing after all.

\*

As Claire walked up her garden path, keys in hand, her phone rang. She turned to wave at Doug as he pulled away. She'd been in such a good mood she'd allowed him to drive her home. He'd been a perfect gentleman. He'd opened the door for her and hadn't tried to wangle his way inside or even kiss her.

She fumbled with her keys in one hand while she pressed her phone against her ear with the other. 'Hello?'

Peggy's voice was low and husky. 'So . . . How did it go?'

'Great,' Claire said, smiling at the memory of the evening as she tried to jiggle her key in the rather old and uncooperative lock. 'It was a fantastic party and I made loads of useful contacts, even got to speak to the top man himself.'

'Yeah, work schmerk,' Peggy said airily. 'Tell me more about the men! I know you said you don't have the hots for Doug, but did he manage to change your mind? And, if not, can I have him? I quite fancy having a sugar daddy.'

Claire chuckled as she finally managed to twist the key the right way and her front door swung open. 'He can hardly be considered a sugar daddy when he's only a couple of years older than we are!'

'Details, details . . .'

Claire did a one-handed manoeuvre to switch her front door key with her flat key and headed up the stairs. 'Yes, Peggy, you can have him. If there's anyone who'll be a match for his mother, I think it just might be you.'

'Marvellous,' Peggy said, with the air of a woman

envisioning a future of pampering and luxury. 'But enough about my love life – it's yours I'm interested in! Was that Jayce Ryder as dreamy as his photos?'

Claire entered her flat and kicked her heels off just inside the door. 'Pretty much.'

'Ooh, do tell more! He's so your type!'

Claire frowned slightly as she padded down her hallway and headed for her bedroom. 'I suppose he is . . .' She'd always liked the smooth, well-dressed sort. 'But there wasn't anything there.'

Hmm. How surprising. She hadn't even thought about that at the time.

'Rats!' Peggy said emphatically. 'So the evening was a total bust then?'

Claire sat down on the bed, smiling. 'I wouldn't say that, but it's late, and it's Thursday night cocktails tomorrow. I'll tell you and Candy all about it then, I promise.'

Peggy grunted. 'I may have died from the suspense by then.'

Claire stifled a smile. 'See you tomorrow evening, Peg. I expect you'll still be very much alive.'

Peggy muttered a reluctant reply then let Claire hang up.

When she was ready for bed, she jumped under her sheet – it was too hot for a duvet – pulled it over herself then turned the light off. She watched the shadows from the street light outside flicker gently on her ceiling and, as she fell asleep, she wondered where in this vast and sprawling city the elusive Nick might be and what he was doing right now.

# Chapter Twelve

# I'll See You In My Dreams

Claire sat down on a stool in Caprice, a cocktail bar on Essex Road, and grinned at the two friends who'd been waiting for her. Peggy was slurping her way through a Cosmopolitan, and Candy was still scanning the cocktail list.

'Spill!' Peggy said, as soon as Claire's bum hit the seat of a stool.

'All in good time,' Claire said, and picked up a menu herself, hiding a smile. Really, it was too easy to wind Peggy up. 'Have you ever tried the Movie Night cocktail?' she asked Candy, her face a picture of innocence. 'It sounds very appropriate for us.'

'No,' said Candy, playing along. 'What's in it?'

'Rum, Disaronno, chocolate sau—'

'Oh, for heaven's sake!' Peggy said and snatched the menu out of Claire's hand. She turned to the barman pointed at Claire. 'She'll have a Mojito . . .' and then she pointed at Candy '. . . and she'll have a strawberry Daiquiri.'

'Hang on!' said Candy.

'Peggy!' Claire shouted at the same time.

Peggy gave them a weary look. 'You always order the same bloody thing every time,' she told them, 'no matter how long you spend picking the menu apart.' She fixed her gaze on Claire. 'Come on then.'

Claire released the smile she'd been hiding. 'Nothing much to tell really. Lovely venue. Lovely party. Lovely people, *darling* . . .'

'That's it?' Peggy asked, sounding more than a little disappointed.

'Just about,' Claire replied. 'Oh, but I did go home with a man's telephone number tucked inside my handbag.'

Peggy squealed and Candy leaned forward. 'What's he like?' she asked, with the kind of vicarious interest reserved for 'happily marrieds' when discussing their single friends' dating lives.

'Nice,' Claire said, her smile growing in wattage. 'Very nice.' She pulled the cocktail glass the barman had just placed on the bar towards her. 'And not my usual type at all and maybe that's a good thing. He's the complete opposite of my ex.'

'Really? How?' Peggy asked.

Claire took a long cool sip of her Mojito and thought for a moment. 'In my experience, the kind of man who likes to project a perfect image is always high maintenance in one way or another. Take Philip . . . No one would have thought that under all that grown-up sophistication lay the heart of a whining little boy.'

Peggy's snorted in agreement. She'd heard all about Philip over the year or so Claire had known her, but Candy was a newer friend and hadn't heard the whole story. She frowned slightly. 'You've never really talked about him much. What do you mean "high maintenance"?'

Claire stared past the bartender to the mirrored shelves. In between the multicoloured bottles lined up there she could just about see fragments of her own reflection. How could she explain it? Many of her 'married life' friends had been just like Candy – nice husband, nice house, nice jobs – and they often hadn't understood why she'd been unhappy with Philip. On the outside he'd seemed so dashing, so charming.

'Oh, I don't know . . . Take my work, for example. Things were fine when I was lower down the ladder at the ad agency, but then I was offered a couple of promotions and he didn't like it much.'

'He told you to turn them down?' Candy was reassuringly shocked at the idea.

'No. He was never that outright about things, much more passive-aggressive. He had this way of making these little comments. They'd sound perfectly reasonable on the surface.'

'Such as?'

Claire shifted position and took another, longer slurp of her drink. 'For example, when I'd tell him I had to stay late at the office, he'd say of course he wanted me to do well at my job, but . . . ' she paused to smile wryly '. . . with Philip there was always a *but*.' She changed her tone to mimic the smooth, soothing one he'd used on her. '*It's just that you work so hard and I miss you when you're not here. Can't you say no? I only ask because I love you so much* . . . And before I knew it I was sabotaging my own career, giving in to please him. It was a long time before I realised he never compromised the same way for me.'

Peggy scowled but Candy gave her a sympathetic look. 'I'm lucky with Mike,' she said, 'but I know what it's like to get a little caught up in being Mrs so-and-so, of wanting so badly for it to work that you're prepared to give a little bit more than you should. Between that and the kids being really little, I kind of lost myself for a while. That's why I joined the film club. I thought it was important to have outside friends, outside interests.'

'Well, we're very glad you did join,' Claire said, smiling back at her, and that was definitely the truth. Candy was often the voice of sanity and reason amidst the other more colourful members of the Doris Day Film Club.

Peggy had been silent for a while, processing. She drained the last of her cosmopolitan and signalled for the barman to hit her again. 'I still don't think that sounds like the Claire I know.'

Claire sighed. 'I know, I know . . . I let him change me, manipulate me to being what he wanted. It was just, after my father, I was so overwhelmed to have a man who loved me like that, who said everything I did was wonderful, that he couldn't bear to be apart from me.'

Her soul had been hungry for those things for a long, long time, but, after a while, instead of feeling like a lovely warm nest she could snuggle down in, those little requests, those little things he asked her to do for him, multiplied and multiplied, until she felt hemmed in, until breathing had felt difficult once again.

'In the end, I realised I'd been allowing him to slowly carve away at me, shaping me into who he wanted me to be.' She paused to let out a low self-mocking chuckle. 'You know what?'

'What?' Candy and Peggy said in unison.

'He reminded me of those insect-eating plants – you know the ones I'm talking about?'

'I think so,' Candy said.

'The kind that trap flies?' Peggy asked.

'Yup,' Claire said, 'that's them. I saw a programme on the Discovery Channel once. Did you know some of them produce narcotic fluid? Once the flies are trapped in the pitcher they don't bother climbing out again. They're so affected by all that lovely, hazy sweetness that they hardly notice they're being slowly digested.'

'Ew!' Candy said.

Peggy just laughed. 'That's a bit dramatic!'

Claire gave her a knowing look. 'Well, firstly, pot calling the kettle black! And, secondly, that's how he made me feel – as if he was slowly squeezing the life out of me, giving me the appearance of freedom, but keeping me trapped buzzing around him with no hope of escape.'

Candy finished shuddering. 'But you did escape.'

'Yes,' Claire said, her tone grateful. 'I woke up. It all happened when he got fixated on the idea of having a baby.'

'You didn't want one?' Candy asked, sounding surprised. 'I think you'd make a great mum.'

Claire felt something warm flood her chest. 'Thank you. There was nothing – *nothing* – I wanted more than to have the kind of happy secure family I never had.'

She'd wanted to have babies, like Candy had, that grew into cute toddlers. She'd wanted to love them and cuddle them and tell them they were wonderful and they could fly and be whatever they wanted to be.

'But contemplating all that with Philip suddenly brought

my marriage sharply into focus. It didn't feel like a dream come true when I thought about it. It felt like a life sentence.'

'So you left?' Candy asked.

Claire shook her head. 'If only I'd been that sensible. I was daft enough to keep on trying. We went to counselling and I felt really hopeful when he said all the right things at the sessions, said how much he wanted to change, but when we got back home he'd just carry on the way he always had. It was like he just couldn't have a grown-up conversation, you know? Instead, he resorted to emotional blackmail and manipulation. Finally, I asked for some breathing space. I couldn't think straight with him hovering around me all the time. The more he tried to hold on to me, the more restless I got. We separated. I suppose a part of me still hadn't given up, although I didn't realise that until he announced he'd found someone else. Claire, mark two.'

Candy looked disgusted. 'What? A younger, more malleable model?'

Claire let out a snort of dry laughter 'Yes, and yes. And the total irony is she actually is called Claire, and she's just as needy and clingy as he is. They really make the perfect couple.'

Peggy made gagging noises and Claire wanted to hug her for it.

'Honestly, Peg, I ought to thank her for taking him off my hands. The longer we've been apart, the more I see that. And Philip isn't a monster. He just isn't the man he pretended to be when we first met. I wish them well.'

'God, you're in great shape about it,' Candy said. 'I'd be a mess if Mike did that to me.'

Peggy nodded. 'Me? When I've been dumped, all I can

do is fantasise about slashing his tyres – or something else vital – and then I curl into a ball and cry for a week.'

'I've moved on,' Claire said simply. She didn't want to think about the other Claire, her belly currently stretched round with her first child, because every time she did she felt a pang of something sharp and ugly. Jealousy. And anger. Anger that Philip had stolen almost a decade of her life on false pretences and that she seemed to have paid the price for that, not him.

'Anyway, I'm not sure how I got on to digging up ancient history, especially as there's a new guy on the horizon – maybe – and he's nothing like Philip.'

'Yay!' Peggy said, returning to her earlier cheeky mood. 'So when are you going to meet up and get naked together?'

Claire let out a throaty laugh then she slurped as much mojito as she could from around the large chunks of ice in her glass with her straw. 'I'm not jumping into anything too fast this time around. I did that with Philip and look where it got me.'

Peggy made a disappointed face. 'You're no fun,' she chided.

'So you're always telling me.'

Claire took once last sip of her drink, making sure she really had got it all, and looked at the woman in the mirror opposite her.

No, no matter what Peggy said, this time she wasn't going to be blinded by whatever chemicals addled her brain at the start of a relationship. She was going to take things slowly, get to know him, *really* check him out. And if he didn't like that, well, maybe he wasn't the right one for her anyway.

# Chapter Thirteen

## A Wonderful Guy

Dominic stood outside Pete's front door, feeling a sense of déjà vu because of the bunch of flowers and bottle of wine in his hands. They were from the petrol station again, but one with a Marks & Spencer food shop, so they were much classier than the previous ones. Pete opened the door. 'Hey,' he said, somewhat less enthusiastically than he had last time.

'Hey,' Dominic said back, then followed his best friend inside.

Ellen was ready and waiting, hair brushed, blouse ketchup-free. She received his peace offerings gratefully and gave him a hug and a kiss. 'I'm so glad you could make it.'

Was he mistaken, or did he hear a soft grunt from Pete's direction?

Ellen shook her head and looked first at her husband then at Dominic. 'I don't think I've ever met two such thick-headed, stubborn men! It's about time you both stopped sulking and made up.' She glanced over at Sammy, who was glued to something with robots and strange creatures on the TV. 'His emotional age is higher than yours at the moment, and that's saying something after the lie-down tantrum he pulled in the supermarket this afternoon.' With that, she stomped from the room into the kitchen, which left him and Pete staring at each other.

Dominic scuffed his shoe on the carpet. 'Sorry I was a bit touchy last time,' he mumbled.

'A *bit*?' Pete said, but he shot a look over his shoulder towards the kitchen and reconsidered the tack he was taking. Ellen might seem sweet and lovely, but both of them knew she was like a rabid Rottweiler when her patience finally snapped. Dominic was guessing that if Pete wanted to get lucky sometime in the next six months he was going to have to do as he was told. 'Sorry I opened my big fat mouth,' Pete mumbled back. 'I don't think you're a loser.'

Dominic let out a weary breath. 'I know. It's just . . .'

Pete nodded, and Dominic knew he knew too. Pete walked towards him and gave him a stiff hug. Dominic patted him on the back and then they pulled apart and looked away from each other.

'Want a beer?' Pete asked.

'Always,' Dominic replied and, just like that, all the tension between them melted away as if nothing had ever happened.

Pete went to the kitchen, where his wife gave him an approving smile, and got a couple of bottles out of the fridge. Dominic went up to Ellen, gave her another hug and whispered an apology for running out on her and her spag bol as well, then he and Pete sat at the kitchen table and sipped their beers, half watching her as she bustled round the kitchen roasting a chicken. Dominic's mouth was already watering, even though it looked as if the bird still had a long way to go.

'What have you been up to since we last saw you?' Ellen asked. 'How's work?'

Dominic shrugged. 'I've been doing more research on that free-diving documentary. It turned out a couple of the top people in the sport were passing through London last week, so I met up with them and asked if they'd like to be involved if I get this thing off the ground. They also gave me some useful pointers about research.'

'Did they say yes?'

Dominic nodded. 'The more I find out about free-diving, the more it intrigues me. I mean, going that far beneath the waves without scuba gear is dangerous. It takes intense concentration and training. I'm not sure I could do it.'

Ellen shuddered. 'Neither could I! All that water above my head . . .'

'I'd do it,' Pete said, with an air of confidence.

His wife turned and gave him a look. 'Give over. You had a panic attack snorkelling in Spain the other year.'

'No I didn't! A speedboat went past and sloshed water into my snorkel, that was all. It was a coughing fit, pure and simple.'

Ellen snorted softly and peered at the chicken in the oven.

'Well, that's what I want to explore,' Dominic said, steering the conversation back on track. 'I want to find out about the sort of people that do this, about their tight-knit community. How do they *not* panic when oxygen is just a distant memory, knowing that people die each year doing what they do? How does knowing they're so far below the surface with no safety net not freak them out of their tiny little minds?'

'That sounds really interesting,' Ellen said. 'Anything else new?'

Dominic sighed. 'I've also been to the physio a couple of times. He's given me a bunch of exercises to do three times a day – which I'm actually doing, mainly just to stave off the boredom. It's all thrilling stuff.'

She made a sympathetic face. 'I thought you loved your job.'

'I do. It's just . . . I don't really like the desk stuff. I only do it so I can get to the good bit, which is going out there and filming things, seeing the big wide world. Unfortunately, all I have at the moment is desk stuff, stretching on forever and ever, it seems. As you can see, I'm finding it all fairly depressing. Can we talk about something else?'

'Okay,' Pete said. 'In other news . . . What's up with you and your upstairs neighbour? Has she hired a hit man to put a bullet through your forehead yet?'

'No,' Dominic replied, chuckling to himself. 'And she's not going to, either.'

Pete gave him a disbelieving look. 'And why, pray, would that be?'

Dominic grinned at his best friend. 'Because for once in my life I've decided to take your advice about women.'

Pete slumped in his sear, pretending to faint, but Ellen poked him with a spatula on her way to the vegetable drawer and he miraculously woke up again.

Dominic didn't mind the theatrics. He knew he was holding the trump card. He kept smiling. 'I'm going to ask her out to an early bird dinner, just like you suggested.'

That's when Pete stopped mucking around and looked as if he was going to faint for real. 'What?'

Dominic just shrugged. 'I'm going to do everything I can to win her round and make her mine, what can I say?'

Ellen stopped heaping carrots onto the chopping board. 'You're serious, aren't you?'

'Deadly.'

There was silence in the kitchen.

'You said I didn't have what it takes to be romantic,' he told Pete. 'You have to admit, if I can woo this particular woman and get her to like me, then you'll have to admit you were wrong.'

Pete held his hands up. 'Hell, I'll admit I'm wrong now if you want! And that's not *exactly* what I said. But, Nic, there's proving a point and then there's . . .' he paused to shudder '. . . proving a point.'

Dominic couldn't hold it back any longer. He burst out laughing.

When he'd finally got his breath back and wiped his eyes, he looked them square in the eyes. 'Don't look at me like that. What I didn't tell you is that the old lady who lived upstairs doesn't live there any more – her granddaughter does.'

The look of relief that washed across his friends' faces almost set him off again.

'Why didn't you say so?' Pete asked.

Dominic grinned back at him. 'Because it was too much fun watching you two do the mental gymnastics.'

'You're a sadist,' Ellen said, as she turned back to her carrots, but she was smiling as she shook her head.

Pete thumped him on the back. 'Good one! Now . . .' He leaned forward. 'Tell me about this granddaughter. Is she hot?'

'I'm standing right here!' Ellen called out over her shoulder.

'Aw, Ellie, you know you're the only one for me,' he crooned, all the while nodding at Dominic, egging him on.

Ellie humphed. 'Come and peel these carrots then and prove it.'

Pete sighed, took his beer with him to the other side of the kitchen and took over. Ellen swiped the beer back while he wasn't looking and went to sit opposite Dominic. 'Is she nice?' she said, getting a dreamy look in her eyes. 'I could do with some female company when you come round. With him and him,' she said, nodding in the direction of first Pete then her son in the living room, 'I'm trapped in a testosterone-filled world, where the punchline to every joke involves bottoms or farts. You raise the standard slightly, but not much.'

Dominic chuckled. 'She's nice. Clever. Funny.' He shot a glance at Pete, hard at work peeling carrots and decided to throw him a bone. 'And blonde.'

Pete punched the air and mouthed the word 'result!' while his wife's back was turned.

Ellen swigged her contraband beer. 'And she's totally forgiven you for being . . . What was it? An "unbearable, egotistical lout"?'

That's when Dominic's grin dimmed a little. 'Not exactly.'

'What does that mean?' Pete said, taking his eye off the carrots and nearly adding his finger into the mix. 'Ouch!'

Dominic stood up and leaned against the kitchen counter. Looking straight into Ellen's eyes across the table was unnerving him a little. 'It's only a flesh wound,' he told Pete as he showed him the minuscule cut on his finger. 'What it means is that, yes, I've met her, but she doesn't know I'm the guy from downstairs yet.'

Ellen frowned. 'How on earth did you manage that?'

'Met her at that party I went to last week, the hotel thing.'

Ellen looked even more worried. 'And she hasn't worked out you live in the same building? How is that possible?'

'We just seem to have very different rhythms,' he explained. 'She's out when I'm in and vice versa.'

Pete plopped the peeled and chopped carrots into a pan and got himself another beer from the fridge, sending his wife a knowing look as he did so. She just smiled angelically at him. 'But this girl—'

'Claire,' Dominic added helpfully.

'Claire . . . You're going to bump into her in the hall eventually, right? You know that?'

Dominic nodded. 'Of course I do. I'm not stupid.'

Pete gave him a look that said he wasn't sure about that. For once, it looked as if his wife agreed with him, because she said, 'Don't you think she's going to be cross when she finds out?'

Dominic shook his head. 'I have it all planned out.'

'Oh, gawd,' Ellen said.

'It's just we had such terrible first impressions about each other that we jumped to all the wrong conclusions. I just need a little bit of time to undo that. Not long. I'll ask her out to lunch or something.' He shot Pete a look. 'Or an early bird dinner . . .'

Pete narrowed his eyes. 'Ha, ha, ha.'

'We'll go out, have a nice talk . . . And when she sees I'm not such a bad guy after all, I'll tell her the truth and we'll have a good laugh about it.'

Ellen shook her head. 'You make it sound so simple. Are you sure it's going to be that easy?'

'Yup. Because in the meantime I'm going to convince her she's got it all wrong about her annoying neighbour.'

Pete sat down at the table again and let out a guffaw. 'How the heck are you going to do that?'

Dominic narrowed his eyes a little. 'Well, obviously, I'm going to stop being annoying.'

'Not possible,' Pete interjected. Dominic ignored him.

'And I've come up with a new gift, one she'll really like, and I've written a really nice apologetic letter. She's always out until about half-ten on a Tuesday, so it'll be safe to leave it on her doorstep and she'll find them when she gets home.'

'What does the letter say?' Ellen asked.

Dominic unfolded a piece of paper from his back pocket and started to read it to his friends.

*'Dear Ms Bixby*
*I realise now that my clumsy attempt at a peace offering may well have been misunderstood, and that, while with the best intentions, my note may have come across as a little patronising. Please accept my sincere apologies. I hope we can start afresh and get to know each other better, as I will be staying in London for the next couple of months and I'm sure neither of us want to be at loggerheads for all that time.*
*Your downstairs neighbour,*
*Dominic'*

'That *is* a nice letter,' Ellen said softly, but then she frowned, 'but I'm still not sure all this sneaking around is the right way to go.'

'What else can I do? If I tell her the truth now she'll never give me a chance.' And, although he hadn't told Pete and Ellen this yet, he really wanted that chance. He hadn't been able to stop thinking about her for the last six days and it was torture knowing she was often so close – right above his head – and yet he couldn't do anything about it. 'What do you think, Pete?'

Pete leaned back in his chair and put his hands behind his head. 'I think it's genius.'

Ellen shook her head and got up. She was halfway to the hob to check the carrots when there was a wail from the living room. She instantly turned and ran to check on Sammy.

A moment later, she shouted, 'Pete! Your son has . . . Well, let's just say you'd better get those rubber gloves on again!'

# Chapter Fourteen

# That Touch of Mink

Claire picked another good 'fashion' film of Doris's for the following week's film club meeting—*That Touch Of Mink*. Who couldn't love those beautiful, understated classic dresses of Doris's? Or Cary Grant?

However, when Kitty, Grace and Abby arrived just before the film started, Abby didn't look as if she'd been made over at all. The vintage girls were looking perplexed and Abby wore a scowl twice as dark as last week's. When the film finished, she shot out of her seat and scurried off before Claire could investigate further. She walked over to Kitty and Grace, who were deep in conversation.

'I just don't get it,' Kitty was saying, 'all of those dresses were gorgeous!'

'I know,' Grace replied. 'And I had no idea she was going to freak out like that.'

Uh-oh. Claire pasted on a smile and joined them. 'How did it go?' she asked, looking from one to the other.

Grace's expression remained aloof, but Kitty pulled a face. 'Not so great,' she said. 'We took along some great stuff – mostly mine, because Grace is taller than me and

Abby. Of course, with vintage, you often need to do a few alterations and Abby's flatter in the chest than me, although I'd kill for her legs—'

Claire put a gentle hand on Kitty's arm. 'What happened?'

Kitty shrugged. 'I don't know . . . One minute we were trying things on and then I said something about none of the dresses fitting and she totally lost it, kept saying things like "Of course they didn't" and then she flatly refused to put one more thing on.'

Reading between the lines of Kitty's very reasonable-sounding explanation, Claire managed to paint herself a picture of what might have happened. She cleared her throat. She was going to have to handle this carefully. 'Do you think that some of the dresses might have been a little . . . full-on . . . for Abby?'

Both girls frowned at her.

'What do you mean?' Kitty said sharply.

'They were divine,' Grace insisted. 'Abby was lucky Kitty would think of lending them to her!'

Claire nodded sympathetically and, while she did, she tried to think of how she could get her point across. 'How do I explain this . . . ?' she started. And then it came to her. 'You two, you're very confident in how you dress and how you look, but Abby isn't like that.'

Kitty humphed. 'That's why we were trying to help her.'

'I know. But think of it this way . . . You two are more like Marilyn but Abby is a little more Audrey.'

For a moment both girls looked at her blankly.

'More classic, less sexy,' Claire explained. 'Don't think *Breakfast at Tiffany's* but "My Funny Valentine", especially the beginning part.'

For a moment their expressions didn't change, but then Grace said, 'Oh,' and her eyes lit up. The revelation hit Kitty a few seconds later.

'She's a little bit shy, a little bit awkward, and not comfortable with this fashion stuff. Do you think you could find something a little less . . . Well, you know.' She added a crafty trump card. 'If anyone can find the right thing, it's you two.'

Kitty and Grace looked at each other, determination in their eyes, and then looked back at Claire.

'We won't let you down, Pres,' Kitty said, giving a little salute. Grace just nodded seriously.

'I know,' Claire replied. 'I'll chat to Abby and see if I can persuade her to give it another go. You can all come round to my place next week, if you like. I've got a spare room with lots of space and a full-length mirror.'

'Oh, that would be wonderful!' Kitty turned to Grace. 'Come on! We've got to go and start planning!'

# Chapter Fifteen
## Three at a Table for Two

When Dominic got home that evening, before ten, just to be on the safe side, he crept into his flat and then crept out again. He stood in the hallway, listening.

Nothing. No sound from upstairs. But then he hardly ever heard her moving around up there except when she left or returned to the flat – the open and close of the front door, her footsteps on the stairs, then the muffled slam of her flat door. Slowly and silently, he made his way up to the first-floor landing. Once there, he placed a careful bundle outside her front door.

No more old lady magazines and corner shop chocolates. This time he'd really put some thought into it, tried to work out what a woman like Claire would like.

It was almost one a.m. when he ventured outside his flat door again. He looked on his doormat for a familiar crisp envelope, but there was nothing. He crept upstairs to see if his gifts and letter had been accepted. Claire's doormat was also empty.

So far, so good, he supposed, although he'd have preferred a more immediate response from her. Patience – at least when he was away from his camera – wasn't one of his strong suits.

However, when he surfaced the next morning, he found what he'd been waiting for on his doorstep. He grinned to himself and ripped the envelope open. He hadn't really paid that much attention to the stationery before, but now he noticed the thickness of the paper, the tissue lining of the envelope. It probably said something about Claire Bixby, but he wasn't exactly sure what.

He unfolded the creamy paper and read the note inside:

*Dear Mr Arden*
*I appreciate your effort at a truce and agree that we need to find a way to coexist harmoniously. Thank you for the flowers and chocolates. I hope you don't mind, but I'm going to emulate your kindness and pass them on to a friend who is in need of a bit of cheering up.*
*Best wishes,*
*Claire Bixby*

He frowned. It was hardly gushing, was it? Not exactly what he'd been expecting. This latest letter still had a hint of the tone of the starchy headmistress, and he guessed that if this had been a piece of homework the words 'could try harder' would be neatly inscribed in red pen at the bottom.

That was always the silent message he'd got from Erica when they'd been going out. He should have paid attention to that, really, especially before he jumped in with both feet and asked her to marry him. That had been his most spectacular fall from grace, one he quickly realised the relationship would never recover from.

But surely every relationship was a compromise? Why couldn't she just have accepted that he wasn't good at that kind of stuff? He'd loved her in every way that mattered.

He grunted slightly and went off to his computer and opened up a lengthy article on the breathing techniques free-divers used. Why did he keep harping back to Erica at the moment? The relationship was over. Had been for a long time.

What really puzzled him was how other guys succeeded where he'd failed. Even Pete, of all people, had managed it. It was if all the other men his age were clued in to some big secret that they were keeping from him. It wasn't fair.

And Claire's dismissal hadn't been fair either. He had tried harder this time. Nice flowers – not from the corner shop but a modern-looking bouquet from Waitrose – and the truffles from Hotel Chocolat had cost an eye-watering amount. It didn't matter. Operation Good Neighbour obviously needed a rethink.

Thank goodness the second prong of his plan, Operation Charm Offensive, was still up and running. Or it would be when he followed up with Claire after their meeting at the party. Grinning, he pulled the small business card Claire had given him from his wallet.

\*

It wasn't hard to find the little travel agency. Dominic saw it the minute he stepped foot inside Old Carter's Yard. Paying virtually no attention to the surrounding shops, he marched straight for it. Through the large bay window at the front, he could see Claire, alone in the shop. He mentally punched the air and, grinning, because he just couldn't seem to help himself, he knocked on the door.

A host of expressions crossed her features when she spotted him standing there – polite interest at first, then confusion and surprise as she recognised him – but they all ended up curling themselves into a welcoming smile. She was pleased to see him too. Even better.

She got up from her desk as he opened the door and walked inside. 'What are you doing here?' she asked, puzzled but still smiling.

'What do most people come to a travel agent's for?' he asked. 'I want to book a holiday.'

The smile dimmed a little, which was a bit surprising. He'd have thought she'd be pleased about that.

'Oh?' she said lightly. 'I didn't think you liked to use travel agents.'

He gave her a playful smile. 'Well, you've got to try everything once.'

'I suppose so,' she replied, looking a little wary. 'Why me?'

Later, Dominic would realise this was the moment where he went wrong, that he should have just told her it had been an excuse to see her, but, in the moment, he was so caught up in not revealing he was her downstairs neighbour before he could win her round, he chose another tack. 'After looking you up online . . .' A lie. He'd meant to before he'd left the house that morning but had run out of time '. . . I decided I need the specialised kind of help only you can provide.'

She nodded. The smile had completely disappeared now. She even looked a little bit sad. What was it with this woman? Every time he tried to get one kind of reaction out of her, he got exactly the opposite. It was like being in a dream world where none of the usual rules applied.

'Of course,' she said, her tone professional and flat, and then she bustled around behind her desk for a moment and sat down in her office chair, the great slab of furniture between them. Even though this was the most logical arrangement if they were going to chat as agent and client, he got the feeling this was a bad thing. He sat down in the chair opposite.

She messed around with her computer for a few seconds then looked him in the eye. 'I'm very happy to share my specialist knowledge with you. I take it you want to book a romantic trip?'

Dominic's grin popped back into place. She was the one to have brought up romance. That had to be a good sign, didn't it, if that was the first thing that popped into her head when she looked at him? He might be halfway to winning Pete's unintentional challenge already. 'A romantic trip sounds good to me.'

However, if anything, Claire looked even more grim. 'Will it just be a romantic getaway, or is there a special reason?'

Dominic lifted his eyebrows. Once again, Claire Bixby was making no sense to him. He should probably just try to go with the flow.

She frowned. 'It's not a significant occasion? Like an anniversary or—' she broke off to swallow '—a proposal?'

Crikey, she liked to move fast. He'd only been there for five minutes and she was already talking marriage? Maybe this wasn't such a good idea after all! He shook his head. 'No. Why would I . . . ?'

He trailed off, looked around the inside of the office. There were picture of couples everywhere, even a bunch of fake flowers and a couple of helium balloons saying 'Just Married'. Either Claire Bixby was a woman with a serious wedding obsession or . . .

The slogan at the bottom of a flyer lying on the desk jumped out at him and caught his eye. *'Far, Far Away – the specialists in romantic travel.'*

Oh, hell. He'd done it again, hadn't he? Gone marching in without paying attention to the details. It was just he'd been so focused on seeing Claire again he hadn't thought about anything else. He blamed his father. It was a trait than ran through all Arden men – the inability to take a moment to look a little bit deeper, to go further than a first impression. His mother never let his father do the grocery shopping any more, not since she'd sent him out for basmati and he'd come home with pudding rice. He'd looked at her helplessly when she'd challenged him about it. 'I just saw something that said "rice" on the packet and picked it up,' he'd explained.

And that was just how Dominic felt now, a little foolish, and desperately scrabbling to work out how he could salvage the situation. Claire was looking at him. Waiting. He knew he needed to say something next, he just couldn't work out what.

'Well,' she eventually said, rescuing him. 'The trip is obviously for two people . . . '

Dominic almost made a quip along the lines of, *Well, you never know* . . . but decided against it. He had a feeling Claire wouldn't find it very funny at the moment.

'And how long for? A weekend? A couple of weeks?'

He said the first thing that fell out of his mouth. 'A week.'

She nodded, scribbled something on a pad. 'And what about destinations? Do you have anything in mind?'

He shook his head. Nope. Especially since he hadn't expected to have to pick something *romantic*. This was a crucial moment, wasn't it? If he was going to prove to Claire, Pete – and maybe even himself – that he wasn't the loser in love that everyone thought he was, he was going to have to pick well. Oh, this would have been so much easier if he hadn't got so carried away with Operation Charm Offensive and had just told her he wanted to book a flight to visit Auntie Pat on the Costa Brava.

'I thought I'd see what suggestions you had.'

Good. That was good. He'd deflected that one for now. Claire didn't seem very pleased, though. That little line he remembered from before appeared between her bunched brows. 'A city break? Or a beach? Or would you prefer mountains or countryside? You must have some idea.'

She seemed to be getting a little irritated with him. He'd probably broken one of those mysterious female rules, the kind that only women knew about, but still prosecuted guys for relentlessly when they broke them.

She sat back in her chair, folded her hands in her lap. 'Is this trip a surprise?'

He let out a rough bark of laughter. 'You bet it is!' he said, and then realised what she meant. Oh. A surprise for *her*, the non-existent woman he was supposed to be going away with. 'Why do you ask?'

She gave him an 'isn't it obvious?' kind of look. 'Well, if it wasn't, I'd assume your girlfriend would be here with you.'

Great. Now he'd saddled himself with a girlfriend. This

was so *not* how he'd envisaged this meeting going. If he asked Claire out now, she'd think he was a total and utter slimeball. He sighed. Just for a moment, he wished the non-existent girlfriend was real. Then she'd be able to answer Claire's rapid-fire questions and he'd have a chance to think. That was the reason he'd backed himself into this corner in the first place.

'Good point,' he said, even though he'd already forgotten what she'd just said. There had to be some way to talk himself out of this, hadn't there?

'Well, if you don't know what *you* want,' Claire said, 'and this is supposed to be a special romantic trip, perhaps you need to think about what *she* would want?'

Now she just didn't seem mildly irritated, she was getting a little snippy. Instantly, he could hear the same voice in his head as there had been when he'd read the notes she'd left on his doorstep.

'I'm kind of stuck,' he mumbled, meaning that he'd dug himself into a hole during the last five minutes, one he was becoming increasingly fearful he was never going to scramble out of. Claire, however, took it another way. The expression on her face softened a little. Odd. When he tried to charm her, she just clammed up, but when he let a little bit of the desperation underneath show, it had the opposite effect.

'Don't worry,' she said. Her voice was gentle, understanding, but there was a distance in her manner too. 'Lots of men get paralysed by the pressure of a romantic holiday. We'll take it step by step.'

'Just the men? Don't the women feel the same way?'

She shook her head. 'Nope. They pretty much have it all worked out. Women tend to pay attention to stuff.'

'What kind of stuff?'

She gave a little shrug. 'Details. Little snippets of information they store away during a relationship to use later.'

Dominic nodded. He knew all about that. Only Erica hadn't stored away things that would help her book a holiday. No, what she'd hung on to was every transgression he'd ever made in word or deed, all neatly catalogued and labelled in her memory, so they were readily accessed every time they'd had a fight. 'I suppose you're right,' he said grudgingly.

Claire nodded. 'Women remember those little things about their partners – a favourite song or dish, somewhere they once said in passing they'd really like to visit. Men? Well, they tend to be more . . . oblivious.'

He disagreed with her on principle more than because he actually had a winnable case. 'No we aren't.'

She folded her arms across her chest. 'Then why haven't you got the faintest idea where, when you've got the choice of the whole wide world, your girlfriend would want to go?'

He had to come up with a good idea. Right now. Somewhere seriously romantic. If he didn't buck his ideas up, she'd think 'Nick' was just as much of a loser as her downstairs neighbour and both his plans to win her round would have bombed out in one morning.

Come on, Dominic. You can be romantic if you try! And there's no one that knows destinations like you. You've got to be able to come up with *something*.

Claire was still looking at him. 'Any ideas?'

'Venice,' he said briskly, almost on reflex. His shoulder

muscles unbunched. There. That was a seriously romantic place.

She blinked. 'Did you say that because it's really her dream destination, or because it was the first thing that came into your head?'

The momentary soaring feeling he'd had faded. He was so busted. For some reason, he found that really funny. Laughing to himself, his bowed his head, shaking it. When he looked up again, she wasn't smiling. 'I panicked,' he said.

Claire just stared at him. He quickly swallowed his laughter and straightened his features. For some reason that just made him want to laugh all the harder. She could see it too, which only made her eyes narrow.

'What kind of woman is she?' Claire asked, starchily, pushing the end of a mechanical pencil so a razor-sharp point appeared. 'Tell me something about her. That will help me come up with some less obvious suggestions, but if Venice turns out to be the perfect fit, then I'll help you do Venice in total, drop-dead style. Okay?' She waited, pencil poised above her pad.

Dominic nodded. Flip, he should have quit when he was ahead. It was bad enough when he'd had to answer questions about places – and he was good with places – but now he had to describe a woman, a thing, according to all sorts of people, he clearly knew nothing about. He might as well confess right here and now to stealing Claire's milk a fortnight ago.

He tried to picture her, this phantom woman, tried to work out if she'd be brunette or blonde, tall or short, fat or thin, but she just stayed a fuzzy lump in his imagination. He searched the posters on the walls for inspiration, but the women he saw were all flat, two-dimensional creatures and, try as he might, he couldn't imagine them any other way. And then his eyes drifted back to Claire, looking calm and very three-dimensional on the other side of the desk.

Why not?

She was the one he was trying to win over, after all. What better way to redeem himself in her eyes than by planning the kind of romantic trip she'd like? He looked at Claire. Really looked at her.

For a moment there was only silence between them, then he started to talk.

'She's bright and friendly,' he said, mentioning the first things that popped into his head about her and, surprisingly, instead of having to root desperately around for more words, they were ready and waiting on the tip of his tongue. 'She's intelligent,' he added, his voice firm and decisive. 'She seems reserved when you first meet her – maybe even a little prickly – but once you get past that, she's warm and funny.'

Claire's blank expression thawed. Her brow smoothed and her eyes widened. She cleared her throat. 'Those are lovely things to say about someone,' she said, her voice a little husky.

Yes, they were, weren't they? Dominic was pretty pleased with himself. When Erica had been in one of her *Tell me why you love me?* moods, his brain had always frozen, and he'd learned the hard way that mentioning great boobs did *not* go down well. He was good with pictures, not words. He'd known that he'd loved her, had told her frequently. Why hadn't that been enough?

However, Claire wasn't wearing that same pinched expression Erica used to have. She had her elbows on the desk, and she was leaning forward, hands clasped, looking at him. He realised that finally, and quite accidentally, he'd said something to impress her.

His plan was working. A warm glow spread inside his stomach. At least, it did until he realised what a doofus he'd been already.

Fabulous, Dominic. Well done. You might be winning her over, but you've gone and invented a fake girlfriend she now thinks you're in love with. He'd really outdone himself in the 'jumping in without thinking' stakes this time, hadn't he?

Well, he might as well book the holiday. At first, he'd just thought about talking it through with her, then he'd realised what he'd said at the party was true: he hadn't travelled purely for pleasure in a long while, and he had plenty of time on his hands at the moment. Maybe a week away somewhere he would never usually go wouldn't be such a bad thing. He could relax and let his shoulder finish healing, just like the doc had said. He'd work out what to do about the fake girlfriend later. At least the holiday idea would give him an opportunity to interact with Claire, show her he wasn't the no-brain caveman she'd taken him for.

'Can I take one of those brochures?' he said, nodding at the rack behind her. 'It might spark some ideas.'

Claire stood, fetched one and handed it to him wearily. 'Let's hope.'

# Chapter Sixteen
# There Once Was a Man

Claire almost missed her stop on the bus journey home. She'd been staring out of the window, so she really should have noticed where she was, but she had to push her way off the double-decker at the last moment, gaining herself a few tuts and dirty looks from the other passengers.

However, when she got to her front door, she discovered she had no desire whatsoever to go inside. She stood there, remembering it had once belonged to someone else, someone she'd loved very much. Emptiness radiated from behind the closed door.

She would have phoned Candy or Peggy for a pep talk, but Candy was probably rushing round cooking the kids' dinner or ferrying them to after-school clubs, and Peggy was out doing a proposal at the London Eye that evening.

In the end, Claire dipped inside her flat for a few seconds, where she dropped off her work bag and picked up the flowers and chocolates she'd discovered on her doorstep the previous morning. She hadn't lied in her note to the suddenly – and rather strangely – solicitous Mr Arden. She did know someone who needed cheering up. She transferred her purse, phone and keys into smaller handbag, picked the gifts up and set off for Maggs's house.

She decided to walk. It would be a shame to be stuck inside the car on an evening like this. An inauspicious morning had cleared into yet another glorious afternoon. Besides, parking in Maggs's road was a nightmare and she'd probably have to find a space five minutes' walk away as it was. The whole journey on foot from her flat would probably only take double that, and she liked walking through the streets of Highbury and Islington.

It wasn't long before she was knocking on Maggs's front door, ready to flourish her gifts. When Maggs opened it, she looked first at Claire and then at the flowers and the Hotel Chocolat gift bag. 'What's all this in aid of?' she asked, but Claire saw the warmth in her eyes as she stepped past her into the house.

'It's most odd,' she said, as she headed through to the kitchen. She put the bouquet and chocolates on the table and started to fill the kettle. 'My downstairs neighbour has suddenly turned over a new leaf. I haven't heard a peep out of him for a week, his bike has been noticeably absent from the hallway and he keeps leaving me presents.'

'Nice flowers,' Maggs said, as she peered into the tissue in cellophane. 'Don't you want them?'

Claire shook her head. 'They're very pretty, but I can't help feeling there's something fishy going on, that he's being *too* nice. Keeping them feels as if I'm agreeing with that, falling for it. I'd be much more comfortable to see them going to a good home.'

Maggs reached for the kitchen scissors and sliced expertly through the wrapping, saving the little sachet of flower food.

She shook her head. 'You're far too suspicious for a girl your age,' she said.

Claire rested her bottom against the kitchen counter and watched the old furred-up kettle start to jiggle and groan as the water began to boil. 'I'm not suspicious. I'm just realistic,' she replied. 'Not sure the leopard downstairs can change his spots, that's all.'

Maggs fetched a cut-glass vase from a bottom cupboard and placed it on the table. 'Maybe that last note of yours did the trick and made him see what a first-class prat he was being.'

Claire pressed her lips together and thought for a moment. 'Maybe,' she said, nodding. 'Maybe I should give Mr Arden the benefit of the doubt. That's what Doris would do, wouldn't she?'

Maggs nodded. 'Probably.'

Claire nodded again. Somehow, through all that she'd been through, Doris hadn't lost her faith in human nature. Somehow, it had helped her stay strong. Claire didn't really understand that. She just kept seeing the stupid, pointless, selfish things people did to each other and it made her cross. Really cross. But she was fed up being angry and sad at the world. It didn't make her any happier. So she'd tried to take a leaf out of her idol's book, change her outlook; she was sure that was the root of her problem.

Maggs started arranging the flowers in the vase, cutting the stems at an angle. She nodded at the now quiet kettle. Claire blinked. She hadn't even noticed it had finished doing its job. Taking Maggs's silent cue, she pulled two mugs from the cupboard and made them both a cup of tea.

'Remember what your gran used to say?' Maggs asked, as

she put a pale pink rose amongst the eucalyptus and laurel twigs in the vase.

Claire nodded as she placed Maggs's mug on the table. 'People are like icebergs – there's always more beneath the surface than you realise.'

Maggs held her gaze for a couple of seconds then went back to arranging the flowers. 'That's right. So, while your Mr Arden is puzzling you at the moment, there's an explanation for it. You just don't know it yet.'

Claire took a sip of her tea. 'I suppose that makes sense.'

'And it might be a less nefarious reason than you suspect.'

Claire didn't say anything, so Maggs glanced over her shoulder at her.

'Maybe,' Claire finally admitted, but the syllables felt as if they'd been dragged from behind her teeth. She shook her head and made a dismissive noise. 'Ignore me. I'm just in a bad mood because I'd met someone nice and I'd thought he liked me too. Seems I was wrong about him. So maybe – and I'm still saying it's a stretch – maybe I'm wrong about Mr Nightmare From Downstairs too.'

Maggs stopped what she was doing. 'Do tell!'

'Well, I suppose the whole bike thing could have been a misunderstanding—'

Maggs shooed away her answer with an impatient hand. 'Not that! About the other thing! The other man . . . Was it this rich fellow who took you to that party?'

Claire shook her head. 'It would be easier if it was. I don't think Doug would ever surprise or disappoint me. But, no, it was someone else at the party.'

'Go on.'

'Well, he came into the shop today, asked for my help booking a holiday.'

Maggs blinked. 'And that's a bad thing? It might just have been an excuse to see you again.'

Claire let out a huge sigh. 'Yes. I thought so too at first, but then he said he'd come to me because of the sort of holidays I specialised in booking. Turns out he has a girlfriend. One he's very keen to impress, by the sounds of it.'

'Ah,' Maggs said.

Claire nodded. 'I know. You should have heard the way he talked about her too.' She sighed again. 'Oh, well. I should have taken Gran's advice, shouldn't I, and looked a little deeper? I'd have probably read the signals if I'd been paying proper attention, not getting all caught up in the way his eyes crinkle at the edges when he smiles.'

Maggs nodded sagely. 'The smile. It'll do it to you every time. That's how Sid won me over, you know. I told him I wasn't interested, but he just kept coming around, smiling that smile of his at me, and before I knew it I was trotting down the aisle!'

Claire smiled. 'It worked out okay in the end, though, didn't it?'

Maggs gave her a weak smile back. 'Yes. Yes it did.'

'I don't know what it is. I know you say I'm suspicious – and I suppose I am – but never when it comes to love. It's like I'm colour-blind, except only I'm man-blind. I have no depth perception where they're concerned. I mean, look at Philip.'

Maggs walked over and rubbed her arm. 'We were all fooled by Philip. Don't you fret about him. Everyone's got a secret side, Claire. Even you. Even me.'

An image of Maggs's hip flask, shiny and secret, flashed through Claire's mind. She started to think she should be more worried about that than she'd allowed herself to be. How had she missed that? How had she not seen what was building in front of her nose?

Maggs nodded to herself as she walked back over to the table and got going with the flowers again. 'And you can't know everything about a person when you first meet them. Sometimes it takes a lifetime to work it all out.'

'That's what makes it all so difficult. The whole thing's such a risk. I thought I was ready to try again, but . . . after this . . . maybe I'm not.'

'Don't be daft,' Maggs said, sounding much more like her usual self. 'At least you know you need to look deeper. Knowing the problem is half the solution.' As she finished speaking, her eyes fell on Claire's handbag. 'And there's another thing you're obviously ready to look below the surface of.'

'What do you mean?' Claire asked, but then she saw the corner of a crumpled envelope sticking out of the side pocket and she knew exactly what Maggs meant. She put her mug down and shook her head from side to side. 'No. You've got it wrong. I haven't read it. I haven't even looked at it since you gave it to me that night. It's just been sitting there forgotten in that handbag. It doesn't mean anything.'

Maggs put down the large fluffy thistle head she was holding and turned to face Claire. 'It doesn't mean anything that you've been carrying his letter round for the last two weeks?'

'No.' Claire frowned. 'Don't look at me like that. It doesn't.'

'There's more going on below the surface in everyone, Claire. Even you.'

Claire picked up her tea again and sipped it, welcoming the scalding liquid down her throat. All the while she peered at Maggs over the rim of her mug. 'Not everything has a meaning. Some things, yes, but not everything. Not that. It's just I haven't used this handbag since that night. I haven't even thought about it – about him. Not really.'

'Then there's probably a reason for that too.'

Claire looked away. 'Now you're just being awkward.'

'No,' said Maggs, and the rustle of leaves told Claire she'd gone back to arranging the flowers. 'You could have thrown it away or put in a drawer out of sight. But you didn't. Why don't you just read it?'

Claire kept looking at the back door, at the blurry green shapes moving in the evening sunshine behind the textured glass. 'I don't want to. I told you that.'

Maggs's voice lowered, lost its ever-present edge. 'Laurie would have wanted you to.'

Claire snapped her head round to look at Maggs. 'You don't know that.'

Maggs nodded. 'I do. I was her best friend, remember. She could tell me things that were too painful and raw to discuss with family. He ran out on her too, when he left. Hardly even sent a Christmas card, although she tried to stay in contact. She always hoped he'd come back one day, older, wiser, ready to be part of your family again.'

Claire felt her eyes fill. It made her cross. 'I didn't know that.'

'She didn't ever get that chance to repair what had gone

wrong,' Maggs said. 'But you have that chance. You can do it for her.'

On the outside Claire stayed very still. Nobody would have guessed that a million conflicting emotions were rushing through her at that moment like an electricity current. Nobody but Maggs.

She felt her lips form into a sneer as the next words left her mouth. 'Then I hate him for that too. For not coming back sooner. For breaking his mother's heart.'

Maggs snorted softly. 'Must admit, I don't much like him, either. But you know what your grandmother was like. She never stopped hoping, never stopped believing in people, even when everyone else gave up on them. If what she prayed for all those years has finally come to pass, I just think it's a shame to waste this chance.'

Claire inhaled then exhaled heavily. 'Is that why you're so keen on me doing it? On reading it?'

Maggs nodded. 'Yes. For Laurie. But also for you.'

Claire was so surprised she let out a little huff of a laugh. 'For me?'

'I see how lonely you are.' Claire started to shake her head, but Maggs continued, 'I see it, because I know what it feels like.' She paused to give Claire a meaningful look. 'But I had a life full of love and happiness with Sid before that happened. You've hardly even begun yours yet and you're intent on cutting yourself off from love.'

Claire felt as if a big hole had opened up inside her and she was teetering on the edge of it. She kept very still, just in case. 'I'm trying not to be like that. I really am.'

Maggs's serious expression thawed a little. 'I know.'

They spent the next few minutes in silence. Maggs

finished arranging the flowers and Claire just watched her, hypnotised. Better that, than delving too far into what Maggs had just said.

Maggs placed the vase on the wide windowsill behind the kitchen table. 'He was a lot like you as a child, you know.'

It took Claire a few seconds to work out who Maggs was talking about. 'My father?' That seemed hardly believable. He'd been made of steel – wrapped up in a deceptively charming coating, to be sure, but made of steel all the same. She'd been neither as a child. Too cowed to be strong. Too shy to be charming.

'He was optimistic and kind. Sensitive.'

Claire shook her head slowly. 'I can't believe that.'

'Too sensitive. His father knocked that out of him quick smart.'

Claire stared straight ahead. She didn't want to think of her father like that. Small. Weak. Trembling behind the lounge door, waiting for her grandfather's judgement. Judgement that might have been meted out with a switch or a strap.

Maggs came over and leaned on the kitchen counter beside her. Close, but not touching. Only an arm's length away. Maggs was quite a bit shorter than Claire, so it wasn't the top of her bottom that rested on the ledge, but the small of her back.

'You see things differently as an adult from how you understood them as a child,' she said simply. 'He became a monster in your mind – a villain – but maybe he's just a man who's made mistakes, one who wants a second chance.'

Claire turned her head to look at Maggs, whose jaw was hard and eyes beady.

'Maybe it's time to find out?'

Maggs looked back at the handbag, at the scruffy corner to the letter sticking out the pocket. Slowly, Claire walked over to it. She pinched just the corner of it with thumb and forefinger. It slid out easily. She felt as if she'd just crossed some kind of threshold, as if there could be no going back, even though the letter was still as snugly inside the envelope as it had been when she'd arrived.

She felt as if she was in a dream world as she pulled out the folded sheet of paper – nice paper, she noticed – and read it. It was as if another Claire was standing there reading the words and she was floating at the corner of the ceiling, looking down on herself.

*Dear Margaret*
*I don't know if this letter will reach you, but I have to try. I am looking for Claire, my daughter. I don't know if you know where she is, or if you remained friends with my mother, but my mother is not the kind to lose friends or family easily. I have learned that one has to be quite determined about it.*

Claire stopped reading. She felt her insides boiling, just like the furred-up kettle had only ten minutes earlier, the anger rising to the surface in great bubbles that shook her so hard, she was sure Maggs must feel the reverberations through the kitchen counter.

Maggs had been right. Gran had tried to keep in touch, but he'd rejected her. She closed her eyes. Why would she ever want anything to do with this man? He wasn't her father. Not really. Just provided some raw DNA to get her going.

'Don't stop,' Maggs said quietly.

Claire looked at her. Her whole jaw trembled as she answered. 'I'm not sure I can continue.' She very much wanted it to rip it into confetti and post it piece by piece down the plughole of Maggs's kitchen sink but, somehow, she managed to focus on it once again.

*I know I have made mistakes. I want make amends. It's the right thing to do. I hope you can find it within you to help.*
*Yours sincerely,*
*Martin Bixby*

Claire looked up at Maggs, her mouth slightly open. 'That's it? You've been going on and on at me about reading *that*?'

Maggs nodded.

Claire didn't know whether to laugh or cry. 'It's nothing,' she said, shaking her head. 'Less than nothing. "It's the right thing to do"? What the heck does that mean? No mention of loving me or missing me or even an "I'm sorry"!' She slammed the letter down on the counter and walked away from it.

Maggs kept her voice quiet and steady. 'He may not say he's sorry, but he might mean it. Why else would he get in contact?'

Claire almost laughed. Maggs clearly had been nipping too much of whatever she kept in that hip flask. 'You're joking, right?'

'No.'

They stared at each other.

'Remember the iceberg, pet. Some people have a hard time saying what they feel. Even if they really, really want to.'

Claire was about to say that wasn't good enough, but then she noticed the grim set of Maggs's mouth, flattened out, the muscles drawn tight to prevent even the hint of a wobble. Her eyes were begging Claire to understand.

And Claire did. Maggs had always found it hard to let her feelings be known too. She chided and nagged Claire, but Claire knew she loved her fiercely, just the way she loved Maggs back. It was just a bit of a stretch to think her father was in any way similar.

However, she owed Maggs a lot. At least giving her the benefit of the doubt about this one thing.

'Okay,' she said hoarsely, nodding at the finality of what she was saying. 'Okay. You can tell him you know where I am, but that's all. We'll see if he can be bothered to do anything with that.'

# Chapter Seventeen

# Bewitched, Bothered and Bewildered

From: clairebixby@farfaraway.com
To: nica453@monstermail.com
Subject: Trip Ideas

Dear Nick,

It was lovely to chat the other morning. I'm really pleased you think Far, Far Away was the perfect place to come to plan your trip. I wondered if you'd had a chance to think about some more personalised destinations? If not, maybe asking yourself the following questions might help you narrow the field down. (Excuse me for using 'she' below, but I realised I didn't ask what your girlfriend's name was):

1. Is she the outdoorsy type who likes walking and sailing or would she prefer to spend time at a spa being pampered?

2. Which would she enjoy most – a summer's day out in the countryside or the bright lights and bustle of a night out in the city?

3. If you think about her clothes and jewellery, are they quirky and individual, from markets and independent shops or does she tend to go for understated and elegant pieces, possibly by well-known designers?

I know the questions seem random, but they really will help me start to pin down the right kind of trip suggestions for you.
Many thanks,
Claire

*

Dominic stared at his computer screen. He hadn't ever thought something as insubstantial as an email could make you feel as if you'd been placed firmly at arm's length but Claire had managed it. It dented the good mood he'd carried with him since yesterday morning a little. They'd been getting on so well until he'd put his stupid mouth into gear without thinking.

Oh, well. The only thing to do was answer her questions and answer them well. He still wanted to prove to her he wasn't the dunce in the romance stakes she thought he was, and he'd been thinking about what to do with his non-existent other half most of last night and had finally come up with a plan.

At first he'd decided to dump her – before any firm bookings were made, of course – then the trip could easily be amended for one person, but after further thought he'd decided that maybe she would dump him instead. Guys would mock, see that as a sign of weakness, but Claire definitely wasn't a guy, and it might just make her feel a little warm and sympathetic towards him too.

Not that he liked to manipulate. That really wasn't his style. But, given the two options, he'd be stupid if he didn't choose the one that suited his goal, wouldn't he?

He pulled his keyboard forward and started to type.

From: nica453@monstermail.com
To: clairebixby@farfaraway.com
Subject: RE: Trip ideas

Hi Claire,

Thanks for getting back to me so promptly, and thanks for the questions – I think! You're right. I don't really get where you're going with these, but I'll put myself in your very capable hands.

The only problem was, now he was definitely going to have to answer those damn questions. Hard enough if the girlfriend had been real. Doubly so now he was basing her on Claire. A woman like Claire would expect him to know stuff about his girlfriend, the kind of stuff he hadn't got a clue about Claire after only two meetings. He stared down at number one:

*Is she the outdoorsy type who likes walking and sailing or would she prefer to spend time at a spa being pampered?*

Hmm. He really didn't know. On the two occasions he'd met her in the flesh, Claire had been immaculately put together, with neat little dresses and high heels. The spa seemed the obvious choice, but then he started to imagine her walking on a hilltop in the Peak District or up on top of a tor on Dartmoor and he could envision her there too. The picture in his head reminded him of an old-fashioned holiday photograph, one of those little ones with the thick white borders held in an album with black pages.

He could see her sitting on a rock, turning to smile at him in red three-quarter-length trousers and a crisp white blouse, the warmth in her eyes hidden by a pair of tortoiseshell sunglasses. He could also see her skipping lightly down a grassy footpath, turning back to laugh over her shoulder at him now and then.

Okay, so he wasn't quite sure about that one. Maybe he should just move on to number two?

Summer afternoon or night out in the city?

He let his lips puff out as he blew out a breath, then gave up keeping his fingertips hovering over the keyboard and instead planted his elbows either side and rested his chin on his hands.

He shook his head. Once again, he could see her doing both. The summer afternoon carried on in the same vein as the little hilltop walking fantasy he'd had going, only this time it involved a long and lazy lunch at a charming little country pub by a stream, Claire choosing to sit under the shade of an umbrella so the faint freckles on her nose didn't darken too much.

Dominic sat up a little. She did have freckles, didn't she? Just a light dusting. He hadn't realised he'd noticed.

But he could also imagine Claire dressed up, looking elegant in a form-fitting dress, hopping from a black cab in the West End, ready to walk, head held high, into a fashionable bar or Michelin-starred restaurant.

He didn't even bother with question three. What did he know about women's clothes? He knew when they looked nice in something, but he hardly paid attention to designers and labels when he was in the back of beyond filming. The only requirements for most of his own clothes were that they didn't fall apart on his rigorous trips and didn't look too bad with a bit of dust or dirt thrown in.

He frowned and repositioned his keyboard. He'd wanted to wow Claire with his insight and detail. Instead, he had nothing. He ended up finishing the email, trying to keep it jaunty and light without letting on he actually had nothing to say.

> As for the questions, I think I've learned after our recent meeting that I'd better give them some thought rather than typing the first thing that comes into my head. I'll get back to you very shortly.
>
> Nic

And then he realised how she'd spelled his name in her email – the same way she'd written it on the napkin at the party.

Not 'Nic', but 'Nick'.

His finger hovered above the 'k' key, but he didn't press it. Just that one little letter felt like a big fat lie. Worse than the ones he'd already told. Probably because he'd stumbled his way into those ones. This one would be a choice.

He sighed and got up from his desk. Bin day tomorrow. He'd better put his recycling out. How he'd actually remembered the right day he wasn't sure. He must be getting into the rhythm of life back here now. He wasn't sure whether to be pleased or fed up about that.

He looked at the stack of magazines standing – well, falling over and spilling onto the floor – in the corner of his spare bedroom. She was right. He did get too many. Not because they weren't useful, but because he wasn't here long enough to digest the information from one a year, let alone multiple subscriptions.

He walked over to the pile, grabbed the top one and tore the plastic wrapping off, then he flicked through to see if there was anything of interest. There wasn't, so he threw it on the floor, making a new pile, and picked up the next one.

Two hours later, the teetering stack was gone, replaced by a large pile of magazines to recycle, a smaller one of issues to keep and a cloud of shredded plastic wrapping in between them. He went to get a bin bag.

He just about managed to fit the discarded magazines in his paper bin and heaved it outside to sit next to the pavement, wearing a hoodie for disguise in case Claire should look out her window. Then, before he went back inside his front door, he carefully tiptoed across the hall to where her recycling bin sat ready for the next morning in the little nook at the bottom of the stairs. He picked it up and took it out to stand next to his. The least he could do after the countless times she'd done that for him.

When he came back in the front door, he looked up the stairs. Was she in there? Probably. It was now close to midnight. Quietly, he crept back inside his flat and reached for a scrap of paper. He was going to use the plain back of a printed leaflet for The Bombay Palace, then stopped himself. He thought about Claire's letters, about the lovely thick paper, the way the blue ink of her fountain pen flowed across the paper.

He didn't have nice stationery. He didn't have much stationery at all. But he could at least use a clean, fresh page nicked from the printer and a fineliner with steady ink, rather than the ballpoint which sometimes decided to deposit sticky blobs of ink on the paper and sometimes didn't. Using both those items, he wrote a short note, letting her know she didn't have to worry about her recycling bin – it hadn't been stolen, just put in the proper place – then he crept up the stairs to post it through her letterbox. Hopefully, she'd find it before she left for work in the morning.

When he got back to his desk, he found the email he'd written to Claire still open on his computer and realised that he hadn't pressed 'send'. It seemed odd, corresponding in these two very different ways. He was having to be so careful on both fronts, not to reveal his identity, not to say the wrong thing. He knew, even though on the face of it he was lying to her – by omission mainly, rather than outright deception, by not putting right what she'd got wrong – it still felt as if it was the right thing to do. The fair thing to do, so they could get past the awful first impressions they'd created and discover the truth beneath.

He stared at the bottom of the email. He couldn't add that 'k'. It was too much. In the end, he hit the backspace key twice until he'd just signed off as 'N'. That much he could live with.

And then, in a moment of pure honesty, he hastily typed the following as a postscript:

Thanks for all your help and sorry I'm so rubbish at this.

It felt good to say something real amongst all the half-truths and sidestepping. Before he could change his mind, chicken out and keep his ego undented, he pressed send and heard the whooshing noise as it disappeared into the ether, travelling from server to server around the country, maybe even the world, only to reappear feet away in the flat above.

\*

Claire heard her phone ping as she lay in bed reading. For a couple of seconds, she stayed absorbed in the thriller, but when she got to the bottom of the page, she leaned over and took a look at her phone on the bedside table. She knew she ought to go back to her book, to find out what happened to the girl being chased through moonlit woods, but she saw the subject header.

Carefully, she placed a bookmark between the pages, put her book down and picked her phone up. She let out a small sigh then swiped the screen to bring it up.

Short and sweet. This man didn't gush, did he? The last bit made her smile.

*Sorry I'm so rubbish at this . . .*

She smiled again. He *was* rubbish at it. But the fact he'd owned it, rather than hidden it all behind a layer of bravado, made her like him more.

It was such a pity he was planning this all for someone else.

She sighed again. She seemed to be doing a lot of that these days.

She pressed 'reply' and began to type with her thumbs.

From: clairebixby@farfaraway.com
To: nica453@monstermail.com
Subject: RE: Trip ideas

Dear Nick . . .

She stopped typing and backspaced, jabbing her right thumb on the right little button, hitting the 'p' a few more times than was strictly necessary along the way, meaning she just had to backspace all the more.

Not 'dear' Nick. That was too affectionate, too intimate somehow, even though it was perfectly proper. She replaced it with 'Hi' and carried on.

\*

Dominic heard his phone chirp as he walked past where he'd thrown it on the sofa on the way to the bathroom. He picked it up and took it with him while he brushed his teeth, savouring the knowledge that she'd not only read his answer but had replied so quickly, but it wasn't until he'd stripped off and crashed onto his bed that he read the full reply.

Hi Nick

Please don't worry about being rubbish at all this – and I gather by 'all this', you mean romantic stuff. I'll let you into a secret... Most men are. Even the ones who come to me to book their holidays. Maybe especially them, because the truly romantic ones can do it all on their own.

There's nothing wrong with acknowledging a weakness and seeking help. No one's good at everything, and that's what I'm here for, after all, to help. It's not only my job, but what I love to do.

I'll let you into another secret: you just need to think outside the box. Most men have a very narrow definition of romance.

They think it's flowers and chocolates and lingerie.

He sat up, his eyes suddenly wider than when he'd lain down. It wasn't? Then why were all those things shoved in front of men's noses at Valentine's Day and Christmas? Was the whole retail industry cynically exploiting this error? He shook his head and read on.

Well, it can be those things . . .

He let out a relieved sigh and rubbed his free hand through his hair.

. . . but it's also a lot more. Romance isn't in the object itself – the gift. You've heard the saying 'it's the thought that counts'? Well, that concept goes a long way for a woman. The gift better be good, but the gift on its own isn't enough, and sometimes the strangest of presents take on a whole new level of meaning and romance when the right thought goes behind them.

I have a friend whose husband made her chips on Valentine's Day one year and she said it was the most romantic thing anyone had ever done for her.

I can almost visualise you scratching your head, Nick. It's very funny. Even so, I'm not going to tell you the rest of the story now. Think about it. And I'll tell you why it was so romantic when you give me the answers to those questions.

Look forward to hearing from you soon,
Claire

Dominic flopped back on the bed and stared at the ceiling. He wondered if the flat layout was the same upstairs. If so,

Claire could be up there right now, mere metres above his head. He wondered if she was still holding her phone too, if she wasn't quite ready to let go of it yet. He brought it up in front of his face and skim read the email again.

It was strange. In person, Claire, while friendly and open, always seemed a little guarded too. There was a 'keep off' quality about her that wove in and out of her engaging personality. However, in her last email, unlike her stiff notes on the doorstep, he felt as if she'd let that barrier down, as if she was whispering those precious secrets she'd told him right into his ear.

He growled with frustration, even as he chuckled and slid his phone onto the bedside table and turned out the light. Now he was going to have to come up with seriously good answers to those questions, and he still had no ideas whatsoever.

# Chapter Eighteen

# A Woman's Touch

Abby, Kitty and Grace turned up at Claire's flat before the film club meeting the following Tuesday. Claire ushered them inside and up to her spare room.

'Right,' Kitty said, sitting down on the chair by Claire's desk. She indicated that Grace and Abby should perch on the edge of the bed, which made Claire smile, as it seemed very much as if Kitty was a queen holding court. She stood by the door and looked on.

'I've found a great dress for you,' Kitty said to Abby. 'Much plainer than the ones of mine I let you try on. I looked to Audrey for inspiration. She had a figure like yours, but she wasn't quite as tall as you. Still, I'm sure this will work better.'

Claire hid a smile. Obviously, she'd done her job well if Kitty had totally forgotten that hadn't been her idea.

Kitty nodded towards her and Claire passed her a garment bag that had been hanging on the back of the door. Abby let out a sigh of relief as Kitty pulled it from the plastic and Claire almost did too. Much better!

There was no lace, no frills, no bold patterns, just a lovely plain cream dress with a pattern of tiny white flowers on it, so pale they almost didn't show up against the background. It had a scoop neck, capped sleeves and a thin red patent leather belt that ran round the middle. Claire was tempted to say she'd have it if Abby wasn't interested.

Kitty motioned for Abby to stand up and start shedding her football kit.

'Come on, girls,' Claire said to the two vintage girls, guessing Abby would prefer a little privacy. 'Why don't we wait outside? If Abby needs help with the zip, she can call us.'

A minute or two later, they heard a soft, 'Ready!' from behind the door and Claire pushed it open so they could file back in.

Kitty squealed and clapped her hands. 'Perfect!' she decreed, and then she and Grace leapt into motion, fussing round Abby, doing the zip up and fluffing the full-ish skirt that came just to her knees. 'You've got really great legs, you know.'

Abby looked over her shoulder to see who she was talking to, but there was no one there. 'You mean *me*?'

Both girls smiled and nodded. 'Great muscle tone,' Grace said. 'Must be all that football.'

'I have great legs?' Abby whispered.

Kitty laughed. 'Better than mine. Why do you think I wear these long skirts? I'd kill for thighs like that.' She stepped back and turned Abby so she could see her reflection in the full-length mirror on the wall.

Abby blinked in surprise. 'It looks… I mean, *I* look … nice.'

Claire smiled. 'I think you look beautiful.'

Abby twisted this way and that. 'Look! I actually go in and out in the middle.'

'That's the magic of fashion for you, darling,' Grace drawled.

Kitty grinned. 'Try looking at yourself side on.'

'Flipping hell!' Abby exclaimed. 'I've got boobs!'

'It's the darts in the bodice,' Kitty told her.

Abby nodded seriously, even though Claire was sure she hadn't a clue what a dart was, and then she frowned. 'How much is it? Is it really expensive? I've only saved a hundred pounds from my part-time job at the sports centre.'

Kitty shook her head. 'I've got a friend who runs a little shop in Greenwich and I've sent a lot of business her way, so she said she'd let me have this one at cost – if it fitted you, of course. Fifty quid. That's okay, isn't it?'

Abby smiled and nodded.

'It should even leave you enough for some shoes,' Claire said.

Abby's face fell. 'Shoes? I hadn't thought about shoes! All I own is trainers! And I can't walk in those things,' she said, pointing to Kitty's stilettos. 'I'll just faceplant in the middle of dance floor at Mum's party and totally humiliate myself!'

Claire looked down at her feet. 'Ballerina pumps. That's what's needed here.'

Abby looked at her in horror. 'Heels are bad enough, but *ribbons*?'

Kitty, and even Grace, burst into fits of laughter. 'Oh, Abby,' Kitty said, as she wiped a tear from the corner of her eye. 'That's one of the reasons we like you. You're so funny!'

'I'm funny too?' she said, obviously still not having come to grips with the legs thing.

Kitty nodded. 'Sometimes.'

Grace, however, was much more focused on the shoes. 'Not Darcey Bussell kind of ballet shoes . . .' She reached into Kitty's suitcase and pulled out some flat black shoes with a little bow at the front. 'These.'

'Oh.' Abby visibly relaxed. 'I think I could manage those.'

'What size are you?'

'Seven,' Abby said and Kitty frowned. 'Damn. Those are a five.'

'I have some that size,' Claire offered. 'They're cream too. I'll just go and see if I can find them.'

'Oh, good. While you do that we can think about hair and face.'

Claire left the door open and, as she walked down the hall and into her bedroom, she heard Grace say, 'Now, you're going to have to keep really still. Liquid eyeliner is a pig if you don't get it right first time.'

She returned with the shoes a few minutes later and watched as Grace worked on Abby's face and Kitty her hair. When they were finished, they prodded their subject in the direction of the mirror again. Abby stared at herself. 'Is that me?' Kitty and Grace both nodded. 'But my eyes look so big! And my lips . . .'

Abby was right. Her eyes did look huge and Grace had painted Abby's full lips the only choice in her palette – pillar-box red. While they looked fabulous, full and plump like Angelina Jolie's, Claire wasn't sure the colour suited Abby as well as it did Grace. However, if Abby wasn't complaining . . .

Abby patted the back of her head, trying to work out what Kitty had done with her hair, and discovered she'd swept it off her face and had twisted it into a bun. She then moved her hand round to the front of her head and giggled softly. 'I don't think I can remember the last time I saw my forehead.'

'What do you think?' Kitty said, and Claire heard a tremor in her usually confident, purring tone.

Abby looked at herself in the mirror again, as if she was beholding an alien being. 'I think,' she whispered, 'I really do look like a girl.'

Kitty and Grace grinned at each other and then Kitty threw herself at Abby again, hugging her tightly, only to be shooed away by Grace in case she messed up the carefully applied make-up.

'Try these,' Claire said, and handed Abby the shoes.

Abby stood up and put them on. 'They fit, just about. A little bit snug over the toes,' she said, as she walked up and down beside the bed, 'but they don't slip too badly.

'Perfect,' Grace said, sighing. 'You're just like Cinderella!'

'Or Calamity Jane,' Kitty said nodding.

'Calamity *who*?'

'Doris Day film,' Claire explained.

Abby smiled. 'Should have known!'

'We're watching it in a couple of weeks,' Claire told her, smiling back. 'I think you'll like Calamity. She's a bit of a tomboy too.'

Kitty took on a dreamy expression. 'Yes, but then there's this scene where she goes to the dance at the fort and . . . Oh, when he sees her! It's just—' She clamped her mouth closed. 'Whoops,' she added. 'Don't want to spoil the story! You'll see.'

Claire looked at the old-fashioned alarm clock on the bedside table. 'Rightio. It's just about time to get going.'

'What?' Abby asked, looking between them. 'What do you mean? Going where?'

Grace blinked. 'To the film club meeting, of course.'

Abby's face turned as pale as her dress. 'You want me to go out like this?'

Kitty looked confused. 'That's the point of all this, isn't it? So you can go out looking nice for your mum's party? People will see you then.'

'But that's weeks away! I'm not ready yet!'

'Maybe a little practice run isn't such a bad thing?' Claire said. 'If you wait until the party and do it all in one go, it might be a bit overwhelming.'

Reluctantly, Abby nodded. 'I suppose so. I don't want to have a stroke or a heart attack. Mum will definitely never forgive me if I steal the limelight away from her on her big night and blues and twos and a trip to A&E would definitely do that!'

Kitty and Grace burst out laughing again. 'See? Told you you were funny,' Kitty said when she'd regained composure. Abby looked perplexed, but pleased and, while she was in a good mood, Kitty pressed her advantage. 'Anyway, everyone at the club really wants to see how it all turned out.'

'You told them we were doing this?' Abby asked.

'Why not?' Grace asked.

'Of course,' Kitty replied at the same time, but there was a look of pride in her features and Claire very quickly understood what this was all about. Good old Kitty was definitely going to enjoy all the adulation that went with being the fairy godmother of this particular Cinderella moment.

'Come on, Abby,' Grace said, thankfully sounding a little more genuine. 'You know it makes sense.'

'It does,' Claire said firmly, even though she didn't quite like the way the other two girls had manoeuvred Abby into this. 'But I think you should only go dressed up if you want to.'

Abby stared at herself in the mirror once more, then nodded to herself before looking back at Claire. She swallowed. 'No. You're right. It's about time Ri – I mean, some people – realised I was a woman.'

The look in her eyes tugged Claire's heartstrings. 'Are you sure?' she asked softly.

Abby nodded. 'Yeah. Let's do it.'

# Chapter Nineteen

## You're Getting to Be a Habit With Me

The familiar music to *By the Light of the Silvery Moon* played, and Claire hummed along inside her head. Anyone looking at her would have thought she was engrossed in the film flickering on The Glass Bottom Boat's huge television, but while her eyes were pointed in the direction of the screen, her mind was somewhere else entirely.

She was thinking about Nick.

They'd been emailing each other since she'd asked him those questions the other day. He still hadn't answered them, but it had led to a back and forth conversation about ideas for his trip, which had led to discussing travelling in general, which in turn had led to sharing funny trip-related anecdotes and disasters.

Nick had many more than she had. He'd been to so many places! And always the most interesting places too, places on her bucket list that she still hadn't made firm plans to visit. While, on the one hand, the conversation about all these exotic locations thrilled her, on the other, they made her feet itch jealously.

He had such a great way of telling his stories, though, that it was hard not to be swept away by the magic of the places he'd been to – Baobab Alley in Madagascar, Machu Picchu, Victoria Falls and up into the frozen north to see the Aurora Borealis.

She smiled to herself as she remembered a silly story of his about getting lost on the Moscow Metro because he hadn't been able to decipher the station names on the map.

If it had been anyone else she'd have wondered if he was interested in her. Sometimes, she forgot it herself when they were bantering back and forth. Every now and then she wondered if she should be communicating with him this way, but if she looked at his emails, dissected and analysed them, they weren't flirty, just friendly, and she'd heard the way he'd talked about his girlfriend, hadn't she? Their emails had definitely wandered from professional into chatty, but that was where it ended.

It was just nice to have someone to tell things to. Silly things. Little things.

She shifted in her chair and tried to concentrate on the film again. They were getting to the bit where Gordon MacRae sang 'Just One Girl' and it was one of her favourite moments.

Most of her emailing with Nick happened late at night, messages pinging back and forth like a conversation. She didn't know where he was when he sent them, but she was usually in bed. She'd cuddle up under her light quilt, fluff up her pillows and then open up the email app on her phone, holding her breath, and see if a message had arrived from him. There was usually one, if not two.

It was totally ridiculous, but she imagined it a bit like the split-screen phone calls between Rock Hudson and Doris Day in *Pillow Talk*. She'd always wanted someone to chat to like that late at night, to give her that warm feeling of talking with someone who 'got' the things you got, who made you feel that, after all, you were not so very alone.

That was where the similarity ended, thankfully. Nick wasn't some nefarious womaniser, out to charm her into bed, and Claire hoped she was intelligent enough not to get duped the way poor Doris had in the film, but really… Falling for a guy who said he was from Texas and called himself Rex Stetson? How gullible could you get?

Anyway, Nick wasn't trying to charm her into anything, was he? All his attention and focus were fixed on his other half. That's why she didn't feel too guilty about roping him into her ridiculous little one-sided fantasy. One day soon it would all be over. She wasn't stupid. She knew her daydreams had a shelf life. The holiday would eventually be booked, and he'd disappear off into the sunset with his wonderful girlfriend, and then all Nick would be to her was another – hopefully – satisfied customer.

She knew all of that. But it didn't stop her feeling giddy when her phone pinged to let her know a new message had arrived.

Perhaps that wasn't such a bad thing, anyway. It showed her that, after more than two years of not even thinking about romance, maybe her heart was healing enough for her to believe that there were a few good men out there, that if she'd stumbled across one then she might be lucky enough to find another. This was a practice run for her bruised heart, safe exactly because it was doomed never to go anywhere.

That might seem like reverse logic, but all Claire knew was that for the first time in a very long time, she was starting to believe not all men were pathological liars.

# Chapter Twenty

## Everybody Loves a Lover

Maggs had thrown George a bone and had consented to let him give her a lift home, so Claire tidied up after the meeting on her own then made her way back down to the ground floor of The Glass Bottom Boat. However, as she turned the corner halfway down she spotted Abby at the bottom, surrounded by a group of boys who were blocking the doorway to the little courtyard at the back of the pub.

'Oh, my God! Preston!' one of the boys said rather loudly. 'What happened to you?' And he started laughing.

Another boy standing next to him snickered.

Abby's face, which had looked so pretty – not just because of Grace's make-up, but because she'd looked happy and confident – fell. She glared at the boy then pulled back her arm, swung and knocked his beer bottle out of his hand.

'Hey,' the boy yelled. "What d'you do that for?'

Abby didn't say anything. In fact, she ignored him, too busy looking past him to the tall boy with slightly floppy hair who hadn't made a sound so far. His eyes were wide, as if he couldn't quite believe what he was seeing. 'Abs?'

he whispered, and all of sudden Claire just knew this must be Ricky.

Abby looked as if she wanted to say something. She shook her head and started to open her mouth, but that's when Kitty and Grace arrived to 'rescue' her. They linked their arms with hers in a show of female solidarity and marched her out of the pub, leaving the group of boys with their chins on the ground.

Claire also marched past the boys, too intent on checking if Abby was okay to pay them much attention. She tried to peer over the heads of the people in the crowded lounge bar, but couldn't see them anywhere. It looked as if the three girls had already made a speedy exit. She was just making sure when something made her do a double take.

It had just been a glimpse, but the sense of familiarity had been overpowering – a shock of slightly messy dark hair, a smile that was both cheeky and warm, the crinkle around the edges of a pair of brown eyes.

She ground to a halt in front of a pair of bar stools. 'Nick?' she said, quite a bit louder than she'd meant to.

He looked round, dazed. His friend too.

'*Claire?*' he said, his voice only a whisper.

He was with a guy. She felt a warm tide of relief rush over her. Thank goodness. She wasn't ready to meet the wonderful girlfriend just yet. Not unexpectedly. Not when she hadn't had a chance to prepare herself. 'What are you doing here?'

He stood up, knocking his pint of lager and spilling a few drops on the dark polished bar. 'It's my – I mean, this is Pete's local. Isn't it, Pete?' He nodded towards his large and burly friend in a checked shirt. Pete nodded dutifully, eyes wide as he looked her up and down. 'Have you met Pete?' he asked, looking back at her.

'I have now,' she said, smiling at the friend, who jumped off his stool, wiped his hand on the front of his jeans and offered it to her. 'Nice to meet you, Pete,' she said, shaking his hand firmly.

Pete was still looking a little discombobulated. He glanced towards the door. 'Yeah, I . . . uh . . . live a couple of roads away.' Then he swallowed and looked questioningly back at his friend.

Nick nodded. 'Just down here having a pint, chewing the fat,' he said, smiling, but his eyes still held a hint of the nervousness she'd spotted when she'd taken him by surprise. 'How about you?'

Claire felt her stomach dip a little. As much as she carried no shame being the president of the Doris Day Film Club, she also knew that some people didn't get it, thought she was a bit weird. She really didn't want this man to be one of those people. 'I attend a meeting in the upper room most Tuesdays,' she said. 'It's a club.'

'Ah.' Nick nodded. 'That makes sense . . .'

She frowned. 'What makes sense?' It was almost as if he was mentally putting jigsaw pieces together about her, and that definitely *didn't* make sense. The man hardly knew her. And how could what she did on a Tuesday evening have any significance for him?

He shook his head. 'Nothing.' And then he turned to Pete. 'Isn't that your phone?'

Pete patted his back pocket. 'Don't think so.'

Nick fixed him with a rather intent stare. 'Are you sure?'

Pete stared at him blankly for a second. 'Oh. Oh, yeah.

Maybe.' He pulled his phone out of his pocket and made a big show of checking it for any recent communication. 'Yep,' he said, glancing nervously first at his friend and then at Claire. 'It's Ellie. She's having trouble getting Sammy to bed. I'd better—' he glanced towards the door '—you know . . .'

Claire spotted his half-drunk pint on the bar. 'But you haven't finished your drink.'

Pete looked longingly at his lager. 'I know,' he said, and sent a hopeful look to Nick.

Nick didn't move, didn't say anything. Pete's face fell. 'But when duty calls – especially in the form of a sleep-deprived mother dealing with the terrible twos . . .' He grabbed the glass and downed as much as he could in one go. When he'd swallowed, he said, 'Nice to meet you, Claire.' Then he shot one last look at Nick and he was gone.

Nick indicated the empty stool. 'Can I buy you a drink?'

Claire hesitated. 'I don't know . . .'

'Come on,' he said, flashing that slightly devilish smile at her. 'It's not long till last orders and I'd like to pick your brains about European destinations.'

She looked at the seat of the stool. 'Okay,' she said, and sat on it gingerly. It was business, after all, and they were in a public place. Nothing was going to happen. She shouldn't feel guilty. 'I'll have a half of one of those,' she said, indicating his pint.

His eyebrows shot up. 'Really?'

She gave him a slightly cheeky smile. 'I don't look like the sort of girl who drinks lager?' she asked. 'What would you have picked for me?'

He shrugged. 'You see, this is my problem,' he muttered,

almost to himself, then he looked up at her. 'I'd have probably gone for the obvious.'

She settled herself more comfortably on her stool. She was starting to enjoy this. 'Which would be?'

He let out a heavy breath, as if he knew he'd be condemning himself with his words. 'Something smart and sophisticated. Wine, maybe. Dry. Or a cocktail.'

She kept smiling and gave a little shrug. 'Well, I like those things too. It's just that sometimes there's nothing like an ice-cold beer.'

He grinned at her and signalled for the barman. 'My thoughts exactly.' Once he'd ordered, he turned back to her. 'So, what sort of club are we talking about?'

Claire looked at him, then she took a deep breath. 'It's a film club. We meet and watch old films. Doris Day films, to be exact.'

He blinked. She could see the amusement playing behind his eyes as he digested that. 'Doris Day? Don't you think she was a bit . . .'

She straightened on her stool and stopped smiling. 'A bit what?'

He shrugged one shoulder. 'I don't know . . .'

'Old hat? Squeaky clean? Goody-goody?' she suggested. She'd heard all those responses before. Usually from people who didn't know what they were talking about.

He shook his head. 'I was going to say "underrated",' he said, his eyes glinting with humour, 'but now you mention it . . .'

She punched him lightly on the arm, then instantly regretted it. It was contact. Physical contact. Even though it had been nothing more than a stupid playground gesture, her awareness of him had now rocketed four hundred per cent.

'Seriously,' he said. 'My gran used to like Doris Day, but what's the attraction for a modern woman like you?'

The barman placed their drinks down on the bar in front of them. Claire reached and took a sip before answering. 'Well, the truth is that my grandmother liked Doris too, and she set up a fan club back in the fifties, and I ended up inheriting the job.'

Nick made a 'too bad' face.

'Oh, no,' she said quickly. 'I really don't mind. I've come to appreciate Doris in my own right. She's an amazing woman. Not just for her talent, but for her strength.'

He looked confused.

'You said she was a goody goody . . . Well, that might have been her image, but the truth behind her life wasn't quite like that. She could never quite understand how she got stuck with that label, but once she had, her fans were very reluctant to let her part with it, and her husband-slash-manager didn't want to disappoint them.'

He smiled and sipped his beer. 'You mean she was an old trout in real life?'

Claire shook her head. 'Nothing like that. What you see coming through on the screen – that warmth, that charm, the honesty – by all accounts that's the genuine Doris.'

He put his glass back down on the bar. The pub was getting rowdy now it was close to last orders and they were having to lean closer and closer to each other to have to be heard. 'You're right,' he said, thoughtfully. 'If I had to find a word to describe how she comes across on camera, that's it. There's a real honesty about her.'

Claire smiled at him. It started off small but just kept on growing. 'I'm glad you can see it,' she said, forgetting to hide the warmth in her voice, forgetting that this was supposed to be a business chat. 'That's what I like most about her.' She let out a heavy breath and looked away. 'Honesty is a rare quality in this day and age.'

When she looked back, Nick was wearing a strange expression. He swallowed.

'Anyway,' she said, shaking herself slightly. 'What I meant to say was that, despite the Technicolor perfection and all-American wholesomeness of her films, her life wasn't like that at all. She went through a lot of hardship.'

'Really?' he said.

She bobbed her head and took another sip of her beer. 'Did you know that she didn't start off singing and acting at all?'

He shook his head, keeping his eyes on her the whole time.

'She was a really talented dancer. So much so, that when she was thirteen, her and her dance partner won a big competition. She was all set to move to Hollywood to see just how far she could go when there was a terrible accident.'

'I didn't know that.'

'It's true. The night before they were due to leave there was a big farewell party. Afterwards, she went to go and get ice cream sodas with friends and the car she was in was hit by a train.'

His eyes widened. 'Was anyone killed?'

'No,' she said. 'They were lucky. But Doris had to be pulled from the wreckage. Her right leg was shattered. The doctors didn't even think she'd walk again, let alone dance.' She sighed. They were close now, faces only inches apart

– it was the only way they could hear each other talk in the noisy bar – and she looked right into his eyes. 'But Doris didn't let it get her down. She didn't mope or feel sorry for herself, like most people would have done. Oh, no. She started listening to the radio while she was stuck at home in bed, and pretty soon she started singing along to the likes of Benny Goodman, Glen Miller and especially Ella Fitzgerald. In the end, her mother took her to singing lessons, and the rest, as they say, is history.'

He was looking right back at her. Something inside Claire told her to look away to break whatever was zapping between his eyes and hers, but she couldn't seem to make herself do it. 'That's an amazing story,' he said.

Claire swallowed. 'And that's only the start of it,' she said. 'There's more. So much more. She was working by fifteen, singing with big bands, travelling all over the country on tour buses with a bunch of older men, holding her own. And then there were the marriages . . .'

Nick let out a bark of surprised laughter. 'There was more than one?'

She nodded. 'Four, in fact. The first one aged seventeen to a man who later ended up killing himself. The rest . . . well, it's a long story. But she's still happy and sunny and trying to help people – and especially animals – the best way she can.' She looked down at her lap, suddenly very serious, then back up at Nick. 'She's a survivor. Not just underrated, but underestimated.'

He looked back at her. The smile also gone from his face. 'I'm starting to see that.'

For a long moment, neither of them said anything, and then the bell for last orders rang, breaking the spell.

She sat back on her stool, took one last sip of her drink then stood up. 'I really should be going.' Not just because it was late, but because she kept forgetting she really shouldn't be socialising with him. If she were his girlfriend, she'd be a bit miffed if he'd bought another woman a drink. She'd be even more miffed that he was looking at said woman the way he was looking at her.

She made sure she stayed just shy of eye contact as she bid him farewell. 'Well,' she said, finally discovering the brisk, efficient business tone she should have been striving for. 'It was lovely to see you again. Do get in touch about your travel plans when you're ready. Bye, Nick.'

And, without waiting for a reply, she turned and walked towards the door, her spine as straight as a dancer's.

'Nick' stared after her. And then he did the only thing he possibly could have done.

He followed her.

# Chapter Twenty-One
## Let's Take an Old-Fashioned Walk

He didn't have to check which way she went when she left the pub; he knew. Of course he did. She was heading home, just as he was. He jogged lightly until he caught up with her. She turned her head to look at him, but kept moving.

'Are you stalking me, Nick?'

Nick. He could hear the extra 'k' when she said it. He didn't know how, but he could.

'No, I'm not stalking you. I just happen to be walking this way as well, and as long as we're walking the same route, we may as well walk together. While I'm a big fan of girl power, or whatever everyone calls it these days, you're still safer if you're not on your own.'

He waited for the rant. Erica had given him one every time he'd tried to do something like this for her, accusing him of treating her like a weak, second-class citizen, but Claire didn't say anything but, 'Well, I'm sure I'd be fine on my own, but that's very chivalrous of you.' They carried on walking.

'Doris came from that era, didn't she?' he said. 'When

men could hold a door open for a woman and still keep their heads on their shoulders.'

'She did,' Claire said, glancing across at him as they walked. 'But she wasn't old-fashioned at all. In her life and in her films, she was a front-runner for women's liberation. She was the wage earner in her family, and she often played intelligent, successful career women, not delicate flowers. Either that or tomboys who could shoot or fix a car or throw a baseball better than the men she was with. You've got to love her for that.'

'You have,' he said, smiling, even though Claire was looking deadly serious.

She sighed and her pace slowed a little. 'It was after watching *On Moonlight Bay* with my gran that I realised it didn't matter if I was a bit of a tomboy, that I could still be that one day and then dress up in frills and bows the next, and still be all girl.'

He looked at how steady her stride was in her stilettos, the easy sway of her hips in her fitted skirt, and shook his head. 'I can't imagine you as a tomboy.'

She stopped giving him the cool treatment and grinned at him. 'Well, I was. I used to like to dig for worms and make mud pies with the boys that lived next door. At least I did until . . .' She trailed off, the smile disappearing as quickly as it had arrived.

'Until what?'

She shrugged his question off. 'Let's just say my father preferred I didn't mix with them, that I was a little more ladylike. Besides, they were older than me and it got to the stage they didn't want a little shadow with pigtails following them around.'

He let out a low chuckle. 'Well, if you ever want to wear pigtails and follow me around, I promise I won't complain one bit.'

That earned him a sharp look. Damn. He'd forgotten about the make-believe woman of his dreams. Better back-pedal, change the conversation to something else. Doris, perhaps. He seemed to pretty safe with that subject, mostly because then Claire was doing the talking and he wasn't opening his big fat mouth.

'So was Doris a tomboy too?'

Claire's expression softened, but he noticed the way she changed her direction a little so they weren't walking so close together. She paused as they crossed the road and headed down a side street. 'You're going this way as well?'

He nodded. 'Take this route home every time I go to The Glass Bottom Boat.'

She frowned at his vague answer, but kept walking. 'Yes, Doris was a bit of a tomboy. Like most women, there was more than one side to her. She liked dressing up in lovely clothes in her films, but she often didn't once she got home, preferring to relax and just be natural. She didn't really do the whole "Hollywood" thing, going to parties and premieres all the time.'

'Really? Wasn't she a really big star?'

Claire looked up at him, just briefly, then down at her feet as she walked. 'She was. Number one female star in Hollywood for quite a few years during the fifties and sixties, but those things didn't really matter to her. They were just numbers, she said, and once you'd got to number one, there was only one direction you could go.'

He nodded. 'Wise words.'

Claire sighed. 'This is my road,' she said, as they turned another corner.

Dominic looked up and saw with surprise that it was. The walk home had been far too short. 'Okay,' he replied slowly, trying to work out what he was going to do when they got to the garden gate. Another thing he hadn't thought through. If he walked on, it was another lie, but if he didn't . . .

Claire didn't seem to notice the battle he was having with himself. She just kept on walking. 'All she really wanted was a home, a normal life, a happy family,' she said wistfully.

There was sadness in her voice that Dominic told himself he should pay heed to.

'I hope her life turned out the way she wanted it to in the end,' she added. 'Sometimes when you're young you make decisions and you don't realise how they're going to come back and bite you on the butt. Especially when it comes to love.' She looked at him suddenly, flushed with embarrassment under the street light. 'Sorry,' she said, 'didn't mean to say that. You don't need to hear me wittering on about life and love, the universe and . . . Doris.'

'Claire?' He reached out and touched her arm.

She jumped away as if she'd been stung. 'What?' she said, more than a bit crossly.

'Which house is yours?' he asked softly, even though he knew. They were there. Home. But Claire hadn't noticed and was just about to walk past the gate.

'Oh,' she said, and stopped dead. 'This one.' Then she laughed. 'That crept up on me!' She turned to look further down the road. 'Which way are you?'

He swallowed. 'Not too far away,' he replied, making sure he didn't look in any particular direction.

'What a coincidence.'

He nodded.

'Anyway . . .' she said and glanced towards their shared front door. 'I'd better get inside. Thanks for walking me back. It was very gentlemanly of you.'

Dominic felt something warm flare in his chest. Even though he knew he wasn't being gentlemanly at all, he hadn't realised how nice it was to hear someone say those words, to at least *think* it wasn't beyond possibility that he could be like that. 'No problem,' he said, aiming for 'casual' but landing on 'slightly gruff'.

She looked at him and he could see her chest rise and fall, just once, in the glow from the street light across the road. Her voice was low and quiet when she spoke. 'Goodnight, Nick.'

The words hung in the air between them, slowing time, but then she turned and started to walk up the path.

'Claire!' he found himself calling out after her.

She looked round, her eyes wide.

He'd told himself he'd just say goodnight, but he heard himself saying, 'I think I can make a stab at those questions of yours now.'

She walked the few steps back down the path towards him. 'You can?'

He nodded.

'Oh.' She sounded disappointed. 'Good.'

'In answer to question one: I think she likes the outdoors, but she probably isn't yearning to bungee jump on holiday.'

He stopped and thought for a moment. 'Although I could be wrong – she's constantly surprising me.'

Even though it was dark and the yellow light from the street lamp across the road fell across Claire's features, she looked a little pale. He decided to carry on while the words were still filling his head.

'I think she enjoys the occasional evening out and has a great time doing so, but she's not a party animal who's at a club every night. Sometimes she just likes her own company and a good book.'

She nodded. 'Good. That's the kind of thing I wanted to know. It rules out extreme sports and isolated destinations where there's no nightlife at all, or hedonistic hotspots where there's nothing but.'

Ah. That made sense. He was starting to see where she'd been going with those questions now.

'I'm answering them in the wrong order, aren't I?' he said. 'That was question two.'

She shook her head lightly. 'It doesn't matter. Carry on, if you like.'

He took another lungful of oxygen. He didn't know where this stuff was coming from but he was going to ride the wave while it lasted. 'I'd say she likes a bit of pampering – like most women – but a spa isn't her thing. She'd much rather be somewhere relaxed and natural, so a summer day in the countryside might be just up her street.'

'Noted,' Claire said, looking very serious, concentrating as if she was committing everything he said to memory.

'And as for fashion . . .' He laughed and shrugged, and even Claire cracked a smile. 'I wouldn't know a designer label if it came up and bit me on the nose, not unless it was of the outdoor gear kind of variety – and I don't think she owns a set of mountain climbing clothes – but she always looks nice, as if she's taken care about her appearance, but that doesn't mean she's snobby about brands and such like either. I think she's somewhere in the middle. I think she probably owns a few nice things, but she chose them because she liked them, because they suited her. She's got her own style, and she doesn't wear something just because someone else tells her it's fashion.'

Claire frowned.

'What's the matter?' he asked. 'Wasn't that enough detail?'

She sighed. 'No. It was plenty of detail. I was just hoping your answer would help me decide between luxury hotel versus something boutique and quirky. From your answer, it sounds as if she's not very easy to pigeonhole that way.'

He looked very hard at her. 'More on the boutique side, I think. Not too quirky, but not too glitzy, either.'

Her brows pinched and she thought hard. 'Nick? You keep saying "I think" when you talk about her. Don't you know?'

Ah. He'd inadvertently given himself away a little bit. Those were the sort of things a man in love should know about the woman in his life. His mind quickly flitted to Erica.

Night on the town. Spa. Luxury hotel all the way.

He smiled to himself. There. He wasn't as hopeless as she'd thought he was. That hadn't been hard at all, even after all these years.

But that didn't help him with Claire, did it? He thought for a moment. 'The old saying's true, I think. You can't judge a book by its cover.'

Her eyebrows rose in lieu of a verbal question.

'For example,' he continued, 'I would have never picked you for a Doris fan in a million years, but since you talked about her on the walk home, it actually makes perfect sense.'

'It does? How?'

Dominic shrugged. That bit he wasn't so clear about. 'I don't know,' he admitted. 'It just does. Anyway . . . What I'm saying is that people aren't always what they seem, even when you've known them for years.'

She let out a snort of dry laughter. 'Ain't that right.'

'You sound like you have personal experience.'

Claire nodded, her expression rueful. 'Yep and I have one ex-husband under my belt to prove it.' She watched his reaction, must have read the surprise on his face. 'You're shocked. Why?'

Again, he didn't know. It seemed he'd got those questions done just in time, because now his flash of insight about Claire seemed to be over. Every time he thought he'd got to know her, she revealed another layer, a new surprise.

He looked at Claire and saw open and warm, loyal and funny. Who wouldn't want to stay married to her? He'd have bet money on the fact that once she had a ring on her finger, the marriage would have stuck.

'I don't know,' he said, shaking his head. She seemed so together, not like the friends of his who'd gone through divorce at all.

But then he looked at her eyes and had the funniest sensation, as if he was looking in a mirror. There was pain there. Well hidden, but there. And disenchantment. Wariness. Suddenly he understood the strange push-me, pull-me effect she had on people, that drawing them close while keeping them at arm's length thing.

She was looking up at him, her eyes wide, saying nothing. It would be so easy to step in and kiss her. He could feel his weight shifting to the balls of his feet to do just that, but he rocked back and stepped away. Now was not the right time, not when she thought he was a decent guy who had a girlfriend. He didn't want to be another disappointing man to add to her list.

'Goodnight, Claire,' he said again.

She nodded. 'Goodnight.'

This time she walked up the path and he didn't stop her, didn't call out. She didn't look back as she slid her key into the lock and opened their shared front door. It closed behind her and he stood there in the darkness, doing nothing but watching where he'd seen the last flash of her dress before she'd disappeared.

Which was stupid, really, as he realised that unless he wanted to be walking the streets of Islington for another hour or two until it was safe to creep into the house after her, that he only had a very small window of opportunity to get to his flat door undetected.

He didn't know how, but he knew she'd look out the window once she got upstairs to see if he was still standing there. And he really shouldn't be – for a whole host of reasons.

He'd have to time his race to his flat just right. Too early and she'd still be on the stairs. Too late and she'd see him coming up the path. He had about fifteen seconds at most – the time it took for her to close her front door and walk to the large bay window at the front of the house. And he could probably make it, if he went right about . . . now.

He dashed for the front door and hid under the small porch while slowly and silently turning his key in the lock.

Somehow he knew she'd just entered her flat. Possibly, because since she'd left him he'd been imagining her walking up the stairs, counting each one, in the back of his mind.

As carefully as he could, he pushed the front door open, closed it just as quietly and in a combination of tiptoed creep and sprint made it to his flat door in under two seconds. He fumbled his keys in his hands and his heart began to pound. Suddenly, his fingers seemed like big fat sausages, incapable of doing anything dextrous, but then he found his door key. Moments later, he was inside his flat, breathing heavily, his back against the door.

He shook his head. This was getting stupid. Really stupid. Was all this sneaking around really necessary?

He took a moment to consider that question. Probably not, although he'd convinced himself it was.

They'd got past the surface layer now, past those first impressions.

It was time. Time to tell her. Time to put his neck on the line and see if she could forgive him for being her oafish neighbour and welcome him as the man she was attracted to. She tried to guard it well, but he could tell she was.

He let out a breath and ran a hand through his hair, relaxing even further against the door. The only problem now was *how* to tell her. Do it wrong and he'd probably lose any chance with her forever, and he really didn't want that. This was about more than proving a point now. When it all boiled down to it, he just really wanted to see her again.

He chuckled as he pushed himself upright and loped into his living room. This was why he liked to move around. When he stayed put somehow he always managed to get himself into a whole heap of trouble. Now he had to work out how to tell Claire the whole story without confirming every bad thing she'd ever thought about him.

He dropped onto the sofa and picked up the remote. Seriously. His life was starting to sound like one of Doris Day's rom coms.

# Chapter Twenty-Two
# I'm Beginning to See the Light

Claire picked up the remote and pointed it at the TV. She itched to go and look back out of the window, but that was just too sad. She'd already seen he wasn't still standing there.

He'd gone home. To his lovely girlfriend. The paragon of femininity he'd been describing to her only moments earlier. She shook her head, silently lecturing herself. Don't torture yourself, Claire.

She stopped flicking channels and marched off to the kitchen. She'd gone past beer and needed wine now. A nice glass of cool Sauvignon. When she'd poured herself a large one, she sank back down on her couch again and stared blankly at the television screen. Some documentary. She couldn't be bothered to keep surfing. Besides, her mind was churning far too much for her to concentrate on anything.

As she sipped her wine, she checked inside herself. She was feeling all out of sorts. Stupid woman, she told herself. You shouldn't have said yes to a drink with him, however innocent. It had only made things a thousand times worse.

Yep. What she was feeling . . . ? She now had a name for it.

Jealousy. Pure and simple.

Because she'd realised that even through the whole of her five-year marriage, Philip could not have answered those three questions about her. He'd always bought her chocolate liqueurs at Christmas, even though she'd told him repeatedly that she hated her alcohol and her chocolate mixed, but that had been Philip all over – too absorbed in himself and what he needed from those around him to truly think about anyone else.

That girlfriend of Nick's? Well, Claire hoped she appreciated him. Yes, he was a little rough around the edges. Yes, he often plugged his mouth with both his feet. But there was something to be said for a man who really, truly stopped thinking about himself for one second, who stopped constantly taking from the woman in his life, and tried to give something back to her. Even if it wasn't easy for him.

Maybe especially if it wasn't easy for him. What he lacked in finesse, Nick got 'A star' for in effort.

See? And she'd gone and got the wine, put the television on to help her stop thinking about him, and she'd done nothing but. Focus, Claire. There's no point mooning over what you can't have.

She took another sip of her wine and turned the volume up on the TV, hoping it would snag her attention better. Instead of flicking through more channels, she decided to just stick with what was on. It seemed much better than quiz show reruns or late-night shows with rude internet videos or reality shows about fishermen, truck drivers or cheating spouses. She wriggled down further amongst the sofa cushions and paid better attention.

It was a documentary about an orphanage in Uganda, one

in the slums of Kampala. It had started more than twenty years ago, by a local couple whose hearts had been so moved by the homeless children they'd met that they'd taken them into their own. The civil war and the sweep of the AIDS epidemic across the country had left countless children with no one to care for them.

It wasn't long before she was completely absorbed in the unfolding story. As she watched, she saw the attitude of some people to the street children, who just saw them as urchins or beggars, who passed them by in the same way as Londoners ignored the *Big Issue* sellers on their high streets or the rattling charity boxes at the entrance to their local supermarkets. But these were *children*. Cold and hungry with sad eyes and quivering lips. They way the story was told showed just how extraordinary the couple with two children of their own had been.

They had seen. They looked past the prejudice others couldn't get round and they had *seen*.

Over the next forty minutes, she learned how they'd secured help from a UK charity through a visiting minister, how their overcrowded house had filled even further, and then how they'd built not one but three schools in the area. How they'd given hundreds of children a home and an education. How they'd stopped the cycle of poverty and disease for so many, helping them to go on to university or get jobs. It was truly remarkable. And all it had taken was two people – not a nation, not even an organisation – who'd had the courage to take their blinkers off and see what was under their noses.

Claire reached for a tissue as the credits rolled and blew her nose. Halfway through making a rather unattractive sound, she froze. Then she hit the pause button and rewound the live feed to watch what she'd seen again.

It was still there, in large white letters on the black background:

*Director*
*DOMINIC ARDEN*

*

She shook her head. Surely not. Surely it couldn't be . . .

But then she thought of all those geeky video magazines she shuffled through like piles of autumn leaves on her doorstep. It was too much of a coincidence to be otherwise.

Well.

She'd have never guessed that in a million years.

She hadn't really thought about what kind of work he did with all that high-tech equipment of his, but if she'd had to think about it, she'd have probably said he did something nerdy like make YouTube clips about shoot 'em up games or, even worse, corporate training videos.

It seemed her annoying downstairs neighbour had hidden depths. Who'd have thought? She took another large glug of wine as she fast-forwarded through the adverts and onto the next programme – a rerun of *Friends*. The one with the Thanksgiving video. She'd seen it a thousand times, but she watched it anyway. She needed something safe, something familiar. Because everyone else – especially the men – in her life were behaving most unexpectedly today.

# Chapter Twenty-Three

## Young At Heart

Claire clattered up the stairs and into the upper room of The Glass Bottom Boat. Tonight, the sky was overcast, making it seem more like April than June, and light rain showered the dusty streets off and on. Even so, she pushed open the sash windows as far as she could, enjoying the freshness of the damp, if slightly chilly, air.

She pulled out her case of DVDs and hooked up the player to the big screen as Peggy appeared in the doorway. 'What is it this week?' she asked.

'*Young at Heart,*' Claire replied, one of Doris's biggest hits, her one film with Frank Sinatra.

Peggy walked over to her. 'I thought that was one of your favourites. You're not looking very excited about it.'

'It is,' Claire said wearily. She usually loved watching it, listening to all the songs, especially 'There's a Rising Moon'. 'It's just I'm not really in the mood for love triangles and white picket fences tonight.'

'Hmm,' Peggy said, studying her intently. 'Does this mean you still haven't heard from lover boy?'

Claire shook her head. 'And he's not my lover, remember? He's got a girlfriend.'

Peggy made a booing noise.

'And, no, I haven't heard from him, not since I bumped into him in after the last club meeting. Looks as if I've lost out on the business front too!'

'You should be a twenty-first century woman and contact him!'

'I have,' Claire replied. That was the annoying bit. 'I sent off a couple of very harmless chatty but professional emails to him and . . . nothing.'

Peggy pulled a sympathetic face. 'Aw, sorry about that. He sounded cute...' she started.

Claire sighed. 'I know.'

'It's always the way,' Peggy said philosophically. 'The ones you want you can't have, and the ones that want you just aren't interesting.'

'I know that too,' she said, nodding. It was a real pain in the backside too. Because that was why Nick had gone silent on her.

They'd had a 'moment' outside her front gate.

Oh, she knew it didn't necessarily mean anything, but she understood why he was keeping his distance. It wasn't as if, after she'd married Philip, that all other men had become anonymous, sexless blobs. Sometimes you saw someone who flicked your hormonal switches. Sometimes you thought to yourself, If I wasn't involved with someone, I'd be interested . . . Didn't mean you were evil. Just that you were human. It was what you did with that thought afterwards that counted, whether you watered and fed it until it became a full-blown obsession or whether you weeded it out before it had a chance to take root.

That was what Nick had done probably. Weeded her out.

Maybe he'd plan his holiday on his own now. Or maybe he'd find another travel agent to help him, which would be a pity. She had a feeling that now he'd made a breakthrough with those questions he'd be even more fun to work with, that they could really let their imaginations fly together.

Maybe she needed to do some weeding of her own.

Thinking about him like this . . . It wasn't productive in any sense or form.

Time to think about something else. Someone else.

And thinking of intriguing men . . .

She hadn't seen her downstairs neighbour in the last week, either, even though she'd been looking out for him, trying to catch him in the hallway when she heard him moving about, but he always managed to dart inside his flat or disappear beyond the tall hedge that protected their squat front garden from the street before she managed to lay eyes on him.

Ever since seeing that documentary, she'd been curious about him. Maybe she'd built up a totally false picture of who he was. Yes, he'd caused her a few inconveniences from time to time, but now he was here more permanently, he seemed to be mending his ways. While at first she'd been sceptical about his promise to make an effort – especially after all those sarcastic notes – she now had to admit that maybe he hadn't been trying to get a rise out of her. Not recently, anyway.

However, before she could contemplate the enigma of her downstairs neighbour any further, the rest of the club members started arriving and she had to put all thoughts of him out of her head.

George arrived first. Claire went and said a special hello to him. He was such a sweet man. If only Maggs would give him a chance. Candy came next, followed swiftly by Kitty and Grace, who seemed to be deep in conversation about something. They sat down close together, thick as thieves, and kept glancing towards the door.

Peggy arrived just on the dot of eight and, a few moments later, as Claire was saying a little bit about the film they were going to watch that night, Abby slipped in at the back. Gone was the dress of the previous meeting, replaced once again by the football kit. She hunkered down and let her long hair fall over her face.

Claire watched her sadly as she finished talking and set the DVD running. It was such a shame. Abby had looked so pretty last week. Not just because of the clothes and hair, but because she'd let down that tough exterior a little and they'd all seen a bit more of the sensitive girl underneath. It didn't escape Claire, as the lights dimmed and the credits started to roll, that Kitty and Grace were whispering furiously to each other and kept glancing over their shoulders at the hunched figure at the back of the room.

Hmm, she thought, as the crooning tones of Sinatra's theme song died away and the camera panned then zoomed through the window of a charming suburban house. Perhaps she'd have a little chat after the meeting, see if she could sort out what was going on.

Claire looked round at the empty chair beside her. Where on earth was Maggs? She often cut it fine getting to the meetings, but Claire had never once known her to be late.

They'd already got to the scene where Doris was singing 'Ready, Willing and Able' on the beach by the time the door creaked and a wiry figure slipped onto the chair beside her.

'Everything okay?' Claire whispered, leaning in close as Maggs put down her handbag.

Maggs straightened and stared at her. The white of her eyes glowed in the gloom. 'Fine. I was on the phone.'

'Oh,' Claire said. That seemed odd. *Young at Heart* was also one of Maggs's favourites.

'Your father called.'

Everything inside Claire went cold. She stared straight ahead at the screen. 'H—how?' she stammered. 'How did he know your number?'

'I wrote back to him after our last chat on the subject,' Maggs said. 'Just like you said.'

'Oh,' Claire said again. It was a completely inadequate word to convey the churning inside her stomach. She knew she'd told Maggs to do it, but somehow it had still come as a shock. She turned her head slightly to look at her, managed to keep her voice light and unconcerned, as if she was asking about the weather. 'What did he say?'

Both Candy and Bev looked over their shoulders, not cross, but clearly the whispering was disturbing them.

'We can't talk now,' Maggs added, dropping her volume even further. 'I'll tell you afterwards.'

'Okay.' Claire turned her attention back to the screen. She'd completely missed the bit where Sinatra had made his first appearance and now he was sitting at the piano, playing a beautiful tune and charming the socks off Ethel Barrymore with his melancholy wit.

*Okay?* In what universe was this okay? Why, oh, why

had she let Maggs talk her into this? The firm and certain knowledge that she'd have rather driven her Fiat off Tower Bridge than see her father again settled in her chest.

But there was nothing she could do about it now. She would just have to sit through the next hour or two and hold off until the meeting was over.

Thankfully, the story was a familiar one, and it didn't matter if she drifted off now and again while they all sat there in the dark and watched the unlikely love between Doris's bright and chirpy Laurie and Sinatra's self-destructive Barney bloom.

It turned out all right in the end, though. Happy endings and wedding bells all round.

Even that had been manufactured. The original story it had been based on had been more like real life, a mixture of tragedy and happiness, Doris's mismatched romance doomed. Claire could never quite decide whether she liked the ending as it was, or whether she wished they'd been brave enough to make it darker, more real. There was always that tension, wasn't there? Between the fantasy and the reality. Ultimately, both were unsatisfying. One for its lack of truth, the other for its heartache.

When the film finished, the club members began to chat again, discussing the performances and songs. Claire took the opportunity to slink to the back of the room. Before she sorted out her own life, she had someone else who required a little bit of attention.

'Hey, Abby,' she said softly, as she sat down beside her. 'I've been thinking about you all week . . . Are you okay?'

Abby hugged herself tighter and nodded.

'I saw you talking to those boys after the meeting last week.'

Abby looked up at her, panicked. 'They're just idiots,' she said darkly. 'I don't care what they think!'

Given Abby's current wardrobe and demeanour, Claire could beg to differ, but she wasn't sure pressing the issue was going to be helpful. 'And the tall one. The one who didn't say anything. Was that Ricky?'

Abby's lip wobbled and she scowled even harder to stop it. 'He's a prat.'

'Have you heard from him since?' It didn't escape Claire that she was asking Abby a similar question to the one Peggy had asked her earlier and, from the look on Abby's face, she was being just as lucky in love.

Abby shook her head. 'And I haven't seen him, because I just stayed in my room all week and didn't go anywhere.' She glanced up at Claire, terrified. 'I can't talk to him, so don't ask me to! It was bad enough before . . .'

'How do you mean "bad"?'

Abby let out a noise that was half groan, half sigh. 'It's stupid . . . It's like my feet grow roots. I can't move – and I definitely can't speak! And then I go hot and cold all over and I just end up stammering and shaking, not knowing what to do with myself. If I'm lucky, I manage to croak out his name!'

'Abby . . . Don't you realise that is exactly how I would have described the way Ricky reacted when he saw you in that dress last week?'

Abby sat bolt upright and stared at her. 'No. Don't be daft. That was different.'

Claire leaned forward slightly, lifting her eyebrows. 'Was it?'

Abby opened her mouth then froze.

'Maybe he just was a little shocked. Maybe – despite what you think – it worked. I think you just might have blown his socks off.'

The look of hope and pain mixed in the younger girl's eyes made Claire mist up a little. 'Really?' she whispered.

'Really,' Claire said, standing up.

Abby rose too, but she looked stunned, as if she just might wander blindly down the stairs, off across the park and not stop until she hit the Thames.

'I think you should find him and ask him to go to the party with you.'

Abby grunted. 'That's not going to happen now. I'm probably not even going to the stupid party.'

'Why not?'

'Kitty kept texting this week, wanting to do another makeover and I didn't want to so I just didn't answer, because I didn't know what to say, and now she hates me and I can't do all that stuff on my own.'

Ah. So that's what all the whispering at the front had been about.

'They'll come round if you're honest with them. I think you have to be brave enough to tell them what you think. There's no use in running away from it. Sometimes you just have to face things head-on.'

Abby looked at her doubtfully.

'Of course they're angry at the moment,' Claire explained. 'They're upset, but I'm sure if you go and tell them what you've just told me and apologise, they'd understand. We've all felt like that in front of a boy once or twice in our lives.'

Abby laughed. 'Not Kitty and Grace! I mean, have you seen them?'

Claire nodded gently. 'Yep. Even Kitty and Grace. I bet you. They often go downstairs for a drink afterwards. Why don't you see if you can find them?'

The girl didn't look convinced, but she thanked Claire and headed off looking determined. Claire turned to find Maggs, arms crossed, looking at her.

'Enough of the delaying tactics,' she said, as Claire walked across the room and popped the DVD out of the player and returned it to its case. 'I'll buy you a drink and we'll talk.'

'I know we said we'd talk, but I wasn't delaying, I was helping. There's a difference.'

Maggs humphed. 'Well, now it's my turn to help you.'

Claire zipped up the DVD case and placed it back in her tote bag, then slung the bag over her shoulder. 'I'm starting to think your brand of "help" isn't much help at all.'

Maggs just gave her a sour look. 'Physician, heal thyself,' she said dryly.

'What?' Claire asked as she turned off the lights and they headed down the narrow stairs.

'I heard what you said to that girl,' Maggs said behind her. She waited until they both had their feet on the ground floor before she looked Claire in the eye.

'About making up with Kitty and Grace? That was just a silly misunderstanding, hardly the same as dealing with the parent who deserted you and hasn't given a toss about you in – what – twenty plus years.'

'No,' Maggs said slowly, fixing Claire with her beady

eyes and then she did a fair impression of her best friend's granddaughter. '*There's no use in running away from it. Sometimes you just have to face things head-on.*'

Oh. That bit.

She followed Maggs to the bar, where the older lady had no problem elbowing her way in amongst the group of sports-loving lads gathered there. 'Well,' Claire said, trying to nudge her way in after Maggs and not quite managing it, 'there's a difference between running away from things and leaving the past behind, getting closure.'

Maggs turned round. 'What do you want to drink?'

Claire sighed. 'Better make it a Diet Coke. I'm driving, after all.'

'One Diet Coke and one double gin and tonic  and don't be stingy on the gin,' Maggs told the barman, who sauntered away as if he hadn't heard.

When they got their drinks, they pushed their way through the crowd to a small table tucked into the corner. Claire let Maggs sit on the upholstered bench while she perched on a rather rickety stool covered in the same worn fabric.

Maggs took a long slurp of her drink, closing her eyes. She put the glass down and opened them again. 'That's a load of tosh and you know it.'

'No, it isn't. I'm applying the Doris principle . . . Leave the past in the past. Concentrate on the present.'

Maggs thought for a moment. 'Tell me, Miss Leave It in the Past, if everything is so over and dealt with, why aren't you more at peace with it? Why are you so resistant to looking over your shoulder and seeing what's back there? That doesn't much sound like the serenity of closure to me.'

Now that Maggs put it like that, it didn't sound much like

it to her either. Damn her for being sharp as a tack, despite her age. Why couldn't she stay indoors and deaden her mind with daytime TV like some other women her age did?

'Okay,' she said wearily. 'Let's not drag it out. Just say what you've got to say. I'll sit here and listen. No running away . . .' she crossed her finger over her heart, the way she'd used to as a child '. . . I promise.'

Maggs just nodded. 'Good girl.'

Claire rolled her eyes.

'He's asked if you'll go and visit him. Next Friday, the nineteenth.'

Claire swallowed. All of this suddenly seemed very real. 'Where?'

Maggs reached into her patent handbag and pulled out a piece of folded paper. She handed it to Claire. On it was the address of a nursing home in Penge, south of the river, but still probably not more than fifteen miles away.

She supposed it wasn't odd that he'd stayed in London, that he was so close, and probably had been for a long time, but she realised that when he'd left, her eleven-year-old brain had always imagined he'd gone far, far away, and her adult brain hadn't done anything to amend that assumption.

She stared at the paper, letting her eyes run over the address again and again until suddenly she couldn't bear to look at it any more. She quickly folded it back up again and stuck in her pocket, then she downed the last of her Coke and turned to Maggs.

'Okay, I'll go. But I've got one condition.'

'Uh-oh,' said Maggs, before taking an extra large slug of her drink.

Claire smiled thinly at her grandmother's best friend,

pleased to be exerting a little control in this situation. 'I'll go and see my father if you go out on a date with George. A proper one. None of this "he drove me to the shops" nonsense.'

Maggs gave her the kind of stare Paddington Bear would have been proud of. Finally, she looked away and grunted. 'Infernal child,' she muttered, and then she turned back to Claire and sat up tall. 'Okay,' she replied, in the manner of someone calling someone else's bluff, 'you're on!'

Claire's resolve, and also her stomach, wobbled. 'And you'd better see if the man in question is still hanging around to give you a lift, because suddenly I'm very much in the mood for a large gin and tonic too.' And she stood up and pushed her way back to the bar.

# Chapter Twenty-Four

# I Got It Bad (and That Ain't Good)

It was eight-thirty on a Wednesday morning, but Dominic wasn't in bed; he'd been up for ages. He was sitting in his spare room, researching top worldwide locations for free-diving, where the biggest communities of enthusiasts hung around, what extra equipment he'd need if he went ahead and did this job. He hadn't done much underwater stuff before, but he had a mate who specialised in it, so it would probably be a lot more sensible to hire him to shoot the stuff that went on below the surface, rather than trying to shoot it himself. He made a scratchy note on a pad to call Tony later on that day.

While he surfed and read articles, he kept one ear on the open door that led to the hallway, waiting for any noise to indicate Claire was on the move. He'd got up at seven, just to be sure not to miss her, and had decided he might as well get something productive done while he waited.

Ten minutes later, his patience was rewarded and he heard her door open at the top of the stairs. He leapt up silently and took quiet steps to his hall, where he held his breath and flattened his body against the wall next to his front door.

He heard her neat footsteps on the stairs, deadened by the carpet, then louder as the heels of her shoes met the tiled floor of the hall. Two clicks and the front door opened. He heard the familiar groan as it swung wide on its hinges, then there was a thud, and silence.

For a second he stayed rooted to the spot, but then he was off and out of his flat, computer forgotten. The front door banged a second time.

He'd chosen his wardrobe for this morning carefully. Running shorts and shoes, which he intended to use, and he'd topped it off with a hoodie. He'd probably get a bit warm, but the anonymity it would afford him was worth it. He flicked the hood up over his head as he got to the end of the garden path and cleared the box hedge that ran behind the garden wall. It was getting a bit messy, he noticed. He'd have to see if he could borrow a pair of clippers off Pete . . .

He quickly looked left and right. For a moment, he thought he'd been too slow, that he'd lost her, but then he spotted Claire walking briskly towards the main road that ran across the end of their street, where there was a couple of cafés, a convenience store, a newsagent's, a florist's and an Indian takeaway.

In recent weeks, he'd grown used to darting off in the opposite direction from whichever one Claire had chosen, but this morning he set off after her. He wanted to jog, but he knew he'd catch up to her too quickly, so tried to keep his paces really, really short and stopped to do stretches every now and then, ignoring the quizzical looks of an old lady with a shopping trolley who was taking great interest in his progress.

God, he'd be rubbish as a spy. If Pete could have seen him now he'd have laughed his socks off.

Claire turned left at the end of the road, confirming his suspicion she was heading for the shops. Which one, though? He suddenly broke into a sprint so he could reach the corner before she disappeared inside one of them. His quads didn't thank him for it.

Once he got there, he jogged on the spot and kept an eye on her blonde head, not fifty feet away, as it made its progress down the road. The old lady with the shopping trolley passed him as he huffed and puffed on the spot, waiting for the moment when Claire would be far enough away that he could resume his surveillance without the danger of getting caught.

'Pervert,' the old lady muttered as she trundled past.

Dominic stopped jogging and looked quite affronted. 'Am not!'

The woman gave him *Yeah, right* kind of look.

'I saw the way you were following that girl,' she replied. 'Ought to be locked up!' And she carried on towards the shops, muttering and turning to give him evil looks over her shoulder every few seconds.

It was only as Dominic returned his attention to his primary task that he realised the blonde head had disappeared. Claire had gone. He swore silently, then jogged softly towards the shops, wondering if the sun reflecting off the windows would prevent him from seeing clearly inside.

He jogged up to the newsagent's and tried to peer past the posters into the darkened shop. As he was standing there trying to work out whether Claire was inside, something heavy squashed his foot. He spun round to discover the old lady passing. Her trolley wobbled as if it had just regained balance after hitting something.

'Hey!' he said. 'Did you just run over my foot on purpose?'

'I'm watching you,' she muttered darkly and carried on her way.

He was just turning round again to see if he could spot Claire inside the shop when something else crashed into him. Or, to be more precise, someone.

'Oh, my God! Nick! What are you doing here?'

His heart did a little hiccup and he took a moment to gather his thoughts before turning to look at Claire. 'Running,' he said breezily. That much was true, at least. He just didn't tell her *why* he was haring round the streets of Islington. 'I don't live a million miles from here and I like to vary my route so I don't get bored. What about you?'

She glanced at the magazine in her hand. 'Just about to get a coffee before I head off to the office. I was going to get one to take away, but . . .' The smile disappeared and she looked at him seriously. 'Do you have five minutes? I've been trying to get hold of you all week about your trip.'

Dominic inhaled. 'Sure.'

That had been his plan all along: to bump into Claire – although not quite so literally – so he could talk to her face to face. He'd composed email after email in the safety of his flat in the last seven days, and then had deleted every single one.

He'd thought about going to her office again, but she seemed to snap into professional mode more easily there. If he was going to come clean, it would be a lot easier if he could talk to the smiling, relaxed Claire he knew out of the office. That would remind her just how well they got on before she had to merge her mental pictures of 'Nick' and 'Dominic'.

She looked over her shoulder at the little coffee shop next door. 'Care to join me?'

Even better. He smiled back at her. 'Only if it's my treat.'

'Oh, no. You don't have to do that. Not when it was my idea to chat in the first place.'

'I want to,' he told her firmly and walked over to the coffee shop door and held it open for her.

As he stood there, he spotted the trolley crone outside the hairdresser's. *Pervert*, she mouthed at him. Dominic might have been tempted to make a rude gesture had he not been holding the door open for Claire. Instead, he turned to the old hag and gave her his most winning smile. 'Consider it an apology for not getting back to you over the last week,' he said to Claire as she passed by him. 'To be honest, I've had a lot on my mind.'

That was the truth. But it had been mainly Claire on his mind, and how he could extricate himself from this ridiculous situation he'd got himself into with her.

'Okay,' she said, frowning slightly. 'If you insist.'

Unlike the big coffee chains, this independently run shop had waitress service and, once the dour-looking owner had taken their orders, Dominic turned to Claire, took a deep breath. 'I need to let you know that I'm having second thoughts about this trip. At least, in its current form.'

He wasn't going to pull the plug completely. That wouldn't be fair to her after all the hard work she'd put in.

'Oh?' she said.

He nodded. 'The more I think about it, the more I realise

this isn't the right time to be planning a romantic trip. I think I've been getting a little ahead of myself.'

'Oh,' she said again, looking even more confused.

He could see her brain working overtime, a million questions zipping through her head, but then he saw her shut all those questions down, one by one. She blinked then smiled at him. 'So, what are you thinking of? Cancelling?'

He didn't like that smile. It was her 'office' smile. Just what he'd hoped to avoid. 'I'd still like to get away,' he said evenly. 'I need time to think about what I want to do next with my life.'

As those words left his lips, he realised how true they were.

Yes, he loved his job. Yes, he loved making films, but the pace had been relentless in recent years. If he kept it up, when it was time to end his career and move back home, he'd discover he was old and lonely. He suddenly realised how much he didn't want that.

Claire didn't miss a beat. 'And you still want my help? From what you've told me, you're more than capable of managing this on your own.'

He nodded. 'Yes. I do want you. I mean, I want your help. I need to do something different. I need to change.'

Claire didn't look entirely convinced. A slight scowl marred her forehead, but at least she wasn't smiling that scary plastic smile at him any more. That had to be a good thing.

'Okay,' she said and fell silent.

Right. He realised he'd made another error. Unlike a lot of women he knew, she obviously wasn't the nosy type. She wasn't taking the bait to ask him why he'd changed his plans. Damn. Since he'd been back in London he'd realised that his interpersonal skills had been severely eroded by his solitary lifestyle.

'Somewhere temperate might be nice,' he told Claire, as the waitress set a cappuccino in front of her and a double espresso in front of him with a surly grunt of acknowledgement. 'As you know, I seem to have specialised in hot and dusty locations in recent years.'

Claire emptied a packet of sugar into her cappuccino and stirred it carefully. 'Have you ever been to Uganda?'

Dominic's stomach dropped. Did she know? Had she worked it out before he could tell her? If so, why was she so calm, making this almost a throwaway comment? When Erica had laid little traps like this for him to fall into she'd watched him like a hawk. 'Yes,' he said slowly. 'Why do you ask?'

Claire shook her head and smiled. 'Oh, no reason. Or at least not a professional one. It's just that I saw this documentary the other night . . .'

He swallowed, and his blood, which had been racing round his veins, cooled and slowed to almost nothing. He knew his first self-produced project had been repeated last week. Had she really . . . ?

'Any good?' he asked, trying to sound casual.

Claire nodded, and a fire lit behind her eyes. 'Really good,' she said. 'So good that I'm seriously considering child sponsorship. I'll have to try to remember the name of it.'

*The Lost Generation*, he whispered mentally.

And she'd liked it? Claire had actually liked it? His blood started pumping again, and this time it was doing a victory march. The oddest feeling swelled inside his chest making him feel lighter, freer, as if the impossible could happen and that he could spill his secret and everything would be okay. It was only as it took him to its dizzying heights that he realised that strange sensation had a name – hope.

'Shouldn't be too hard to work out,' she added and then she laughed. 'That was the funny thing about it. It turns out it was made by my – oh!'

She frowned and reached into her handbag, which sat on the floor by her feet.

'By your . . . ?' he prompted, willing her to carry on. It would be the perfect way in to saying what he needed to say, but Claire didn't take the hint. Instead, she pulled out her phone and looked at it.

'I'm sorry,' she said, shaking her head and smiling, 'but it's Doug. Do you mind if I take this?'

Dominic shook his head. What else could he do?

Claire pressed the screen of her phone and then held it to her ear. 'Hello, Doug? How can I—' She stopped mid-sentence and frowned. 'Oh, I see . . . Yes . . . Yes . . . Well, obviously that wouldn't be suitable at all. I'll get to work on it as soon as I—' She paused to pull a face at Dominic, indicating the conversation she was having was as difficult as he'd been imagining. 'Okay . . . Okay . . . Listen, don't panic. I can't do anything right now, but all the files are at the office. I can be there in less than half an hour. Yes . . . Yes . . . Okay. Goodbye, Doug. Try to breathe a little for me, will you? Okay. Bye.'

She finally ended the call, placed her phone on the table between them and gave him a 'would you believe it?' kind of look. 'I'm so sorry,' she said. 'An emergency involving Doug's South Pacific trip. Would you mind terribly if we . . .'

Dominic felt his whole body sag, but he smiled and said, 'No, of course.'

'Email me,' she said, and gave him a slow sweet smile that flipped his heart like a freshly tossed pancake.

'Sure,' he replied, as she tucked her phone back into her bag and signalled to the waitress that she'd like a takeaway cup for her coffee. Before Dominic could form a coherent thought, she'd hurried out of the shop and disappeared.

Emailing? That meant he was back to square one.

Fantastic.

# Chapter Twenty-Five
## Perhaps, Perhaps, Perhaps

Claire was supposed to be doing some work on Peggy's Paris proposal trip. She was sitting cross-legged on her bed in her pyjamas. Her laptop was balanced — unsurprisingly — on her lap and the TV was on low, switched to a baking show.

What she was actually doing instead of working or watching the towering sugar-work creations on the screen was fretting about Nick. It had been a lovely surprise to see him the day before. She'd really missed their chatty little email conversations when they stopped, and she hadn't realised just what a rush of endorphins she'd get at seeing him in the flesh again. She went a little bit tingly just thinking about it.

*This isn't the right time to be planning a romantic trip.*

That's what he'd said, hadn't he? But what the heck did it mean? The question kept chewing away at her, preventing her from concentrating on anything else for more than five seconds. She was driving herself crazy.

At first, he'd just been a nice-looking guy. Maybe a little bit shallow, but attractive all the same. Someone she'd have been happy to flirt with, maybe go out on a few dates with.

For her, that was big, big progress. But then he'd gone and ruined it all by revealing he was a nice-looking guy with a girlfriend. A serious girlfriend, if he was going to expend all that money and time and energy booking her a surprise trip.

That had been fine too. She'd been able to handle that.

Or at least she had until he'd gone and started opening up to her, showing her just what was under the 'nice-looking, but shallow' tip to his iceberg, until she'd really started to like what she'd seen.

He could be thoughtful and intuitive. He was very observant, although she'd bet he didn't realise that was one of his strengths, and, when he put his mind to it, he could be very romantic indeed. It was strange . . . He possessed all these qualities, but it was obvious that he was more than a little rusty in using them, even though he was in a serious relationship. Why?

She sighed. She really shouldn't want to know. Because the more she thought about him, the sicker she felt that some other cow had got to him first. But . . .

*It's not the right time for a romantic trip.*

Did that mean there was trouble in paradise?

And was she the lowest form of human scum for being just a little bit elated at that thought?

She buried her face in her hands and let out a frustrated shout. Between her fingers, on screen, she could see that someone's spun sugar tower had crashed to the studio floor. She rubbed her face, breathed in and sat up straight, returning her fingers to her keyboard.

She'd just fire off an email to him.

Not to ask about the girlfriend, of course. That would be truly unprofessional. However, if he got a little chatty with his reply and let something interesting slip . . . Well, that could hardly be considered her fault.

From: clairebixby@farfaraway.com
To: nica453@monstermail.com
Subject: Sorry
Dear Nick,
I wanted to apologise again for dashing out on you yesterday. It was lovely to bump into you . . .

Claire bit her lip. 'Lovely to bump into you?' Did that sound too keen? She backspaced.

What a coincidence seeing you there.

Yes. That was better.

I would like to ask you a couple of things about your upcoming holiday, especially now . . .

She'd been going to type 'it's not going to be a romantic holiday', but that sounded far too blunt. Heck, how did she put this without sounding either insensitive or nosy. Or both? She sighed and carried on.

. . . especially now the focus . . .

Yes, that was a good word.

. . . of your trip has changed. You can either email me back, or you can call me or drop in at the office, whichever is more convenient.

Best wishes,

Claire

P.S. I realise I forgot to ever tell you the story of why those chips were so romantic. If you want to know, you just have to ask . . .

She resisted the urge to add a little 'x' after her name and pressed send. There. A totally cool and professional email – mostly. Her halo was still intact.

About a minute later, her inbox pinged. She instantly clicked on the reply.

From: nica453@monstermail.com

To: clairebixby@farfaraway.com

Subject: RE: Sorry

Hi Claire,

Seriously, there's nothing to be sorry for. It wasn't as if we'd arranged an appointment. Take me up on a rain check for that coffee, though. I mean it.

Claire, who'd leaned forward to read Nick's reply, sank back against her pillows. He was asking her out for coffee? Did that sound like a guy who was currently involved with someone else? Or was he just trying to be friendly? Maybe he just wanted to keep her sweet so she got the best possible deals for him. Argghh! Who could tell?

So what disaster of Doug's took you away from me? I'd bet a hundred quid and my left kidney that it had something to do with his mother. Have you ever met her? Picture me shuddering!

N. x
P.S. I am practically exploding with curiosity about the chips!
You have to put me out of my misery.


Claire's heart soared at the sight of that extra letter after
his usual sign-off. Calm down, she told herself. Maybe he
does that all the time. Maybe he just forgot he was talking
to you and not someone he was close friends with.
But, still . . .
She smiled as she typed her reply.


From: clairebixby@farfaraway.com
To: nica453@monstermail.com
No, I've never met her, but I feel as if I have! Not only does Doug
go on about her constantly, but I've been (un)lucky enough to
see the holiday pics. Doug emailed me loads to prove what a
wonderful time they'd had.

   This latest crisis was to do with the first-class menu on the
airline I was proposing, one that Mrs B. had never used before.
She's always a bit wary of aeroplane food after being served
something yellow and spongy she couldn't identify on a trip
back from Indonesia. Apparently, the uncertainty of what lay
on her plate spoiled her whole journey and much of the rest of
her year.

   I've tried to explain to her that one can't get airline menus three
months in advance, but she's not taking no for an answer.
C.


Her finger hovered above the 'x' on her keyboard. His
might have been a throwaway gesture. Completely
platonic. Knowing hers was not made her chicken out.

Nick's reply pinged back quickly.

From: nica453@monstermail.com
To: clairebixby@farfaraway.com
Did you manage to solve the problem in the end? And please don't leave me hanging about the chips. It's the sort of thing a guy like me might actually be able to pull off!

Claire typed again.

From: clairebixby@farfaraway.com
To: nica453@monstermail.com
I'm hoping providing some sample menus may soothe her worries. Otherwise she wants to book with someone else, which is doable, but it'll cost more and involve an extra connection, which means they'll lose another half day of the holiday.

Don't suppose you fancy a trip to the Cook Islands? That would solve all our problems. I could do you and Doug a great group discount rate. You could share a villa ;-)

And if you want to know about the chips you may well have to bribe me with wine . . .

She closed her eyes and pressed 'send', then winced. Had that been too much? Had she been too cheeky, too forward?

From: nica453@monstermail.com
To: clairebixby@farfaraway.com
Ha ha. I think I'd rather take a three-week tour of the London sewer system than spend that amount of time with Doug's mother.

Besides, I'd like to go somewhere I've never been before.
And I reckon the wine thing is totally doable. :-)

Claire's pulse did a little skip. They'd always been playful and chatty in their emails, but did this mean they were now flirting? It was a pity she couldn't type lying down, because suddenly she'd come over a little dizzy.

From: clairebixby@farfaraway.com
To: nica453@monstermail.com
You've been to the Cook Islands? I'm so jealous. Is it really as lovely as the pictures in the brochures?
Btw, the sewer tour could be arranged, if you really want it. ;-)
And you could take me out for that drink afterwards.

Oh, Lord. She hoped her instincts about the disappearing girlfriend were right, otherwise she was being very, very bad indeed.

From: nica453@monstermail.com
To: clairebixby@farfaraway.com
Yep. It really is that lovely. White sand, waving palm trees, crystal water. The one place I've been where the brochure pics really don't need any retouching. Unless you're there during monsoon season. Then it's not quite so much fun.
Btw, let's forget the sewers and just do the wine.

From: clairebixby@farfaraway.com
To: nica453@monstermail.com
I could see that about the Cook Islands! Anyway...

Claire paused. She needed to ask this question. Even from a professional point of view she needed to ask this question, but the fact her request for information also had a personal edge made her feel a little shaky. She had to know for sure before they kept going like this. She took a deep breath and carried on typing.

. . . When you said you were changing the type of trip you wanted to book, was it just the overall feel, the romantic element? Or are there other changes?

From: nica453@monstermail.com
To: clairebixby@farfaraway.com
What kind of changes?

Claire swallowed.

From: clairebixby@farfaraway.com
To: nica453@monstermail.com
Like the number of people going.

There. She'd said it.

Are we still booking for two?

She pressed send.

A minute or two passed. Gran's big old sunburst clock on the wall seemed to tick extra loudly. Claire began to get worried that she'd overstepped the mark. Had she? It had seemed an obvious question to ask, given the way the conversation had been going. She'd tried to tell herself she'd have asked it anyway, even if she hadn't been nursing this silly crush, but she wasn't sure if she was kidding herself or not.

Quite a few minutes slipped past and it got to the point where she suspected she'd just prompted another patch of radio silence from Nick, maybe even lost herself a customer, so when her email alert pinged quarter of an hour later she almost jumped out of the little dent she'd made for herself in her stacked-up pillows.

From: nica453@monstermail.com
To: clairebixby@farfaraway.com
Good question. And one I really should have made clear before now. I didn't realise I hadn't.
Yes, things have changed.

Claire's heart began to beat double time.

I'm looking at a trip for one now.

She punched the air in triumph, but then realised that was a really insensitive thing to do, even if Nick couldn't see her.

Oh, Lord, she wanted to ask a million questions. All of them nosy. All of them inappropriate. Her fingers itched to commit every single one of them in writing. Instead, she composed something that sounded sympathetic rather than predatory, because, seriously, what guy was going to respond to a girl who threw herself at him when he was at his most low?

Okay, so *a lot* of guys would take that opportunity, but Nick wasn't one of those guys, was he? He wasn't shallow, only out for a quick fling; his devotion to his ex while he'd been trying to plan her dream holiday had proved that.

Stupid woman. Didn't she know what she'd thrown away?

From: clairebixby@farfaraway.com
To: nica453@monstermail.com
I'm so sorry to hear that.

And, despite her personal interest, she truly was. She knew how hard it was when a relationship you'd invested your whole self in ended, even if it wasn't a good one. Even if it was a toxic one.

She exhaled and sank further into her pillows.

Wow. She hadn't realised it before, but she could feel the ripples of that pain still reverberating from her break-up with Philip, even though she'd known it was the best thing for both of them, even though she'd felt so free at the time.

She started to type again, this time not thinking about what she wanted from Nick, but about what she could give him.

I know I can't make the situation any better for you, but I can book you a wonderful relaxing holiday to help give you time to lick your wounds and come back refreshed and ready to get on with life.

In that case, I recommend we stick to Europe. No long-haul flights. Pretty easy choices with currency. Lots of great culture and perfect weather this time of year, before the summer starts to bake too hard. What do you think?

And, Nick? If you ever . . . Well, if you ever need a friendly ear, someone to talk to. You know I'm here.

C. x

She didn't know why she'd written that last bit, but she'd hit send on automatic before she'd been able to stop herself. It was out there now. Nothing she could do to call it back.

She waited again. The show on the TV had changed to a nature documentary while she hadn't been paying attention. Darn. She was going to have to go and see who won that round of the baking show on catch-up.

From: nica453@monstermail.com
To: clairebixby@farfaraway.com
Thanks. N. x

His last email was proof enough that he was still feeling raw. Just that one word. And he'd proved himself a pretty chatty guy up until that point. It was time to draw this to a close this evening, wasn't it? She'd said enough.

She composed one last email, saying she'd be in touch during the week with some ideas for his trip. She signed it without the 'x' she'd boldly added to her previous message and then closed down her laptop and put it on her dressing table without waiting for a reply, then she picked up the little throw cushion she kept on her bed and hugged it to herself.

# Chapter Twenty-Six

# Julie

The opening credits of *Julie*, one of Doris's more critically acclaimed dramatic roles, were playing when Claire picked up her phone to turn it onto silent and realised she'd missed a text from Nick. She smiled, tapped in a quick answer, then turned her attention back to the film.

There were only a couple of movies of Doris's she'd never seen before and this was one of them. It had been hard to track down a DVD copy in Region 2 format, but eventually they'd managed it, ordering a Spanish version – *El Diabólico Señor Benton* – and choosing the English soundtrack and turning off the subtitles. For some reason, her grandmother hadn't had this one in her collection. As the film progressed, Claire started to see why.

'I can't believe she married the psycho!' Kitty exclaimed loudly, as the man on the screen pinned Doris down and told her he'd kill her if she ever tried to leave him. 'I mean, how could you get that close to someone and not know? He killed her ex just to have her for goodness' sake! And now he's going to kill her too?'

A few of the other group members murmured their

agreement, but Claire stayed quiet. So did Maggs. They looked at each other, silent agreement zapping between them, and then looked back at the screen.

Easily, Claire thought. It was too, too easy to see what you wanted to see. Thank goodness her mistake had been with a man who was just a greedy child deep inside, unable to give as well as take, but he hadn't been violent.

After half an hour, Claire had had enough. She wanted to get up, flip the lights back on and declare the meeting over, but that wouldn't be fair to the rest of the club members, who were enjoying a well-written 'woman in jeopardy' tale, and Doris was acting her socks off.

Claire decided to concentrate on that and not get sucked into the story. It wasn't real, after all. Just people pretending to be other people, props, sets, cameras. She kept concentrating on these things, focusing on the film-making techniques, instead of looking into Doris's eyes on the screen, instead of letting herself see the terror there. Because that felt real. Very real.

Claire knew there was a reason for that. She'd read loads of books about Doris over the years, including Doris's autobiography, but it had been some time ago. Now pieces of information kept coming back to her about this film.

Doris, without really knowing what 'method acting' was, had used that technique to get into her parts, and for this one she said she'd revisited just how she'd felt when she'd been married to her first husband, when she'd lived this kind of role for real. By all accounts, filming it had left her on the edge of a breakdown. She'd been ill too, in pain and needing surgery, but her manager and third husband had refused to shut filming down so she could see her doctor. It had been a dark time for Doris. When she'd finally got to hospital, they'd found a tumour – benign, thank goodness – the size of a grapefruit inside her. She'd ended up with a hysterectomy, ending any hope of having a second child.

While it was hard to watch, brave Julie found her freedom in the end – and so had Doris. She'd made many films after this, had come through her surgery well, and carried on to live to a ripe old age.

That thought carried Claire through the rest of the film, to the credits and beyond. As she was packing away, Maggs collared her.

'I'm coming with you on Friday morning,' she said.

Claire shook her head. 'No, it's okay. I'm a big girl. I can manage seeing my father on my own.'

'I know you can,' Maggs said, 'just like I can get the bus home on my own, or do my own shopping, or make myself a cake now and again, but you come and do those things for me anyway.'

Claire smiled. 'It's because I love you, Auntie Maggs.'

Maggs huffed. 'You haven't called me that in at least two decades. Anyway, that's my point.'

Claire leaned in and gave her a kiss. Maggs wouldn't say the words, but she knew the old lady felt them with every fibre of her being. 'Thanks,' she said. 'I'll pick you up at ten.'

She was still smiling as she packed away her things, but it gradually faded. While the thought of having company on Friday was nice, her conversation with Maggs had just served to remind her the day was looming. She'd been doing very well at ignoring that up until now, thinking she'd just leave the worrying to the morning itself, but now, as she walked down stairs and out of the pub, there was a cold knot in her stomach.

# Chapter Twenty-Seven
## Cuddle Up a Little Closer

Dominic was sitting on his sofa in just a pair of old tracksuit bottoms that had been cut down into shorts, doing research for his free-diving project on his laptop. He'd found a site outlining some of the training procedures and had become fascinated with it. He'd ended up following the instructions, just to see what it felt like, and had been doing prep exercises for the last half an hour: breathing in deeply and holding it briefly before 'purging', blowing it all out again. He was now ready to see how long he could go. He set his laptop aside, brought up the stopwatch on his phone and sat it down next to him on the sofa.

Keeping his body relaxed and positioning himself so he could stay still, he breathed in deep and filled his lungs to eighty-five per cent.

His efforts at holding it were ruined when, forty seconds in, an alert for an email from Claire popped up on his screen. *Chips!* The subject line read. He let the air out so fast that he felt a bit dizzy afterwards. He didn't care, though. He swiped his phone to pull up the message.

From: clairebixby@farfaraway.com

To: nica453@monstermail.com

Subject: Chips!

Okay, Nicholas . . . Is your name Nicholas? I suppose I've assumed it is, but it could be something entirely different, couldn't it?

Dominic stopped breathing again, but this time it was for a very different reason. She was getting a little too close to the truth there, wasn't she?

Anyway . . . I've decided to put you out of your misery about the chip thing, although I'm still holding you to that promise of a glass of wine!

He was counting on that. They'd been emailing back and forth for almost a week since that first chat where he'd told her he didn't want to book a romantic trip. They'd lost all pretence of keeping it business-related now, even if a bit of travel chatter slipped in quite frequently. There was joking, there was banter. Plenty of flirting. There was more than that too.

There'd been talking. Well, typing. Proper communicating. The way he'd never been able to do before. He'd told her all sorts of things he'd never told anyone else, not even Pete. Well, maybe, especially not Pete . . . Somehow it was easier when it came out of his fingertips instead of his mouth, when he wasn't looking at an angry female face that was expecting him to come up with the perfect answer right here, right now.

They'd also graduated from email to texting, although

when they wanted to discuss longer subjects email was still their preferred medium. It was like they had their own private little universe going where no one else existed, no one else mattered.

Maybe that was why he'd told her about Erica. Not everything, but bits. The start of the truth. In return, she'd begun telling him about her ex-husband. The guy sounded like a real wet fish and Dominic was endlessly grateful to him for that, because if he hadn't been such a waste of space Claire would still be married to him and he'd never have got to know her.

A part of him knew he should hold back, but he couldn't seem to stop himself. That same part knew this was dangerous. Usually he played it safe in relationships, leaving the daredevil stuff for his job. Now, however, with an absence of anything but office-based work, it seemed he was letting his daredevil urges seep into other areas of his life. Somehow he couldn't seem to care about that either. He was having too much fun.

He shook himself and realised he'd yet to read on about these now infamous chips. He rectified that immediately:

I'm afraid after all this build-up, it's going to seem a little bit tame, but I'll tell the story anyway:

My friend's husband was not the romantic sort at all, of which she complained frequently and loudly. He was also rubbish at cooking and she got fed up having to do it night after night for the pair of them.

Anyway, one year he decided to up his game. Not only did he go an a secret cooking course on the run up to Valentine's Day, but on the day itself he cooked her favourite meal – steak and chips, with Béarnaise sauce and everything – and the crowning glory was his artistry with the potatoes.

He didn't just cut them into strips or wedges. He saved a few back and carved them into letters, so when he presented her with her plate of gorgeous food that she hadn't had to lift a finger to prepare, the words 'I love you', were spelled out in hot, crispy potato letters across her plate.

She told me she cried for ten minutes and her steak went cold!

So there we go . . . There's my ultimate example of how something as unromantic as potatoes – especially if they're muddy – can be turned into a romantic experience to top all others. It's all about knowing the person you're making the gesture to and the amount of thought and effort that's gone into it.

You're going to tell me that's really lame now, aren't you?

Sigh.

Claire x


Dominic smiled as he read the end of the email. In a funny way it did make sense, but only if he thought about it very hard.

He shook his head as he read through it a second time and then let out a long, drawn-out breath. He needed to tell her, didn't he? And he'd been planning to, but somehow all these emails had been stalling him, probably because he didn't want it all to end.

However, he knew he couldn't keep it up much longer. He'd had a couple of close calls in the last week, moments when he'd only just slipped inside his flat in the nick of time, or had almost run into her in the street and had to duck into someone else's garden. He knew he was playing Russian roulette, that it was only a matter of time . . .

He'd made the mistake of letting the deception drag out way past its sell-by date.

If this thing was going to go anywhere between them, it had to move beyond emails and texts. He was going to have to do this communicating stuff face to face eventually. He just hoped he could take what he'd learned and turn it into actual, real live conversation.

A thought dropped into his brain, cool and simple and perfect.

He wanted to tell her the whole story in person, but that didn't mean he was restricted to email. After all, he had her phone number . . .

He picked up his phone and started to dial, but then he realised there was something else he needed to do urgently. He flipped open his laptop and logged onto Facebook. Once there, he searched for 'Erica Conway' and, as soon as her profile page popped up, he clicked on the button that said 'Friends' and chose 'unfriend' from the drop-down list.

*

Claire had been glancing at her phone on her bedside table while she'd been reading, hoping it would ding with a reply from Nick, but when it actually rang she almost dropped her book. She picked it up, heart beating.

'Hello?'

She knew it was him from the caller display, but she could hardly believe it.

'Hey.'

Claire closed her eyes. It was him all right, with that

rich, warm voice that always held a hint of laughter. 'Hey,' she breathed back, cradling the phone with both hands and hugging it to her a little. She was only sad it was a thin little sliver of a thing, not one of those big chunky phones with a curly wire that Doris had used in *Pillow Talk*. This moment felt just like that.

She knew she was being a total and utter sap, but for some reason she just didn't care. She imagined her grey vest top and shorts away and envisioned herself in a filmy blue negligee the colour of a summer's sky.

'You got my email about the chips, then?'

He chuckled and the sound seemed to curl right out of her phone and wrap itself around her. 'Yes, I got it, but I also "got" it, I think.'

'Good.' She sat up a little. 'Don't take this the wrong way, but why are you phoning me? Is there a problem?'

'No problem,' he replied casually. 'Just wanted to hear your voice.'

Oh, *good* answer.

She draped her arm on the pillow above her head as they started to chat about anything and everything.

# Chapter Twenty-Eight
## Won't You Dance With Me, Papa?

Claire pulled up outside a nursing home in a wide and leafy street not far from Crystal Palace Park. The road was full of massive red-brick Victorian villas, the sort that must have been owned by wealthy middle-class families when they were first built, but now had been carved into flats or converted into private schools and old people's homes. She got up and stared at a huge oak tree towering overhead. The passenger door clicked open and soon Maggs was standing beside her.

'Are you sure you don't want me to come in with you?'

Claire shook her head, still staring into the branches of the tree. 'No. It's fine. I want to do this on my own.'

Maggs looked in the direction of the park, which could just about be glimpsed at the far end of the road. It was a pleasant afternoon, sunny, not too hot, with a light breeze. Strange weather for something like this, Claire thought. Everything seemed so pleasant, so benign. It should be thundering or, at the very least, overcast.

'I'll take a stroll, then,' Maggs said. 'I'll get back here in about forty-five minutes.' She patted her handbag. 'If you need me before then, text.'

Claire nodded. 'Will do,' she replied, but her voice was soft and faint. She transferred her gaze to the red-brick building in front of her. Someone on the staff must be a keen gardener, because there were window boxes overflowing with colourful flowers.

Maggs walked over and pressed a kiss to her cheek, saying nothing, and then she turned and walked down the road. Claire watched her go. Some old ladies stooped, their backs irrevocably rounded, a lifetime of poor posture solidifying their muscles and bones, but Maggs was ramrod straight as she walked away.

Claire wondered what Maggs was going to do about George. She'd told him he could take her out to lunch, as long as it wasn't somewhere 'full of old farts', but Claire was still worried for poor George, and once she started worrying about him that got her on to worrying about Maggs, but then she realised she was only doing it so she didn't have to think about what came next.

She relaxed her tense rib muscles and dragged in a breath and, following Maggs's example, pulled herself up and walked through the gate and up the path of St Elwin's nursing home. A friendly nurse met her and said she'd show Claire to one of the smaller lounges, where she confirmed she and her father would have a bit of privacy, then she gave Claire a sympathetic smile and left her standing outside.

Claire stared at the door. It was panelled. Once varnished wood, she guessed, but now it had been painted in brilliant white gloss, recoated so many times over the years that the beading inlaid in the panels had started to lose its definition.

She knew she should knock, but she didn't. She just stood there, feeling the cold creep up from her toes, chilling her calf bones, making her thighs tremble.

That suffocating feeling was back, that horrible, frozen state she remembered from standing in the yellow hallway of her parents' home, waiting for a bark of an instruction to enter, to come and receive judgement. She found she couldn't speak, couldn't move. All she could do was let it wash over her in a stinging icy wave and hope the first surge would be the worst, that after that she'd be able to ride it.

No voice came from the other side of the door. No command to enter. He must have known she was there. He must have heard the nurse talking to her. She seriously considered turning tail and racing through the corridors until she could burst through the front door and out into the fragrant June air again.

But then, almost without consciously deciding to do it, she lifted her hand and pushed the door open.

She stepped into a small lounge with a sofa and a collection of assorted armchairs. The carpet was a rich royal blue and the walls, in an ironic twist of fate, were the same bright buttercup that her mother had chosen for her house. French doors led onto a well-tended mature garden. She could see an elderly couple taking a stroll and a nurse pushing a woman in a wheelchair. Only when she had taken in all these things did she look at the only other person in the room.

The door whispered shut behind her, the fire-regulation closer attached to it having slowed its progress. Just as well, there was nothing her father hated more than a door being slammed. This place must be like heaven to him.

Her father. She looked at him. Mentally totted up the

years since she'd last seen his face. Twenty-three. That was
two-thirds of her life just about. They stared at each other.

'You came,' he said flatly.

'Yes.'

'I wasn't sure you would.'

Claire said nothing. She hadn't been sure she would
either, but she wasn't going to tell him that. She didn't
want to agree with him about anything.

'What do you want?'

He nodded to one of the other armchairs. 'Sit,' he said.
It wasn't an order but a request, but Claire still felt the tiny
hairs on the skin covering her spine lift, and she sat in a
different chair from the one he'd pointed out to her.

She sat on the edge of the seat, knees together and palms
on top of them, and then she lifted her face.

He looked her over thoroughly and, for the first time since
she'd entered the room, Claire took a really good look at
him too. It was if, in the shock of the moment, she hadn't
been able to process all the information her senses had been
sending her, and now it all arrived a bit late, jumbled and
out of breath.

He was sitting in the chair, arms on the armrests, gripping
the ends with his long fingers, as he always had, but that
was where the similarity to the man in her memory ended.
She remembered him with black hair and dark slashes for
eyebrows. There'd always been something quite regal about
him, as if he'd always known he was born to rule others,
but the man who sat in front of her was grey and balding,
his shoulders slumped and, even though he was still broad
and tall, his limbs seemed skinny inside his clothes.

Was this the monster? The one she'd run from all these years?

'You look a lot like your mother,' he said, startling her out of her observations.

Claire kept staring at him and answered in an even tone. 'I know.' She had her mother's snub nose, her freckles and her smile.

'Your eyes are mine,' her father added.

She showed no trace of emotion on her features. 'No,' she replied firmly and slowly, as she stared at a pair of eyes that matched her own for blueness and shine. 'They're nothing like yours.'

He frowned. Claire realised it was only the second time in her life that she'd contradicted him. During her childhood, once had been enough. It gave her a sense of power. She ought to have felt happy about that, but somehow that emotion was swallowed up in the deepening and darkening furnace that was burning inside her.

'Are you ill?'

He didn't flinch, didn't bat an eyelash. He'd always been that direct himself, she supposed, so maybe it didn't surprise him that she'd been so blunt. It bothered her that she remembered things about him like that, especially after she'd done her best to erase him from her consciousness, but little details, little comparisons, kept popping into her mind the longer she sat here opposite him.

'Yes,' he replied.

'Are you going to die?'

He blinked. For a ghost of a moment, she almost thought she saw something resembling dark humour in his eyes. 'Yes, because that fate is shared by us all, Claire.'

Her stomach lurched when he said her name. She wanted to lunge at him, push it back inside his mouth. She didn't want to hear him use it.

'But, no, I'm not about to die. Not just yet, although I probably won't reach the ripe old age of my mother's darling Doris.'

Good, Claire thought. And she meant it.

'So what do you want with me?' she repeated. 'Why summon me after all this time? Have you got something to say?'

There was a long silence as he folded his arms in his lap and continued his appraisal of her. Claire refused to look away. She had a feeling she'd never forgive herself if she did.

He drew a large, heaving breath. 'I wanted to see how you turned out, that's all, to see what kind of person the child I produced has become.'

Through no thanks to you, Claire answered silently. She realised she could have said it out loud if she'd wanted to, but she didn't bother. Somehow it didn't seem worth it.

'That's all?' she said, nodding gently to herself, answering her own question before he did. Of course that was all. It was curiosity, plain and simple, that had caused him to call her here. Not love. Not remorse. Not a sudden and transforming need to redeem himself.

For the first time since they'd started talking he looked away. 'Yes.'

'In that case, I'm going to leave,' she said, standing up. She'd only been sitting for five minutes and yet her limbs felt stiff and unfamiliar. 'Please don't contact me again.'

She promised herself she wouldn't look back as she walked away. Even so, she couldn't help it as she passed through the doorway. Afterwards, she was never sure it was because she'd been weak or because her head had just naturally turned that way as she'd passed through the doorway. For some reason that bothered her.

He was slumped even further in his chair, looking steadily and determinedly out the window.

She thought all hope had left when he'd answered her question, but she found it was this moment that erased it completely. With shame, she realised that if he'd turned and looked, if his eyes had begged and said what his mouth had not been able to, that she might have sat down again. What a sad, deluded loser she was. Maggs might talk about icebergs and hidden motives, but there was nothing beneath the surface of this man but hardness and coldness, just as one would have expected.

She walked to the exit, passing the smiling nurse without reacting. How odd, she thought, as she crossed the threshold into the sunshine. She'd expected this moment to tear her neatly ordered world apart, but instead she found herself totally and completely numb.

*

The numbness pervaded as Claire walked through the main gate of Crystal Palace Park and down the wide avenue of beech trees. Maggs couldn't have got far. They'd left each other maybe fifteen minutes ago, max. Claire decided to take a wander and see if she could spot her, and if that didn't work, she'd text.

It was quiet, even though it was close to eleven o'clock on Friday morning. There were a few people in sensible shoes walking their dogs, a handful of parents and children in the playground. As Claire went past the sprawling play area, a child's shriek cut through the birdsong and sound of gently rustling leaves. She quickly turned her head to see where it had come from, sensors on high alert, but the alarming noise was quickly followed with a high-pitched giggle. Another shriek. Claire scanned the playground.

It wasn't hard to identify the source. A lone pair was at the swings – a father pushing his daughter, aged six, possibly seven. She was calling for him to push higher and higher and when he did she let out a scream of half joy, half fear. Her long wavy hair fluttered behind her like ribbons as she swung forward, then flipped to cover her face when she changed direction.

She looked so happy, an expression of pure bliss on her features every time she swung high. Claire stepped forward to the edge of the black-painted railings that ran round the edge of the playground. She stayed there watching them, feeling the momentum of the swing, its rhythm, tug at something inside her.

She transferred her attention to the father. He was grinning too, wider every time his daughter shrieked. His eyes shone, never leaving her, not even for a second.

The tugging inside continued, but now it became uncomfortable.

The unravelling happened so suddenly that it took Claire completely by surprise. One moment she was experiencing a simple moment of joy in a beautiful park and the next a trapdoor opened inside her, revealing a pit that was vast and dark.

And then she felt the heat that billowed from it. It started in her feet then rushed up her legs and into her torso, threatening to suffocate her, burning away the mist of numbness that had been clouding her since she'd left St Elwin's. Her hands began to shake.

A fireball exploded through her, scorching where it touched. She had to grab the railings in front of her to steady herself and heaved in a lungful of warm air and closed her eyes.

Oh, how she hated him for dragging her back into his orbit again, for making her feel like the little girl who had starved for his approval, even before she'd left. And she hated herself too, for still wanting it from him, even after all he'd done to her and her mother and her grandmother.

He wasn't worth it. He didn't deserve this emotion. Not one bit of it.

Tears blurred her eyes and shame washed into the mix with the other swirling emotions.

She was vaguely aware of a hand being placed on her arm.

'Claire? Are you all right?'

She recognised the voice. She knew she recognised it, but for a fleeting second she couldn't match it with anything in her memory banks. She turned her head and found Maggs looking at her, face full of concern. She slapped Maggs's hand away and her features contorted in disgust. 'This is all your fault,' she said in a low, growling voice. 'You made me come! You made me believe there was more, that maybe I'd misjudged him, done the wrong thing by keeping away all these years!'

Maggs couldn't have looked more shocked. 'I—'

'Don't!' Claire shouted. 'Don't you dare defend yourself!'

She had to get away. From this woman who'd manipulated her into coming here today by cooing about how much it would have meant to her grandmother. From this place. From anywhere close to where *he* was. She needed to get back on her side of the Thames.

She turned sharply and started to stride towards the park gates. She knew she was walking faster than Maggs could keep up with but she didn't care. She hardly noticed her journey back to her car, because her mind was full of shouted conversations, with Maggs, with her father . . . And all the time she could see him hunched in that chair, pretending, once again, that she didn't exist.

She unlocked the car, got in and turned the keys in the ignition. She sat there for a few seconds, looking towards the end of the road. There was no sign of her travel companion, but she still took the handbrake off, put her foot on the accelerator and drove away.

She'd gone three streets before she turned round and went back for Maggs. She was still angry, but the fireball was starting to burn itself out. As much as she wanted to yell and scream at her grandmother's friend right now, she couldn't leave a seventy-year-old stranded in Penge, of all places, miles away from home.

But when she got back to St Elwin's, Maggs wasn't standing outside, looking this way and that, wondering where Claire was.

Claire began to panic. She drove up and down the road, trying to spot her. Maggs, while fit for her age, didn't walk fast. She drove round the block looking for her and when she came up empty she parked back outside the home and pulled her phone out of her bag. Why hadn't she thought about that earlier?

Her calls just went through to voicemail. That was when

she really started to get scared. Oh, God. What had she done? How could she have treated Maggs that way? Finally, everything she'd been feeling caught up with her. She laid her head on the steering wheel and sobbed.

She didn't know how long she stayed there. She lost all sense of time and space. All she could do was listen to the ugly howling, feel the shape and depth and colour of her own sorrow. It blotted everything else out, raging like a storm, wearing itself out with its own fury.

*Flip*, she thought to herself, in a tiny lucid moment when she seemed to be watching herself, as if she was in the passenger seat of her own grief, *there's been a lot locked away for a long time, hasn't there?* She hadn't even cried like this when her grandmother had died, had just stuffed those unwanted feelings down into the pit, believing she'd disposed of them.

It was just as another of these cogent moments stretched out to form a semblance of normality that she heard a short rap on her window. She looked up, face tear-streaked and soggy, to find Maggs standing there. Claire rolled down the window. Maggs was looking rather grim.

'I'm so sorry . . .' she began, but then the tears took over again. A moment later, she heard the passenger door open, the squeak of a seat as Maggs sat down. Then the door closed again and they were cocooned in the shell of Claire's tiny car. Claire looked across, eyes pleading with Maggs to understand.

It was the one bright flicker in this afternoon of misery that the look on Maggs's face suggested she did.

'I'm so sorry,' Claire began again, speaking between hiccups. 'I shouldn't have left you like that! I shouldn't have—'

Maggs held up a hand. Claire was grateful. Even if she'd known what the rest of that sentence was going to be, she didn't know if she'd be able to get through it.

'It's okay,' Maggs said seriously. 'I might not know exactly what went on in there between you and your father, but I understand.'

Claire reached into her handbag for a tissue and blew her nose. While she was mopping up her eyes she said, 'Where did you go?'

Maggs nodded towards the nursing home. 'In there.'

'Why?'

'To see the bastard for myself.'

Claire kept staring at Maggs. 'And?'

Maggs shrugged. 'Why don't you tell me what your visit was like first? It might help make sense of mine.'

Claire closed her eyes. She didn't want to go back to that bland little lounge with its floral sofas and sunny windows, not even in her imagination. 'There was nothing,' she said in a whisper, eyes still closed. 'Gran was wrong. There was nothing beneath his surface.' She opened her eyes and looked at Maggs, who was unusually quiet. 'He didn't want to see me, not really,' she explained. 'He just wanted to jerk my puppet strings and see if I would still dance for him.'

Maggs raised her eyebrows. 'You really believe that?'

Claire nodded. 'I don't know . . . Maybe being ill has made him feel weak. Maybe he needed to exert some power over the one being in this world he'd always been certain of controlling.' Tears sprung to her eyes again. 'But I didn't let him, Maggs. I didn't let him.'

Maggs reached over and patted her knee. 'I know,' she said, nodding.

Claire took some comfort in that. She blew her nose again, used a fresh tissue to mop up her face, then heaved in a deep breath. 'What did he say to you?' she finally remembered to ask.

Maggs was silent for a moment. She looked down at the hands in her lap. 'I don't think now is the right time to tell you,' she said simply and then she looked at Claire, a gentle smile in her eyes. 'Why don't you drive me home and I'll make you a nice cup of tea?'

# Chapter Twenty-Nine

## What Does A Woman Do?

The ringing on Claire's doorbell was so insistent that she sprinted down the stairs to open the front door. When she did, she found Abby there, party dress on, make-up half done and a large brown stain spreading across her cream skirt. Abby couldn't say anything, just shook her head and looked as if she was about to burst into tears. Claire quickly leapt into action and ushered her upstairs to her flat where she let Abby borrow her dressing gown while she tried to scrub the stain out of the dress.

'What on earth is this?' she asked. 'It just won't budge!'

'Coke,' Abby said glumly. 'I had some on my dressing table while I was getting ready and I knocked it over when I was trying to put my mascara on myself.'

Claire stopped scrubbing and looked at the stain in despair. It had faded a little, but not enough, and even if she did manage to get it out, she didn't know how they were going to get the dress dry again in time for the party. She didn't have a tumble drier – which would probably have ruined this vintage dress anyway – and Abby was due at The Glass Bottom Boat in under two hours.

'I thought Kitty and Grace were going to help you?'

Abby nodded. 'They were, but it was hard enough to stay calm as it is, and they get so giggly and . . . *girly.*'

Claire smiled. She knew exactly what Abby meant.

'I asked them to show me how to do some simple make-up and I've been practising all week. Getting dressed on my own wasn't a problem. Or, at least, I didn't think it would be.'

'Come on,' Claire said, leading Abby to her bedroom, where she threw her wardrobe doors wide. 'There's got to be something in here that will work. My style's a lot less...' she searched for a word that wouldn't sound rude '. . . well, a lot *less* than Kitty's.'

It turned out that style wasn't the problem, but length and fit were. Abby was taller than Claire and much more up and down where Claire went in and out. The bits that were supposed to be filled with curves were baggy and the bits that were supposed to skim were stretched tight. After three dresses, Abby looked as if she might really cry this time.

'It's fine,' Claire said, giving her a quick hug. 'I'm going to call for reinforcements.'

She prayed silently as she dialled, hoping the magic could happen once again.

Ten minutes later, Kitty was knocking at her door with a familiar blue suitcase at her side. Claire almost didn't recognise her at first, because her face was scrubbed of make-up, her hair in a loose ponytail and she was wearing jogging bottoms and T-shirt. Kitty rolled her eyes. 'I know . . . But I was having a slobby afternoon at home while Grace is at work. Anyway, what I look like doesn't matter.' She tapped the suitcase. 'I came prepared for Plan B,' she added, with all the seriousness of a general going into battle. 'Where is she?'

Claire nodded upstairs and they both rushed up to her spare room, where Abby was waiting. 'Right,' Kitty said, looking her up and down. 'I haven't got anything as good as the white dress, but I've got a few things in here that might work. I borrowed a few pieces from my vintage shop owner friend when we were looking for that one . . .'

'Oh, Kitty,' Abby said, a tear leaking down her face as she ran up and hugged her. 'I don't know what I'd do without you!'

Kitty who was momentarily – and rather surprisingly – silenced by Abby's unexpected display of affection just mumbled, 'That's what friends are for, isn't it?'

\*

'I can't wear this!'

Claire and Kitty stood behind Abby and joined her as she looked at her reflection in the mirror. 'I admit, the other one suited you better, but it fits,' Claire said helpfully.

Abby twisted her head to look at Kitty. 'I really appreciate your help, I really do, but it's . . . it's . . .' She turned her head back to stare in the mirror.

It was a bit, Claire thought. While a similar shape to the cream dress that was now soaking in Claire's sink, this one had a large white collar and cuffs and the main fabric had a dark red background and was covered with polka dots as big as golf balls.

'We'll have to go more dramatic with the make-up, of course,' Kitty said, pulling a tube of lipstick out of her bag. Abby looked as if she was going to bolt.

'Kitty, why don't you go and put the kettle on and make us all a cup of tea,' Claire said, sitting down on the bed and gesturing for Abby to do the same. For a moment it looked as if Kitty was going to argue, but then she put her lipstick down on Claire's desk and slid from the room.

'I know this isn't what you envisioned,' Claire said to a clearly terrified-looking Abby, 'but it's a dress, and you'll only have to wear it for a few hours.'

'I—I c-can't walk down the road like this.'

'I'll give you a lift. You just have to go in and out, if you like, just let your mum see you. I'm sure she'll just be pleased you made the effort and, for what it's worth, although I know you think it's not your style, I actually think you look very pretty in it. Not many people can pull off that red, but you've got just the right skin tone.'

Abby's lips crumpled and she shook her head. 'I don't know . . .'

While Claire's heart squeezed with sympathy for Abby, she decided it was time to get a little firmer. Abby would kick herself later if she bottled out now. She waited for her to look her in the eye and then she simply said, 'I suppose it depends how badly you want those tickets.'

Claire would have offered to lend her the money to pay for them, but she had a feeling that this showdown between Abby and her mother had been a long time coming and that it was something she really needed to see through.

Abby nodded and Claire could see her mulling those words over. They sat there in silence until Kitty came back with three cups of tea on a tray. 'No offence,' Kitty said to Abby, 'but could you take the dress off before you drink yours? One vintage disaster a night is about as much as I can take.'

Abby stood up and reached for the zip at the back of her neck, but then she stopped and her hand fell to her side. 'No,' she said. 'I'm not going to take it off. I'm going to wear the bloody thing.' She looked up at Claire, a new fire in her eyes. 'Everything else in my life might be messed up at the moment, but I am flipping well going to that match!' She looked at Kitty. 'Hand me that lipstick.'

# Chapter Thirty

# Between Friends

Ellen had promised Dominic a spaghetti bolognese to make up for the one he'd missed, so on Saturday evening he found himself round at their house again. Pete was minding Sammy in the lounge while Ellen cooked and Dominic joined him. For some reason, they ended up on the floor playing with a wooden train set that had enough track to make a branch line that went out into the hall and back again. Sammy was completely absorbed, making gentle chuffing noises as he pushed his train along the track.

Pete looked across at Dominic as he tried to work out how to use up the last few pieces of unlaid track. 'Did you see the doc yesterday?'

Dominic nodded.

'What did he say?'

'It's good news, really. As long as I follow a few ground rules while I'm working and keep up with the physio exercises, he says I should be able to work soon, as long as it's nothing too extreme.'

'What does that mean for the China thing?'

'While the location's a bit exotic, the camera work

shouldn't be that strenuous. It's a history documentary, not a piece on extreme sports or Triad gangs, after all.'

'Great!' said Pete, grinning. 'So you've told the BBC guys you can do it?'

Dominic inhaled. 'Not yet.'

Pete frowned. 'I thought you were stoked about getting that job.'

'I was—I mean, I am,' Dominic said with conviction. He fiddled with the wheel on a wooden engine Sammy wasn't using. 'I just thought maybe I shouldn't jump into anything too soon, you know. Maybe I should take up the offer of doing that London-based job after all.'

Pete let the piece of track he was holding fall to the floor. 'What? The hotel thing?'

Dominic nodded.

Pete blinked, then frowned. 'But you said – and I quote – I'd hate every minute of making that film and I'll hate myself even more when it comes out and everyone sees my name attached to it!"'

The tiny wooden train became very fascinating all of a sudden. Dominic spun one of its wheels faster and faster while he thought. 'I know . . .'

'Mate? What's really going on? Is it this girl? The Doris fan?'

Dominic looked up. 'Maybe.'

Pete smiled. 'She forgave you, then? Even after you fessed up to being the neighbour from hell?'

Dominic shifted uncomfortably. 'Ah. About that . . .'

Pete stared at him. 'You haven't told her yet, have you?'

Dominic shook his head. 'Not exactly.'

Pete stood up and called to his wife in the kitchen. 'Did

you know that this plonker hasn't told that girl – Claire – who he is yet?'

Ellen appeared in the doorway a few moments later holding a wooden spoon. She gave Dominic the kind of look he'd seen her give Sammy when he'd done something sensible, like trying to flush his blankie down the toilet. 'I always used to think you weren't as much as an idiot as him,' she said, nodding towards her husband, 'but now I'm not so sure.'

'It's complicated,' he muttered. 'I am going to tell her. Soon.'

He'd made the decision days ago.

He looked from Pete to Ellen. Neither looked convinced.

'What's stopping you?' she asked.

Dominic shook his head gently. 'Nothing, really . . .'

Only the memory of how Erica had looked at him when she'd handed back his engagement ring, when she'd told him he was the last kind of man she needed. He really didn't want to see that same expression on Claire's face.

Pete picked up Dominic's phone, which he'd left on the dining table in the back half of the room and held it out. 'Come, on. Do it. Rip the plaster off.'

Dominic took the phone, but shook his head. 'I can't do it over the phone.'

'Then don't,' Ellen said, sounding firm but looking sympathetic. 'Arrange to meet her.'

He nodded. He knew it was the right thing to do. And if Claire didn't want to see him again, he could hardly blame her. It was just he was having so much fun emailing her, texting her, calling her . . . He couldn't remember when he'd last been so into someone, when the stupid little beep his phone made when a message arrived had made him grin quite so widely.

They were right, though. He woke his phone up and wandered into the hall, stood inside the loop of Sammy's branch line, while Sammy pushed a train around his feet then back into the lounge, and composed a text that read:

You know you offered to listen if I ever wanted to talk? Would you be able to meet me later? You can say where. There's good news and bad news – something I need to tell you about my girlfriend. N. x

Although he'd said all he needed to say at the moment, he kept composing the rest of the message – what he'd really wanted to say – inside his head.

*Like the fact she doesn't exist.*

*Like the fact I'd like her to be you.*

And then he stared at the back of Pete and Ellen's front door, sat, phone in hand, cold swirling around in his stomach, and waited for it to buzz its reply.

A minute later, it arrived: *Okay. I'm on my way to The Glass Bottom Boat for something else, but I could meet you outside in an hour.*

Dominic stared at it and then he walked back into the living room in a semi-daze. Both Pete and Ellen wore expectant expressions. 'Sorry, Ellie,' he said. 'Looks like I'm going to miss out on your spag bol once again.'

Ellen just walked across to him and kissed him on the cheek, then she shoved him out the door.

'Hey! It won't take me that long to walk to the pub!'

'I know,' Ellen said, starting to close it, 'but it will to

take a shower and change those ratty cargo trousers for something presentable, find a T-shirt that doesn't have a big hole in it.'

Dominic looked down rather offended. Yes, this T-shirt was a little well loved but it was his favourite. Anyway, the hole wasn't that big. More like a tiny catch. You could hardly notice it. He opened his mouth to argue, but Ellen gave him one of her looks and gently closed the door in his face.

# Chapter Thirty-One
## The Party's Over

Claire parked quite a way down the road. It was always busy here on a Saturday night and because of the party at The Glass Bottom Boat, there seemed to be fewer spaces than ever.

'Oh, man,' Abby said, as she stared out of the passenger window and looked at the pub in the distance. There were a whole lot of people milling around between here and there. She'd seemed quite confident all the way here, but now her face was looking a little pale under Kitty's foundation. 'I wish Ricky had said yes so I wouldn't have to go in there on my own.'

Claire thought for a moment. She still had twenty minutes before she'd arranged to meet Nick. 'Do you want us to walk up with you? Safety in numbers and all that?'

'Would you?'

''Course we would,' said Kitty and she winked at Abby. 'Secretly, I'm hoping to crash so I can see your mum's reaction to your dress.'

'We're not going to crash,' Claire said firmly, and instantly saw the disappointment on both Abby and Kitty's faces. 'But we could stand at the door for a few minutes, if you want us to?'

Abby nodded, her expression grateful.

'Okay, let's go then.'

When they got to the pub, Abby stopped walking. 'Crap,' she said, staring at the double doors that had been propped open with fire extinguishers. 'It's packed.'

'You'll be fine,' Claire told her, feeling a little wobble in her own stomach on Abby's behalf. This lot were rather rowdy.

Abby clutched her middle, where a wide white belt cinched in her waist. 'I think I'm going to puke.'

'Not in that dress, you don't' said Kitty quickly and rather sternly.

Abby looked up at her and nodded. 'Right.'

They pushed past the people crowding around the entrance so they were standing just inside. Claire couldn't really see much above the crush, but hoped that Abby could. 'Can you spot your mum?' she yelled above the noise.

Abby squinted and looked round the room. 'No,' Abby yelled back, looking from left to right, but then there was a loud cackle from somewhere near the bar and Abby's head snapped round. 'There she is!'

Kitty pushed herself up onto tiptoes and Claire tried to move so she could see round someone's head.

'The petite woman in leopard print, with the big hair and six-inch heels,' Abby said. Both Claire and Kitty looked back at Abby in shock. 'Yeah, I know,' she said. 'Sometimes I wonder if the stork really did bring me.'

Claire gave her a quick, one-armed hug, as much as the

space constraints would allow. 'It's your moment,' she said. 'Good luck.'

'Knock 'em dead,' Kitty said in all seriousness.

Abby nodded, took a deep breath and headed on through the crush. In the wake she created, Claire and Kitty were able to sidle a little bit closer.

Abby pushed her way to the edge of the circle of people surrounding the guest of honour and waited, but nobody said anything. Claire was trying to work out why they were all being so rude, when she realised it was just like when she'd seen Kitty on the doorstep – for a moment not even her own mother recognised Abby.

Abby stepped forward. 'Mum?'

Her mum stopped in the middle of a story and turned to face her daughter. Her face was completely blank, and then, slowly, so very slowly, recognition dawned in her eyes. 'Abby?'

Abby nodded.

Her mother looked her up and down. 'What the bloody hell are you wearing?'

'A dress,' Abby said, looking perplexed.

Claire had a bad feeling about this. She'd expected a joyful, almost tearful expression, but Abby's mum wasn't looking very happy at all. Claire tried to push a little bit closer.

Abby, whose expression had been both scared and hopeful, started to slouch and she hugged herself around her middle. 'You said you wanted me in a dress, so here I am in a dress.'

'I know I said I wanted you in a dress,' her mother said, hands on her hips, voice tense, 'and I know you didn't like the idea. But it doesn't give you the licence to come along to my birthday party and bloody take the mick!'

Abby's mouth dropped open. 'I'm not!'

'Polka dots? Little white collars? Seriously? What's wrong with a bit of Lycra, for goodness' sake? Who do you think you are? Doris bloody Day?' And then she nodded to herself. 'That's it, isn't it? You didn't like me making you go to that club and this is your way of paying me back. Well, it's not going to work, you know!'

It was at that unfortunate moment that the DJ had chosen to change tracks and her voice rang out in the silence. Everyone turned and looked at Abby. Everyone. Claire's stomach dived. She knew Abby didn't do well when cornered, and she was proved right when Abby let out a string of rather unladylike words.

Her mother stared at her, face rigid, and then she began to shake. She thumped the woman standing next to her on the arm while still keeping her eyes on her daughter. 'Give me my handbag.'

The woman handed it over.

Her mother rummaged inside and then produced the pair of tickets Abby had been dreaming about all these months. Then, carefully and very deliberately, she gripped them in her blood-red talons and tore them in two.

'No!' Abby shouted and dived for the pieces, but they'd fluttered to the floor and were now being kicked this way and that by the rest of her mother's guests.

She stood up again and looked at her mum. 'I hate you,' she yelled, just before the music started up again, and then she pushed her way through the crowd and out the door with something approaching superhuman strength. It must have been, because Claire tried to follow and found herself blocked in.

She looked this way and that, searching for a better exit route, and that's when her eyes locked with those of the guest of honour. Abby's mum's eyes narrowed and she started marching towards her.

'You put her up to this, didn't you? You and that sad little club of yours!' she spat at Claire. 'You helped her.'

'Yes, we did,' Claire said, any wobble that had been in her stomach gone. She pulled herself up taller. 'And I'm proud of it. That girl tried really, really hard to impress you. You have no idea how scared she was to come in here and face you and all your friends, and you threw it all back in her face! You should be ashamed of yourself – at the very least you should have let her explain.'

The other woman put her hands on her hips. 'Oh, should I?'

Claire just raised her eyebrows and let the other woman work it out for herself.

'Well, there's something else I should do, because I don't think I remember inviting you to my party.'

'Don't worry,' Claire said, as she turned towards the door. 'I'm going.' And the stunned crowed parted before her like the Red Sea until she reached the door.

When she walked into the cold night air, her heart was pounding, partly from the adrenalin rush of the confrontation, but partly because she was just so angry on Abby's behalf, especially because she knew what it was like to have a parent who judged you and found you wanting, no matter how hard you tried.

Kitty was already outside the pub, looking up and down the street.

'Did you see which way she went?' Claire asked.

Kitty shook her head.

'You go that way,' Claire said pointing to the left, 'and I'll go the other.'

Claire checked the alley down the side of the pub and found no trace of Abby, but then she had a brainwave. She crossed the road and headed into the park, towards where the football goals were. When she was maybe thirty feet away she started to wonder if she could see a group of large white dots collected near one of the goalposts and, when she got closer, she realised she was right.

'Oh, Abby,' she said and drew the girl into a hug. Abby was stiff against her. 'Do you want me to take you home? I'll have to find Kitty first, though.'

'Kitty's right here,' a voice said behind her, slightly breathlessly. 'I saw you going into the park and followed.'

Abby peeled herself away from Claire. 'I don't want to go home. Ever.'

Claire decided not to push the point, even if she knew Abby would have to set foot across her own doorstep at some point.

'You can come back and stay at mine and Grace's,' Kitty said firmly. 'We were going to have a Katherine Hepburn movie marathon when she got in from work, and I'm positive she won't mind.'

'Are you sure?' Abby said hopefully.

Kitty nodded. 'Cross my heart,' she said, drawing one glossy nail across her ratty T-shirt. 'You can kip on the sofa.'

Abby closed her eyes. 'Do you think I could go to sleep and wake up somewhere else, better still, *someone* else?'

'If you lie still long enough, Grace will probably give you a makeover,' Kitty said. 'Does that count?'

For the first time in what seemed like months, although it was actually probably only an hour, Abby smiled. 'Can't hurt to try,' she said, as she Kitty and Claire walked back across the park towards the gate.

# Chapter Thirty-Two

## It's Better to Conceal Than Reveal

Dominic waited for Claire outside The Glass Bottom Boat. He couldn't go inside, because there was some kind of private party going on, and he couldn't see her anywhere. He'd tried texting a few times and had even left a voice message, but she wasn't answering her phone.

Finally, after he'd been standing there ten minutes, he saw her walking up the street towards him. She was wearing a simple yellow dress and she looked like a ray of sunshine in gloomy shadow cast by the tatty old pub.

She spotted him and smiled. His stomach lurched, half in anticipation, half in fear. He had no idea how the end of this evening would turn out.

'Sorry I'm late,' she said, sounding a little breathless. 'Had a bit of a crisis.'

He frowned. 'Everything okay?'

She nodded. 'Yes. For now, anyway. But what about you?' There was concern in her eyes and it made everything about her look soft. 'You said you needed to talk. Has something happened?'

He shook his head. 'Not really. Look, this isn't a great

place to chat.' Loud music was pumping from inside the pub and noisy party guests kept spilling out or barging their way back in again. 'There's that new wine bar a couple of minutes away. Shall we go there?'

The wine bar was also busy, but thankfully, instead of The Glass Bottom Boat's dingy yard, it had a large garden outside, filled with tables and chairs, potted olive trees and topiaries. They found a recently vacated table in the far corner, just big enough for two. A large row of lavender bushes gave them a little privacy.

'I still owe you that wine,' he said, as she sat down.

'Wine would be lovely.' She smiled, but he could see the worry in her eyes. It didn't help that he knew things were going to get even tougher here on in. He headed off to the bar and his nerves grew the whole time he was standing there.

When he returned to the courtyard, Claire was staring into space. To the casual observer, she'd look perfectly content, he supposed, but there was something about the way she was so still that told him things weren't right. Usually, she looked bright and alert, ready to break into a smile at the slightest opportunity. This evening she looked as if something invisible and heavy was sitting around her shoulders.

He put a glass of questionable Pinot Grigio down in front of her. 'What was this crisis? Can I do anything to help?'

She inhaled sharply, as if he'd surprised her, and turned to face him. 'What?'

He sat down and placed his pint on the table. 'You look as if something is bothering you.'

She shook her head. 'No. Tonight's crisis wasn't mine, thank goodness, but you're right – I have been feeling a little off-kilter for weeks, but you're only the second person who's seen beneath my attempt to cover it up.'

'Who was the first?' For some reason he was instantly and intensely jealous of that person.

'My grandmother's best friend.'

'Ah.' He dialled his memory back, remembered a feisty little old lady who'd often visited Laurie – he'd remembered her name now – and had once given him a flea in his ear for leaving muddy bike tracks in the hallway. Suddenly, he wasn't quite so jealous any more.

'So what is this thing you're trying to cover up?'

She shook her head. 'I thought I was supposed to be here to listen to your problems, not the other way round.'

'And I thought friendship was supposed to be a mutual thing, share and share alike?' Okay, that wasn't quite the right expression, but she got his meaning. At least, he thought she did, as her elusive smile made a brief appearance.

'We're friends?'

Yes, he realised. They were. He nodded.

He wasn't quite sure how that happened. Usually, he had girlfriends and he had girls who were friends. Women fell into one camp or the other with him. Somehow, it didn't surprise him that Claire had been the one to straddle the line.

His non-verbal answer seemed to be good enough for Claire, because she started to talk. She started to tell him about what she'd done the day before, a visit to a nursing home to meet a man she hadn't seen in more than twenty years, and then the whole story of her childhood came out, thick and fast.

'I just can't seem to stop being angry with him,' she

finished quietly. She'd been staring at the table, and when she looked up at him he could see that her eyes were large and glossy. On instinct, he got up, circled the table to where she was, crouched down and put his arms around her. She burrowed her face into his neck.

For a while they stayed like that, breathing together, and then Claire pulled back. 'So,' she said, trying to surreptitiously wipe a bit of moisture away from the corner of her eye with her finger. 'That's my life story. Now it's your turn. Starting with this good news of yours.'

Dominic didn't answer straight away. For some reason the residual sheen of a mopped-up tear on her cheek hit him like a punch in the gut. He tore his eyes away from that damp patch and refocused.

The words were there in his head – the truth – but he couldn't seem to unlock his teeth and let them out. He returned to his seat, where he inhaled and then slowly exhaled. 'My good news is that I don't have a girlfriend.' He searched her face, looking for a sign that he hadn't read her all wrong. 'At least, I hope that's good news for you.'

'Oh.' Claire couldn't have looked more shocked if he'd told her he did lion taming in his spare time. 'You broke up?'

Dominic started feel queasy. 'Not exactly.'

Okay, this was it. Now or never.

How he wished he had a magic remote control, one that would let him fast-forward over the next few minutes so it would all be over. He leaned forward, made sure he looked Claire squarely in the eyes.

'I never had a girlfriend.'

Claire almost choked on her wine. 'You mean you're a – that you've never even . . .'

'No! I mean, not that. I mean I have had girlfriends. In the past. Lots of them.'

He closed his eyes. Oh, hell. This was not the clear and precise speech he'd hoped he'd give at this moment. Claire was looking at him, eyebrows raised. He was hoping he could see a glimmer of amusement behind her surprise, but maybe that was just wishful thinking.

He took a deep breath, tried again. ' I mean that I didn't have a girlfriend when I came to see you at your shop.'

'Oh!' The little wrinkle above her nose deepened. 'Then why did you say you did?'

There was no way to make himself look good in this scenario, was there? No way to spin it. He might as well just give it to her straight. All his efforts to be clever about it – good news and bad news, and all that rubbish – had only got him into trouble anyway.

'Actually, I didn't say that I did. You assumed and I just . . . Well, I just didn't correct you.'

Claire looked as if she was trying to do a particularly difficult bit of long division inside her head. 'Why on earth not?'

He started to laugh, a low, dry sound, and the worst possible thing he could do at that moment, but he couldn't seem to help himself. 'Because booking a trip was a good excuse to see you again, but I didn't realise you specialised in romantic holidays, so when you said that, it kind of caught me on the hop.' He shielded his eyes with his hand. 'And I didn't want you to think I was a complete idiot, so I just went along with it.'

Claire folded her arms. 'And how did that work out for you?'

He removed his hand from his eyes and looked at her. 'Fabulously. Can't you tell?'

His attempt at a bit of self-deprecating humour fell completely flat. Claire just blinked. Her arms remained firmly crossed.

'Listen, I know it was stupid thing to do and I know I should have told you sooner – I even tried to the day I bumped into you at the newsagent's, but you got called away . . .' He paused, took a breath. Collected himself. 'But I like you, Claire, and there's more to the story. I wanted you to see I wasn't such an idiot before I came clean and you started looking at me the way you are now.'

Claire's eyeballs moved side to side, as if she was replaying images and conversations inside her head.

'I'm sorry I lied to you, Claire, even by omission. You know me well enough by now to know that sometimes I jump into things with both feet without always thinking. I don't do it because it's part of some big master plan.' He gave an exasperated sigh. 'I do it because I'm a total numpty.'

There. Right there. One corner of her lips twitched a microscopic amount. He had no idea why his total and utter humiliation pleased this woman so much. If he was sensible, he ought to run screaming from the pub right now. However, he'd already proved quite nicely that he was nothing of the sort.

She didn't say anything for a few seconds. For a moment, he thought she was going to make a joke, but then she started frowning again. 'I don't get it,' she said slowly. 'All those emails . . . All those questions I sent you! If this girlfriend of yours was a complete invention, who the heck were you talking about?'

He exhaled again and his shoulders sagged. 'You.'

Claire froze, her eyes wide.

Dominic didn't know what to make of that. When she didn't move, didn't speak, he decided to give her some space. He walked away to the back of the garden, where there was a small raised flowerbed full of plants that smelled nice in the warm evening breeze.

A moment later, he heard movement behind him. He turned round and found Claire standing there. He couldn't read the expression on her face. She didn't look confused any more, but she didn't look cross either. He was just wondering what stupid thing would come out of his mouth next when she saved him from himself.

She did that by stepping forward, closing the distance between them and kissing him.

*

Claire had not planned on doing this. But here she was, kissing Nick, and she had to say she wasn't regretting her decision much. If at all.

After a second of frozen surprise, his arms had come round her and she'd leaned into him. It had been a long time since she'd kissed or been kissed. The last man had been Philip, and he'd always been a little bit full on – too clingy, too affectionate. Maybe she'd felt that way because there had always been a hidden agenda with him. A kiss had never been a simple kiss.

But this kiss right now? Simply lovely.

Because Nick hadn't hidden anything from her, had he?

Not only did she know there was a better man that hid beneath the 'wandering soul' persona he used as a disguise so well, but he'd come clean with her, been totally honest. She'd been able to see it in his eyes. Either that, or he'd chosen the wrong profession and should have been a multi-Oscar winning actor instead.

That's why she'd kissed him. Because she was attracted to him, yes, but also because he was the first man she could remember in a long time who'd willingly let her see beneath his walls. That alone deserved some kind of reward.

When she pulled away, she rested her forehead against his. 'Wow,' she whispered softly.

She felt rather than heard his grunt of gruff laughter. 'You're not kidding.'

And then lips met lips again. Claire let go, just sunk into it. It was only as she did so that she realised just how tired she'd become keeping a tight grip of control of everything in her life, of how nice it was to let it all fall in a heap at her feet and forget about it.

She'd been feeling so raw since that meeting with her father, and this was the perfect salve, the perfect way to help her forget about scheming, manipulating men who only wanted to trick women, who only wanted to push them around for fun.

He pulled back. 'Claire? About the other thing—'

She placed a finger over his lips. 'No,' she whispered, looking him right in the eye. 'No bad news. Not tonight. Please? I've had enough to deal with this week already.'

'But—'

She shook her head and shut him up with another kiss. 'Save it for another day.'

# Chapter Thirty-Three

# I Love the Way You Say Goodnight

This time, when Dominic walked Claire home, it took a lot longer. Mainly because they stopped at every other street light to kiss. She kept smiling at him. A smile he hadn't seen before. A smile that made him want to start dancing like that guy from *Singing in the Rain*, even though there wasn't a cloud in the warm summer night sky. He frowned for a moment. Was Doris Day in *Singing in the Rain*? He wasn't sure.

They talked as they walked too. 'Forget your father,' he told her. 'The man obviously has mental problems if he doesn't want you in his life. If he doesn't get down on his knees and beg you for forgiveness, he's a goddam fool.'

Claire responded to this by grabbing hold of his T-shirt and pulling him towards her and kissing him again. He grinned stupidly back at her. He liked seeing her happy, and it made his chest swell a little – and his head, maybe, but he wasn't going to admit to that – to think that he'd helped lift her mood. It wasn't often that he managed to say the right thing to a woman at the right time, but with Claire somehow it was getting easier and easier.

Even with all the unplanned stops, they reached their shared front gate way sooner than he wanted to.

He very much wanted to tell her everything, he realised. This pretence felt like a heavy winter coat he was stifling under, one that he couldn't wait to shrug off.

But not tonight. He was going to respect her wishes. She needed a breather, time to think and regroup. Tonight he would be the perfect gentleman. He walked her to the gate, kissed her thoroughly but didn't push for an invitation inside, and this time, when she finally closed the door behind her, instead of sneaking in after her he kept on walking.

Ten minutes later, he was back at Pete and Ellen's. Pete answered. He was wearing his pyjamas. 'Sorry, buddy!' Dominic said, looking at his watch. Crikey! Was that the time?

Pete yawned but motioned for him to come inside. 'No problems,' he muttered. 'I hadn't gone to bed yet. Ellie's gone up, but I was watching *Die Hard*.'

Through the backs of your eyelids, by the looks of it, thought Dominic, but he didn't say so. Pete grabbed him a beer from the fridge and they sat down in the dark, only the flickering blue light from the TV screen to light them, and watched in silence while Bruce Willis took on a tower block full of terrorists single-handed. And barefoot.

When the adverts came on Pete, still staring at the screen, said, 'It didn't go to well, huh?'

Dominic swigged his beer bottle back. 'What makes you think it went badly?'

Pete turned to face him. 'Mate . . . You've arrived unannounced at close to midnight and you're being awkward as hell.'

Dominic allowed himself a small smile. 'Well, if by badly you mean kissing her, then I suppose it went terribly.'

Pete slapped him on the back. 'All right!' Then the grin slid from his face as he took a long hard look at his best friend. 'So why aren't you doing a Tom Cruise and jumping up and down on my sofa?'

'I am excited, it's just . . . I still haven't told her everything and I promised myself I would before I let anything happen between us.'

'Hang on, rewind,' Pete said, suddenly looking very serious. 'You haven't told her everything?'

Dominic shook his head again. 'I tried. I got as far as debunking the mythical girlfriend and then she kissed me, and then she asked me not to tell her any more. So we just kept on kissing.'

Pete sighed. 'You tell a woman you've been lying to her for weeks, inventing a fake life, and her first reaction is to kiss you? Mate, if I could bottle what you've got I'd be a rich man!'

Dominic frowned. 'You're making it sound worse than it is. Anyway, do you think I've overstepped the mark?'

'Nah,' said Pete, who now had one eye on the TV screen, because the adverts had finished and Bruce had made a reappearance. 'She kissed you first. Not your fault. End of.'

Dominic nodded. There was that. Technically, he was in the clear.

Then why did 'technically' make him feel a little bit slimy?

'Wanna crash here the night?' Pete asked.

'Could I? It would be much easier than trying to creep around and not bump into Claire in the hallway.'

'Sure. You can have the sofa.' Pete turned to him and grinned. 'But not yet, right? Cos *Die Hard II* is on straight after this.'

Dominic grinned back and they clinked beer bottles.

'Tell her tomorrow,' Pete said matter-of-factly, more of his attention on Bruce Willis – who was tying up a bad guy, dressing him up as Santa and sending him down in the lift with a message to the baddies written across his chest – than on his best friend.

'That's what she said . . . just about. I want to, but I'm just not sure it's the right thing.'

'Really?' Pete mumbled, not taking his eyes from the screen.

Dominic nodded. 'There's this whole thing with her father.' He glanced across at Pete and decided going into detail would be a lost cause. 'It's complicated. I don't want to make things worse for her. I think she's going to be upset when I come clean, and she's got enough on her plate to deal with at the moment, you know?'

Pete grunted his agreement.

'But *not* telling her could be a huge mistake. What do you think I should do?'

Pete didn't answer for a moment.

Dominic stopped watching the TV and looked at his best friend. 'Pete? Are you listening?'

Pete nodded. 'Of course.'

Dominic raised his eyebrows. 'Then what did I just say?'

'Don't tell her and save her feelings or do tell her and make her upset,' Pete reeled off.

Dominic glared at him. He hated it when Pete did that. He knew it drove Ellen nuts as well. Pete had a point, though.

His no-frills summary had clarified things very nicely. 'So you don't think I should tell her the rest, then? Not yet?'

Pete shook his head and flinched as another bad guy took a bullet.

Dominic nodded to himself. Okay, he felt better about it now. While he didn't like lying to Claire, he was doing this for her, and that was what she'd been teaching him, hadn't it? To think about what the woman in his life needed and act on it?

'Got any leftovers of that bolognese?' he asked Pete.

Pete nodded. 'Fridge,' he all but grunted, and Dominic got up and headed towards the kitchen.

Upstairs, Ellen lay sleeping, the sheet thrown off her, totally unaware of the advice her husband was dispensing in her absence. Had she been privy to it, though, she might well have rolled her eyes and said, 'Oh, Pete . . . What on earth have you gone and done this time?'

*

Claire couldn't sleep. She was sitting up in her bed, pretending she was reading a book, but actually she was just sitting there, grinning. She couldn't keep this to herself any longer. She picked up her phone and fired off a quick text to Peggy. Thankfully, there was a good chance she'd get a reply. Peggy was a bit of a night owl. There was no point disturbing Candy, because she had probably fallen into bed not long after her kids.

*You'll never guess what!* she typed, knowing Peggy would never be able to resist such a text, even if she was sleepy.

*What?!!* came back, almost instantly.

Claire grinned to herself. The lovely warm feeling inside kept on growing. *I saw loverboy tonight.*

The next text was pure Peggy. *!!??!!?* While she was still chuckling about it, another one arrived: *Is that good or bad?*

*Good,* Claire replied. *Definitely good.* And then she decided to put poor Peggy out of her misery. *He hasn't got a girlfriend.*

She could feel the stunned silence at Peggy's end. She recovered a few seconds later, though. *He chucked her?*

Claire inhaled. There was no easy way to explain the conversation she'd had with Nick this evening via text, so she decided to leave the explanations for later and just stick to the juicy details.

*Long story . . .*

*But he kissed me.*

Peggy sent back a string of characters that Claire couldn't understand. She twisted her phone ninety degrees to see if that helped, but eventually she gave in and just sent a message back saying, *Huh?*

*I was trying to do an emoticon version of me fainting,* Peggy replied, *but it obvs lost something in translation.*

*But OMG!!!*

Claire just grinned at her phone. Indeed. She waited, knowing the full inquisition would soon start.

*Was it good?*

*Is he still gorgeous?*

*Did you ask him inside?*

And there it was. *Yes, yes and no*, she replied, and then they spent the next ten minutes messaging back and forth until Claire was yawning hard and going cross-eyed trying to focus on her phone screen.

She said her goodbyes to Peggy, turned off the light and snuggled down into her pillows, still smiling, but after a few seconds she sat bolt upright again, her eyes wide.

Oh my goodness!

She'd been so caught up in walking home with Nick and all that delicious kissing that she'd totally forgotten she'd left her car parked down the road from The Glass Bottom Boat!

# Chapter Thirty-Four

# The Thrill of It All

The following Tuesday, Claire, Peggy and Candy met early before the film club meeting. They ordered drinks and then took them to the upper room, where they could talk undisturbed for a while. Claire filled them in on all the details of her evening with Nick.

Peggy frowned when Claire told them about the whole 'fake girlfriend' business. 'Hmm,' she said. 'I still think that all sounds a bit fishy.'

'Aw, no,' Candy replied. 'I think it's sweet. He can't think straight when he's around her.'

Claire looked from one to the other. 'I know.'

'Who are you agreeing with?' Peggy asked. 'Me, or her?'

'Both of you.'

Candy and Peggy looked at her funny.

'What I mean is that I feel a bit the same way. It was very sweet, but it also . . . I dunno . . . rang some of my alarm bells. That's why I wanted to ask your advice about something.'

'Fire away,' Peggy said.

'Of course,' Candy replied.

Claire folded her hands on the table in front of her as the other two leaned in. 'I want to know if you think I should invite him to the Doris Day Film Club. Next week. Or do you think that'll scare him off?'

Peggy and Candy looked at each other and then back at Claire.

'Erm . . . Is it really his kind of thing?' Candy asked. 'He sounds a bit more of an action man than a sit indoors and watch films kind of guy.'

Claire shifted in her seat. 'I really don't know, but I have to admit, I have an ulterior motive for asking.'

Peggy grinned. 'Ooh, do tell!'

'Well, everything inside me is telling me this is the real deal, that I should go for it . . .'

'But?' Candy said.

Claire looked at her. 'But I keep thinking about how my "man radar" is broken, that I really can't trust my own instincts. That's why I need you – both of you and the rest of the Doris Day Film Club – to help me. I might not be able to tell fact from fiction where a good-looking man is concerned, but I trust you lot to do it for me.'

Candy sipped her wine. 'In that case, I think you should definitely bring him.'

'Me too,' Peggy said, 'and it has nothing at all to do with the fact I'm *dying* of curiosity to see who this god of a man is!'

'So . . . It's kind of like a test,' Candy said slowly.

Claire nodded. 'Exactly. If he passes, then I know I can take things to the next level without getting all paranoid and suspicious.' Then she'd really be able to let her whole self go where her heart wanted to drag her.

It wasn't long before the rest of the film club members started arriving and Claire got this week's selection out: *The Thrill of It All.* She was definitely ready to see a light, frothy – in more ways than one – romantic comedy. The way she'd been feeling since Saturday night had almost erased the memory of that visit with her father. Almost.

Claire was pleased to that Abby had returned to the scene of Saturday night's crime and had come along to watch the film. The pain of her mother's outburst must still be pretty fresh because, as far as Claire could gather, Abby hadn't been home since and was still staying with Kitty and Grace.

However, living with the two girls was obviously having a positive effect on her – at least in the fashion department. Today, she looked comfortable in skinny jeans and a T-shirt that didn't totally swamp her athletic frame. Grace had been right. Abby really did have great legs, and was that a bit of mascara Claire could detect on her eyelashes?

They were just about to get going when there was a knock on the door. All of the film club members looked at each other. They were all here. Who on earth could that be?

Claire got up and opened the door. She found one of Abby's 'lads' standing there, the tall one. She cleared her throat and stepped aside. 'Abby? I think there's someone here to see you.'

Abby looked up from where she was sitting and her mouth dropped open. 'Ricky! What are you doing here?'

'I came to see you.'

She shook her head in disbelief. 'Here? Now?'

'Well, you haven't been answering your messages and when I called at yours, your mum slammed the door in my face. Apparently, I'm in trouble for something.'

Abby grunted. 'That makes two of us!'

He grinned at her and she smiled grudgingly back at him. Claire could clearly see the strong friendship between them, along with a little flash of something more, but then Abby seemed to remember that she was upset with him and her smile faded. 'It's not the right time,' she said, shaking her head. 'I can't deal with all of the stuff with my mum *and* you right now.'

Ricky, too, stopped smiling. 'Please?' he said.

Abby's eyes were large, but her mouth was a thin line and she shook her head.

Ricky stepped forward. 'I came to your mum's party, you know, but by the time I'd got there, everyone said you'd left and I couldn't find you. I looked for ages.'

Abby's eyes grew even wider. 'You did?'

'Oh, go on,' Maggs said, giving Abby a nudge. 'Give the poor lad a chance!'

Kitty, Grace and even Peggy shuffled a little further forward on their chairs. Claire narrowed her eyes at them. 'Why don't you two do this in private,' she suggested and quickly shooed them out the door.

'Spoilsport,' Peggy said.

Claire gave her a look that she'd inherited from her grandmother. 'You should know better.'

'It's okay,' Kitty squeaked excitedly. 'He's taken her outside and they're standing right under the windows. Look!'

'Kitty!' Claire began to say, but she was drowned out by the stampede as the rest of the film club members – including Candy, even though she hung back a little – fought for position at one of the two sash windows. Claire sighed and shook her head. It seemed, when it all boiled down to it, they were all joined by their love of a good romance. She sidled a little closer. Just to make sure everyone was behaving themselves, of course.

'He's saying he's sorry,' Kitty yelled over her shoulder, 'and that she looked very pretty in that dress the other week.'

There was a murmur of agreement from the film club, but they hushed again quickly so Kitty could give them the next instalment.

'And he's saying he's sorry for being such an idiot . . . That he was scared when he thought their friendship might change . . .'

'Aw,' Candy said, turning to look at Claire. 'That's so sweet! I hope my boys are like that when they're old enough to have girlfriends.'

'Shhh!' Maggs said, giving her friendly elbow.

Kitty held up a hand. 'She's speaking now . . . She's saying that she just needed to show him she was a girl . . . Awww.'

'What?' said Grace sharply, who was squeezed in behind Kitty and couldn't hear as well. 'Don't just go "awww"! Tell us what he blooming said!'

'All right, Grace. Don't get your frilly vintage knickers in a twist! He just said he *always* knew she was a girl – Ooh! Look! Now they're kissing!'

Everyone pressed forward again and there was a round of applause. Claire was worried someone was going to tumble out of the window and onto the pavement below, and she was worried that someone was probably going to be Kitty, because everything upwards from her hips was leaning out the window and, with those boobs, she was a little top-heavy.

She moved a little closer and hooked a finger under Kitty's

wide red belt, just to make sure, and, as she did so, she took the opportunity to rise onto her tiptoes and take a peek herself.

Yep. Abby and Ricky were definitely kissing.

# Chapter Thirty-Five

## The Man Who Knew Too Much

'Are you sure you want to do this?' Claire looked steadily at Nick, trying to detect a flicker of fear, any hint that he was lying to her, but she saw nothing.

He shrugged and smiled at her. 'Why not?'

Why not indeed. She had no idea why she was so nervous about this, no idea at all.

'Okay. Let's go then.'

She took a deep breath and headed up the narrow and winding staircase at the back of The Glass Bottom Boat. She pushed the door to the upper room open and was met with a sea of smiling, happy faces.

'Hey, everyone,' Claire said in a rush. 'Sorry I'm a little late!'

'Only five minutes late,' Maggs said from her vice-president's chair.

Claire fussed with her DVD case as she put it down on the table. 'Yes, I know, but still late. However,' she said, turning to Nick, 'I have a good reason. I've brought a guest. I hope you don't mind.'

'We totally don't mind,' Peggy said, grinning.

'This is Nick.'

Nick waved at the group. 'Hi,' he said. 'This is my first time, so be gentle with me.'

That earned him a collective chuckle and even more smiles.

'Are you a new member?' George asked, looking quite serious. Claire wasn't sure if he was feeling territorial or glad of some male company.

'Give the guy a chance. He's only just got here. Let's just say he's an interested visitor, and why don't we at least let him see a film before he makes up his mind?'

Most of the group nodded.

Kitty piped up, a naughty twinkle in her eye. 'I don't 'spose you need a dress too, do you?' And then she whispered to Grace, 'I wouldn't mind getting him down to his underwear!' Unfortunately, Kitty's version of 'subtle' was one step down from using a loud hailer, and half the room heard her, including Claire. She didn't dare look at Nick.

Grace dug Kitty firmly in the ribs with her elbow and blushed a fierce red. It was the first time Claire had ever seen her look so flustered. 'Shut up!' she whispered back.

'What?' Kitty mouthed at her. 'Just sayin'!'

Claire slipped her arm through Nick's and closed the distance between them. 'Anyway, I hope you'll all give Nick a warm Doris Day Film Club welcome.'

There was a chorus of 'Hi's, 'Hello's and 'Welcome's from around the room.

'Hey, Abby,' Claire said, seeing her sitting next to Kitty and Grace and looking very pretty, with her hair pulled back off her face and yet another new pair of skinny jeans on. 'How are you?'

'Great,' Abby said, both beaming and blushing.

Claire smiled. 'I take it things are going well with Ricky?'

Abby blushed harder. 'And not just that . . .' She reached into her back pocket and produced a pair of tickets, which she flourished proudly.

Claire's mouth dropped open. 'But I saw your mum tear them up!'

Abby nodded. 'Ricky convinced me to talk to her, and we cleared a few things up. She even said sorry for what she said at the party, then yesterday she came up to my room and gave me these.'

'I thought you said it was all sold out?'

Abby shrugged. 'Mum wouldn't say how she got them, only that she "called in a few favours". I don't really care how she did it, as long as Ricky and I can go together.'

Claire smiled. 'I'm so glad it all turned out well in the end. You know what,' she said to everyone, 'as a club we did a great job helping Abby. I think that deserves a round of drinks to celebrate. What does everyone want?'

She spent the next five minutes taking orders and then nipped downstairs. When she returned with a barman in tow carrying a tray of drinks, everyone cheered. Claire looked for Nick. He was deep in conversation with George, Maggs and Bev, and all three of the old generation of the film club were smiling and laughing as he told them about a trip to Morocco that had gone terribly wrong.

That gave Claire an idea about what film they should watch that evening. They had been planning on *The Ballad of Josie* – not one of her favourites, but you had to give them all a fair go – but suddenly she realised she wanted Nick to be impressed by Doris, to see her as a serious actress as well as a bright and bubbly musical star.

She sat down next to him. He didn't miss a beat telling his story, but the smile he gave her made her stomach do a perfect triple somersault.

'So what do you do, Nick?' Maggs asked.

'He's a journalist,' Claire said proudly. 'Does travel pieces.'

Much to his surprise, Nick shook his head, but he had just taken a sip of his drink, so she had to wait for him to swallow it before he could give a proper answer.

'You're not? I thought Jayce Ryder wanted you to do a "piece" on The Hamilton?'

Nick swallowed. 'He did.'

How had she not known this? How had she managed, once again, to jump to conclusions without even digging deeper? Mind you, when they chatted they tended to talk about her work more than his. Why hadn't she noticed that either? And on the few occasions he'd told work stories, the details had fitted within her idea of what he did well enough for her not to ask more questions. For some reason, the fact she'd missed this made her feel more than a tad uneasy.

They all looked at him, waiting for him to say more. Claire could see he was weighing something up very seriously. Finally, he nodded, almost to himself, and looked her in the eye. 'I do tell stories about the places I visit. Let's just say they're more visual than verbal.'

He was watching her closely, as if he was waiting for something to happen, for a particular response. Claire wracked her brains. 'Like a photographer?'

'Kind of.'

He kept looking at her intently, as if he was willing her to understand something. It was making her nervous. And when Claire was nervous, she had a tendency to do one of two things: clam up or babble. Unfortunately, on this occasion she seemed unable to do anything but the latter.

'That's so cool! I've always thought what a wonderful job that must be. Oh, the things you must have seen! Have I seen your pictures anywhere? Hey, Peggy,' she called across the room, 'isn't Nicole's husband a photographer too? What's his name?'

Peggy gave her a strange look. 'Alex Black,' she replied slowly.

'Oh, yes! That's him.' Claire tuned back to Nick. 'Have you met him? Alex Black?'

Nick's eyes were a little wide and he was staring at her too. 'No, but I've heard of him.'

'He's married to Peggy's business partner,' Claire said, totally aware her mouth had run away with her, but powerless to apply the brakes. 'He does landscapes, mostly British—'

Maggs cut her off. 'Good for him,' she said firmly. 'Now, do you think we're in danger of watching a film tonight, or are we going to spend the whole evening extolling the virtues of Peggy's friend's husband?'

Claire could have kissed Maggs.

'Yes. Yes, of course.' She stood up and walked over to her DVD case. 'Change of plan, if everyone's happy? How about *The Man Who Knew Too Much*?'

There was a firm and loud murmur of agreement, much to Claire's relief. A few moments later, the lights were off and the credits were rolling. She sat down between Nick and Maggs, feeling slightly out of breath and settled down to watch Hitchcock's classic thriller.

Maggs leaned in close and nodded towards their guest. 'I reckon he's a keeper,' she whispered in Claire's ear. She could see Candy and Peggy sitting next to each other, both gave her thumbs-up signs.

Claire's heart rate slowed further. She made herself breathe in and out slowly. Yes, he was, wasn't he? He'd charmed them all – every single member of the Doris Day Film Club – which meant he'd passed her little test with flying colours. She settled down to watch the film knowing she shouldn't really feel quite so scared any more.

*

Dominic was starting to get scared. Not because Claire had almost stumbled upon part of the truth, but because she hadn't. It was as if she hadn't wanted to go down the trail of breadcrumbs he was trying to lay out for her.

He watched the family on the screen talking to someone in the back of a bus, but really didn't pay much attention to what was being said. He'd waited too long, hadn't he? He shouldn't have been such a coward.

It was just the more time he'd spent with her over the last week or so, the more he'd come to realise how seeing her father again had shaken her up. At the time he'd told himself he was protecting her, but now he was starting to wonder if it was because he was chicken.

And yet he still couldn't tell her. Not yet.

Earlier on that afternoon he'd called the BBC documentary team and had let them know he was just about fit and able. Pete had been right – he'd have hated himself if he'd done

Ryder's thing – and he knew he couldn't stay in London indefinitely. It was time to go back to his real life, see if he could try and merge it with the new one he was building for himself at home too.

Only, the director had some surprising news of his own. The job was still Dominic's if he wanted it, but the schedule had changed, something to do with filming permissions and needing to grab a window of opportunity before it closed. They were going to Yangcheng three weeks early. If he said yes, he had to fly out tomorrow.

So how could he come clean to Claire now? He couldn't drop a bombshell like that and run, leave her to stew on it for a month before he returned.

He glanced across at her as she watched the film. Her features were lit with the soft blue light from the TV screen. She was totally absorbed in the unfolding story. He didn't think he'd ever met anyone quite like her. Forget about Doris Day. He reckoned he could sit here all night and look at Claire and he wouldn't get bored.

Eventually, he managed to tear his eyes from her and focus his attention back on the screen, knowing that was what she wanted. It turned out to be a really good film, a tense thriller about an ordinary couple caught up in an assassination plot with an exciting and dramatic climax. He also hadn't realised this was the film that had made 'Que Sera, Sera' a hit. He'd have put money on the fact it had come from a cheesy musical or something like that.

They stayed and chatted some more to the rest of the group after the film had ended. He had to admit he was surprised by the diversity of the Doris Day Film Club members – old and young, male and female, well-off and not so well-off.

They were an interesting bunch. He could see why Claire was so enthusiastic about her hobby and why she threw herself into her role as president whole-heartedly.

They walked back to Claire's house afterwards. It seemed so familiar, so natural now to walk this way with her that he could hardly believe the first time had only been four weeks ago. He felt as if he'd known her for years.

As always, he walked her to the gate but stopped shy of going up the path to the front door. He looked down at her, wondering how on earth he was going to break the news. He wanted to tell her the truth – the whole truth – so badly it hurt. He was so tired of papering over his own cracks, of running, scared that if he slowed down and someone took a really good look at him, they wouldn't like what they saw.

'Claire? I've got something to tell you . . . not great news.'

She smiled at him.

'I've had a call from some colleagues of mine,' he told her. 'I've been offered a job.'

Her expression didn't change. 'The sort of thing you do is freelance, right? You have to take the opportunities when they come?'

'Yes,' he replied. 'I do. I need the money and the profile this one will give me. Hopefully, it'll take me to the next level of my career.'

Claire hugged him tighter. He could feel her grinning against his neck. 'But that's good, isn't it? I thought you said this was bad news.'

He peeled himself away from her, looked her in the eye so she could see everything he was thinking and feeling. 'I catch a flight to Shanghai tomorrow. I'll be gone for four and a half weeks.'

That was the arrow that pierced her smile and sent it fluttering to the ground. 'Oh.' For a long time she didn't say anything and then she pulled him towards her and delivered the sweetest, sexiest kiss yet. It was a double-edged sword, because he knew he didn't deserve it.

'Nick?' she whispered. 'As romantic as this is, kissing at the gate like teenagers, one day you're going to have to come inside.'

He froze. *Don't say it,* he begged her silently. *Don't make this harder than it already is.*

But it seemed that Claire was blind to the subtle signals he'd been sending her all evening. She started to back away up the path, let her fingers join with his and then tugged him to go with her.

Feeling like every fibre of his being was screaming at him to not be an idiot, to just give in and join her, he shook his head. As much as he wanted to, he couldn't do it, not while there was so much unsaid left between them. 'I can't,' he said, pulling her to him and burying his face in her hair. 'I want to but I can't. Not tonight.'

'Early flight?' she said shakily.

He didn't reply, too sick of half-truths and misdirections to let even one more out of his mouth.

'I'll miss you,' she said, and her voice sounded all scratchy.

Dominic swallowed. His throat had suddenly got very tight. 'I'll miss you too.'

He just held her for a while, breathing her in. He didn't want to let her go, but he knew that he had to. When he had finally gathered the strength, he pulled back, brushed her hair from her face and held it in his hands.

'Whatever happens after this,' he told her, surprised by

the depth of emotion in his voice. Erica had always told him he sounded like a robot when she'd wanted him to get deep and meaningful. 'I want you to know that you're the most amazing person I've ever met.'

She shook her head, but he carried on.

'Yes, you are. You've been through so much, Claire, and yet you haven't let it scare you into living small, running away . . .' Like he had. 'You're generous and big-hearted and caring, and you've always got a kind word and a smile for everyone you meet.'

She blinked and a tiny trail of moisture formed on her cheek. 'Oh, I don't think I'm too different from most people.'

He smiled and shook his head. She didn't see that, either, but maybe that was what he loved best about her. 'You're so strong,' he told her. 'So strong . . . I meant what I said about being amazing, and when I get back I'm going to do everything I can to make you see it too.'

Her face stretched into a wide smile. 'You still want to see me when you come back? This isn't a brush-off?'

He decided words weren't doing a good enough job, so he decided to persuade her with his lips. Finally, he mumbled, 'Of course I do, you daft woman.' And then, before he could weaken any further, he kissed her one more time, turned and walked down the road without looking back.

# Chapter Thirty-Six

# I'm Not At All In Love

'They've introduced a new range of cocktails, have you seen?' Peggy said excitedly. She passed the menu to Candy, who then showed it to Claire.

'We have to have this one!' Claire said, tapping at the menu with a fingernail and grinning at the other two.

'It would almost be unpatriotic not to,' Peggy agreed. She flapped the menu closed and signalled for the barman. 'Three Doris Days, please,' she said, batting her eyelashes at him.

He smiled back at her. 'Coming right up.'

Candy sighed. 'I liked the look of the Ginger Rogers too, but we really have to drink Doris first.'

'What a genius idea,' Claire said. 'Inventing cocktails named after old movie stars.'

A few minutes later, the barman returned with three long glasses, filled with ice, alcohol and decorated with sugar round the rim. All three women looked at their cocktails.

Candy squinted at hers. 'It's very . . . um . . .'

'I think the word you're looking for is "pink",' Peggy said helpfully.

They exchanged looks then picked up their glasses and put the straw in their mouths. Claire took a long hard sip, then put hers down on the bar, frowning. 'Wow,' she said.

Candy nodded. 'It starts off sweet, almost sickly, and then – bam!'

'I got that too!' Peggy said. 'There's a warmth to it, reminds me of brandy, but it isn't brandy.' She smacked her lips. 'Nope, can't tell what it is. I wish they'd label the ingredients of these things. I don't like blind cocktail drinking.'

'I did ask,' Claire said, taking another long slurp, 'but he said these are secret recipes and that if he told me he'd have to kill me. I don't like it that much, even if it is named after Doris.' She paused as another layer of flavour hit her taste buds. 'Ooh, have another taste! There's something else, too. Something almost—'

'Sharp?' Candy suggested. 'No, that's the wrong word. It's more refreshing and clean, despite the warm notes. I don't think I've ever tasted anything quite like it.'

All three of them nodded as they sat on their bar stools.

'I'm not sure we'll ever work it out,' Peggy said.

'Maybe we're not supposed to,' Claire said. 'After all, it's surprising and complex, a bit of a mystery. A bit like the woman herself.'

The other two smiled at her.

'I think you're right,' Candy said. 'Perhaps we should just enjoy its indefinable qualities without analysing it.'

'You go ahead,' Peggy said, fixing her eyes on the bartender, who was serving someone at the other end of the bar, and smiling. 'I think I might work on getting the secret out of that one there, and I don't think he'll shoot me afterwards, either.'

Claire chuckled. 'Peggy, you're incorrigible.'

Peggy sighed and took another sip of her cocktail. 'I know. Fun, isn't it?'

'So . . .' Candy said, leaning forward. 'What's the news on the hunky Nick? Have you heard from him recently?'

Now it was Claire's turn to sigh. She shook her head. He'd been gone for two weeks and two days, which meant he was roughly halfway through his trip. It was torture. 'He's off in China, in the mountains. He said he might not have any signal for a couple of days.'

'Aw, you're missing him,' Candy said.

'It's fine,' Claire replied. 'When he does have Wi-Fi we totally make up for it.' Since he'd left, their messaging and emailing had gone into overdrive, way more prolific than it ever had been before, and way more intimate, too. That last night had changed things between them. She sighed. 'I don't know if this sounds stupid, but I feel like I don't have to hold anything back from him. I can tell him anything.'

Candy smiled at her. 'I don't think that sounds stupid. I think it sounds pretty wonderful.'

Claire nodded. It was. She sat in bed each night, phone on the pillow beside her, and waited to hear from him. He was eight hours ahead, so he'd often get in contact when he got up bright and early before work. Sometimes she'd hear from him just before she started work, after he'd come back to his hotel after a long day.

'He seems like a great guy.'

'Pretty easy on the eyes, too,' Peggy chipped in. 'Has he got a brother?'

Claire laughed. 'What about the poor barman? Is he yesterday's news already?'

Peggy gave her a cheeky smile. 'Just keeping my options open.'

Claire frowned. 'Actually, I don't know if he has a brother. I'll have to ask.'

'You've been seeing each other for . . . how long?' Candy said, 'And you don't know about his family?'

Claire stared at her half-finished drink. How odd. No, she didn't. She realised there were great big gaps in her knowledge of him, like those holes in a lump of Swiss cheese.

She didn't know if he'd always lived in London, for example, or had moved here after university. In fact, she didn't even know if he'd gone to uni, or what he'd studied. She frowned harder. How did she not know these things, especially when they'd spent hours messaging back and forth? She'd thought they'd covered everything there was to know.

But she did know everything that really counted. She knew how Nick thought, how his brain worked, that he was funny and loyal and    like Doris, really – had much more going on under the surface than he let people see. And she knew he thought she was amazing . . . and strong. Surely, those things were more important than knowing if he was an only child or had chicken pox when he was five.

'I'll ask him when he gets back,' she told Peggy.

'Ask who what?' Peggy said.

'Ask Nick about his brother.'

Peggy and Candy both burst out laughing.

'What?' Claire asked, starting to get a little irritated.

'We were having that conversation five minutes ago,' Candy explained. 'Now we're arguing about what Fred and Ginger's first film together was. I say it's *Flying Down to Rio* and Peggy says it's *The Gay Divorcee*.'

Claire blinked. Had she really tuned out for that long?

'Somebody's got it bad,' Peggy teased in a sing-song voice. 'Somebody's falling in *lurve*.'

Claire said and knocked back the last of her Doris Day. 'Don't be ridiculous,' she said.

# Chapter Thirty-Seven

# Love Me or Leave Me

Dominic kicked his hotel door open and threw his rucksack on the floor. The first thing he did was head straight for the shower, where he washed the dirt and grime of five days in the mountains near Yangcheng off of himself. His crew had retraced part of Gladys Aylward's route through the mountains and, even for him, it had been exhausting. He had no idea how a tiny Cockney woman had managed it with a hundred orphans in tow, the advancing Japanese army an ever-present threat.

Once he was clean, he dried himself off, threw some clean clothes on and pulled his phone from his bag. He lay with his head on the pillow, fighting sleep. A host of messages from Claire popped up on the screen the instant he turned it on.

He had so much to tell her. But not now . . . His eyelids were trying to close, no matter how hard he tried to keep them open, and his arms were finding the weight of his tiny phone too much. He should send off a quick message, telling her he was back in Wi-Fi range and that he'd be in touch soon. In a minute, though . . .

His phone dropped to the mattress and he closed his eyes.

He'd missed her. Just for five days they'd been out of contact, and he'd really missed her. He'd missed telling her things, about the places he'd been to and the things he'd seen.

He loved telling Claire things, full stop. She never scowled or judged. She never shut him down for not putting things the right way.

He smiled as his brain started slowly switching off and began the descent into unconsciousness. For once, he had good news to tell her. Although it hadn't been good news for the director and producer, that had been for sure. They'd manage to fall foul of complex Chinese bureaucracy and filming privileges had been denied for the next leg of the trip. They were going to have to either sweet talk their way back into the right people's good graces, which could take weeks or months, or see if they could find library footage to fill the gaps in what they already had.

All in all, it meant one thing: he was going home. At least for now. And instead of the vague sense of dissatisfaction that often came with that knowledge, there was a feeling of warmth, of peace. He breathed out heavily and patted the bed beside him for his phone. He really should tell her . . .

That thought circled round his brain a few times, and his last semi-lucid thought before sleep overtook him was that maybe he should just let it be a surprise.

*

It was another forty-two hours before Dominic arrived back in London. There'd been a hold-up for his connecting flight in Shanghai and he'd spent the night on the airport floor. Not the first time, he'd reasoned, and probably not the last. Thank goodness for an inflatable pillow and his iPod, that was all he could say.

The thought of getting the Piccadilly line filled him with dread, so he found a taxi and slept from the moment it drove away from Terminal Four right until the moment it pulled up outside his front gate. He stumbled out of the cab, not even thinking about what time of day it was and crashed his way into his flat. Thankfully, it was mid-afternoon, and Claire was safely installed in her office near Clerkenwell, too far away to witness his noisy homecoming.

Five hours later, Dominic woke up in his clothes on his bed. He blinked back the drugged feeling of a deep sleep, rolled over and stared at the ceiling. He smiled and almost drifted off again. Not some anonymous hotel ceiling or the cracked and crumbling walls of a dodgy hostel. He was home.

Home.

That one thought dragged him back from the brink. He sat bolt upright, his heart pounding. He looked up at the ceiling again. Home meant Claire. He checked his watch, which he hardly ever took off when he travelled, even when sleeping, mainly so someone hadn't snaffled it by the time he woke up again.

Eight-fifteen.

She might be up there right now.

His heart began to pound even harder.

But then he did a bit of mental maths and realised it was a Saturday evening. Hopefully, she was out. He hadn't seen a light on or any sign she was upstairs when the cab had pulled up outside. He rubbed his hand over his face and stumbled out of bed and headed towards the kitchen.

Thankfully, he knew he didn't have to resort to cold kidney beans for breakfast.

He opened the cupboard and spotted a row of cereal boxes, all full size, ready and waiting to be chosen and eaten with some long-life milk, which he pulled from the cupboard next door. Not as good as fresh, to be sure, but definitely better than nothing.

He made himself a cup of tea in between shovelling spoonfuls of Shreddies into his mouth and then sat at the table, munching away, until his brain was firing on all cylinders and his stomach was full. It took three cups of tea and two bowls of cereal, but it happened eventually.

The only thing he could think about, more than his recent travels, more than when his next flight was booked, was Claire. He couldn't wait to see her.

His smile dimmed a little.

It was time. No more excuses, no more stays of execution. He had to tell her everything, and he had to do it as soon as he saw her. Things had got way too serious for him not to.

He tried to ignore the little quiver that started in his stomach, that sloshed his recently consumed cereal about until he started to feel a little queasy and regretted that second bowl.

What if she told him to get lost? What if she never wanted to see him again?

He couldn't think like that. He had to hope. And there was reason to hope, wasn't there? He'd wanted her to get to know him before she judged him, but what he hadn't counted on was that she'd get to know him better than any other woman had, that he'd open up and let her see so much. That had to be more than enough, didn't it? Even when she realised what an idiot he'd been, she'd have to weigh it up against the rest of the truth she knew about him.

He hoped so. It made sense to him anyway, or maybe that was his sleep-addled, jet-lagged brain talking to him.

In any event, he decided that immediate action was probably not the best thing. For one thing, he really needed his wits about him when he talked to her. There was no point doing it when he couldn't even form a coherent sentence. For another, he really needed a shower and a shave. If he approached anyone now – even the smelly dog that lived next door that liked to roll in poop it found in the park – they'd run a mile. Not the effect he wanted to have on the woman he . . . Well, the woman he really, really liked.

So tonight was out. He'd have to be content with staring at his bedroom ceiling and knowing she was up there. Tomorrow morning, however, would be another matter entirely.

He hoped he could pull it off. What was that DVD Erica had loved, the one where Tom Hanks had known he was emailing the blonde chick – the one who'd *really* liked her apple pie in that other movie? He couldn't remember the name of the film or the actress, but he knew he wanted his revelation to hit Claire the same way. He wanted her to punch his arm, frown, then cry, then finally kiss him and tell him she'd wanted it to be him all along.

Maybe he should see if he could find it on Netflix tonight? Do a little research.

He yawned and jumped in the shower. When he was clean and dressed again, he went to check his overflowing inbox on his computer and, as he deleted most of them and responded to a few, he started to work on a plan . . .

He was going to knock on her door in the morning. Not too early, so they'd both had a good night's sleep, and then he'd invite her out to breakfast. Only he wouldn't take her to the little café where they'd almost had cappuccinos last time. No, he'd bring her downstairs to his flat, and lead her through to the kitchen, which, of course, he would have cleaned before then.

Hmm. That's where the plan hit a snag. He didn't think Shreddies were going to cut it as a romantic breakfast. Girls liked things like croissants and strawberries and freshly squeezed orange juice, didn't they?

He stopped himself. No. He was thinking in general terms again, going for the obvious.

What would *Claire* like for breakfast?

He got up and paced round his spare room while he chewed that over. It took a while, but eventually he came up with something he thought she would like: a fresh fruit salad with a tropical twist, including mangoes and pineapple, guava and, yes, strawberries. Not because they were obvious, but because he reckoned Claire liked a little bit of British tradition alongside her taste for travel. Her crisp white notepaper alone told him that.

And after that he'd serve proper cappuccinos, one made with his little Italian coffee pot that sat on the stove, the one piece of kitchen equipment he was truly a maestro at using, and after that he'd make *chilaquiles*, tortillas simmered in salsa with avocado and scrambled eggs. He suspected Claire would like a bit of spice with her breakfast. He hadn't cooked it in a while, but he learned from an old Mexican lady with no front teeth. For some reason, when he had the time, the inclination and the right ingredients – well, any ingredients – breakfast was the one meal he excelled at.

Once that was decided, he checked his watch to make sure he had time to go shopping and get back in again before Claire was likely to return and then he headed off to the supermarket.

# Chapter Thirty-Eight
# Quiet Night of Quiet Stars

Claire rushed back from a night out at the cinema with Peggy as fast as humanly possible. She left her phone on the passenger seat of her car after dropping Peggy back home and kept glancing over to see if it had sprung to life with a new message. Unfortunately, it stayed depressingly silent.

Was he okay? He said he'd be back at his hotel yesterday at the very latest. She really should have heard from him by now. She pulled over and picked up her phone, opened both her message app and her emails to make sure she hadn't missed anything, but all she saw was the last email he'd sent almost a week ago:

I'll miss this . . . Will tell you all about the mountains when I get back. Next stop, the Yellow River and then on to Xian. Hope you're not too jealous. Promise you I'm working very hard and it's actually very boring. It'd be so much more interesting if you were with me. :-) Sleep tight, lovely Claire. Promise you'll dream of me? N. x

She put her phone down on the passenger seat again and placed her hands back on the steering wheel.

*Honestly, Claire, you're losing it. You couldn't even wait four more minutes to get inside your front door to check your messages? Just how hung up on this guy are you?*

Pretty hung up, she admitted to herself. She hadn't yet resorted to crossing off the days until he returned on her calendar with red pen, but she was perilously close. Anyway, she didn't need to. It had been three weeks and one day. In just over a week he'd be home.

She drove home and pottered around her flat aimlessly for a bit before giving up and heading for bed. She wasn't sleepy, but it was almost around the time Nick might send a message so she decided to get comfy and read while she waited to see if one came.

About an hour later, she yawned and checked her phone again. Still nothing. She hoped that didn't mean anything. She hoped he was all right. What if something had happened to him?

There was a sudden loud noise from downstairs and she almost jumped out of her skin. Her pulse drummed in her ears, stopping her from listening properly to see if she could hear it again. Was it him? Her neighbour? She hoped so. She'd assumed that he'd shipped out again sometime in the last month, because it had gone awfully quiet. The only other alternative was burglars.

Stop it, she told herself. You're just letting your imagination run away with you.

She was just settling down again when she heard another noise from the flat below. Was that a hoover she could hear? She sat there for a moment, listening. Yes, it was a hoover!

Thank goodness for that. She'd never have thought she'd be so pleased to hear her neighbour's night-time wanderings. He must be back from wherever he'd been.

Oh, well, she thought, shrugging her shoulders. Everyone's got to do their housework some time, and she supposed it was just white noise. It might even lull her off to sleep. That sort of thing worked on babies, didn't it? He might even be doing her a favour.

She turned off the light, lay her head on the pillow and stretched out, staring into the darkness of her bedroom. Sleep didn't come, not immediately, anyway. Instead she started thinking about Mr Arden from downstairs, about his documentary that had made her cry and that maybe, just maybe, she'd been a little bit tough on him.

The more she thought about it, the more she realised she was right. The same way she'd done with Maggs the day she'd gone to visit her father, she'd been taking her anger out on the wrong person. Yes, he was annoying occasionally, but he hadn't really deserved the ticking-off she'd given him, especially in that first note. It was just that once she'd got caught up in all the back and forwards bickering she hadn't been able to see straight.

Once again, she found couldn't get the idea of him out of her head. After half an hour of lying there, trying to fight it, she decided to deal with it the only way she knew how. She got up, walked to her kitchen and got out her notepaper and fountain pen.

When she'd finished writing a softer, more conciliatory sort of letter than her others, she folded it, placed it one of her tissue-lined envelopes and licked the flap to stick it down, then she wrote his name on the front and stared at the letter sitting in front of her on her kitchen table.

Unlike her first note, there was no reason to want to call this one back. No sharp words, no misdirected anger. It would be okay to go and deliver it right now, so he'd find it first thing in the morning.

She continued to stare at the letter, wondering if she should just leave it on the table anyway, but in the end reasoned she'd be much more likely to get back to sleep if the whole job was done, so she stood up, shoved her feet in a pair of fluffy slippers so she didn't make too much noise on the stairs and headed off out of her flat.

She was just stepping onto the tiled hall floor when she heard a noise from his flat and froze. For a moment, she stood there, heart racing, tempted to sprint back up the stairs and dive into her nice warm bed, but she made herself breathe evenly and slowly, waited for her heart rate to slow.

There were no more noises after that. The house was silent, and it would be stupid to go back upstairs, the letter still in her hand, when she was mere feet away from his front door.

Stop being such a wuss, Claire. The only danger you're facing is accidentally bumping into him in your skimpy love-heart pyjamas. Hardly blood-curdling stuff. Anyway, even if he did hear her and come out to investigate, it would take a short while for him to reach his door, and by then she'd have sprinted up the stairs and be safely back in her flat.

Slowly, working through her feet like a ballet dancer, she crept across the hall, hardly daring to breathe. She was just about there, crouching forward and reaching that last distance to prise the letterbox open with her free hand, when all of a sudden there was light in the hallway of his flat, movement and a strange rustling sound.

Claire tried to reach for the letterbox, but it swung away from her. It took her a split second to realise it was because the door to the downstairs flat was opening.

Oh, heck. No running now.

She closed her eyes momentarily to prepare herself for the awkwardness that was sure to follow and then she stood up straight, opened them again and looked her annoying downstairs neighbour in the face for the very first time.

# Chapter Thirty-Nine
# You Should Have Told Me

Claire began to laugh nervously, trying to work out how she was going to explain she wasn't a stalker, even thought she was sneaking around outside his flat in her pyjamas in the dead of night, but then reality seemed to do a sort of weird shift and it wasn't her downstairs neighbour she was face to face with, but Nick.

For a second elation rushed through her – she'd been waiting to see him for so long – but then everything shifted again, and instead of feeling wonderful, as if it was all part of some lovely dream, it turned into a very different kind of dream altogether. Details began to jar and nothing made sense.

How was he . . . ? When did he . . . ?

And then the puzzle pieces began to fall, slotting themselves into place one by one.

The final piece hit with the force of a ten-ton truck, so powerful that Claire almost thought she was going to fall over. She dropped the envelope she'd forgotten she'd been holding and backed up, some primal instinct propelling her away from him. She kept staring at him, unable to believe what she was seeing, but then something snapped and she turned and ran up the stairs.

She heard a rustle as the rubbish bag he'd been holding hit the floor then his feet thudded on the stairs behind her. 'Claire! Wait!'

She turned suddenly, just before she got to the top step. She was shaking and she couldn't stop herself. Her stupid hands were trembling. 'Just what kind of sick game are you playing?'

'I'm not!'

She folded her arms tightly across her chest, as if trying to hold herself together. She felt as if her bones would shake themselves apart if she didn't.

'I should have known you were too good to be true,' she said in a whisper that was hard and cold. 'I should have remembered that every time you peel back the lid on a man, all you find is a selfish bastard who wants to control and manipulate people for his own ends.'

He shook his head, looking so much like a lost little boy that she wanted slap him. 'No, it wasn't like that. You've got to believe me!'

'No,' she said, as she started moving again, wanting to get away from the feeling that her flesh was crawling and she was going to vomit. 'No, I don't. I don't ever have to believe anything you say ever again.'

Then she turned and fled into her flat, slamming her front door behind her.

# Chapter Forty

# Do Not Disturb

Dominic strained his ears all night listening for Claire, but she was as quiet as she'd ever been up above him. It wasn't until the next morning, when he was lolling on his sofa, feeling bleary and weary and only just conscious, that he heard a noise from the hallway. He hauled himself up with superhuman effort and ran outside.

She was coming down the stairs, dragging a small wheeled suitcase behind her.

'Claire!'

She ignored him. Just kept thudding the case down the next step and then the next.

'I want to explain.'

She banged her case down one more step. 'Actually, I don't want to know what twisted little game you're playing.'

'I'm not!'

'Oh, so you haven't been lying to me all along?'

He opened his mouth and closed it again.

'Running into you at that party, that was a set-up, wasn't it? Go on, admit it! You were tricking me the whole time! God! I'm such a fool. I almost fell for it too.'

For a moment another emotion broke through the anger. The look of hurt on her face made something deep inside Dominic's chest squeeze, but then her features hardened and contorted again.

'And you were very clever about it,' she added softly, calmly. If anything, that was even worse than the shouting had been.

Dominic shook his head, tried to tell her that it was pure stupidity and stupidity alone that had got him into this mess, that there hadn't been anything remotely clever about it, but he seemed to have lost his new-found skill of communicating with a woman he cared about. All that came out was a grunt.

'You played it just right,' she continued smoothly, 'reeling me in with your "I need help being romantic with the girl I'm devoted to" nonsense—'

She stopped. Her eyes widened, and then she let out a laugh so loud and hard it made Dominic flinch.

'Hah! A girlfriend who didn't actually exist!'

She brought a hand up to her forehead, massaged her temple, and then she laughed again, but this time it was soft and croaky, barely there. 'It's all starting to make sense to me now.'

Dominic finally found his missing voice. 'No! It wasn't like that!'

She pulled her case down the final step to the floor, paused for a moment to catch her breath and shot a sideways glance at him. 'I don't believe you.'

'At first I still thought it was your grandmother living upstairs. I didn't know you'd taken over her flat. Neither of you told me!'

Claire's expression became blank. 'Well, she wouldn't have. She died.'

Oh, hell. He should have worked that one out, shouldn't he? 'I'm sorry,' he said gently. 'I didn't know that. I always liked Laurie.'

Claire stared at him hard, as if he was doing something sneaky by being nice to her. He supposed he could understand that. At the same time, he could see her brain working behind her eyes, processing the information. He was thinking of those early notes he'd written her, about hearing aids and cocoa and knitting. It seemed she was too, because after a long pause she said, 'Well, that certainly explains a lot.'

'See? I didn't know the whole time.'

She tipped her chin up. 'But you knew before me.'

He nodded.

'When? When did you know? Just now? Yesterday? Last week?'

'I worked it out at the Hamilton party.'

Her mouth made tiny movements, as if she was trying to form words, and then she just shook her head and headed for the door. She flung it open then paused. 'Okay,' she said, hardly able to get the words out she was so angry. 'You want a chance to explain? Tell me one thing.'

'Anything.'

A single word left her mouth, '*Nick?*' She watched very carefully for his reaction. 'I know that's not your real name.'

Ah. That. He swallowed.

'It is 'Nic'—N I C—short for Dominic. I didn't realise you had thought it was spelled differently until later. And I didn't tell you that was my name. You just picked it up from Doug. He's always called me Nic. Most of my friends do.'

She gave him a look that suggested she was surprised he had any.

'I didn't lie to you,' he said, pulling himself up a little bit straighter. 'But I also didn't put you straight.'

'Why? Why did you do it? Why base it all on lies right from that very first moment? You didn't have to, you know.'

He nodded. He knew that now. God, how he knew that now. He just was stupid enough not to have known it back then. 'I worked out who you were when you were telling Doug about the ridiculous gift I'd left you that morning, when you showed him my note.'

A magazine and some cheap flowers? How had he ever thought that appropriate? He astonished himself with his own cluelessness once again.

'I knew you'd never give me a chance if I told you who I was right at that moment. You'd already made up your mind about who Dominic Arden was, without even meeting me, so I decided to make use of the misunderstanding about my name to buy myself a little time, so you could get to know me before you judged me.'

He'd been hoping an explanation might soften her anger a little, but she was standing there, hand on her case, staring at him as if she'd like him to explode on the spot.

He cleared his throat. 'I know that was wrong now . . . but I didn't think it'd go on for so long, get so complicated.'

Her features hardened. 'If you'd come clean right at the start, I might have found it funny. I might even have realised I'd got you all wrong and given you a second chance.'

He sent her a heartfelt, pleading look. He knew that underneath all her anger, Claire had a generous heart, that she was ready to give everyone the benefit of the doubt.

He just needed to convince her he deserved some of that generosity. 'Could you give me that second chance now?' he asked softly.

She shook her head. 'I can't. I can't be with a man who lies and manipulates to get what he wants. I can't be with a coward who pretends to be something he's not. Even if I could forgive you, there could never be anything between us. You're simply not good enough for me.'

Dominic had thought he couldn't feel any worse than he already did, but he'd been wrong. Her words hit him right in the chest, in the heart she'd softened up nicely for him. The sad thing was, he didn't blame her at all.

Everything got very numb then. It was as if he was on overload and his systems started shutting themselves down one by one. All he could do was blink and try to stop himself feeling as if he might float away. He looked at her smart red case, trying to focus on something solid and real. It was cabin luggage size, stuffed to the brim. 'You didn't tell me you had a holiday booked.'

She wrestled her case towards the door and muttered, mostly to herself, 'I blooming well *could* do with a holiday.'

He did the gentlemanly thing and opened the door, held it for her so didn't swing back and send her flying. 'Where are you going?'

Despite his chivalrous behaviour, she refused to look at him. She pulled the trolley handle on her case all the way up. 'Away from you.'

'You can't move out! Not because of me. Not because of this.'

Claire looked over her shoulder at him as she bumped her case over the threshold and onto the front step. 'Watch me.'

And then Dominic was left standing on his own in the hallway, wondering if this was what open heart surgery felt like and what on earth he was going to do with all the eggs and avocados and tomatoes he had sitting in his fridge.

# Chapter Forty-One
## I Didn't Slip, I Wasn't Pushed, I Fell

Claire hadn't had a firm plan about where she was going to go at eight o'clock on a Sunday morning. All she'd known was that she wanted to get out of that house, that she couldn't bear another moment knowing that lying, scheming, rotten Nick was probably less than twenty feet away, no matter where she went in her flat.

No. Not Nick. Dominic.

Slipping up on that just made the rage swirl higher again. How could she have been so stupid? Hadn't she told herself not to get hoodwinked? Hadn't she told herself to be careful? How had she missed all those really obvious clues? She couldn't believe she'd done it all over again.

Well, that was it then. No more men in her life. She obviously couldn't be trusted to pick the good ones. Otherwise she'd choose someone like Doug, who was sweet and kind, charming and . . . well . . . rich. The only other option was to cloister herself away for the rest of her life and stay celibate. Which meant she probably should give up Doris and start crushing on Julie Andrews instead.

She threw her suitcase into the back of her car and then got in and started to drive. It was an irritatingly lovely morning. The clear golden light was dancing through the leaves on the trees that lined the roads and the birds were singing. It was the kind of morning for making love and having long lazy breakfasts that lasted until three. It annoyed her immensely that the faint possibility of those things had now been wiped completely from her horizon.

She stopped and got a cappuccino from a café she didn't normally go in, but was far enough away from her flat that there was no danger of . . . him . . . that man . . . stumbling into her. Her stomach rolled with shame again.

Oh, she'd thought it was so cute that he'd kept popping up everywhere, like it had been fate or something, and all the time he'd probably been following her like a creepy stalker. She shuddered so hard that some of the foam from her cappuccino slopped onto the tabletop and she had to dab it up with a napkin.

This was good. Thinking things like this about him was good. She had to keep her anger burning bright and hot, because if she let it go out . . . If she got close to admitting to herself that she'd started to feel something deep for him, something real . . . Well, that big trapdoor might open up again inside her and she'd fall in and never, ever make it out. So she sat there, sipping her cappuccino and ignoring the gnawing feeling tugging at her insides.

After two hours of driving around North London, wondering if she should get a hotel room, she headed for the only place she could think of that might give her a friendly welcome.

She stood on Peggy's doorstep, feeling like a stray puppy as she rang the doorbell. Peggy answered, not looking too sleepy, thank goodness, in a kimono and high-heeled fluffy pink slippers.

'Claire!' she exclaimed when she saw her standing there, red case at her heels. 'Jeepers! What happened?'

Claire, who had been ready to launch into a plea for sanctuary, promptly burst into tears. Peggy, bless her, didn't bat an eyelid, but just wrapped her arms around her friend and held her until the sobbing turned into hiccupping.

'S-sorry,' Claire stuttered as she pulled away, trying to mop the worst of her tears up with the ends of her cardigan sleeves. 'I didn't mean to do that.'

Peggy gave her another sympathetic squeeze. 'Looks like you needed to.'

Claire sniffed. 'And I'm sorry for barging in on you so early on a Sunday morning. It was just . . .' she broke off to do a percussive little sob '. . . I didn't have anywhere else to go. I would have tried Maggs, but she's in Bournemouth this weekend, visiting her brother.'

Peggy waved her apologies away and shooed her into her flat. Once Claire had been ordered to sit on the leatherette sofa in Peggy's fifties-themed living room and brought a cup of coffee and a couple of chocolate digestives, Peggy sat down in an armchair and looked steadily at Claire. 'What on earth happened?'

Claire closed her eyes. She didn't even know where to start. All sorts of explanations whirled round her head, most of them half finished. In the end, she grabbed hold of the simplest one – the reason why she was here.

'Can I sleep on your sofa for a couple nights?'

Peggy smiled at her. 'I can do better than that. My new flatmate – the one I got after Nicole moved out to get married

– is away with her boyfriend in Vienna. You can have her room. I'll send her a text. I'm sure she won't mind.'

Claire nodded gratefully. 'Vienna's lovely this time of year,' she said, her voice sounding strained and damp.

'I'm sure it is,' Peggy said, fixing her with a determined stare, 'but that's not the issue here, is it? What's all this about, Claire? Is something wrong with your flat?'

Claire felt the tide of tears rising again, so she clamped her mouth shut and just nodded. When she felt as if she'd found that balance between letting go enough to be able to talk, but not so much she descended into sobbing, she very carefully let a few words out her mouth. 'It's more what's underneath my flat.'

'Dry rot?'

Claire shook her head. 'Worse.'

Peggy's eyebrows shot up. 'A sink hole?'

Claire shook her head harder. 'A no-good, rotten, lying scumbag of a man.'

Peggy nodded. 'Know the breed,' she muttered then sank back into her armchair. 'But I thought you were seeing Nick. Is he the scumbag? And what's that got to do with your flat?'

Claire launched into the whole story, starting with the day she'd fallen over that stupid bike in the hallway and ended up with marching out on . . . that man . . . this morning. 'So Maggs was right,' she said, as she came to the end. 'There was certainly a lot more to my downstairs neighbour than I ever imagined!'

Peggy just stared at her, shaking her head in amazement. 'Flipping heck,' she said. 'It's like you've got your own little Doris alternative universe going on!'

Of all the things Peggy could have said, Claire had not

been expecting her to say that. She leaned forward in her chair and stared at her. '*What*?'

Peggy just gave her a you-can't-mess-with-fate kind of look. 'Your life . . . It's turned into the plot of *Pillow Talk*.'

Claire, despite her recent crying jag, began to laugh softly. She'd obviously crossed over from despair to hysteria, the way people did at funerals, when everything had got too much and the only way to cope was to go a little crazy. 'No it isn't! I haven't got a party line and I'd definitely know if that rat had a piano in his flat and was singing to women all day long!'

'Not the *exact* plot!' Peggy said, slightly exasperated, as if Claire should know that instinctively. 'The mistaken identity him sussing you out before you'd realised it was him. Then there's the emails and texts, the twenty-first century version of all those intimate pyjama-clad phone calls. The fact he's been trying to charm you, but digging himself in even deeper.'

'Trying to charm himself into my knickers, don't forget!'

Peggy winked at her as she swung her legs round to drape them over the arm of her chair and dunked her digestive in her coffee. 'Would that be such a bad thing? He is pretty hot!'

Claire suddenly wished with a passion Maggs had been home this weekend.

'Yes! That would be such a bad thing!' she said loudly, then frowned. Just for a moment she'd reminded herself of Doris in that scene with the phone company man, the one where she's complaining of sharing a party line with a sex maniac and ends up coming off all uptight and frigid instead of squarely in the right. Which she was. And so was Claire.

'Because . . . ?'

'Because he's no Rock Hudson and I'm no Doris Day!' Claire replied, feeling all hot around her ears. 'And because this is real life, not a sixties romcom. He's not going to come good in the end and ask me to marry him.' She folded her arms. 'I wouldn't even if he did! There's no way to gloss over what he's done and pretend it's okay.'

'I suppose you're right, but it would be cool if it did turn out that way.'

Claire sighed too. Yes, it would. She'd always thought how much fun it would be to be in one of those madcap comedies of Doris's, but now it was actually happening to her she realised it wasn't as nearly as much fun as she'd thought it would be.

'So, what will you do now?' Peggy asked. 'You can't let him drive you out of your own home.'

Claire nodded and contemplated that concept, let her mind wander and cook up ways she could drive *him* out. Fun though that was, she wasn't being very realistic. There really was only one thing she could do.

'I'll just have to go back,' she said forlornly. 'You're right. I'm not going to leave my lovely flat just because some scumbag happens to own the flat downstairs. I will just have to take the Doris approach.'

Peggy raised her eyebrows as she sipped her coffee. 'Which is?'

'Pretend the thing I don't want to deal with doesn't exist. I shall just ignore him. It's been easy enough to do so far, and he'll probably be off to God-knows-where again soon.' She fantasised briefly about all the sticky ends he could come to on his travels – falling down a crevasse in a glacier, being kidnapped by guerrillas, eaten by head-shrinking cannibals in some remote jungle – but was interrupted by Peggy, who was being annoyingly sensible.

'Are you *sure* that's going to work? You wouldn't have turned up on my doorstep if you were able to do that.'

Claire thought for a moment. 'I just need a couple of days to steady myself, to get my head in the right place. I mean, if Doris can use this technique to get over everything in her life, why can't I?'

Peggy swung her legs back over the arm of the chair and placed them on the floor, then she leaned forward and looked at Claire. 'I hate to tell you this, honey, but I'm not even sure it works for Doris all the time.'

Claire stiffened. 'What do you mean? Of course it works. By all accounts, Doris is happy and sunny and living to a ripe old age. Sounds good to me.'

'Another coffee?' Peggy asked and headed for the living room door.

Claire nodded. Last night hadn't included a lot of sleep. The caffeine would certainly help keep her vertical for a few more hours.

Peggy turned at the threshold. 'Even bright, perky Doris Day can't be Doris Day all the time. I bet there are times when she's sad or lonely or angry too.'

They stared at each other in silence, contemplating that fact, then Peggy finally said, 'Actually, how about we go out and have breakfast at the little café down the street? They do proper Italian coffee – much nicer than my cheap instant – and wonderful pastries.'

Claire looked at her suspiciously. 'You're paying this

time. You never did give me the change back from that Frappuccino the other week.'

Peggy looked blank. 'Didn't I?' she replied innocently. 'Okay, then. It's my treat.'

Peggy's treat? Those didn't come around too often, so Claire nodded and Peggy grinned at her. 'Give me ten minutes,' she yelled, as she dashed to her bedroom.

Claire watched the open door for a while then picked up a book from Peggy's coffee table. Ten minutes in Peggy time meant at least half an hour. She might as well keep herself occupied while she waited.

# Chapter Forty-Two
## I've Only Myself to Blame

Once again, Dominic found himself standing on Pete and Ellen's doorstep. However, this time, instead of a bottle of wine and a sad bunch of flowers, he was carrying an overnight bag and wearing a hangdog expression. Ellen opened the door and Dominic saw Pete trail into the hallway after her, curious to see who was knocking on their door this early on a Sunday morning.

'Flipping hell! I thought you were in China!'

Dominic shook his head. 'Long story . . . I'm back.'

Ellen looked carefully at Dominic. 'Hmm. Something's up.' And then she turned and looked at her husband. 'This is your fault, isn't it?'

Pete looked both surprised and mildly offended. 'You can't say that! We don't even know why he's here yet! And how can it have been my fault when he's been thousands of miles away for the last three weeks?'

Ellen just made a dismissive noise. 'This has got the whiff of your shonky advice all over it,' she told him as she stepped aside so Dominic could enter.

He was too tired to argue, or even to help Pete and Ellen

argue. He just dropped his bag in their hallway and followed Ellen into the kitchen. 'Do you think I could borrow your sofa again for a few nights?'

'We can do better than that,' Ellen replied. 'You can use the attic room. Technically, because it hasn't got a fire door, we can't call it a bedroom yet – not until someone chases up that builder who said he could sort that out for us . . .' she paused to give her husband a sharp look '. . . but we can put an air mattress up there. At least it would give you a bit of privacy and peace and quiet. Sammy likes to get up at five-thirty most days, and I expect you don't want him bouncing on your head at that time in the morning?'

Dominic shook his head. At that moment a small boy streaked through the kitchen, wearing not one thread of clothing.

'I thought you said you got him ready to go out to the park to play footie,' she said to Pete, looking unconvinced.

'I did!' said Pete. 'He must have taken it off again! How was I supposed to know that—' He stopped and looked at Ellen's expression then sighed. 'I know . . . my fault. I'll go and find it.' He chased after Sammy, who was trying to unlock the back door. 'Sam! Where d'you leave your football kit? Come and show Daddy and then we can go and get your ball.'

Sammy reluctantly allowed himself to be led away.

Ellen motioned for Dominic to sit at the kitchen table and busied herself making them both a huge cup of tea. When she'd finished, she sat down opposite him. 'Come on, then,' she said. 'Out with it.'

He sighed. 'You were right and I was an idiot.'

One corner of her mouth kicked up. 'That much is glaringly obvious. Care to go into specifics?'

'It's Claire . . .'

'Uh-oh. You told her?'

He shook his head. 'She found out.'

Ellen just pulled a face. She didn't need to say anything more.

Dominic nodded. 'Yeah, I'd say your prophetic powers are spot on. I bumped into her in the hallway. It did *not* go well.'

Ellen took a large sip of her tea, all the time looking at him from over the rim of her cup. 'That I can imagine. If a woman hates anything – more than being told, yes, her bum *does* looks big in that – it's being lied to. Especially by a man.' She shook her head, gave him a pleading look. 'I thought you were going to come clean?'

He nodded again. 'I was. It was just . . .'

Ellen didn't say anything. She just waited.

Dominic looked down into his giant mug of builders' brew. 'The more time I spent with her, the more I realised how much I liked her, and the more I liked her, the harder it got to say something that would blow it all to smithereens. I kept telling myself I was doing it for her, but really I think I was being a big fat coward.' He looked up and found Ellen staring at him. Her expression wasn't fierce, but it wasn't very sympathetic, either.

'You're right. You are an idiot,' she said.

'I didn't want to lose her. What am I going to do, Ellie?'

He must have been looking pretty pathetic, because her face softened a little. 'I don't know,' she said, 'not exactly. But you're going to have to give her time – and space.

Moving out was probably the best thing to do, so you can borrow our attic room as long as you like. You'll have to push Pete's crates of all his comics and model aeroplane junk to one side, though.'

Dominic almost managed a smile. 'He still has that stuff?'

Ellen chuckled. 'He tells himself – and me – that he's saving them for Sammy.'

He sobered a little. 'And what about after that? After I've given her time and space?'

'Look, I know you're a pretty great guy underneath. You've always been there for Pete, even when he's been a total plonker, and I know that Erica hurt you badly. You just can't let it stop you living your life.'

Dominic looked back at her in surprise. He was about to say that he lived his life at full pelt, that he did things other people just dreamed about, but then he realised what she meant. Hadn't it been creeping up on him ever since he'd come home, this feeling that when it came to the things that mattered – relationships – he was stuck wading in the shallows? 'How do I do that?' was all he eventually said.

Ellen played with the handle of her mug. 'It's not going to be easy,' she told him firmly. 'The first thing you need to do is apologise – properly.'

He nodded. 'I tried that, but she really didn't want to listen.'

'Of course she didn't! She's still spitting angry. But she won't stay that way forever. You're just going to have to be patient. Don't give me that look. I told you this wasn't going to be easy, especially not for you – Mr When The Going Gets Tough, The Tough Get Going.'

Dominic really wanted to contradict her about that, but

he needed the rest of Ellen's wisdom on this subject, so he kept his stupid mouth shut. 'Okay, then what?'

'Then – and this is the hard bit for most men – you're going to have to let down a few of those walls, let her see who you really are, and do it not just in words but actions and, no, flowers and chocolate will not be good enough.'

He nodded. He knew that now. Boy, did he know that now. 'I did let her see who I was, that's the problem.'

'Nope,' Ellen said firmly. 'It's the solution.'

'But she hates me! She hates what she saw!'

She sighed. 'Men . . . You're so literal sometimes, only able to think about stuff on one level. She wouldn't be so upset if she didn't like you. A lot. And she's angry at the moment because she's confused. She's not sure who you are – the wonderful guy who's been worming his way into her heart – or the manipulating toad she's scared you might be.'

He supposed that made sense. Didn't mean he had any answers, though. And which one was he? Even he wasn't one hundred per cent sure any more. 'So how do I do that?'

Ellen gave him a rueful shrug. 'That, my darling boy, is up to you to figure out. Even if I knew, I wouldn't tell you.'

Dominic chuckled softly. 'Or you'd have to kill me, right?'

She gave him a *don't be a wally* kind of look. 'I wouldn't have to,' she said, draining the last of her tea and standing up. 'I think there's a queue.'

'Right,' Pete said, bursting back into the kitchen with his son under one arm. 'I have child. I have clothes – *on* the child – and I have a football.' He looked hopefully at Dominic. 'Want to come across to the park with us?'

Dominic almost said yes, but then he realised the peace and quiet of an empty house might be a better choice. He shook his head. 'Not this time.' He risked a glance at Ellen. 'I have some thinking to do.'

# Chapter Forty-Three

## Foolishly Yours

Claire arrived at The Glass Bottom Boat for the film club meeting the following Tuesday feeling more than a little flustered. She was running out of clothes and she knew that she'd have to sneak back to her flat very soon.

She thought, come Monday morning, she'd be ready to go home. But she hadn't been ready. She hadn't been ready at all. Just the thought of seeing his face again made her want to shout and scream and cry. It was most unsettling. She really needed to get herself under control.

Peggy's flatmate had arrived back on Monday afternoon too, so Claire had packed her bag and turned up at Maggs's house. Maggs had taken one look at her, given her a fierce hug and had marched her up to her spare room. Claire had never been so pleased to see eighties striped wallpaper, a dado border and frilly peach pillowcases in her life.

If only she knew what his schedule was. If he'd had a proper job she'd have known she was safe during office hours, but of course he didn't have a proper job, which just meant she really knew how to pick 'em.

*But what about the documentary?* a little voice inside her

head whispered. *The one that was deep and sensitive and made you cry.*

Shut up, she told herself. She didn't want to think about that documentary. As far as she was concerned, it had been made by someone else. And that wasn't the point anyway. The point was that she didn't want all the awkwardness, all the drama, of bumping into him unexpectedly. It would be much better if she could pretend he didn't exist at all.

She parked her car and she and Maggs got out. It was only as she neared the entrance to the pub that she looked up.

She saw him standing there and a sensation rather like lightning shot through her. Not the nice kind of lightning, with a crackle of attraction, but the horrible kind, which made you feel hot and cold all at once and fried your brain cells so that grunting monosyllables became an effort. In fact, that was just what Claire did.

'Wh—Buh—Yuh—' was all she managed. Even she didn't know what she was trying to say. This was exactly why she hadn't wanted to bump into him unprepared.

He fixed her with those big, brown puppy-dog eyes. 'I know you don't want to see me,' he said softly.

Claire nodded, her jaw tense, her lips pursed. Part of her was really glad he knew what she was thinking so she didn't have to try to say it herself, another was insanely cross with him that he could read her so well.

'But if you'd just let me explain . . .'

She shook her head, the movements tiny and staccato, and then she closed her eyes so she couldn't see him, turned to face where she hoped the door of the pub was, opened them again and marched away towards the staircase out the back of the lounge bar. She could hear him calling after her, even crashing through the crowd a little behind her, but she screened those noises out, heard them, but filed them in a corner of her brain marked 'not important', and somehow it worked. Somehow, when she got to the top of the stairs and let herself into the function room, she was felt as if she was gliding above it all, like a swan across a millpond.

Maggs appeared a few moments later, puffing. 'Are you sure you don't want to give him a chance to talk?'

Claire just carried on unloading this week's DVD selection from her bag. *Calamity Jane*. One of her favourites. Well, nearly everyone's favourite, as it turned out. The club had been unanimous in choosing it for their next screening.

She was saved from Maggs nagging her further by the arrival Kitty and Grace, who had Abby in tow, and then George came in, his eyes searching the room for Maggs then coming to rest on her. Claire sighed. When was Maggs going to put the old boy out of his misery? Claire had fulfilled her part of the bargain. It was high time Maggs lived up to hers.

Still, there'd be time after the film to talk about that. The rest of the club members arrived and after a short discussion on the next four films that should be shown during their Doris film season they settled down to watch *Calamity Jane*.

Usually, Claire could sing along with every song – inside her head, of course; she wouldn't want to inflict her singing on her fellow club members – but this evening she kept drifting off, unable to settle and pay attention. She sighed. She normally loved this story of a woman and two men, only the right guy turned out to the wrong guy and the wrong guy turned out to be Mr Right. Maybe it was because, up until the other night, she thought she'd had a Mr Right and a Mr Wrong in her life, but now they'd inconveniently merged into the same person. Somehow that took the shine off the story.

Real life wasn't like that. All it took was one kiss for 'Calam' and Bill to wipe away every bit of animosity from the past and start planning a future together. That was hardly going to happen to her. Even if Dominic – yes, she was using his proper name now – was pretty good in that department, it would have to be a kiss that reached the equivalent of number ten on the Richter scale to dislodge all the baggage they'd got going. And she didn't want to kiss him again anyway. So there.

Still, she wished she really was more like Calamity Jane. Brave. Tough. Ready to face arrows and Indians and ridicule to get what she wanted. So instead of feeling buoyed up as she usually did after seeing the film, she left the meeting feeling deflated, as if she'd held herself up to an idea and come up lacking. All in all, she felt more like poor fake Katie than Calamity.

She was still mulling that over when she tramped down the stairs to the ground floor of the pub. She looked up as she hit the bottom step. Big mistake.

'Seriously?' she said, forgetting she was supposed to be ignoring him. 'Have you been waiting here all evening?'

Dominic gave a very determined nod. 'Yes. Because I need to explain, and you need to listen.'

Claire gave him a tight smile. 'That's where you're wrong, Mr Arden. I don't need to do anything some man tells me. So, if you'll excuse me?'

She moved to go past him. He didn't stop her. But he did follow her as she made her way through the pub.

'Well, if you won't listen to an explanation, at least listen to this: there's no reason for you to stay away from the flat. I've moved out.'

Claire stopped, but didn't turn round.

His voice came closer when he spoke again and she could tell he was standing right behind her. 'I'm staying with Pete at the moment and after that . . . Well, I can always rent it out, find something else for myself. I'm hardly there much of the time as it is anyway.'

Claire straightened and started moving again. 'Do what you want,' she said. 'It has no effect on me either way.'

He didn't follow her this time. Claire knew. Not because she glanced over her shoulder to look, but because the air at her back grew colder and colder the further she walked away from him.

Good riddance, she thought to herself as she headed to her car. The sooner he vacated his flat the better, then she'd never have to think of him again.

# Chapter Forty-Four

## My Kinda Love

Despite what Dominic had said about staying with his friend, Claire remained at Maggs's house until the weekend. While she'd been able to wash her meagre collection of clothes, there were other things she needed from her flat. It was time to go home. She couldn't stay at Maggs's forever.

Since Gran had owned the flat outright and had left it to Claire in her will, she supposed she could rent it out, but she didn't want to leave it. She didn't want someone new, someone who'd never known her gran, to come in and wipe away all those memories.

She came downstairs for breakfast on Saturday morning and told Maggs of her decision.

'Good,' Maggs said. 'I'll get my bathroom back to myself.' Then her smile faded. 'It'll be very quiet here when you're gone.'

Claire nodded. She knew that. She'd always thought of Maggs as a bit of a loner, but in the few days she'd been staying here Maggs had hardly let her out of her sight, insisting she cook for Claire too so they ate meals together, suggesting things they could watch on TV or board games they could play. Maggs was lonelier than she'd thought. Just as well the reverse blackmail attempt of getting Maggs to go out with George had finally paid off.

'So . . .' she said, smiling her best I'm-trying-not-to-be-nosy smile. 'How was your date with George last night?' They'd gone out for an early dinner at a local carvery and then on to see a film.

'Food was okay, film was crap,' Maggs replied, as she filled the teapot and set it in the middle of the breakfast table.

That wasn't what Claire had been asking and Maggs knew it.

'I meant, how did it go with George?'

Maggs set out the teacups and poured the tea, taking her time over every little bit of the job. When there was nothing else left to do she sat down and looked at Claire. 'I wish I could like him that way, but I don't.'

Disappointment washed over Claire.

'Don't look at me like that,' Maggs said grumpily, as she plopped two sugar cubes into her tea and stirred.

Claire hadn't been aware she'd been looking at Maggs like anything.

'I could pretend there's more there than there is, but in the end it wouldn't be fair to either of us. George wants to be devoted to someone, and after a while I think I'd find that a little . . .'

'Wonderful?' Claire said hopefully.

Maggs gave her a look. 'Irritating.'

'Sounds nice to me,' Claire murmured. How she had a man knocking down her door to be devoted to her, someone who cared more about making her happy than making himself happy. For a while she hadn't thought men like that actually existed. George was a nice reminder that they did, even if they were rare specimens. Mind you, in all his sixty-five years George hadn't found one woman who deserved all that devotion – apart from the silver screen version of Doris – so maybe men were just as screwed as women when it came to finding the perfect partner.

Claire looked at Maggs. She knew she had to bring something up that neither of them wanted to talk about, but with the hope of George no longer on the horizon, she couldn't put it off any longer. 'So what are you going to do? You know the answer isn't in that little silver hip flask of yours, don't you?'

Maggs went very still. 'Ah, so you've noticed that, have you?'

Claire nodded. 'More and more frequently in the last couple of months. Maggs? I'm worried about you.'

Instead of telling her to shut up and mind her own business, which was the reaction Claire had expected, Maggs just nodded sadly. 'I've started to be worried about me too. It was just that a little tipple helped blur the edges on the nights when this tiny house still seemed too empty, or when I was out in a crowd and aware of the hole at my side.'

Claire swallowed a lump in her throat. She knew how hard it was to lose someone you'd been close to your whole life, how the ache never quite seemed to go away. Losing her best friend less than two years after losing her husband must have hit Maggs hard.

Claire was going to reach out and touch Maggs's hand, but Maggs suddenly stood up and got very busy cutting bread. Only when there was a little toast rack full of even, browned triangles did she sit down and stop moving.

She took a breath and paused, as if she was gearing up to saying something. 'It's not a proper problem yet,' she said, and glanced up at Claire, 'but I think I have to admit it could grow into one. If I let it.'

This time Claire did reach out and cover her hand. 'You know I'm here for you if ever you need me.'

Maggs patted Claire's hand in a way that reminded her of her grandmother. 'I know that, but you're a young woman. You've got your own life to lead.'

Claire took a crisp triangle of toast from the rack. 'I know but . . .'

'But nothing. I'm not letting you move in here with me and become old and crusty before your time.'

Claire started to laugh. 'Maggs, you are definitely not old and crusty!'

Maggs stole the butter dish just as Claire was reaching for it. 'Yes, I am,' she said, with a defiant twinkle in her eye. 'And don't you forget it. Besides, I stayed up last night after my date with George thinking, and I've come up with a plan.'

'You have?'

Maggs nodded. 'I think I know exactly where I can find my Mr Right, and you're going to come and help me pick him.'

*

After breakfast, Maggs commanded use of her personal chariot and chauffeur – aka Claire and her Fiat – and instructed that she should be driven to an unspecified

destination. She just kept her referring to an old battered
*A–Z* on her lap and told Claire when to turn right or left or
go straight on.

Claire listened to the instructions with one half of her
brain, but with the other half she was trying to work out
what on earth Maggs was up to. Had her friend gone senile
overnight? Should she call a doctor? And when she wasn't
worrying about Maggs, she was cooking up scenarios about
what finding 'Mr Right' might mean.

Not long after they'd crossed Blackfriars Bridge, Maggs
suddenly said, 'Before you move out, I need to tell you
about my visit with your father.'

Claire kept her expression neutral. 'Do you really have
to?' That was another man she really didn't want to think
about.

Maggs nodded. 'Yes. I think I do.'

Claire sighed. She knew she might as well let Maggs spit
it out. She'd only keep badgering her about it if she didn't.
'Go on, then.'

Maggs frowned. 'He looked so different . . . Not the man
I remembered at all.'

'I know.'

'And that wasn't the only thing that was different, either.'
She shifted in her seat to face Claire more fully, even though
Claire was staring straight ahead, keeping her eyes on the
road and following Maggs's intermittent directions. 'Left
here.'

They paused as Claire navigated her way through a busy
junction, and then Maggs carried on talking.

'Do you know, that after your father was six, I never saw
him cry ever again?'

Claire shook her head. No, she hadn't known that. She wasn't sure she wanted to know it now.

'Your grandfather was responsible for that. The bastard was always quite proud of himself for beating it out of his son. I was actually quite glad when he got run over by that bus in 1976. I think him dying set Laurie free from a miserable marriage.'

Claire paused and let a car through in the middle of a street crowded with parked cars. 'And this is what you talked about, is it?' She wasn't really in the mood for a trip down memory lane, and would rather this conversation was over as quickly as possible.

'Oh, no,' Maggs said, shaking her head, as if that should have been obvious. 'In fact, we didn't speak at all.'

Claire shot a glance at her passenger. They hadn't? Then what on earth was this all about, this big secret Maggs needed to tell her so badly?

'That was the thing,' Maggs said softly, as if she couldn't quite believe what she was about to say. 'When I marched into that room to give him a piece of my mind, he was hunched up and facing the window . . .'

Yup, thought Claire. That was pretty much the way she'd left him.

'. . . and he was crying.'

A horn blared, and Claire realised she just cut someone up quite badly. She made a 'sorry' face and waved a hand to apologise. She couldn't quite work out what Maggs had just said.

'He was . . . ?'

'Crying,' Maggs repeated. 'And he wasn't too pleased about me catching him at it, either. I just thought you ought to know. Maybe your visit affected him more than you thought.'

'Thanks,' Claire said. But she wasn't sure she did want to know. What good did it do? What was the point of him having feelings after all if he was too much of a coward to let them out? It wouldn't change the way he'd treated her, would it? Even if a tiny part of him did really love her, did really feel sorry about how he'd treated the people in his life, he was too proud, or too scared, to show it.

Thankfully, Maggs told her they should now look for a parking space. She found a spot in a rather industrial-looking back road in Battersea and then Maggs led her a short distance to their destination.

It was only as Claire saw the famous blue logo with a dog wrapped around a cat that she realised where they were. She blinked and looked again. *Battersea Dogs & Cats Home?* This was so not what she'd been expecting.

Maggs just gave her a smug smile and led the way inside.

'I've been looking online,' she explained, as they were led back to the kennels, 'and there's someone I'd like you to meet. He's called—' She suddenly stopped and looked at the name tag on an enclosure. 'Oh!'

'What?' Claire said, frowning.

'Well, this isn't the dog I came here to see,' Maggs replied, 'but look . . .'

Claire did look. The name tag said 'Barney'. And inside the enclosure was a medium-sized dog with a curly mass of chocolate-coloured fur.

'Hello, boy,' Maggs said, bending down. The little dog tilted its head and looked at her. After a couple of moments' thought, it trotted towards her and sniffed her hand. Maggs looked up at Claire and smiled. 'Barney . . . like Frank Sinatra in *Young At Heart*, Laurie's favourite. I think it's fate.'

'I think it's going to eat you out of house and home and leave hair on your couch,' Claire said. 'Maggs, are you really sure about this? Don't you need some time to think about it?'

Maggs stood up. Barney stayed where he was and watched her, wagging his tail. 'Actually, I've been thinking about it for a while now. I just hadn't got round to doing anything about it, but after last night it all just sort of came together in my head.' She bent down again and scratched between Barney's ears. He closed his eyes and leaned into her hand.

As much as Claire was still reeling from the surprise, she had to admit they did make an adorable pair. Doris, with all the animal rehoming charity work, would certainly approve.

'You're giving up men for a dog?' she asked.

Maggs just smiled. 'Yup.'

And she looked so happy that Claire couldn't quite decide whether she was the craziest person she knew or the sanest. The way things had been going in her own love life, maybe she should try it.

# Chapter Forty-Five
## The Game of Broken Hearts

Maggs was so happy to start the rehoming process for Barney that Claire couldn't help getting caught up in the excitement. He really was a sweet little dog. She just hoped Maggs knew what she was letting herself in for. Once they got back to her house, Claire gathered together her belongings, shoved them in her little red case, then clumped it down the stairs and left it in Maggs's hallway.

'Well, that's me ready then,' she said to Maggs when she found her in the kitchen.

Maggs, who had been washing up, dried her hands with a tea towel. 'As much as it's been lovely to have you here, we both know you need to go back and face things . . . face *him*.'

'Oh, I'm not going to face him,' Claire said breezily. 'I'm going to cut him out, not think about him any more. Besides, he said he was going to go and stay at a friend's.'

'Did he? That was very nice of him.'

Claire snorted. 'Who knows whether he was telling the truth. Every word that comes out of his mouth is a lie.'

Maggs looked as if she was going to say something, but in the end she just shook her head and put her tea towel down and followed Claire out of the kitchen and into the hallway, where Claire picked up her case. Maggs stood with her hand on the door jamb as Claire trundled her case down the path. She stopped at the gate and looked back.

'Just remember,' Maggs said, her beady eyes boring into Claire, 'not every man is like your father – or even like that Philip.'

'Can I just remind you of what you said back at the dogs' home?'

Maggs gave her a questioning and innocent look.

'You don't seem to be too interested in giving men a second chance,' Claire said. 'You know, you ought to give practising what you preach a chance some time!'

Then again, maybe she wouldn't be Maggs if she did.

'That was different,' Maggs replied, crossing her arms.

'How?'

She shook her head. 'I did give George and I a second chance. We took a good hard look at what was under the surface of our friendship and found there was nothing there. It wouldn't have been fair to either of us to pretend otherwise.'

'Well, there's nothing there for me and Dominic either.'

Dominic. That was the first time she'd said his name out loud. His real name.

Maggs just gave her a disbelieving look and waved her off as she drove away.

When Claire got back to her flat, she stood at the gate, looking up the path. She had that weird 'familiar but not familiar' sensation, that feeling you get when you've just come back from holiday and you know you're home, but it takes twenty-four hours or so before it feels that way.

She chose to carry her case up the path, not wanting to

announce her arrival any more than necessary. Once on the front step, she pulled her keys from her bag and opened the locks. The old heavy wooden door swung open.

The hallway was bare. Quiet. Everything was perfectly in place, which in itself was odd. Not a stray piece of junk mail, not a takeaway leaflet to be seen. It seemed emptier than usual and Claire fought the feeling that the bike that *wasn't* propped up against the wall was missing.

Her flat was just how she left it. There was a magazine on the floor in front of the sofa, some unopened mail she'd dumped on the kitchen table and had forgotten and her peace lily looked in desperate need of a drink. Once she'd attended to that, she put her case on the bed and started to unpack, throwing the contents into different piles – clothes for washing, toiletries to go back in the bathroom, shoes for the wardrobe – and then, when she was finished, she stood in the middle of her flat and listened to the silence.

She sighed and rubbed her hands over her face. How was it possible to miss him when she hated him so much?

It was only as she crossed from the bedroom into the kitchen and glanced down the hallway to her front door – something she'd actively avoided doing since she got back, just in case she was tempted to look out for him – that she realised it hadn't shut properly, that it had bounced open again. She walked down and pushed it closed and, as she did, she saw a single white envelope on the mat.

A shiver ran up her spine. She recognised that handwriting. And there was no stamp, no postmark. There was only one person it could have come from.

Only this time it wasn't a scrumpled scrap of paper or a reused envelope that held his note. It was a beautiful envelope in a vintage sage green, long and elegant, the kind of stationery Claire would usually kill to get her hands on.

She bent to pick it up and found her hands were shaking.

She walked, just staring at it, until she got to her kitchen and then she sat on one of the chairs that surrounded her little square table and stared at it some more. Finally, something delicate inside her snapped and she gently tore it open along one edge.

The paper that fell out was just as beautiful, and he'd written in ink, deep indigo ink. The kind of ink that should always fill a fountain pen, because that precise colour made everything that came out of it seem important. She held her breath as she read:

*Dear Claire,*
*This is the last note I will send you. You don't want to talk and, after what I did, I don't blame you for that. I was stupid and short-sighted, but I want you to know that I really didn't set out to deceive you. I know you may not believe that, but it's the truth.*
*I have to confess, it would have been easier to come clean if a) I wasn't so good at letting my big mouth dig me an even deeper hole and b) I hadn't liked you quite so much. And I did like you, Claire. I still do. And it had nothing to do with your knickers and everything to do with the brave, kind, resourceful woman I've come to know you are. You are every bit as captivating and sexy and funny as Doris Day.*

She stopped reading at that point, not wanting to spoil his horrible attempts at good penmanship on that lovely paper by making the ink run. She put the letter down on the table and dug the heels of her hands into her eyes to rub away the tears and then she stood up and walked across the room to stare out of the tiny window that looked across the back gardens of the houses in her street and the one beyond.

Had it all been an act?

Probably not, although that's what she'd thought at first, but there was still this feeling of something tugging her towards him deep inside, something she neither wanted nor understood, that just wouldn't let her neatly file him away under the heading 'terrible mistake', as she had done with all her past relationships.

She was going crazy, wasn't she? To even think of still liking him.

Even if she did, it didn't change anything. He'd still lied to her, whatever the reasons. He'd still thought of saving his own skin first before making life easier on her, and she didn't need that kind of man in her life. Not again. Not ever.

So, without reading the rest of the note, she folded up the lovely green paper, slid it gently back into its envelope and then she walked over to the stove and turned on the gas. She held it there, the blue flames licking it until it caught and blazed yellow, and then she dropped it on the stainless steel hob and watched it burn away until nothing was left but ash and tiny curls of blackened paper.

# Chapter Forty-Six

# (Now and Then There's) A Fool Such As I

Dominic stood outside the Victorian terraced house and drew in a large gulp of air. He knew he shouldn't be here. He knew this might only make things worse, but he had to do *something*.

He'd hoped Claire would have softened after she'd got his letter. He knew she must have found it, because he'd walked by the house every evening and on Saturday the lights had been on upstairs. It was odd, he'd never really thought of his flat that much as 'home', but now he was tucked away in Pete and Ellen's attic room, he was really missing it.

Anyway, he still hadn't heard anything from Claire and he realised he never would. And he'd have been able to let that go if he hadn't thought that, deep down, she knew there was more to him, that they had a chance at something good.

But words were cheap, weren't they? And he and Claire had exchanged a lot of words over the last month or two. What he really needed to do was show her. And that's why he was here.

He mustered up his courage, walked up the front path and

knocked on the door. A few seconds later, it opened and he was looking at Claire's grandmother's friend, Maggs.

She looked him up and down. 'Look who it is,' she said dryly. 'Mr Arden.'

He nodded. 'Hello. I know I'm the last person you'd expect to see on your doorstep, but I'd like to talk to you about Claire.'

The old lady folded her arms. 'What Claire does – or doesn't do – with her love life is entirely up to her.'

'I agree,' he said, which earned him a look of surprise and also curiosity. 'But I'm worried about her.'

Maggs just looked at him. He could tell she was thinking hard. In the end, she backed away from her front door and indicated with a nod of her head that he should enter. 'So am I,' she said, 'but I have to say that you are responsible for a lot of what's bothering her at the moment.'

He followed her into a narrow kitchen and sat at the pine table as instructed. 'I know that. And that's why I want to do something to make it up to her.' He looked at the knotty surface of the table then up at his host. 'She told me about her dad, about how she'd been to see him.'

Maggs's eyebrows shot up. 'She told you that?'

He nodded. 'Yes. And I know that it hurt her even more than she let on. And I realise now how my own stupidity just stuck the knife in. I understand.'

Maggs sat down opposite him and eyed him shrewdly. 'Maybe you do, maybe you don't. What's that got to do with me?'

Dominic swallowed. This was it. He had an idea. An idea that might give Claire the boost she needed, something she would never think of doing for herself, but the problem was he couldn't do it alone. He needed to convince this suspicious old lady to work with him, and that was going to be no mean feat.

'I think I'm falling in love with her,' he said slowly.

He hadn't planned on saying that, hadn't even realised it, but now he heard the words out of his own mouth he knew he couldn't deny it any longer.

Maggs's expression didn't change much. He couldn't read what she thought of that statement at all.

'But nothing I do or say at the moment will convince her of that,' he added.

'How do I know you're telling the truth?'

He shrugged helplessly. 'I can't prove it to you either. I don't even know if I'm any good for her, but I really want to be.' He paused for a moment, hoped the old lady could see the sincerity in his eyes. No talking himself up, no glossing over stuff and hoping it would be okay. He was being as honest as he could be. 'I certainly know she's good for me. She's clever and warm-hearted. She makes me think about stuff I'd never realised was important.'

Maggs was staring at him, unblinking and very, very still.

He exhaled. 'All I know is that we'll both regret it if we're too scared to take this chance, if we chicken out of diving in and seeing what's there.'

For a long time Maggs didn't say anything, just stared at him and then she finally opened her mouth. 'Okay,' she said. 'What do you want from me?'

'Your help,' he said plainly. 'And that of the Doris Day Film Club.'

# Chapter Forty-Seven
## Softly, As I Leave You

The evening sun was still hovering at the tops of the trees when Claire stepped into the shady garden at the back of St Elwin's nursing home. Here and there mottled patches of sunlight spattered the grass, growing longer with every passing minute. She searched the garden and spotted her father sitting on one of the benches at far end of the lawn, one of the last places enjoying full sun.

She waited for the familiar feeling to come, that tightening of her chest, the sense of growing doom, but all she could feel was the breeze on the bare skin of her arms and the sound of bees dancing through the waving lavender in complex patterns, like little girls round a maypole. Hear heart rate was steady, her breathing even. She walked calmly across the grass to where he was sitting.

'Hello,' she said. 'They told me you'd be out here.'

The shock on his face would have been funny if the whole situation hadn't been so horribly sad. 'Wh—why . . . ?' He seemed to recover himself a little. The surprise hardened into suspicion. 'You came back.'

'Yes,' Claire said, sitting down on the far end of the bench. 'I did.'

She saw the question in his eyes, the one he really wanted to ask, but his lips remained a grim slit. Fine, she thought to herself. Be awkward. I don't care any more.

'The nurse told me you had bypass surgery.'

He glanced towards the building, scowling. 'They shouldn't have told you anything.'

'I'm family,' Claire said simply, 'and I asked. You didn't leave any instructions that relatives shouldn't be told.'

She saw anger and discomfort in his eyes and guessed the reason: he hadn't told the nursing home that, because he hadn't expected anyone to ask.

'When are you going to go home? They said you came here to recuperate because there wasn't anyone to stay with you.'

He glared at her. 'You volunteering?'

'No.' She looked away at the bright flowers in the well-tended borders. 'Where do you live?'

As the words left her mouth, she thought what a strange question it was to ask one's own father. She turned back to find him studying her. His eyes narrowed.

'Why do you want to know?'

She was tempted to laugh. Had he always been this way? So paranoid? So untrusting? She hadn't seen that about him as a child, but she took a few moments to sift back through her memories and realised there'd been a sense of it then too; she'd been too scared of him to see it.

'Fine,' she said. 'Tell me or don't tell me. I thought that's what people did when they were trying to get to know each other. Is there anything you want to know about me?'

He thought for a few seconds. She could tell he still thought he was walking into an ambush, but he asked the question anyway. 'You were always a sharp little thing . . . What do you do? For a living?'

'I'm a travel agent. I used to work in advertising, but I run my own business now.'

'Why that?'

She gave a little one-shouldered shrug. 'For a long time I wasn't sure. I'd always wanted to travel. But recently I've been thinking more about it, trying to look back and see where it all started. I think it's because I used to sit in my room at night with my atlas that had all the pictures in and dream of where I could escape to when I was old enough to leave home. I suppose I have you to thank for that.'

Not an easy thing to say. Not an easy thing to hear, either. But it was the truth. She was tired of dancing around with him, of trying to find the right thing to say to please him. It might not be pretty, but it was clean and simple. Liberating.

For some reason, he seemed to respond to that better than if she'd been nice to him. He stopped looking at her as if she was about to pull out a knife and stab him. He stared away at a clump of pampas grass in the centre of the garden. 'Lewisham.'

Claire frowned. 'Pardon?'

'You heard. It's where I live now.'

She nodded. 'I live in Highbury. In Gran's flat.'

At the mention of his mother, the shutters came down again. His jaw tensed and his nostrils flared slightly, but Claire quickly realised it wasn't her he was angry with. He wasn't even upset that his mother had left her granddaughter the flat that should have been his. He was angry with himself.

Of course he was. In her father's world, everything was about him.

It was odd. She'd never been able to read anything but displeasure from him as a child, but now, as she stepped back from her own emotions and viewed him objectively, watched his body language, she found it surprisingly easy to tell what was going on inside his head. Guilt. Frustration. Rage. Self-pity. They were all there, but well hidden so only the tiniest ripples showed on the surface.

'If you want, I'll come and visit you again,' she told him. 'But if you don't want, I'll leave and you won't have to see me again.'

He grunted, not giving an answer one way or the other.

'It was you who asked to see me in the first place. You must have had some reason for that.' Claire watched him carefully as she said this. 'Or was it really just because you wanted to satisfy your curiosity?'

He glanced at her and looked away. Claire waited. She realised with a jolt that she could feel the struggle that was going on inside him, the war between the bit of him that wanted to reach out to her and the bit that wanted to push her away, as he always had done. The very air around them seemed to pulse with it.

He did care, just as Maggs had said. He just refused to show it.

Because he was afraid.

That didn't make sense to her; he'd always seemed this towering presence in her mind, one that had wielded terror instead of being cowed by it, but as she thought about it more she realised it was the only thing that did make sense – the frightened man made others fear him, so he didn't feel so weak and vulnerable himself.

It might have kept him safe, but it hadn't made him very happy. And now he was a lonely old man who'd had to come to a nursing home after major surgery because he'd driven everyone who truly cared about him away.

He still hadn't answered, so she stood up. 'It's up to you.'

She realised there was one last thing she needed to know, especially if this was going to be the last time she saw him. That, as she had told him, would be up to him, but she had to take this chance while it was presented to her.

'Why did you wait all these years before contacting me? Why didn't you get in touch when Mum died? Or when Gran died?'

He shook his head. The anger was back, but also the guilt, so heavy she thought she saw his shoulders bow under it. He kept staring at that damn pampas grass as he spoke, and his voice took on a gravelly tone. 'I knew I was no good for them – for Cathy or my mother. It was easier not to think about them, not to think about you. I just . . .' he turned an looked at her '. . . put you all out of my mind.'

That's when Claire's anger flared. It broke away from her like a horse about to bolt. She drew in a breath to answer him, to tell him what the hell did he think of by pretending she didn't exist, but something stopped her.

Wasn't that what she'd done too? Father was horrible, so bury him away, never think about him? Had she learned this survival mechanism from him? She kept trying not to be like him and, in doing so, she only seemed to conform even more tightly to his pattern. And she didn't want to end up like this – a broken person beneath an iron husk.

The only way to slip from his grip would be to take back control, the control she'd never had and he'd always guarded so tightly, and she could think of only one way to do that, only one way to stop herself nursing her hurt and anger, like he had, and using it as armour against an unfair world.

'Dad?'

He looked round at her, surprised as she was at the word that had just come from her lips.

She had to forgive him, as unfair and counterintuitive as that seemed. It was the only way she'd be able to let go. Of the hurt, of the anger, of the wilful blindness. She had to do it for herself, not for him.

But she wasn't going to beg. From now on they'd meet as equals or not at all.

'I need to know. I'll come and visit again if you want me to, but you have to tell me you want me to.'

He stared up at her, and somehow she glimpsed a younger man inside that shell, a man who was angry and hurt and afraid. Still he didn't speak.

She pulled a business card from her bag and handed it to him. 'These are my contact details. If you change your mind, use them.'

She took one last look at him and then she turned and walked back across the lawn and into the house, knowing that it was probably the last time she'd ever see him.

# Chapter Forty-Eight

## It's Magic

Although, technically, the Doris Day film season had ended, because the Doris Day Film Club met on the first Tuesday of the month, they were back together the following Tuesday, the fourth of August. They watched *Lover Come Back*, Doris's second outing with Rock Hudson. Not as well-remembered as *Pillow Talk*, but some critics said it was better. Claire thoroughly welcomed being transported into the make-believe world for a couple of hours. Funnily enough, it was this film and the work they'd done in their rival advertising businesses that had got her interested in that profession when she'd been ready to work out what she wanted to do when she left school.

When the film was over and people were drifting away, Maggs cornered her. 'Before you go, I've got some good news to share.'

Claire looked up, surprised. Maggs hadn't breathed a word to her about this so far this evening.

'You know I like my competitions,' Maggs said. 'Keep the mind sharp. Well, finally I won more than a year's supply of cat food or a free iPod thingy that I don't know what to do with.' Maggs took a deep breath. 'I won a holiday.'

Claire grinned. This was exactly what Maggs needed to cheer her up. 'Congratulations!'

Maggs gave her a rueful smile. 'But I don't think I can go.'

Claire's face fell. 'Oh, no! Why not?'

Maggs shrugged. 'Barney. I can't possibly leave him just after he's just come to live with me. It wouldn't be fair.'

'You have to take the trip now?'

Maggs nodded. 'Yep. It's in the terms and conditions. Have to fly out before the end of August. It's one of those "now or never" kind of things.'

Claire pulled a glum face. 'That's too bad.'

Maggs cleared her throat. 'That's why I want you to take it. I want you to have the holiday.'

Claire blinked. She had not been expecting Maggs to say that. When the shock wore off, she laughed softly. 'Me? Isn't giving a travel agent a holiday a bit like taking coals to Newcastle?'

Maggs gave her one of those looks. 'It would be if you ever took one. When was the last time you had some time off, Claire?'

'I . . .' she fell silent. Cripes. Maggs was right. That trip to Prague with Philip had been three years ago. 'What sort of holiday?'

Maggs smiled. It was a happy smile, but it was a kind of mischievous one too. 'This is the good bit. It's a week, all expenses paid, in California.'

Claire's eyes popped open.

'Three days in Hollywood and another three in Carmel-by-the-Sea.'

Claire's mouth dropped open. 'But that's—'

'Exactly,' Maggs said, nodding. 'That's where Doris lives. Now do you see why I want you to go? It's fate, I tell you.'

Claire made a dismissive noise with her lips. 'Maggs, you don't believe in fate!'

Maggs suddenly looked very serious. 'I do since I got Barney. That seemed like a lucky coincidence at the time, but that dog is the best thing that ever happened to me.'

Claire stood up and tidied her chair away again, then she walked over to where she'd left the DVD collection and her handbag and began bustling around putting things away. 'Even if that' s true, I can't possibly just drop everything and fly away for a week. Not before the end of August.'

'I know you're good enough at what you do that you could wrap up all your loose ends by then. Even travel agents have to travel sometimes!'

'Erm . . .' Claire had been tempted to disagree, but maybe Maggs had a point.

'And you could do with a break,' Maggs added sweetly. A little too sweetly, maybe. 'It's been a hard couple of months, what with the situation with your dad and the business with . . . well, you know . . . with the flat.'

Claire nodded. That was also true. She was feeling tired and drained. The idea of being able to escape it all, to fly away and be somewhere else for a week began to take hold.

'The chance may never come again,' Maggs prodded.

Claire looked at her. She was right. This was definitely not the sort of thing she would have thought of booking for herself, although now she thought about it, she wondered why. The thought of walking down Hollywood Boulevard, seeing all the stars on the pavement, visiting the studios and doing the tours, was suddenly very appealing. She knew it was all very touristy, but that's what she'd be for a change, wouldn't she? A tourist. And the thought of being able to visit the lots and sound stages where some of her favourite movies had been made . . .

And then there was Carmel, the idyllic little seaside town that Doris had fallen in love with when she'd filmed *Julie*, and had finally retired to. She'd always wanted to see it, to walk along the pale sandy beaches with the crashing Pacific surf, even if the likelihood she'd bump into Doris herself was slim to none.

'Can I take anyone with me?' she asked.

Maggs nodded. 'It's a trip for two. So, who do you think you're going to ask?'

# Chapter Forty-Nine
## Sentimental Journey

The Doris Day Fan Club were gathered—minus their president—in Maggs's front room. Bev, Maggs and George took the three-seater settee, Peggy, Candy and Abby perched on chairs brought in from the dining room and Kitty and Grace were sharing an armchair, which had started off with much giggling and comments about how much fun it would be snuggling, but had descended rapidly into squabbles about whose elbow was where and just exactly how much of the other's fat bum was hogging the seat cushion.

That left one armchair up for grabs. Or it would have done, if Dominic had not been sitting in it.

'Thanks for coming here this evening,' he said, looking round the group. His heart was pounding. He knew these people were important to Claire, and he knew he had to win them round to have a chance of getting her back.

Abby scowled a little. 'Somehow it doesn't feel right… Meeting without Claire.'

The rest of the group looked from one to another in uneasy agreement. Dominic swallowed.

'We trusted you,' Candy said, her arms folded across her flowing grey cardigan. 'Claire trusted you. I don't even know what we're all doing sitting here!'

He shot a pleading look at Maggs. She sent him one back that very clearly said, *You asked to meet them, now it's up to you, sunshine.*

Great. He'd only just got the hang of saying what he felt to one woman. Now he had to deal with a whole roomful. Still, if that was what he needed to do, that was what he was going to do. He glanced at George, wondering if he might find a male ally, but George was glaring at him as hard as if he'd had the audacity to wound not just his president, but his darling Doris.

He cleared his throat. 'I guess that you know all about me now.'

That didn't win him any points for honesty or ingenuity, just a few more hard stares, a few more arms folded across bodies.

'It's very long story, and most of it is my own stupid fault, but I really didn't want to hurt Claire, and I can't tell you how sorry I am that I did. She's . . .' He broke off, horrified by the hoarse tone in his own voice. He shook his head and looked them in the eyes as he carried on talking. 'Well, you all know how special she is . . .'

There were a few grudging nods amongst his audience.

'And, well, you see . . .' He closed his eyes. There was really only one thing for it, wasn't there? He had to rip the plaster off and let it all out there, no matter how much it stung. He licked his lips and opened his eyes again. 'I'm a stupid fool who didn't come clean when he should have, because I thought she was far too good for me and would

tell me to take a hike, and I really didn't want that, because
. . . because I've fallen in love with her.'

Peggy, who'd been pinning him with a laser-beam stare
he'd been trying to ignore since he'd entered the room, said,
'But which guy is in love with her? Too-good-to-be-true
Nick or the guy who steals milk and leaves sarky notes?'

He shrugged helplessly. 'Both of them.'

All of him.

'And I think she was starting to feel the same way too, but
I managed to mess things up in a most spectacular fashion.
I've learned my lesson, really I have, and I'd do anything
to have a second chance with her, but I need your help to
do that.'

Bev, who didn't often say much, piped up. 'That's all well
and good, dear, but why should we help you? We don't want
any part in seeing our Claire hurt again.'

A murmur rumbled round Maggs's living room.

'Perhaps it would make things clearer if I told you just
how I needed your help?' he said.

Peggy and Candy looked at each other, some silent
message passed between them and then Peggy said, 'Go
on. This I'm dying to hear.'

Okay. Dominic sucked a quick breath in. This was it. If
he fluffed this up, they'd never say yes and he'd never get
Claire to forgive him. 'A friend told me I had to show Claire
how much she means to me. Not just in words, in actions.
So . . . I've been planning something.'

Candy raised her eyebrows. 'More secrets? More
surprises?'

He shook his head. 'I've been planning a holiday for her.'

Candy frowned. 'But she's already going on—' Then

she stopped and her mouth fell open. She looked at Maggs and then back at Dominic. 'That's you? This Hollywood competition thing is *you*?'

Dominic nodded. The film club took a few moments to gasp and comment and mutter to each other about the revelation.

'It came to me in the middle of the night. Claire and I have talked loads about travelling, about holidays and places we'd like to visit, but I know for a fact that she hasn't taken a trip herself for quite some time.'

Maggs nodded. 'This was why I let him come and talk to us. I thought we should at least hear him out. That girl works too hard and doesn't think enough of herself.'

Dominic continued, 'I'd been planning a nice, relaxing holiday for myself with Claire's help, but I suddenly realised I wanted to do it for her instead.'

'Okay,' Peggy said, looking slightly less fierce. 'You can keep talking . . . for now.'

Dominic sat forward in his armchair. 'At first I thought of white sand and palm trees.' But he'd almost instantly discarded that as too obvious. 'And then I thought of all the questions she asked me about my travels, and wondered about a safari or a trek to some remote location.'

'She would like that,' Kitty said. 'She always talks about the most interesting places. Some I've never even heard of!'

'That's because you thought Caracas was a musical instrument,' Grace said smoothly and earned herself an elbow dig for her trouble.

'Girls!' Maggs said sternly. 'Let's keep to the point!'

All eyes turned back to Dominic. Okay, here goes, he thought. This was not only his moment of inspiration, but the ace up his sleeve. 'But then the other night I turned on the TV and I stumbled upon an old film on one of the movie channels. Usually, I'd have just kept flicking. I almost did. But then I saw a familiar pair of blue eyes on the screen, along with a snub nose, freckles and a dazzling smile.'

'Doris!' Abby said, so loudly she surprised herself and blushed.

'Yes,' Dominic said. 'Doris. It was a film about a woman fighting with a train company about lobsters.' He frowned. 'Since I missed the beginning of the movie, I never did work out why.'

'Well,' Kitty said, sitting up straighter, 'it was all because they . . .' She trailed off as she caught Maggs's eye. 'Sorry,' she mumbled. 'Not the point.'

'No,' Dominic said, allowing himself a little smile. 'And the lobsters didn't really have anything to do with my idea, either, but I had a flash of inspiration as the credits rolled. I realised I needed to scrap safaris and palm-fringed islands and think about Hollywood instead.'

'That's all very nice,' Candy said. Her expression hadn't thawed one bit. 'But isn't it just another excuse to manoeuvre her into doing what you want? She goes on what she thinks is a prize-winning trip, only to discover you waiting in her hotel room?'

'Oh, no,' Dominic said quickly. 'I'm not going with her.'

'Oh,' Candy said, the wind firmly removed from her sails.

'There are no strings attached. If she comes home and she still doesn't want to talk to me then I'll take it on the chin. At least I'll have given it everything I've got.'

'Including the contents of your bank account,' Grace said. 'A trip like that can't be cheap.'

Dominic shrugged. 'She's worth it, isn't she?'

Peggy uncrossed her arms. 'You really are thinking about her, aren't you?'

He nodded. 'I'm trying to. Do you all think it's a good idea?'

One corner of Peggy's mouth curled up and she nodded back at him. 'I think she's going to love it.'

'I hope so. It's already booked. She goes at the end of next week, the twenty-third. Flights, hotels, transfers.' Once again, he took the time to look each of them in the eye. 'So what do you say? Will you help me?'

Peggy and Candy looked at Maggs. 'I think we need a moment to ourselves to discuss that,' Maggs said.

Dominic nodded, rose and left the room. He wandered down the hallway and stood in the middle of Maggs's kitchen, just to be sure he was out of earshot. It was an agonising ten minutes before she summoned him back in.

He couldn't waste time walking across the room and settling himself back into that armchair, so he just looked at them from the door, holding his breath. 'Well?'

The vice-president stood up, disturbing the little dog at her feet. 'The verdict is that we'll help you.' Before Dominic could get too excited, she added, 'But if you do anything to mess with my Claire again, I'll deep-fry a sensitive part of your anatomy and feed it to Barney here. Are we clear?'

Dominic nodded. 'Crystal,' he croaked, resisting the urge to cross his legs, and then watched as one by one, wary smiles began to break on the faces of the Doris Day Film Club. Kitty clapped her hands together and squealed. 'This is so exciting!'

Candy leaned forward in her chair. 'One thing I don't get

. . . If it's all booked already, what do you actually need us to help with?'

'The basics are there,' he explained, 'but I know from Maggs that Claire has wanted to go to Hollywood since she was a little girl and, of course, we all know how much she loves Doris.'

Sighs and muttering all round. The atmosphere in the room was definitely thawing.

'What I need from you lot is some ideas for Doris-related things she can do while on the trip. I did a bit of research myself, thought she might like to visit the house in Beverly Hills that Doris used to live in, and maybe even the one at Toluca Lake, but aside from that I'm stumped, and I thought your collective knowledge would come in useful.'

Now he got proper smiles from a few of them. 'Of course we'd be happy to help with that,' Bev said. 'If anyone deserves a trip like this, Claire does.'

They spent the next hour making suggestions, looking up things on phones and tablets. Dominic made copious notes and they all drank gallons of tea. When they'd finished, he had more than enough material to keep Claire busy in California for a month.

'Thanks,' he said again and again, as the film club members eventually drifted away, back to their own lives. 'I'm really grateful.'

And then he was left with just Peggy and Maggs. 'Right,' said Maggs and stood up, waking the curly-haired thing that might be Cockapoo sleeping on her feet. 'Time to get serious. I say we drag ourselves into the kitchen, set up at the table and whittle this wish list down to something usable.

I've got a particularly nice lemon drizzle cake to help us along our way, even if I do say so myself.'

Peggy and Dominic smiled at each other and followed her down the corridor.

'Are you sure you don't want to go on the trip instead of me?' Peggy asked, this time without the saucy look in her eye. 'You could surprise her. It would be very romantic.'

He shook his head.

'Don't you even want her to know it was you who did all this?'

'I've asked Maggs to tell her when she comes back.'

Maybe the trip might have changed her perception about him by then. Maybe it wouldn't. Maybe she'd think he was trying to worm his way back into her good books and throw it all back in his face, but he had to try. At least he'd have dug deep and given it everything he had.

They arrived in the kitchen and Dominic spread his notes out on the table.

'Now,' said Maggs, easily slipping into the role of commander-in-chief, 'which of these zillion and one Hollywood tours do we think she'd like?'

# Chapter Fifty

# I Don't Want to Be Kissed
# By Anyone But You

Claire sat in bed and started to compose a text, but then she threw the covers off and marched into her living room and sat down on the sofa to finish it. She couldn't do that in bed any more, not even if she was only sending a message to Peggy. It reminded her too much of him . . . Nic.

She sighed and finished typing with her thumbs. *Guess what?* she said, aiming for chirpy and upbeat, and realised all she was doing was getting irritated at her own perkiness. Even so, she refused to backtrack. *Doug asked me out to dinner.*

Thankfully, Peggy was one of those people who got the shakes if she was parted from her phone for more than thirty seconds. Strange, for such a retro-crazy girl. *What's new?* she shot back.

Claire took a deep breath. *This time I said yes.*

*!!!!!!!!!!!*

That made Claire smile. A heavy sort of lopsided smile, to be sure, but it was the first time she'd done that in days. *Details!!!!*

She'd known that request would be coming and she was already halfway through typing in the time and place. *Saturday night at The Wardesley.*

*Oooh, posh!*

*I know,* she replied, then there was a pause. She guessed both of them were chewing this news over.

*Don't stay out too late,* Peggy said. *The taxi is coming to get us at five-thirty. A.M.!!!!*

Claire nodded. She knew. It wasn't the best timing, but she'd needed to squeeze this in before she went away.

Her phone stayed silent for another couple of minutes. She was starting to think Peggy must have dozed off, when another message came through. *You're really going to go?*

*Yes,* she tapped in firmly. *I think I need to.*

It was time to move on.

*

Dominic had heard a car pulling up outside as he'd passed through his hallway and walked through his darkened living room to see who it was. Anything to distract him from the job of packing things into boxes. Despite his love of travel, he really, really hated moving. It reminded him he had too much stuff weighing him down.

He pushed a slat in his blind out of the way so he could see better.

Through the gap in the hedge for the garden path, he could see a sleek black car, not the usual sort of thing that parked down his road. That was surprising enough, but when Doug Martin got out of the driver's side, he was even more shocked. He raised his hand to knock on the window and wave.

It was weird that his friend had chosen this moment to pay him an unplanned visit, but he'd be really glad of the distraction. However, as he saw Doug circle round the front of the car to the passenger side, something made him hesitate and his fist never met the glass.

Every cell in his bloodstream seemed to explode into fire when he saw who emerged from the car.

Claire.

For a second, all he could think of was how pleased he was to see her again, even from a distance, even if she didn't know he was there, but sixty seconds later he wished he hadn't seen what came next.

He saw Doug stand close as she emerged from the car. He saw the way his friend moved in, instead of stepping out of her way. And he saw the way Claire wound her arms around his neck and kissed him as if her life depended on it.

It was at that point he decided his eyeballs had taken enough abuse for one evening. He dropped the blind slat, pulled it closed and walked away, heading for his kitchen.

Unfortunately, it meant he was just passing his flat door as the outside door opened. He froze, knowing that Claire might see the movement past his glazed front door, knowing that she'd probably be happier if she didn't know he'd popped back.

He waited as he listened to her make her way up the stairs. He had to glue himself to the wall of his hall with every bit of strength he had. That was what it took to stop himself rushing out there so he could see her again. Considering what he'd just seen in the road outside, that was a pretty pitiful state to be in.

Thankfully, he knew the perfect solution. He was

intending to medicate with Jack Daniel's straight from the bottle. It had always worked when women had been giving him trouble before.

He sloped through to his kitchen and rummaged in the cupboard until he found the square bottle he was looking for, then he unscrewed the cap, hung it lazily between his fingers and carried it back into the living room. There was nothing more to see behind the closed blinds. It was safe now.

He'd only planned to come back for a few nights while Claire was away, partly because he felt as if he'd been clogging up Pete and Ellen's house for far too long, and partly because he knew he needed to do a bit of tidying if he was going to show it to a rental agent.

Well, that's it, then, he thought as he slumped onto the sofa. He'd definitely made the right decision about this place.

He was too late. Claire obviously wasn't sitting around moping. She was going out. Dating. He wanted to believe she was just making herself go through the motions like he was, and maybe he could have convinced himself of that – if it hadn't been for that kiss.

He couldn't even be furious with Doug. After all, as far as Dominic knew, the guy had no idea there'd been anything between him and Claire. He could hardly blame him for stepping in and proving himself the better man.

He put the bourbon bottle down and scrubbed his closed eyelids with the flat of his hand. This is what he'd been afraid of. That, even if he pulled this whole Doris Day trip off, he still wouldn't be good enough for her. In his braver moments, he told himself he'd be fine, happy that he'd given it his best shot. In reality, he knew he'd be crushed.

# Chapter Fifty-One
## Hooray for Hollywood

The sun was just rising above the tarmac of Heathrow's runways. Claire stood at the gate, her face close to the plate glass window, watching the planes tootle in and out. Peggy came and stood beside her. 'Excited?' she asked, smiling widely.

Claire nodded. 'Of course.'

'You're not sounding very excited.'

Claire turned to look at her. 'I am. It's just . . .'

'Nic,' Peggy finished for her. 'Or Dominic, or whatever he wants to call himself.'

Claire sighed, walked over to one of the rows of seats facing the window and dropped into one. 'I should be over this by now. Nothing really happened. Just a few kisses. How was I so stupid, Peg?'

Instead of starting an anti-scumbag-men rant, as Claire had expected her to, maybe had even been secretly hoping for, Peggy sat down beside her. She chewed her lip for a moment. 'Tell me the whole story again, right from the beginning.'

So that's what Claire did. She started with takeaway

leaflets and bikes and ended with the last note she'd had from him. Just as she finished their row numbers were called for boarding. They got up and shuffled through the queue to show their passports and only really had a chance to talk again when their hand luggage was stowed away in the overhead lockers and their seat belts fastened.

'Don't hate me for this,' Peggy said, as she picked up the safety card and pretended to read it. 'But I kind of understand why he did it.'

Claire was speechless. She stared at Peggy. 'You do?' she croaked, when she finally regained use of her vocal cords.

'You know, sometimes you can come across as a little . . .'

Claire raised her eyebrows.

'Well, a little too perfect,' Peggy continued, with a grimace. 'It can be a bit intimidating.'

'Really?' she asked, not quite able to believe it. If anyone knew they weren't perfect, it was her. She'd been struggling against it her whole life.

'Yeah,' Peggy said. 'But once people get to know you, you're really lovely. It's just that first impression, you know.' She went silent for a moment as she carefully put the emergency landing card back in the pocket in front of her. 'Did he really trick you? About everything? You said you felt there weren't any barriers between you, that you could tell each other everything.'

'I thought so.' She gave Peggy a dry look. 'But it seems there was quite a lot he left out.'

'Details,' Peggy said, her tone slightly dismissive.

'Important details,' Claire reminded her.

Peggy looked intently at her. 'But were they really the most important ones?'

Claire didn't want to think about that. She'd been churning that over in her head for weeks and she still hadn't arrived at an answer. 'How did I miss it all? Am I really that pathetic?'

Peggy shook her head. 'I think you should give yourself a break. We're all guilty of seeing what we want to see sometimes.'

The plane jerked as it pulled away from the stand and began to taxi towards the runway. Claire folded her hands in her lap and stared at the back of the seat in front of her as Peggy peered out the window.

Had she? Had she only seen what she'd wanted to see? Had some of the fault been hers too? She thought back over the weeks she'd known Dominic. He'd tried to tell her things a few times, hadn't he? She'd either brushed off and hadn't thought any more about it, or had cut him off. He'd even dropped a whopping great clanger at her feet and she still hadn't tripped over it.

Maybe, instead of asking herself why she hadn't picked up on the hundreds of little clues that must have been around her every day, she should ask herself why he'd done that, why he'd tried to blow his own plan to smithereens.

She shook her head. He still hadn't done the right thing. Even if she'd helped him along in his deception. Even if Peggy was right, that he hadn't been completely fake with her, she still wasn't sure she could trust him ever again.

The engines began to roar and Claire's heart began to beat that little bit faster. She always loved this bit of a plane journey, often grinned in her seat while other people gripped their armrests, and even today she felt her spirits lift a little as the jet began to surge forward.

Anyway, she was flying away from all that mess for a week, leaving it all behind. She'd work out what she thought about Mr Dominic Arden when she came home again.

*

Claire stood on one of the upper levels of Hollywood and Highland, a bustling shopping centre in the middle of Los Angeles. Around her, the crowds and tour groups came and went, but she just stood there staring at the vast 'Hollywood' sign off in the distance, high on one of the hills overlooking the city.

It had been an amazing couple of days. Despite the eight-hour jet lag, she and Peggy had packed a lot in. They just finished walking the length of Hollywood Boulevard, looking for Doris's two stars, one for film and one for music. Peggy had even had a little map with the details of where each one was.

Claire had been most surprised at that, because as far as she could see Peggy really wasn't that organised. When she'd asked where the map had come from, Peggy had just mumbled something about a 'friend' giving it to her. Claire hadn't pushed it. She didn't really care, and they'd found the stars quickly and easily, rather than having to hike round the block, inspecting however many thousand there were to find the ones that read 'Doris Day'.

Yesterday, they'd done a limousine tour of stars' homes, including both of Doris's that had been in the area, then they'd gone to the Chinese Theatre, the Griffith Observatory. Earlier, they'd spent most of the day at Warner Brothers' Studios in Burbank. Not only had the trip included a VIP tour, where they'd got to go and look at props, watch things being filmed and peek at bits the usual hoi polloi didn't get to see, but they'd also had a special private tour too.

Their guide had been Lyle, a former employee of Warner Brothers, who had started there as a runner in the glory days of the studio. He joked that he couldn't keep away from the place, even now he was retired. When they'd mentioned Doris his eyes had lit up. He said he'd been told that some Doris fans were coming from England and, as he showed them various sound stages and places on the back lot where Doris had made many of her early films, he told them stories of how he'd met her a few times when he'd been little more than a boy.

He'd told them about the bike Doris had loved to ride to get around the studio – the only thing she'd asked for when she'd signed her first contract – and taken them to the wardrobe department where a lovely lady called Josie had had some of Doris's gowns for them to see. It had been amazing. They'd spent almost all day there and had come away dazed and utterly, utterly star struck.

'Hey! You still staring at that old sign?' Peggy said, after bouncing up beside Claire. She'd disappeared to do some shopping and now had several bags looped over her arm.

Claire nodded. 'I always thought it was smaller than that when I was little, and that I'd be able to stand beside it and have my picture taken. Now that I'm here I can see how immense it is.'

'Right. Well, I can see another tour group arriving to gawp at it, so we're going to have to move, otherwise we're going to get crushed.'

As they left the viewing area, she turned and took one

last look at the sign. It was starting to go a warm yellow as the sun started to dip towards the Pacific.

'It's a Thursday,' Peggy said, 'and you know what that means . . . Cocktails! I'm for Sex on the Beach. How about you?'

Claire laughed. She was glad she'd asked Peggy to come with her. She was always full of fun and energy, always ready to have a new adventure or cause a little mischief. Without her, Claire thought she might have just wandered round in a daze, not really taking anything in. For some reason, she was feeling lethargic. Maybe it was the heat of this city in late summer. She was looking forward to travelling up to the Monterey peninsula tomorrow, where they'd hopefully catch a bit of fresh sea air.

'So,' Peggy said, as she dragged Claire into a bar and ordered a cocktail for each of them, and a third to sit on the bar, in honour of their missing cocktail night companion. Claire had no doubt that Peggy was a good enough friend to Candy to help her drink hers once she'd dispensed with her own. 'You never did tell me how your date with dear old Doug went.'

Claire stirred her Titanic – an iceberg-blue martini with ice and fake gems in the glass – and looked at her friend. 'Kind of like the drink,' she said, nodding towards it.

'Disastrous?' Peggy asked, wincing.

Claire gave a half-shrug. 'More like, promising start but ended up not being quite what I'd expected or hoped.' She gave Peggy a sideways look. 'I kissed him. Or I let him kiss me, to be more exact.'

Peggy was so shocked she almost fell off her stool. 'You *what*? I mean, how could you? I thought . . .' She paused for a moment, recovered herself. 'What I meant to say was, I thought you didn't like him that way.'

'I didn't, but I wanted to.'

She'd had to do something to stop herself endlessly reaching for a mirage.

She didn't want to, but she missed Nick. Stupid, really, as the man wasn't real, just an invention conjured up by her downstairs neighbour so he could get his own way. It really shouldn't be possible to ache for him the way she did. It annoyed her that she couldn't get the fantasy of him out of her head, especially as he would keep wearing rotten, horrible Dominic Arden's face.

'I gave that kiss everything, Peg, but there was nothing there.'

'Poor Doug,' Peggy said.

'Poor both of us,' Claire said glumly. 'He didn't feel it either. Seems he's been barking up the wrong tree all this time.' She exhaled. 'I suppose it at least leaves him free to continue his search for the next Mrs Martin.'

When Claire had drunk her iceberg and Peggy had worked her way through her own cocktail and Candy's 'Wish You Were Here', they caught a cab back to their hotel, travelling down the avenues with the outrageously tall palm trees that waved against a painful blue sky. Claire found herself sighing. It wasn't that she didn't love being here. She did. It was everything she'd thought it would be and more, but that magic she'd hoped to feel was missing.

She watched the other tourists, oohing and aahing at the sights. None of them seemed to feel a vague sense of disconnection from all the glitz and glamour, and Peggy certainly seemed to be having a whale of a time doing exactly the same things she was.

As they hurried from the cab into the welcome chilliness of their air-conditioned hotel, Claire had to wonder whether it had nothing at all to do with the magic of Tinseltown being missing and everything to do with one particular down-in-the-dumps visitor. It was such a shame, especially as someone up there had served up everything she'd dreamed of and given it to her on a plate.

# Chapter Fifty-Two
# He'll Have to Cross the Atlantic

At four a.m., Dominic's phone vibrated on his bedside table, pulling him out of a patchy and unfulfilling sleep. He rubbed his eyes and reached for it. When he finally managed to focus on the screen, he found a text from Peggy that read: *Studio tour done. Lyle amazing! Where did you find him?*

Dominic grinned. It hadn't hurt that he worked in the TV industry. While he was pretty disconnected from the big Hollywood studios, he'd worked with a few people over the years who did and had prodded a few contacts.

*I know people who know people,* he replied, and then he added, *Did C like it?*

His heart seemed to bang in his ears as he waited for her reply. It arrived twenty seconds later.

*She LOVED it!*

He texted a smiley face back and sat there in his bed, the glow from the phone screen lighting up his face, feeling pretty pleased with himself. Peggy had been keeping him updated this way since she and Claire had left for America.

He tapped in the next text: *So all going well?*

There was a longer wait for Peggy's reply this time.

*Yes . . .*

Dominic stared at the little dots at the end of that lone word. They seemed to speak more than the actual letters did. *What's up?*

A few seconds later, his phone rang. It was Peggy. He picked it up. 'Is everything okay?' he asked, frowning so deep lines appeared on his forehead.

'Mostly,' she replied. 'Hang on.'

There was a lot of bumping and banging and muffled noise on the other end of the line.

'Right. I'm out in the hotel corridor now and I can speak a bit more freely,' Peggy said. 'We're just chilling in the room after having our dinner.' She giggled. 'All this texting back and forth with you . . . Claire thinks I've got some man wrapped around my finger. If only she knew, right?'

'Right,' he said. 'Peggy? What does "mostly" mean?'

'Ah.'

'I know you said Claire enjoyed the tour, but is she not enjoying the trip as a whole? Is there something else I need to do?'

Cripes, this was difficult. Is this how Claire felt every time she planned a trip for someone, always worrying she'd made the perfect choices, got them their money's worth? If it was, she never seemed fazed by it.

Peggy cleared her throat. 'It's something I couldn't quite put my finger on at first. Claire just doesn't seem her normal self.'

Dominic's pulse started to pound. 'Do you think she's ill? Do you need to take her to a doctor? I got great insurance if you do!'

'No. Nothing like that. Calm down. It's more that I get the sense something's missing from the trip.'

'Well, what can I do? How can I make it right?' He started wracking his brains for the thing he must have left off his list, the thing he needed to book to make Claire's holiday perfect. 'What do you think that missing thing is?'

Peggy laughed softly. '*You*, you big lummox!'

Dominic tried to process that, and failed. 'Me?'

'Yes, you. She's experiencing all these emotions about these wonderful experiences you've been giving her and I don't think she knows what to do with them, because the person who created it all is not here. On some deep level that I'm not even sure she's fully aware of, I think she knows there's more to this trip than meets the eye.'

'Me going out there was never part of the plan,' he said gruffly.

'Well, change the flipping plan then!' Peggy replied, sounding more than a little exasperated. 'You need to get your butt on a plane right now.'

Dominic shook his head, even though a part of him was aware she couldn't see him. 'I don't think that's a good idea,' he said slowly. Wouldn't it just look as if he'd been manoeuvring behind Claire's back for his own ends? She'd hardly respond well to that.

'Dominic? What are you afraid of? Just come. She needs you.'

Then there was shuffling, scuffling noise and muffled talking. He could hear Peggy saying something along the lines of, 'No . . . No . . . It's fine . . . I'll be finished in a minute.' Then her voice came loud in his ear. 'That's Claire getting suspicious. Gotta go!'

And then she really was gone. He stared at his phone.

Go to LA? Was she nuts?

She'd wanted to know what he was scared of? Everything!

He had no idea if Claire was even ready to see him again, let alone speak to him, let alone turn up on her dream holiday. It was a long way to go to get shot down in flames.

He knew how badly that felt, how much it stung when you put everything you had on the line for a woman and she looked you up and down and decided to return you for a refund. But one thing that Peggy had said kept worming its way through his brain. She'd said Claire needed him.

He couldn't remember the last time a woman had thought that about him, but he also didn't want to be the one to let Claire down again.

While he was turning that thought over in his mind, looking at its shape from every possible angle, his gaze drifted to the indistinct lump of his rucksack that he'd slung in the corner of his bedroom.

# Chapter Fifty-Three
## Que Sera, Sera

Claire and Peggy had been in Carmel-by-the-Sea for a day and a half. It was the most amazing place, tucked away on the south edge of the Monterey peninsula. The drive up here in an open-topped sports car, provided as part of the competition prize, had been amazing — a winding highway, curving round a dramatic coastline with the pounding Pacific breakers below.

The town itself was unlike anything Claire had ever seen in America before, a hub for artists and creative types. The houses were small and quaint, a far cry from the skyscrapers of downtown Los Angeles. It sort of reminded her of the Cotswolds – on speed. There were quirky little cottages everywhere, so tiny she could hardly believe a family could fit in them. Many had tall stone chimneys and leaded windows in odd shapes and their roofs rose into high, pointed gables. She wouldn't have been surprised to see a fairy tale princess sweeping the steps or a group of hobbits through the window, sitting round the fire and trying to outdo each other with their tall tales.

Even the shops fitted with the overall storybook feel to the town. Some were built in the same fashion as the cottages, others were painted in bright pastels, bevelled glass in their front windows, flowers spilling out of boxes beneath. But the stores weren't cheap and cheerful. They were expensive little boutiques that fitted with the overall sophisticated feel of the town, which was filled with fine restaurants and more art galleries than Claire could count.

And then there was the beach. Oh my, the beach. A gentle arc of almost white sand, surrounded by rolling hills and framed by twisting Montercy cypresses.

The strangest thing was that the town had a 'no stilettos' policy, something that had sent Peggy practically into hysterics. She'd had to go out and buy both canvas shoes and flip-flops and she moaned long and hard every time she had to put them on.

They were staying at The Cypress Inn, something Claire couldn't quite get her head around, because it was actually owned by Doris Day. What were the chances of that happening when Maggs had just won a random competition?

It was rumoured that sometimes Doris made an appearance, but she hadn't been spotted there in months, maybe even years. If she had been there recently, the tight-lipped locals were being very discreet about it. Even so, every time Claire came down from her room into the lobby, she had such an adrenalin spike – just in case the almost impossible happened – that she ended up feeling a little queasy.

This afternoon, she and Peggy were having a total Doris fan-girly day. After visiting the Pebble Beach Country Club, where Doris had shot the opening scenes of *Julie*, they'd taken the car up into Carmel valley, which overlooked the town, and driven to the Quail Lodge Resort and Golf Club.

They wanted to get a glimpse of Doris's house, perched high above the golf course on a small cliff. Every year on the third of April, some of Doris's loyal fans gathered there under her terrace to sing her 'Happy Birthday'. Claire knew what the house looked like from photographs, but she discovered that now they were actually there, working out exactly where it was wasn't as easy as it seemed.

She turned on the spot, shielding her eyes from the sun with her hand. 'You've got the map,' she said to Peggy. 'Which way do you think we need to go?'

Peggy scrunched up her face. 'Dunno. From what I can gather, this is more an "artistic impression" of the resort than an accurate map. I can't quite seem to find my bearings.'

Claire sighed. 'Shall we just walk around the perimeter and—'

She was cut short by the ringing of Peggy's phone. *Again?* That girl seriously had a devoted admirer. She'd been texting at every available opportunity, even sneaking off into secluded corners to have hushed conversations. She glanced at Claire, frowning, and then walked off out of earshot. Claire couldn't help but wonder why she was being so secretive. Was the guy married?

Anyway, from previous experience, she knew this probably wasn't going to be a twenty second call, so she started strolling towards the next green. She made sure she didn't go too fast, so Peggy would be able to catch her up easily.

A few minutes later, she heard Peggy squelching through the dewy grass behind her and prepared herself for a half-hour moan about how her plimsolls were hurting her feet.

'Why don't you hand me that bit of paper and I'll see if I can make head or tail of it?' she said, reaching her hand backward but still keeping her gaze on the scenery at the edge of the golf course.

'Here.' The word was simple, just what she would have expected as an answer to her question.

The voice, however, was not.

It wasn't Peggy's husky tones, but something much lower, much richer. A sound she'd been aching to hear for weeks. She spun round and found Dominic standing there, holding a concertinaed bit of paper out to her.

His hair was messy and there was dark stubble round his jaw. He looked rumpled and crumpled, as if he'd just jumped out of a jeep, and before that a plane. In short, he looked absolutely delicious. She hated herself for thinking like that.

'Try this one,' he said. His eyes were warm, but his voice was serious. 'I told you I never go anywhere without a good map.'

She took it from him dumbly, because that was the only thing she could think of doing at that present moment. 'Wh—what are you doing here?'

He smiled at her, but it wasn't his usual overconfident grin. 'I'm here to be your tour guide.'

She shook her head. 'What?' she said again, but Dominic didn't answer. He just took her by the hand and led her to the eighteenth green. From there she could see the familiar shape of Doris's house, the arched window, tiled roof and long balcony that ran the width of the cliff.

For a long time all she did was stare at it. Was it daft that a tiny piece of her was hoping against hope that she'd see a scuffle of movement and then an old lady with white hair and maybe some dogs bounding across the length of the terrace?

Even though she stood there in silence, Dominic beside her, for more than ten minutes, her wish didn't come true.

When she finally snapped out of whatever spell she'd been under, she folded her arms across her middle and turned to him. 'What are you really doing here?'

He didn't reply. She'd been grateful for the silence while she'd been hoping to catch just a glimpse of Doris, but now she wanted him to speak up. 'Dominic?'

That was the first time she'd called him his name to his face. It felt weird after all those times she'd called him Nick. She shifted her weight onto her back foot and retreated a little, even as she waited for his answer.

He swallowed. 'I'm afraid I have another confession to make.'

\*

Claire just stood there and stared at Dominic. She couldn't quite process what he'd just told her.

There'd never been a competition? This was all some plan cooked up by him and Maggs and the Doris Day Film Club? He'd planned all of this? For her?

She really needed to sit down. And where on earth was Peggy?

It was at that point that some golfers arrived, wanting to finish their game, and she and Dominic had to stroll off the fairway. They walked to a shady spot under a tree next to a pond.

Claire wasn't quite sure what to feel. Half of her was swept away that he'd done all of this for her, the other half couldn't help feeling uncomfortable that, once again, he'd done things behind her back.

She finally turned to him. 'Thank you for all this,' she said simply. 'But I don't know what to do with it. It would be different if we were friends, or if we were in a relationship, but I feel like I don't really know you. I just don't know how to take it.'

Dominic turned so his body was fully facing her and looked deep into her eyes. 'You're wrong. You do know me.'

'No. I knew "Nick".' She closed her eyes before she said the next bit. 'It was him I was falling for.'

When she opened them again, he was still looking at her. They seemed to have got closer. All she could see were those chocolatey brown eyes, crinkling slightly at the edges as he wore the faintest of smiles. 'I am Nick.'

She shook her head. 'You're Dominic. That's the real you. Nick was a total fake.'

He became very serious. 'The fake one was better than the real one. You got the best deal.'

She looked away, moved her hands in an effort to explain what her mouth couldn't. 'But that's the whole point of fakes, isn't it? That they're not what they seem? That they look better than they really are? You're not really selling me on this.'

Dominic pressed his lips together and thought for a moment. A gentle breeze sighed through the leaves of the cypress above their heads and softly blew Claire's fringe across her face. She pushed it back with her fingers.

When Dominic spoke, it was with a determination that she'd never seen in him before. 'The reason the fake me was better is because you made him that way. He started off as clueless as the other one. It was you, pushing me to be better that made Nick who he was. I was a better man with you as Nick than I ever have been with any other woman as Dominic.'

Fake was real and real was fake? Claire's head was starting to hurt.

Dominic breathed out, steadied himself. 'If you tell me to clear off, I'll clear off, but I'm not going to throw all of this away. You changed me, Claire, and I don't want to change back.'

Claire closed her eyes. Looking into those painfully sincere brown eyes was messing with her head. Oh, she so wanted to believe him. She so wanted to believe that this was all true, that he really did care for her that much. What other motive could he have had to do all this? It was way beyond a skilful seduction, and she realised there were times in the past – before she'd known the truth – when he could have pushed that door but hadn't. She'd practically tried to drag him inside one night and he'd still walked away.

She opened her eyes and looked at him helplessly.

'I've been sitting on the surface of my own life for too long,' he said, a hint of finality in his tone. 'But you encouraged me to dig deeper, to *be* deeper. All this . . .' He looked round a golf course and let out a soft laugh, but Claire knew he was talking about more than Quail Lodge. He was talking about the whole holiday. 'I didn't even know I was capable of it.'

'It's been perfect,' Claire whispered. And it had been. It was as if he'd peered inside her head and dug out her daydreams and then inside her heart to find her deepest wishes. She'd even wished for him to be here, even though she'd fought it so hard, and here he was, waving his magic wand over her yet again.

Could this be true?

Men like her father or Philip couldn't have pulled all of this off. They didn't have the capacity to extend themselves that way. The hard lesson she'd learned from them was to measure a man not by what he said – because that was always a lot of flannel – but by what he did. Was she brave enough to believe that what Dominic had done for her had exposed what had been beneath her horrendous impression of him from the start?

He stuffed his fists in his pockets. 'I've got one last thing to say, and after that I'm going to go back to Carmel and leave you alone. And, no, I'm not staying at the Cypress Inn. I didn't want you to get the wrong idea.'

'Okay,' Claire said croakily. 'What do you want to tell me?'

'That I love you.'

A tide of emotion rose in Claire's chest. Not just because of the words he'd said, but because of the look in his eyes. It was all there the love, the pain, the fear at what he'd just said and the greater fear that she'd slap him down and reject him.

No one could have faked that.

She sniffed back the tears that were building behind her eyeballs. 'Actually, there is one last thing that would make this trip utterly perfect,' she said softly.

Somehow she could feel his heart beating hard as he considered her statement. A slight frown pinched his eyebrows together. 'Which is?'

'I think you should kiss me, because I love you too.' Even though she'd fought it with everything she had.

No one could ever have accused Dominic of not being a

'spur of the moment' kind of guy, because before she could even blink he scooped her up into his arms and did just that.

*Could real life be as good as it was on a Hollywood movie screen?* Claire thought hazily, as she kissed him back, reaching up to wind her arms around his neck. *Perhaps, perhaps, perhaps . . .*

\* \* \* \* \*

# You'll never forget your first Fiona Harper!

Find these and more great reads from the queen of rom-com at
**www.millsandboon.co.uk/fiona-harper**

# If you enjoyed this book, try more from Sarah Morgan

Following the success of the Snow Crystal trilogy, Sarah Morgan returns with the sensational Puffin Island trilogy. Follow the lives and loves of Emily, Brittany and Skylar as they embark on new journeys and unexpected encounters.

Look out for these titles, coming soon in 2015!

***Some Kind of Wonderful*** – July 2015

***Christmas Ever After*** – October 2015

**Find out more at
www.millsandboon.co.uk/first-time-in-forever**